+ ERIC J. VANN +

SOUL WEAVER

To my family,
Whose love and support made writing this story possible.

The Great Wilds

The Blightlan

Ruins of
Ishna Noan

Anoria

**Kingdom of
Anoria**

The Dark Tidings Sea

Esan Slashen

Najem

Ishna Shylaen

Daicen

Ejen

**United Princedoms
of Odana**

Souls R

Rifun

Atheen

Whiter

Pichen

**The
Central W**

Iuxlen

Gent

Colin

Ejani Empire

Tarn

Eirma

**Kingdom
of Maiv**

Ana

Nen

South Ejani Sea

Taren

The Frozen Wilds

ack Spire

na Thalas

Vidoria

Geskian
Theocracy

natin Empire

The Shattered
Isles

Thalish Isles

Maryme

Free State
of Tijar

The Silver Channel

Tijar

Es

Morna

Ashepar

Samal

Republic of Archigal

Forril

Three Flames

North Fjani Sea

he Southern Wilds

Dragon's Roost

KADORA
Eastern Peninsula

PROLOGUE

"Sir, the reports for the day," the young man with messy brown hair announced, placing a sheaf of documents on his superior's desk.

The long-haired elf sitting behind it did not look up. "Let me guess, Negan. Nothing new?" He turned a page in the small but thickly-bound book he was studying.

"Actually," the young man began, "there *was* something different…"

The elf stopped what he was doing to look up at once, his silken blond beard trailing across the desk. "Really?" he asked, a hint of excitement in his voice.

"Of course not." Negan grinned. "After all these years of waiting, do you think this place would be so calm if anything had happened?"

The elf sighed, but then a small smile graced his face. "Oh, I wouldn't say that. You could actually act like the trainee you're supposed to be and read something." He gestured to the endless shelves stacked with books around them, before turning back to his own book. "You are standing in the greatest collection of knowledge ever collected in one place, after all."

"What has you so engrossed in this one, Vhal?" The young man stepped around the desk to stand beside him. "I thought you read everything in here already?"

Vhal adjusted his spectacles and again glanced up, one eyebrow raised. "It would take a hundred years to read everything in here. And you know you're not supposed to shorten my name or act so friendly, Negan. I am your mentor and superior, after all."

"But you elves of noble houses have such long names! And speaking to you is the only fun thing I can do here. The rest are always so *serious*."

Vhal tapped his finger a few times against the desk and stared at his trainee with a passive expression. The younger man began to fidget slightly, before finally sighing in defeat.

"Vhal'nuel, what's so interesting about that book?" he asked in an overly polite tone.

Vhal shook his head. It was always like this with the newer ones. "We just received a new shipment of books from the capital. I must say, the emperor's decree that all books and documents entering the empire be copied was a masterstroke. This one is a particularly interesting find. It goes into great detail regarding the nature of the necrotic arts—it even has a few spells and rituals... fascinating stuff, really."

Negan smiled. "If only I could be so excited about books." He took a seat beside Vhal and started whistling lightly, causing the elf to flinch.

"Is that truly necessary, Negan?"

His trainee seemed about to reply when the sound of clanking metal made them both turn. Two armed and heavily armored-men had entered the library from the direction of the restricted section to the rear, holding nondescript boxes in their arms. Both were wearing gold-lined black cloaks with a silver phoenix embroidered at the center, the heraldry of the Caelian Empire and its Imperial Family.

As they passed, one of the guards glanced at Vhal, their eyes meeting for a moment. There was something there, but Vhal couldn't put his finger on it.

"The Imperial Guard has been around a lot lately, and the

regular guards have all but vanished as well," Negan whispered when the men were out of earshot. "Do you think the emperor is here?"

"The Imperial Family has every right to be here," Vhal replied crisply. "The Facility and everything within it, including you I might add, belongs to them, and their ancestors invested a lot of time and resources in making it comfortable over the years. You must know that expanding this place in any way is a colossal undertaking... The mountain rock makes sure of that."

Vhal did not usually pay much attention to the comings and goings of the guards, but was Negan right? It was not his place to question such things... but there was something else which scratched at his mind. He did not recognize these guards. They were not the same men who usually accompanied the imperial family.

Vhal closed the book before him with a loud thud, startling his companion. He stood and slipped the book into an inner pocket of his multilayered black robes, then picked up the documents on his desk and began walking away. Negan jogged after him to keep up.

"I hear there's is a lot of trouble brewing all over the empire," the young man whispered. "Something about the Jannatin tribesmen being up in arms. And of course, the Ejani never lets a chance like some internal strife go by without taking a swing at us." He glanced quickly to either side. "I even heard there were riots in the capital," he continued ominously. "You wouldn't know anything about that, would you? You must have some access to the outside."

Vhal stopped, frowning, "Other than having my own room and office, I have no other privileges as the lead researcher." He raised one eyebrow. "But do tell: how did you come to hear such rumors?"

"Uhhh... well, the guards like to talk when they think no one is around..." Negan replied, a little guiltily.

Vhal sighed. "How many times do I need to tell you this, Negan? That part of the Facility is off limits. You'll get yourself killed, or worse, over silly rumors. Why does it matter to you what happens on the border? We have our hands full with researching the artifact, for the greater glory of the empire. Anything else is a distraction."

Negan took a step back, looking Vhal straight in the eye. "I can't help it! We're practically *prisoners* here. We can't leave or send letters to anyone—and all in the name of secrecy for a project so old most of us don't know when it even *started*!" His hands balled into fists at his sides. "Meanwhile, the emperor and his daughter come and go as they please. I've heard that the emperor has even brought guests with him on more than one occasion. How secret can this place really be if—?"

Vhal grabbed the young man and pushed him against the wall. "Have you lost your mind, child?" he growled. "What if one of the Imperial Guards heard you speak of such things?"

Negan blinked, shocked. Slowly, Vhal released him and let out a deep breath.

"Listen to me for once, Negan. You can resent the fact you are here due to events not within your control, but you must accept the situation and move on." Vhal's tone was not without sympathy. "You are here and you will remain here, so you must make the best of it."

Negan looked down at his feet and closed his eyes for a few seconds before replying. "I really hate it here, you know," he said. "I miss the capital, the open air... and, of course, the girls," he added, with feeling. "I might have been a second son, but I am still from a noble family. I don't understand why they couldn't get some commoners in here instead."

Vhal sighed. It had already been a long day. "We are all from noble families. You should be thankful to the emperor for giving you the opportunity to study, learn, and serve the empire's interest here, instead of some far-flung outpost in the middle of nowhere. These *commoners* you speak of would beg for a fraction of what you're getting. Now go back to your studies, I have important tasks to attend to."

At that, Vhal turned and strode away, giving his trainee no

chance to respond, his path illumined by red crystals affixed to the library walls.

Inside the sanctuary of his office, he hardly glanced at the murals painted on the carved rock walls, depicting different events in the history of the Empire. Large piles of documents, files, and leather-covered books were haphazardly strewn around the room dominated by a large oak desk and chair. To Vhal's surprise, his chair was already occupied.

"Took you long enough," the blue-eyed elf sitting there said. She smiled and coiled a lock of blonde hair between her fingers. She wore robes of the same design as Vhal's, though hers were green instead of black.

"Eleanor," Vhal said as he walked closer to her. "I believe you're in my spot."

"Oh, my mistake. I knew something felt different," she replied coyly, getting up and allowing Vhal to sit—only to plant herself on his lap a moment later. "That's better," she cooed.

Vhal chuckled and gave her a light kiss on the lips. "As much as I love our time together, I do need to go over today's reports."

Eleanor grinned, then slowly moved her hands to reach under his robes. "You know as well as I do that it's just business as usual with the artifact, Vhal. Let's do something a bit more *fun*."

"I really do hate hearing people refer to it as that," Vhal complained, but he was already leaning back, his eyes closed, enjoying her attentions.

"Yes, dear. We've heard you rail about it being a living thing a million times before. But we are researchers, and until we find some actual evidence… well, we'll go with what we know," she said, a touch wearily, but her hands never stopped working.

Vhal leaned back further, letting his mind drift pleasantly. He had been in this place for most of his long elven life. How different would it have been if he hadn't been chosen for this assignment? In a different life, perhaps, he and Eleanor would be married and have their own family by now. He sighed contently, before pulling his lover close into a deep, passionate kiss—only to be interrupted by an ear-splitting whistle. Eleanor jumped at the sound, bumping her head lightly against his in surprise.

"What in the world?" she shouted, in an attempt to be heard over the racket. They both looked up to see a small, white, almost translucent crystal descend from a hidden compartment in the ceiling. The crystal was spinning rapidly. It appeared to be the source of the awful noise.

It took a moment for all this to register in Vhal's mind, but when it did, he sprang to his feet, dragging Eleanor with him as he dashed from his office.

"That's the general alarm!" he yelled. "We must get to the storeroom, quickly!"

Eleanor nodded, finally realizing what the sound represented. As far as Vhal knew, this was the first time it had ever been activated.

They ran past several smaller offices, then a portion of the library, before passing through a large metal gate and into the part of the facility Vhal had only recently warned his trainee not to enter. As they did, others joined them, each wearing different-colored robes indicating their research and magic specializations.

"Where are the guards?" one called out from behind.

"I don't know," Vhal yelled back, "but we can talk about this after we get in there!" They passed through another large metal gate leading to the storeroom. The alarm still rang as Vhal quickly took a head count, then slammed his hand into the center of the metal gate. A low hum sounded from deep within as the intricate engravings on its surface glowed. The light spread quickly, taking only a few moments to cover the whole surface. When it did, the entire gate—which Vhal estimated to weigh several tons—groaned and slowly began to swing shut.

Even with the powerful enchantments in place, it took a few moments for the heavy gate to seal itself fully with a loud clang.

Thankfully, there was no alarm crystal in here, but they could still hear a muffled version of it from the other side of the gate.

Vhal let out a breath he didn't realize he'd been holding. "All right everyone, just stay calm. Once things are safe, the alarm will be shut down and the gate should open on its own."

"Uhhh... sir?" a familiar voice asked from behind the circle of researchers.

"Yes, Negan?" Vhal sighed. "What is it?"

"This place is completely empty. All I can find is some cutlery and a bunch of random books."

Vhal frowned. When he pushed his way through, he found to his surprise that Negan was right. The storeroom—which was just an elongated room dug into the mountain rock—was meant to be stocked with enough food and medical supplies to last several months. But the boxes were cracked, strewn about the floor, while the cupboards had been thrown open. Everything was empty. He would almost call it *looted*... but that was impossible. It would have been easier to rob the Imperial Palace than to get in here.

Before Vhal could rearrange his erratic thoughts, the muffled alarm fell silent. He turned and along with everyone else, stared at the gate, expecting it to open. But it stayed exactly as it was.

"Vhal'nuel?" a short girl wearing blue robes asked.

Vhal blinked a few times, then walked briskly up to the gate. He placed his hand on the center and spoke the password he had been taught when he first became the lead researcher.

"Aslan Da Caelian."

He had always thought using the name of the first emperor as a password was somewhat weak, but it wasn't his place to do anything about that.

The gate hummed for a moment. Then a bright spark shot through Vhal's palm, slamming him backward as he screamed in pain.

His ears were ringing. He could hear Eleanor yell something, along with a few gasps from the others behind him, but he couldn't understand any of it. His whole body felt like it was on fire—he was fairly sure the area where the spark struck him *had* been for a brief moment. Thinking he must have pronounced the name wrong, he gritted his teeth and placed his hand back on the gate.

"*Aslan Da Caelian*," he said again.

The second shock brought him to his knees.

Hands, including those of his trainee and his lover, grabbed to pull him away from the gate.

"I don't understand," Vhal whispered hoarsely. "It should have opened. Why isn't it opening?"

Eleanor placed her hand on top of his, and a cloud of green mist seeped out of her fingers and swirled around him. Vhal closed his eyes as his injuries began to heal. Eleanor leaned closer, whispering calming words until his breathing returned to normal.

"Someone out there will notice we are missing," she said. "Soon, they will open the gate."

But Vhal thought about the missing supplies, and the rather suspiciously short period the alarm had kept running after they had locked themselves in. He didn't want to add to the stress and panic the others were feeling, however, so he nodded reassuringly.

They were trapped in here. And he couldn't help but think it was by someone's design.

Vhal clasped both his hands tightly, one around his lover's hand and the other around the book he had forgotten he still had tucked away in his inner pocket. His mind raced: how and why could such a thing have happened to them, and who could have reasonably pulled it off? It was an exercise which oddly helped to calm his fears, yet fanned the rage that was starting to build in his heart.

CHAPTER 1

As the morning sun slowly crept into the sky, Celia jerked up from her improvised bedroll, gasping. Her eyes were frantic and her skin glistened with sweat.

Safe, she told herself, until her breathing calmed. *You're safe.*

Slowly, she wiped away the sweat with a ragged cloth, a remnant of an old shirt. Then she packed up the few belongings she owned, covered any tracks she had left, and buried the ashes from last night's campfire. As she did, her thoughts returned to the dream again. She had thought she'd gotten over this particular one, but every now and then it came back to haunt her.

It had been just over ten years since the fateful night that led to her transformation, resulting in her fleeing her home for strange lands and ending up here, in self-exile among the Central Wilds. Before that, she had been a normal fourteen-year-old human girl living with her parents in a small, dreary farming village within the Jannatin Empire. Celia was one of the relatively few fortunate humans found to be gifted with the ability to weave magic in her village, so the regional mages' guild had sponsored her attendance at special classes in the nearby town. Celia had spent every possible moment she could there. She loved learning about the world, its history, and how to weave her gift. It had been a mostly quiet life.

But after that night, everything had changed. Celia retrieved a worn-out green cloth from her bag. Her fingers traced the knitting as her lips broke into a small smile. It was the only item she had left from home, the last remnant of her old life. Her mother had made this for her to keep her warm on her way to and from mage school, but now she was using it to keep warm at night and hide what she had become during the day. Celia's smile evaporated as she wrapped the cloth around her head and neck. She let out a deep breath before she strode into the dense forest.

For many years after her transformation, she had kept moving, staying only short stretches of time in any one place. Most of this time was spent in the Kingdom of Maiv, a poor and relatively young country nestled between two hostile and much larger nations—to the west lay the United Princedoms of Odana, known for their massive palaces and slave markets. To the east, the country of her birth, the Jannatin Empire, a militaristic and economic powerhouse in the region, but for the fact it had so many different groups vying for control of their own piece of it.

Even as young as she was, Celia knew she had to stay hidden—most would kill her if they knew what she had become. She avoided the larger cities and kept to small towns and villages. The few valuables she had taken from home before her escape helped pay for the little food and necessities she required, but she was still forced to sleep on the streets or in the countryside most days.

Celia shook her head and let out a bit of air through her nose. Now that she thought of it, she was actually quite fortunate. The Kingdom of Maiv's struggling economy had resulted in an increase of beggars and orphans, which helped her blend in. Another factor was that the Inspection skills, which would enable someone to view her personal details such as her name and race, were relatively rare amongst ordinary folk. The fact that Inspecting someone without a valid reason was considered rude and in many cases, illegal also helped. But as more time passed in hiding, Celia had noticed a problem.

Her body had grown far faster than was natural, both in height and proportion. People who had seen her on more than one occasion stared and gossiped about her unusual rate of growth. Not to mention the sudden increase in male attention it brought along with it. That sort of attention was dangerous.

But that wasn't her only concern. As her body matured, so had a deep unyielding hunger within her. A hunger she could not satisfy no matter what she ate or drank. By the third year, it'd become impossible to ignore.

It was shortly after when she'd had a particularly close call. Whilst she looked for a place to sleep for the night, she had walked down a small street when she felt a shiver travel across her skin. It was a sure sign of an Inspection being carried out. Someone had gotten too curious. Fearful for her life, she'd fled that town. She never discovered who had tried to Inspect her, or whether they had succeeded.

After that incident, she had decided it would be best to leave the kingdom and the rest of the civilized world behind, and struck out for the untamed Central Wilds to the north.

* * *

Celia clicked her tongue in annoyance as she pulled her clothes down to cover herself. She wore an off-the-shoulder long-sleeved dress that clung to her skin, right down to her upper thighs, and below that, long black boots. It wasn't practical, and the dress was a mess from being slept in on the ground, and from being exposed to the constant heat and humidity of the forest for so long, but it was all she had.

She had looted it from an abandoned carriage that looked to have already been ambushed by bandits at some point along the more well-traveled southern plains of the Wilds. Whoever had attacked the caravan didn't seem to have been interested in the dress.

Now, as she followed an animal trail through the dense foliage, she cursed in frustration as it kept getting caught on branches, rucking up to expose more of her skin. She wondered who would wear something so impractical—but then again, practicality might not have been its purpose.

Finally spotting a rabbit burrow at the end of the path, Celia crouched behind a bush and patiently waited for her prey to emerge. It had been a while since her last meal, and she was already feeling the hunger within her begin to wrest control. She needed to act, and fast.

A rustling sound snapped her out of these thoughts. Something was moving in the tall grass nearby.

She quickly raised her right arm and willed her Inspection skill to activate. On her wrist, a diamond-shaped mark, slightly larger than a fingernail, began to heat. A moment later, small gray runes appeared before her, invisible to all but herself.

You have successfully Inspected your target.

Name: Horned Rabbit
Race: Beast
Rank: Critter
Level: 1

The runes only remained for a few moments before dissolving into nothing. Celia grinned, her eyes tracking the rabbit. They glowed brighter as she prepared to lunge—but at that moment, a *thwock* rang out from the surrounding ancient forest, followed by a *thud* as a crossbow bolt embedded itself into the helpless creature.

"Got it!" a male voice yelled.

"Good shot," another voice replied. Two men emerged from the bushes across from Celia. The first, who had a small blade strapped to his side and wore a muddy green shirt with a vest made from an assortment of furs, picked up the rabbit by the ears and showed it to the other. This man wore similar clothes, but was shorter, and wielded a light crossbow.

Celia felt her heart seize for a moment, her tongue reflexively brushing against her upper lip. Of all the inhabitants of the Wilds to cross her path, it had to be men.

She felt a familiar heaviness began to wrap around her heart as the hunger flared within her. She closed her eyes and turned away in an attempt to stop herself from losing control, accidentally rustling the brush beside her. The men froze at the sound.

"Did you hear that?" the taller man asked, as he moved toward her hiding place, his hands gripping the hilt of his blade. The man suddenly dashed forward, grabbing Celia by the shoulder and pulling her out into the open. A cloud was beginning to form within her mind.

"Well," the man said, surprised, as his eyes moved over her skimpily dressed body. "Garish, looks like we caught more than just dinner this time." The shorter man giggled at this whilst shouldering his crossbow.

"Are you lost? The Wilds is a dangerous place for a woman, you know, especially for one like you," the taller man continued, his grin growing wider as he moved closer, placing a hand on her waist. "Scary monsters and hungry man-sized insects lurking about. Good thing I found you. I can keep you safe, and you can keep me—" He stopped and looked at his companion before correcting himself, "*us*—company… it's the least you could do, right?"

Celia kept her head down, paying no mind to the bandit's obvious intentions. She was losing her last vestiges of control.

"Run," she whispered through her teeth. "Please."

The two men stared at her for a moment, then began to laugh. "We can't do that," the taller man said. "Leave a woman stranded in a place like this? No, you're coming with us." He glanced around before addressing his companion. "Want to get a round in?"

The other man chuckled. "It's been a while… but you go first,

Ever since she had become a fully-grown demon, Siphoning had become a major part of who she was. It was her only method for obtaining the demonic mana she needed to simply survive. That first accidental Siphoning over ten years ago had exposed her to the demonic mana that resulted in her transformation. It had also allowed her to live for years without having to do it again—perhaps because she was still young and hadn't been using her abilities much. But out here, her hunger was a constant struggle.

Like all other demons, she had two methods of satisfying it. The first was a basic Siphon. Although this was easier, it also was extremely inefficient—most of the mana usually dispersed into the environment before she could absorb it.

The second method was far more powerful and efficient. It depended on the type of demon attempting it. A vampire, as a half-demon, could Siphon through consuming blood, while canine demonic beasts could do so by biting or consuming the flesh of their prey while they still lived.

For a succubus such as herself, the Siphon worked around pleasure.

Celia shook her head in dismay. "Of all the demonic races I could have turned into..." she mumbled. Celia had tried to research the reasons as to why a creature would turn into a certain type of demon instead of another, but the little information she was able to gather was theoretical at best. Some believed there was some sort of predisposition, based on bloodlines or a myriad of other factors, while others simply argued it was sheer luck. No one really knew.

The mark on her wrist again began to heat as she willed her personal log to appear. Just as before, runes manifested before her, depicting her personal information.

```
Name: Celia
Race: Demon, Succubus
Rank: Lesser Enlightened
Mana: 200/200
Level: 7
```

```
Attributes:
Strength: 2
Reflex: 4
Mind: 3
Vessel: 4
```

```
Skills:
Charm (Level 2)
Demon Claws (Level 2)
Small Blades (Level 1)
Inspection (Level 1)
Mana Siphon
Dark Vision
0 Skill points available
```

```
Traits:
Fire Weaving
```

Seeing that her mana vessel was now full, Celia flicked her hand to one side, dismissing her log. Ever since her hunger became powerful enough to affect her daily life, she had fought against her basic urges to ravage whomever she came upon. She had been raised in the Jannatin Empire, after all, which had conservative views on these sorts of things—at least in the outlying villages.

Turning into a demon might have transformed her body, but she was still a product of her upbringing. Every day was a struggle. It was as if she had two aspects to herself, the human and the succubus, locked in a constant fight for control. But as more time passed, she had surrendered more and more to her instincts. In the end, hunger and temptation always got the better of her.

Just like these two men, her victims were often bandits or criminals who used the lawless nature of the Central Wilds to conduct their trade. They had often been in isolation for long periods and suffered from depression and a creeping loneliness. Playing a damsel in distress was usually enough to get them quite excited about doing the deed—especially with someone who had her figure and beauty.

It always puzzled Celia how the idea of something being too good to be true never seemed to cross their minds. And if it did, they ignored the nagging thought until it was too late. She could not argue with the absolute ecstasy it brought her, both during and after the act, but she despised being beholden to such urges. It was for this reason that she found herself venturing deeper and deeper into the Central Wilds—or, more importantly, away from the civilized world.

Celia rearranged and patted away some of the dirt that clung to her clothes. Now that her hunger would not be an issue for a while, she could get back to the real reason why she was here in the first place. It had happened four days ago, and the event led to her traversing deeper into the Wilds than she had ever dared to travel.

A powerful earthquake had shaken the valley. The sheer violence the event wrought left a physical mark on the land itself. Celia could still remember the loud rumble that had blanketed the area as she felt the ground beneath her shift. But that paled in comparison to what had happened directly after: a massive surge of mana had erupted from somewhere and had kept spilling at an unbelievable rate into the environment. There had been no sign of it stopping or weakening since.

Celia usually kept her explorations to a minimum in the Wilds. She especially avoided going deep into the thickly forested valley as much as possible. She didn't know what sort of dangerous beasts and monsters might have made their homes there. But in this case, she had made an exception. If she got her hands on whatever it was that was causing this massive outpouring of mana, then she would never again need to hunt and be intimate with strangers for sustenance. These hopeful thoughts guided her forward, toward the mountains to the north.

CHAPTER 2

By nightfall, Celia knew she was getting close. The air had that heavy feeling, more than ever before. The feeling of raw magical power.

She was sure that by now the surrounding kingdoms and empires would have sensed this massive outpouring of mana. They would soon be sending in adventurers, or maybe even mages, to investigate. The mana was unlike anything she'd felt before. But it also felt *right,* like it somehow belonged.

Something did bother her, however. The closer she moved to the source, the fewer creatures, monsters, or anything other than vegetation she found. What was puzzling was that this went against everything she understood about how creatures behaved. Usually, they would be attracted to powerful sources of mana, just like she was. But right now, the opposite seemed to be happening. The whole situation made her uneasy.

Celia emerged from the forest and into a large clearing. She found herself at the base of one of the mountains that made up the Forli mountain range, named after the man who first mapped them. The range started in the north, by the southern shores of the Dark Tidings Sea, and stretched down to the Central Wilds. This particular mountain was one of the more massive ones, but Celia did not know if it actually had a name. Not many things did, this deep into the Wilds.

Celia walked carefully through the clearing. Debris, large boulders, and shattered trees lay strewn across it. Just as she stopped to examine the corpse of an unlucky deer lying crushed under a large rock, she was unexpectedly struck by a wave of mana almost bringing her to her knees.

"Damn it!" she cursed, whirling to face her assailant.

But there was no one there. All she could see was a peculiar opening at the base of the mountain.

She would have called it a cave, except it wasn't natural; it had been *made* by someone—or something. She could make out a large rectangular doorway, flanked by two massive, thick metal gates that blended in with the surrounding rock in both color and texture. No doubt some sort of advanced magical enchantments were involved.

If not for the heavy damage they had sustained, she could have walked right past them and not noticed them at all. What really had her attention, though, was the flood of mana she sensed gushing out through the gap in the bent and twisted gates. It wasn't dense enough to form a visible mist, but it had to be close.

Now that Celia was aware of it, she couldn't help but notice other curious things. While the whole clearing was decently green, with grass and small trees growing in between the patches crushed by the rocks, the flora in and around the direct path of the gushing mana was thicker. The grass was longer, its color more vibrant. Long vines hooked and grappled up and along the mountain side. It was the kind of growth she would have expected deeper in the forest, not by the side of the mountain.

To avoid the torrent of mana, Celia shuffled along the mountainside until she arrived at the doorway from the side. There, she reached out with her right hand as if testing the temperature of water—and her skin tingled as it was bathed in energy. It was a strange feeling, a mixture of both pleasure and pain. She drew her hand back as she thought about the possible cause.

Honestly, she didn't have the faintest idea.

She looked down at her hand, which still had a lingering, tingling feeling, then back to the bent gates. *What could possibly go wrong?* she asked herself. It was just a hidden door on the side of a mountain deep in the Central Wilds. This isn't the sort of thing that usually leads to endless torment and untold misery... right?

For a moment, she wished she had the ability to use the Analyze skill. It acted just like Inspection, but would provide details on objects instead of living things. Analyzing these gates might have given her some small clue about this place. Celia rubbed her arms to get rid of the goosebumps that covered them—just the thought of walking in there caused her to shiver.

But there was nothing else for it. Celia straightened up slowly then willed her feet forward into the darkness beyond.

It took a few minutes for her body to get used to the tingling she felt as she walked through the gates and into what appeared to be a long, dark hallway. Her every footstep echoed off the walls.

The walls were mostly smooth, she noticed, but other than clear signs of damage such as cracks, there were small patches of what she guessed were paint and engraved metal. It was impossible to say if they formed a part of a bigger picture, as most of it seemed to have been lost to time. She brushed her hand along the walls—they felt cool to her touch, something to be expected this deep within a mountain. There were square-shaped holes placed at regular intervals, which she assumed were where torch brackets had once sat. But it was the mana that presented the greatest mystery of this ancient-looking place.

Whatever this strange mana was, it was wreaking havoc on the more sensitive areas of her anatomy—the same feeling she had when she Siphoned demonic mana from her victims. Celia tried to distract herself from the pleasure she was experiencing by imagining how someone might react if they walked toward her from the other end of the hallway. All they would see would be a pair of faintly glowing golden eyes, hovering in total darkness. For once, she was glad to be a succubus—the ability to see in the dark was proving quite useful.

She came upon a rectangular opening. Celia could make out some small indents in the rocky sides, indicating there had been a door here at some point, but it seemed to have rotted away a long time ago. Cautiously, she poked her head through the opening. The chamber beyond was large, circular, and full of what seemed to be bookshelves—thousands of them, holding what must be millions of books and scrolls.

A library…? Well, that was the last thing she had imagined finding in here.

She stepped carefully toward one of the bookshelves and pulled out the first book she could reach. How could books have survived this long when even the door to this place seemed to have rotted away? Turning the leather-bound book to face her, she glanced at the title.

A Tale of Forbidden Love, Book 2 of 6.

She rolled her eyes and placed the book back onto the shelf. Moving a few paces down the same aisle, she pulled out another.

Burning Desires: A Champion's Lust.

Celia's body twitched, and she breathed out an exaggerated breath. She stared at the book held between her hands in disbelief and, without a word, slipped it back onto the shelf.

She had started to make her way back to the main hallway when her eyes opened wide, a realization striking her. She pulled a third book from the shelf and studied it.

"Th-this text is ancient Caelian!" she gasped.

That was impossible. The Caelian Empire had fallen a thousand years ago. Most of the languages in the Eastern Peninsula were a slightly modified version of ancient Caelian, which itself was a slightly modified version of an even older dialect. History had long fascinated Celia, but nothing more so than the history of the Caelian Empire and its treasures.

But that was not the point. The mere existence of such books here meant this library was beyond ancient.

Celia slowly drew her fingers across the book's leather cover. Anything Caelian was rare and valued by collectors and historians alike, which only made these books an even bigger enigma. She again examined the volume, noting its good—if dusty—condition.

"These books should never have survived this long," she said out loud, trying to give herself a moment to think. "Unless…"

Moving briskly now, she began brushing her hands across the wooden frame of the bookshelf, throwing up dust as she did so. She coughed as she breathed some of it in, but that didn't stop her from continuing. It wasn't long before she found what she was looking for.

Three small, different colored crystals, embedded in the wood. Fire, earth, and water. That certainly explained what kept these books in such good condition. The markings on these crystals meant they were enchanted, making them even more valuable. But who could possibly have loved their romance novels this much?

Her gaze drifted toward the numerous bookshelves that surrounded her. Smiling, Celia placed the book back on the shelf. If she collected and sold all the crystals in this library, she would be rich. *More* than rich. And that wasn't even considering the books themselves.

Running her fingers over the three crystals again, she grinned as she thought of the things she could buy. There were places who would tolerate a demon such as her for the right price. She could live with some semblance of comfort even. She leaned forward and planted a kiss on the surface of one of them.

Celia turned back to face the opening she had come through. The passage she had been in continued deeper into the mountain. She thought for a moment about simply taking all the crystals she could carry and running for it, but she had already made it this far. Perhaps there were even more valuable items deeper within.

And there was still the question of where all that mana was

coming from. If she gained control over the source, she might never need to worry about Siphoning ever again. *Nothing* was more valuable than that.

With that in mind, she strode out of the library and back into the passage.

The air became heavier and heavier as she moved on. Although the mana wasn't actively attacking her, she had to physically push herself through it, her body was struggling with the sheer weight pressing down on her from every side. If it had been any denser, she would have been blind, shrouded in a mist of mana. Then there were the added effects she was experiencing due to her succubus body. Celia leaned against the walls for support as even breathing became difficult. But she was close, so close now. Just a bit more and she should reach the source.

"This… better be… worth it," she wheezed, each word requiring an effort.

Finally, she could make out a low, dim glow at the end of the passage. There was an open doorway ahead. She dragged herself forward, and then stopped at the entrance, open-mouthed.

The walls and ceiling of the large chamber beyond glittered like stars on a dark night sky. Ahead of her rose four pairs of massive crystal pillars, lining either side of a well-worn path that led deeper into the chamber beyond. Everywhere she looked, mana crystals covered her view—there must have been thousands of them, their collective glow illuminating the chamber.

At the sight of such wonders, Celia forgot about all the hardships her body had been suffering. She stepped onto the path, eyes wide with fascination, trying to take in everything around her. She passed one pair of the incredibly large crystal pillars, then another. As she neared a third pair, she could see far enough into the chamber to make out what must have been the source of all these marvels.

Before her stood a curved rock, almost in the shape of a seat, which protruded out of a sea of small crystals. On top of that rock was what she thought was a glowing yellow egg.

It wasn't solid, however. It looked more like a dense golden mist, ribbons of light dancing within it.

Hypnotized by the shifting and turning of the lights, Celia didn't notice how close she had come to the glowing egg until she bumped her forehead against something hard, causing her to stumble backward and fall.

Celia groaned as she rubbed her sore head. She picked herself back up, now noticing the glass cylinder which encased the misty egg—as well as the spider-web of cracks which spread across its surface. The impact had shocked her out of her reverie and allowed her to start thinking more clearly. She couldn't even begin to explain what the object in front of her was, or why it was encased in glass, but she knew it was the source of this strange mana.

Copious amounts of dark-gray mist flowed from it and leaked into the chamber through the cracks. She instinctively tried Inspecting it, even though she couldn't possibly get anything back—the misty egg was just an object after all.

But to her surprise, she did. Her diamond-shaped mark began to heat up, and she quickly brought up the runes for viewing.

You have failed to Inspect your target.

Error logged. An overseer has been alerted.

Celia's eyes narrowed as she tried to understand what this meant. All these runes were notifications which came directly from the World Seed, a mysterious force no one understood. It governed and controlled practically everything in this world, and it did that through its mark, which every living thing was born with. Celia's eyes lingered on the mark on her wrist, but this was the first time she had seen anything even close to what she just received. What, or who was this "overseer"? Perhaps it was another part of her Inspection skill she wasn't aware of. She sighed, promising herself to work harder on her skills in the future.

Walking around the rock, Celia couldn't help but feel that something was amiss. She couldn't quite put a finger on it, not until she faced one of the crystal columns again.

The crystals… they were gray. None of the manas she knew of had a gray color. It was just another mystery, in a place which seemed to be full of them.

As she circled the glass casing a second time, she again started to experience the effects of the mana on her body. It was time to go. She thought about taking the strange egg with her, but it was far too large. Besides, she didn't want to risk what would happen if she came in direct contact with it. Instead, she decided to Siphon it for all she could, then go back to the library and collect her loot.

Celia placed her right hand on a small crack in the glass and used the same Siphon she had a hundred times in the past. A light-green beam shot out of her finger toward the center of the yellow egg, and the moment it connected, it was as if she had been stuck by lightning. Her mind went blank as ecstasy coursed through her. Her knees buckled, and her eyes rolled back in pleasure, a moan escaping her lips.

But just as suddenly as it started, it stopped. She stared at the strange egg in confusion and then in horror as she was abruptly flung backward a few feet, slamming into the rough floor, then sliding across it.

She gasped and rolled to one side as her body argued with itself about whether it was supposed to feel pain or pleasure from the torrent of mana being channeled into her. As she struggled to regain control, a flurry of notifications began to appear.

Congratulations, you have gained one point of Vessel.

Error logged. An overseer has been alerted.

The rest of the runes began to blur with her surroundings. It was as if her body was being ripped apart, only to be followed by mind-shattering pleasure, which then flipped back again to intense, searing pain. Not able to handle the conflicting sensations coursing through her body, Celia's vision began to darken as she drifted into unconsciousness.

CHAPTER 3

SWATHES OF GOLDEN sands shifted and spread before him without end. Amber mounds and mountains alike rose and fell as the environment passed him on his never-ending travels. Sprays of dust danced along with the winds, blocking his view, affording him a brief pause to collect his thoughts.

He was but a child when he first woke in this place; it had been a long time since then. At first this world had been a mystery, full of new and interesting things to discover. He had traveled the land to witness and experience all it could offer, but it had not taken long for him to realize it was all an illusion, a simple imitation of a real world.

No matter how far he traveled, it was the same. The same ground, the same sky, the same lake. After much time spent exploring, he realized this world was in actuality quite small. It only stretched from horizon to horizon—once he crossed that threshold, he found himself back where he had begun. The most distressing thing, however, was the fact he was alone, truly alone in this world.

He spent most of his time playing with his own mana. He had released so much of it in his time here that it was a permanent presence in this world. A never-receding gray mist which he was able to manipulate freely and easily, it was by far the largest source of entertainment in this unchanging place.

Often, he spent his time trying to remember how things had been before he'd found himself here. But no matter how hard he tried, only a few memories came back to him. Large white feathered wings attached to a vague female form wearing a long white dress, a black mask with purple eyes shining through, and one word… *Aziel*. Was it his name? It felt oddly personal to him, but he did not know why.

There was no way to tell how long he had actually been in this place. There was no moon or sun to help measure time, just a static starry night. He walked and walked and reviewed those memories countless times in his head, but he could not find an answer for how he had arrived here. He suspected the white-clothed woman must have had something to do with it, but he could not be sure.

That, however, didn't stop him from feeling a deep sense of rage and resentment about his current situation. What could he possibly have done to deserve this? He wanted answers, but how? There was no way out.

But then, he had sensed something enter his world… It felt familiar, but not entirely so. He stood, brushing away the sand which stuck to his skin and gazed once more across the landscape he had come to know so well. There it was: a tiny oval of gray mist, very much like his own mana. He stared directly into it, focusing intently, and strange symbols he had never seen before began to take shape before his very eyes, accompanied by a sudden and terrible headache.

He blinked and shook his head, and the symbols disappeared, as if they hadn't existed in the first place—along with the pain.

A moment of confusion followed, but then he saw a new mist appear. It manifested around the gray oval, and while the two looked similar, this new mist had a greenish color. It also appeared to be growing as it consumed everything around it.

He realized this strange mana was actually consuming *him*, along with the world around him. The mana-heavy air was being sucked into it, but the rate at which it was doing so was so slow and inconsequential, he wasn't alarmed by it at all. On the contrary, it captivated him.

He moved forward to study it more closely. He sensed this strange green mana was not entirely new; it was just different. At its foundation, it was still the gray mana he knew so well—but with some minor imperfections causing it to look and behave differently.

He had known different manas existed, but had never been exposed to any other than his own. Or at the very least, he didn't remember if he had been. He prodded and poked the strange mist, hoping to learn something new. After a moment, he decided to take direct action. Focusing his will, he raised his hand and the surrounding gray mist swirled around the intruder before solidifying into a solid translucent shell, halting it.

The pale green mana tried to break out of its confinement. It pushed and scraped against the shell but was too weak to overcome it. Watching it struggle, he was disappointed at how easy it was to contain. Hoping for a more interesting result, he dissolved the shell and allowed the intruder to continue its feast. He then started to channel his own mana directly into it.

In response to this force-feeding, the strange green mist flared and expanded rapidly, gleefully consuming all it could. As it grew larger, it also became unstable, quickly losing its form as whatever kept it going seemed to come undone… until it finally collapsed into itself.

As soon as the greenish mist dissipated, the mana he had been channeling into it shifted and flooded into the original oval of gray mana which was left behind.

Its reaction was completely different. Instead of growing, the gray mist appeared to latch onto the channel as if holding on for dear life. A few moments later, the channel between them glowed brighter. He stared at it in utter confusion, as starting from the far end, the misty channel connecting them morphed into a beam of light and started moving toward him.

The moment that light reached him, his mind was blasted with a rush of information. He recoiled and fell to his knees as he tried to comprehend all the new images and words. Most of it seemed to be some sort of language, but it wasn't only that. There were flashes of images depicting strange creatures, and other assorted objects. It was all words without meaning and pictures without context.

It took a few moments for the barrage of information to run its course. When it ended, he knew an entirely new world had just been opened to him.

More importantly, he knew the gray oval he had somehow forged some sort of connection with was not just a random speck of mist. It was something called a mana vessel, and it belonged to another living being.

Using this new link as a guide, he focused and tried to pull himself toward it. The world around him groaned in response. He could feel the very fabric keeping it together beginning to tear as an increasing amount of gray mist flowed and curled around him. Large fissures appeared in the ground and sky, and the world started to lose its color.

Then, with a sudden and deafening boom, he was free.

* * *

The first thing he perceived was how bright and constricting everything was.

He was stuck within a sphere of golden light, and so he shook and struggled in an attempt to free himself. With every twist, the golden light started to dim, and its strength grew weaker along with it. The walls stretched, and with every bit of extra space, he felt better, as moving his limbs became easier. He was so focused on releasing himself that even when a loud shattering noise rang around him, he paid it no mind.

As the pressure around him lifted, the sphere of light became transparent, allowing him to finally take his first look at the new world he had entered.

He was in a large, rocky cavern. Translucent gray rocks jutted out of the ceiling and walls, glittering. His mind worked hard as he tried to connect what he was seeing with the words and images which were just dumped into his head. The connections came so quickly that he wondered if he knew what they were all along. Crystals. Mana crystals.

The oval of light was now so thin he was sure he could simply step through it. He took a tentative step down from the curved rock he found himself atop, and his feet ripped through the thin sheet of light, only to cause him to fall heavily onto his side. He groaned as he again tried to stand, but his legs were shaky and awkward beneath him. His body didn't look any different, but for some reason, it felt as if his legs had never before been used. None of it made sense to him—he had been walking for long periods of time in that world, so how could it be that his body was not used to the movement?

He looked back up at the curved rock, where the last remnants of the golden light were fading. At that point, understanding dawned on him.

He had not been moving at all; he had been trapped within that sphere of light all this time. So, had that world been all in his head? Was it some complex mental exercise he had created to keep himself busy? Or was it part of whatever that golden sphere had been? He didn't know, and he felt that familiar rage and resentment start to burn deep within him again.

His hands trembled as he grabbed the curved rock with both hands, using it to pull himself to his feet. Carefully, he emulated the walking movement he had made in that last world. His first steps were wobbly, and he almost fell to the ground again more than once, but soon he started to grasp the rhythm of it. He would need to practice if he ever wanted to attempt a sprint any time soon, but at least he could now move around.

Curious, he shuffled closer to a gray crystal. He could sense his mana within every single one of them, but it was the larger crystal columns that really caught his attention. They were near bursting with mana! And while that was reason enough for interest, what really struck him was the strange sensation they were giving off. He couldn't explain it, but they felt almost *alive*.

He could probe that in more detail later. For now, his excitement and curiosity demanded the rest of the cavern be explored. It was both tall and wide, and a straight path which did not look natural cut through its center, running between the eight crystal columns that dominated the space.

He began walking down the path, placing every step with care, until he noticed a figure on the ground beside him.

He could tell this creature was the one he had established a direct link with. He could sense it, his mana coursing through the link and into it. He knelt beside the creature, his heart thumping in his chest, his eyes transfixed. There was a strange attraction connecting them, but the creature otherwise looked unfamiliar to him. A humanoid form, its overall shape somewhat resembled his memory of the white-clothed woman from his memories. He wondered if all females shared the same shape. Other than that though, nothing fit.

This woman wore black clothing, and a pair of small black horns protruded from her head. He again tried to connect what he saw with the information he had just received.

This was far more difficult than the crystals, the connections in his mind failing to reach any firm conclusions. There seemed to be large gaps in the information he was given, and many images of the creatures it did include shared the same basic bipedal shape. Several ideas came to mind—was she human? Perhaps an elf? No, elves didn't have horns as far as he knew.

Not satisfied by this answer, he stretched his hand toward the woman and brushed his fingers gently against her white skin. He felt her stiffen a little, but there was otherwise no response. He proceeded to caress and probe every part of her. It was a strange sensation. Until now the only living thing he had felt was himself.

There was also that odd attraction to this woman he couldn't explain. The whole experience was thought-provoking… but also pleasant. She was soft and warm, and for some reason, her whole body seemed to now jerk a little at his touch, but that did not stop him from continuing his explorations.

When his hand touched the woman's chest, her whole body convulsed for a few seconds, and she let out a strange high-pitched noise. Surprised, he jolted upright and pulled his hand back. Wondering what had just happened, he looked at his fingers, then back at the woman still lying on the floor.

Not wanting to harm her without realizing, he reluctantly decided to leave the unconscious woman alone for now. He took a step back, then turned and struggled as he placed one foot in front of the other and made his way farther along the path toward the open doorway at the far end. The surrounding area was saturated with his mana—he could feel the larger crystal columns slowly feeding it into the surrounding environment—but it was nowhere near as dense as it had been within that prison of a world.

This lower concentration had one consequence: it made him extra sensitive to its whereabouts. Other than the unconscious woman behind him, he also sensed two new mana vessels moving toward him. They were both small, but one was much larger than the other.

They were getting closer; he could hear muffled voices now, coming from just beyond the doorway. Not knowing what to expect, he backtracked and hid behind the farthest column, where he waited for the two new visitors to appear. Would they look like the unconscious female? Or would they be completely different? His mind rushed through all the possibilities as he anticipated his first encounter with this world's denizens.

"Dammit, Elsie, you know how time-sensitive this mission is!" a male voice growled. "We can't install these ridiculous instruments every time we stop."

"The high commander ordered us to bring back as many readings as we can." That was a female voice, full of annoyance. "How else will we study this anomaly, Silus? And we didn't even stop to check the other room."

"High commander? I am a mage of the Maiv Order, you stupid girl! I don't take orders from your *high commander*!"

Their voices echoed through the chamber, making it easy to eavesdrop even from this distance.

He saw the pair step into the main chamber. The one presumably called Silus was leading, with the girl named Elsie following closely behind. They looked very different from one another: Silus had brown hair that brushed the top of his shoulders and hid the nape of his neck. His strides were smooth and graceful, his long, open red robe swishing from side to side revealing a decorated black shirt and pants.

Elsie, however, had a more youthful appearance, with short black hair cut into a long side bang that covered a third of her face. She was hunched forward, a heavy leather bag on her back, and she wore a tight-fitting brown leather tunic with metal plates attached for extra protection. With every movement, her short sword clanked against them.

"Look at this place!" Silus exclaimed. His gaze drifted across the many crystals while his voice echoed through the chamber.

Still watching and listening to the pair from behind the far crystal column, he couldn't help but smile. Unlike the unconscious female, he was able to identify these two; they were definitely human.

CHAPTER 4

SILUS STOOD OPEN-MOUTHED, gazing around the cavern they had just entered.

"Have you ever seen so many mana crystals?" He spread his arms wide, then turned to his companion, feeling his face break into a large grin. "Do you have any idea what this could mean, Elsie? If we can get these crystals back to the capital, then all our troubles would disappear. The damn Jannatins and Odanians wouldn't dare touch us."

His eyes were instinctively drawn to the greatest source of light in the chamber, and he gasped when he noticed the large crystal columns that flanked the pathway.

"By Adara's blessed flame… look at the size of them! Those are Capital Crystals, eight of them." He hurried to one to run his hand over its cold, smooth surface. "Never mind keeping them at bay, we can utterly *crush* them with these!"

"If you say so, Silus," Elsie replied flatly. When he turned to look at her, he saw she had already started unpacking the large bag she was carrying. She seemed completely uninterested in his discovery. These crystals would change the balance of power in the region for generations to come, he would be showered with praise for discovering them—and she had barely given them a second glance. Then again, she was no mage. He should have expected such ignorance.

One of the items Elsie had pulled out was a small square box with a funnel on top. When she clicked a button set into its side, the contraption hissed as it pulled in air. She studied the device, her eyebrows slowly inching upward. "This place has a very high concentration of mana. It's like nothing I've ever seen or even read about before... here, take a look."

She held out the device to him, and Silus recoiled as if she had offered him a plate of rancid meat.

Many of these devices were old, thousands of years old. Depending on their function, they used different types of crystals as a power source.

Silus hated these "Magitech" devices, as they were called, and so did most other mages. It would take years of studying and hard training to gain the needed skills to conduct an effective Analyze or Detect Magic. Not only did these devices perform a service that previously only mages such as himself could offer, but also, Silus didn't understand how they worked. Thankfully, very few did.

While some Magitech engineers had been successful in recreating simple devices like the one Elsie had just used, the more complex and much more sought-after devices such as ones used for long distance communications and war were still far out of their reach. The majority of these engineers only really had the expertise to repair salvaged devices suffering from minor damage.

"I am a mage and a detector; I don't need these silly devices to tell me how much mana is around me." Silus took a deep breath to calm himself. His expression softened as he again gazed upon the crystal columns in front of him. "Besides, even a simpleton with no affinity for mana at all would feel it here. It's astounding... though it does have a strange feeling and color. Which leads to a more pressing question: what mana type is it?"

Elsie smirked. "What? A detector of your caliber can't tell?" she teased, but shrank back when Silus wheeled around to glare at her.

"Impudent brat!" he yelled. "How dare you speak to me in such a manner? I'll make sure your precious high commander hears of this when we get back to the capital." His jaw clenched tightly before he continued, more in control of himself. "Now be useful for once and do your damn job. Use that monstrosity of a machine you've been lugging around and figure out what we have here."

Elsie's face had drained of color, as she scrambled to unpack the rest of the equipment. "Y-yes of course, Adept Silus! I apologize," she mumbled.

Silus felt his rage ebb at her fear. Why shouldn't she fear him, he reasoned—he was a mage after all. Elsie was just a soldier, a woman who had joined up after the king decreed they be allowed to be part of the armed forces. A desperate act for a desperate kingdom. Women had no place in war, in Silus's opinion—it was a situation that only made these crystals even more important.

Silus sighed; he knew he was being too hard on her, but it was still so frustrating. As a detector, he had specialized in skills that allowed him to sense the amount of mana in the air around him and within other people. The mage guild valued detectors, as they were highly useful in classifying magical items as well as identifying persons with the ability to weave spells, which they could then conscript into the guild. This power was why Silus had been chosen for the task of investigating the mana anomaly in the first place.

But no matter what he did or tried, his skill had failed to detect what kind of magic lay within any of the crystals here. He could see and feel the mana heavy air in this place; it just wasn't as clear as he was used to. The Detect Magic skill was supposed to provide him with exact numbers representing mana totals, as well as the breakdown of the type of mana present. Instead, he kept receiving a notification of some error and a mysterious overseer getting alerted—it was a notification he had never seen before, something he would report to the archmage once he got back to the capital. Elsie didn't need to know about his failings.

Silus crossed his arms and waited for Elsie to put together another device she had pulled out of her bag. "What's taking so long?"

"Just the last part," Elsie said, placing a white orb on top of the device and clicking it into place. "Let's see what we have here," she whispered, pulling a small lever. The device began to hum and click repeatedly. After a few seconds, the orb started to spin. Elsie crouched beside it and peered into a small peephole at its side.

Her eyes opened wide at what she saw. "That's impossible!" she gasped.

Silus wrenched his attention away from the crystal column he was lovingly stroking, feeling his irritation rise again at her words. "Stop talking to yourself and speak up, woman!" he snapped. "What does it say?"

She turned around to face him.

"All of them."

"All of what?" he spat.

"It's detecting *all eight* primary mana types, as well as demonic."

He glared at her, eyes narrowed. "Just to be clear here, what you're telling me is that we dragged that thing all across the Central Wilds, and it's broken?" His voice had a dangerous edge to it.

"No! It's not broken! It's just… I don't know! Let me try calibrating it again."

Silus closed his eyes and pinched the bridge of his nose. It had to be broken; it is difficult not to notice demonic mana, even in small quantities. They would be struggling to keep themselves from turning into demons if they were surrounded by it, or at the very least feel its intrusive corruption. Silus ran a hand through his hair and glanced at Elsie as she went over the many parts of her device. Much to his chagrin, he had to admit her Magitech device was usually quite accurate in its analysis. But *all* mana types? How was that *possible*?

He pulled out a small wooden case from his own sack, unhooking the clamps securing it. When he flipped the lid open, three small glass-like spheres were revealed. The archmage had given him these just in case things went sideways. Each sphere had a trace of a specific mana type trapped within it and was made of a material which reacted when exposed to that same type of mana. Silus hated resorting to such methods, but he really didn't have a choice at this point.

Gently, he picked each of them up and laid them on his open palm.

At first, nothing seemed to happen. Then, slowly, each glass bead started to glow a different color, before they began breaking down into dust.

"Impossible…" he whispered, as he stared wide-eyed at his now-empty palm. At that moment, a sound came from deeper within the cavern, and both he and Elsie looked up to see a naked man struggle to balance as he walked toward them.

Silus's whole body stiffened as he stared at him in utter shock. The man sported black hair and had a fit, muscled body, he looked human in every way, but through his sensitive detector eyes, he was something else entirely. The sheer amount of mana coursing through the stranger meant he shone like the sun at its brightest. Silus didn't even need to actively use his skills to know how monstrous this being was.

Silus's whole body went numb as his mind struggled to process what he was seeing. Elsie drew her blade and screamed out a warning.

Hearing this, the stranger froze in place, his head tilting to one side.

"Silus… Silus! Snap out of it!" he heard Elsie shout, but he could not break himself out of his trance. Elsie slowly backed farther away while maintaining her defensive stance. "Who are you and what are you doing here?" she barked, her blade pointed toward the stranger.

The man looked at them oddly, then slowly raised his arm—but as soon as he did so, Elsie yelled again for him to stop.

"Answer me!" she shouted, holding her short sword in front of her. "I am a soldier of the Maivian Army under orders to secure this place. Name yourself or I will strike you down!"

"Name...?" the naked man asked. He looked genuinely confused by the question, but then he lowered his hand to his side and gazed back at the now-agitated Elsie.

"My name is Aziel," he declared, in a stronger voice than before.

Even in his shocked state, Silus was aware that Elsie was trembling lightly, and her cheeks were flushed. "Why are you naked?" she snapped.

"Naked?" the stranger said, before he examined himself briefly.

"Yes, naked! Why are you not wearing any clothes?" Elsie's cheeks appeared to be getting redder and redder the longer this conversation went on.

The man named Aziel again tilted his head. "I have always been this way."

Elsie stared at him a few more seconds, then took a step toward her large bag. Kneeling beside it, she pulled out one of their travel blankets.

"Here, cover yourself with this," she said, tossing it to the man.

The stranger looked at the blanket, flipping it back and forth as if he had never seen anything like it before. He glanced at Silus then at his clothes, his eyes narrowing as if trying to figure something out. He then draped the blanket over his shoulder, pulling and rearranging the fabric so it mimicked a robe in some sense. Luckily for Elsie, the blanket was large enough to cover him.

Elsie let out a long breath, the tension leaving her.

She turned her attention back to Silus and took a few steps toward him to grip his shoulder. "Silus! What is wrong with you?" she hissed into his ear, shaking him. "Snap out of it."

Silus was still staring at the stranger, who shone brighter than anything he had ever seen. "There's so much..." he whispered.

Elsie blinked in surprise, looking from him to the stranger with both curiosity and concern. She wouldn't understand; she couldn't see the same thing he did.

As the paralyzing shock began to wear off, Silus leaned in closer to whisper into her ear. "We must kill him," he hissed.

Elsie was taken aback. "Why? He isn't attacking or doing anything wrong."

"He is a monster!" Silus snapped. "You must trust me in this, we can't let a being such as him go free, he must be disposed of!"

Silus could see her mull over his words, the doubt in her eyes. But then her body tensed, and she gripped the hilt of her blade tighter.

Silus nodded, then turned his head to face Aziel, who had remained where he was, confused. When their eyes met, Silus's expression hardened.

"Now!" he yelled.

He lifted his right hand and swept it in front of him, leaving behind a cloud of red mist. Silus had never been a powerful mage in an offensive sense; he had focused on his detector skills at the cost of the others. But he had to kill this abomination before it had a chance to use its magic.

The stranger looked surprised by his actions. Instead of moving to protect himself, he stared at the spell Silus was weaving, captivated by it with an almost childlike curiosity.

"Is that fire mana?" he asked, but Silus ignored him. He was too busy trying to get the symbols he was weaving to manifest. He cursed to himself for not taking weaving classes seriously. At that moment, the last symbol began to glow red, and Silus grinned triumphantly then grunted as he rearranged the separate symbols into a single intricate glyph. Without hesitation, he directed it toward the stranger, crying out, "Die, monster! Immolate!"

The effect was almost instantaneous. With an audible *whoosh*, the air around the stranger erupted into flames, engulfing him. But he reacted—almost too quick for Silus to perceive—releasing a gray mist that swirled and solidified into what looked to be a translucent barrier, creating a protective dome around him. Despite this, Silus could see the flames had managed to strike the stranger.

The man stared grimly at his trembling right arm. His skin was red and even charred black in some spots.

Elsie, meanwhile, had taken a long route to avoid his flames and had finally been able to flank the stranger. She leapt and slashed her sword down on top of the protective dome. A loud clang rang through the cavern as sparks flew from the point of impact, but her strike didn't seem to do much against the barrier.

Silus let out a frustrated grunt and again released another cloud of mana. They needed to end this.

The stranger frowned as Elsie continued to strike his dome. He then took a step back as if anticipating something, at that moment, Elsie raised her sword high and yelled, "Power Strike!"

Her hands quickened to a blur, and the blade struck the barrier with much greater force, causing it to buckle inward and crack as sparks discharged from the surface. The stranger raised his hand and pointed his palm toward her.

Elsie took a step back as three tendrils of concentrated gray mana coalesced and shot toward her at a blistering pace. She tried to defend herself by slashing her sword downward, but the tendrils moved too fast, and she yelped as they smashed into her chest, throwing her off her feet and slamming her hard against the far cavern wall. As Silus watched, she slid to the floor where she sat, unmoving, her head slumped forward.

Silus hissed and refocused his attention on weaving his spell, but just as he neared its completion, he felt the wind around him picking up speed. He glanced up, and his eyes opened wide.

A massive wave of gray mist was rushing in his direction. He had no chance to react before it engulfed him, its force knocking him onto his back. The spell he had been painstakingly weaving blew away, disappearing within the cauldron of gray mist.

But it didn't stop there. The mist began to coalesce into a single thick tendril, and Silus could only watch in horror as he saw his death approaching from above. It slammed down into him, crushing him against the rocky ground.

The tendril continued to grow, its weight pressing down harder and harder. Silus squirmed, his eyes bulging. He grunted and tried to beg for his life—to say something, anything—but the air had already been squeezed out of his lungs. His face contorted in pain and tears fell from his eyes. His blood began to pool around him as the sound of his own cracking bones reached his ears. A single notification appeared before him, the runes flashing, as if demanding his attention.

Warning: you are suffering from critical injuries and require healing!

The bitter taste of his blood coated his mouth as his vision began to darken. His last thoughts were of the fate of his home, his race, and the evil and destruction about to be unleashed upon them by this catastrophe made flesh.

* * *

Looking around himself, Aziel registered the complete silence that now filled the cavern. This had not gone how he imagined. All he had wanted to do was interact with these two humans—to speak to the inhabitants of this new world, to learn from them. Instead, he was forced to defend himself, and now both lay still and silent.

There was also the strange sensation he had felt at the moment of the man's death. It seemed he had somehow absorbed a small portion of his mana. It wasn't large enough to be visible, but Aziel had sensed it quickly make its way toward him. As soon as it connected with his chest, he felt a wave of strength flow through him. But then he felt a slight burning sensation in his wrist followed by strange gray runes appearing before his eyes. Surprisingly, he was able to read and understand them.

Error logged. An overseer has been alerted.

Aziel had no idea what to make of this. Instead, he tried reliving the events that had just occurred, pondering their meaning. The girl mentioned she was part of the Maivian Army, and he remembered the man saying something about a Maiv Order. Perhaps he could find out something about himself from them.

He took a quick glance at the girl, still lying slumped against the wall, and then back at the man's corpse. The man had seemed angry before he started attacking, but why? What had initiated this conflict? Aziel had already scanned all the images and words that had been dumped into his mind through the new link. As far as he could tell, he should not have looked particularly dangerous. Elsie didn't seem troubled by his overall appearance, only his nudity. So why had the man taken such drastic action?

Aziel stared in disappointment at the man's crushed body. He knelt beside him, shaking his head as he began to undress the corpse. As he threw off the now-singed blanket he was wrapped in, Aziel noticed the burns on his own arm had been healed.

He dragged his fingers across his new, healthy skin and smiled. He wasn't sure what had healed him, but he was thankful nonetheless. He then began the process of putting on the mage's bloodied clothes, which should at least solve the nudity problem, for now.

Glancing back in the direction he came from and where he had left the other unconscious women, Aziel scratched the back of his ear. He would come back to check on the woman later. The girl named Elsie had mentioned another room. Perhaps it was time to begin his exploration of this new world.

CHAPTER 5

GRADUALLY, CELIA RETURNED to her senses. At first, she felt groggy and barely aware of her surroundings. But as the seconds passed, the fog which clouded her mind lifted and was replaced by a surge of adrenaline. Recalling what had happened, she scrambled to her feet and glanced anxiously at her surroundings.

The first thing she noted was that she had been moved. Someone or something had positioned her to lean comfortably against the cavern wall, instead of being sprawled out on the rocky ground. The second and more immediate issue though, was the overwhelming numbness permeating her muscles. It reminded her of the pain she experienced after sleeping on her arm for too long, but she felt it everywhere. How long had she been unconscious?

The moment her Siphon had connected, she had been awed to discover how vast and full that mysterious egg's mana vessel was. It was endless. She could have kept going for days and would not have caused a ripple in the vast ocean of mana simply sitting there. But whatever that thing was, it had noticed her, somehow halting her Siphon almost as soon as she began.

It hadn't stopped there, however; it then did something that should not have been possible. It had created a mana link between them. The amount of mana used to create the link was so immense it had completely overwhelmed her. She could still feel—even see—that link if she focused on it.

Celia closed her eyes in an attempt to understand what had happened. Just one look at the glass cylinder previously housing the egg told her it was no longer sealed away inside, but through the link, she could tell it was still nearby.

Well, it hadn't killed her, she thought, so that had to be a good sign. It still might not be wise to go looking for it—but then again, she had to find out what sort of mess she'd gotten herself into.

Focusing on the link within her was surprisingly easy. Even more surprising was that the thing was still channeling mana into her. Only a small amount, just enough to take the edge off, but the realization shook her to her core.

Celia knew of only one class of beings who could bestow their mana onto others: the Ascended. They were rare and extremely dangerous, the closest thing to what one might consider as gods. But how—? Something wasn't clicking into place.

Other races had the ability to passively absorb the different mana types which were naturally occurring in the environment; it was like breathing to them. Humans, orcs, beastkin, or even simple horses or dogs, they could all do it. But not Celia, not demons.

Demons could only absorb demonic mana, which could only be created by Siphoning it out of other living things, killing them in the process. True, Celia could weave other mana types if she had the corresponding traits, but she still couldn't absorb them. Unless that egg was a demonic Ascended, it couldn't possibly be feeding her mana.

A demonic Ascended... Celia cringed at the very idea; she didn't know if such a thing could even exist. She remembered her wry thoughts before she had entered this cursed place. Endless torment and untold misery, indeed.

Quickly, she placed her left hand on her mark and tried to pull up her personal log. But instead of the familiar breakdown of her attributes and skills, she only received the same concerning notification.

Error logged. An overseer has been alerted.

She tried again and again, but the result was the same. Unsettled, she scanned her surroundings once more.

How could she have been so stupid, playing around with mana sources of that magnitude! She clicked her tongue, chiding herself.

She couldn't even get away—the link forged between them made sure of that. Whatever was linked to her could use it to track her wherever she went. Given the amount of mana used to bring it into being, breaking it was probably impossible. And now she couldn't even access her log. What did that even *mean*? Was she no longer bound by the World Seed?

No, that was impossible. *Everything* was bound by the World Seed.

Frustrated, she kicked at a medium-sized crystal jutting out of the floor beside her, and it rang from the blow. The chime echoed several times around the large chamber before falling silent again.

Her face paled as she realized how loud that had been. She leapt behind the nearby crystal pillar and crouched low, bracing herself. She was certain whatever it was that linked itself to her must have heard and would come back to finish whatever it was it had been intending to do. But as the minutes rolled by, nothing happened.

Celia sighed with relief, then giggled at herself. "Okay… okay," she muttered. "I need to calm down and think this through." She closed her eyes and took a deep breath.

Calmer now, she stood and moved toward the curved rock that had housed the misty egg. The glass had been shattered, and the shards mixed with the sea of small gray mana crystals around the rock.

To her relief, it was much easier to move around now. The air was still thick with the same strange mana, but it wasn't anything close to how dense it had been when she first entered. It no longer felt like walking through a thick syrup while carrying a large sack of grain over each shoulder.

She knelt and brushed her fingers along the surface of one of the small gray crystals and felt that familiar tingling inch up her fingers and spread from the point of contact. Again she wondered what this mana was. One thing was certain though, it was not demonic as she had first feared, but it still felt similar.

Not knowing what to make of this, she gave up trying to understand. Instead, she turned to face the well-worn path and the eight large crystal pillars that flanked it and shook her head in disbelief.

When she had first entered here, she had been so overwhelmed by the mana and the view that she hadn't put two and two together. Now that she was calm and thinking more clearly, she easily identified the columns for what they were: Capital Crystals.

She had seen many mana crystals of different sizes and types before. They were the foundation of the civilized world, after all. But she had never seen a capital class one. She had heard and read of them while in the Kingdom of Maiv, however. The Maivians, like every other nation, used crystals for practically everything. But as a kingdom, they only had a single Capital Crystal in their possession. A fire type, if she remembered correctly.

Celia smiled wearily as she tried to foresee the impact these Capital Crystals would have. Nations throughout history had fought wars of annihilation just to secure a single one of these things. One of the major reasons the time following the fall of the Caelian Empire had been so chaotic was the scramble for control over their six known Capital Crystals.

And here were eight rather large ones just sitting here before her, doing nothing.

Celia recalled the lessons the mages taught her during class. Mana crystals were simply mana made solid. Unlike normal mana, however, a crystal's solid state made it difficult—and therefore inefficient—for someone to absorb mana directly from them. Crystals, while valuable in their own right, were only as useful as the enchantment placed upon them which would allow for the use of the mana stored within to perform a specific function.

Every type of mana crystal had specific areas it excelled in. Celia remembered how happy her parents were when they could finally afford a tiny enchanted fire crystal, which they had used to heat their small farmhouse and cook their food.

Of course, nothing was without cost or risk. Mana crystals were notoriously difficult to find. They only formed in places with a naturally higher than normal concentration of a particular mana, but those places were few and far between. Some types were rarer than others, due to their nature, and the only other way of harvesting involved hunting down live creatures.

It wasn't a widely understood subject, but when a creature died, a portion of its mana vessel—the place where mana collected within living things—sometimes solidified into a crystal. The type of crystal was usually linked to the creature's nature. Celia wondered how small hers would be if she ended up creating one. It wouldn't be a demonic crystal, as those didn't exist. Given her ability to weave fire mana, it was a good bet that it would be a fire crystal, but since she would have to be dead to find out, she supposed it didn't really matter.

Crystals were also not infinite. Once the mana within was depleted, they would shatter into tiny dust particles, forcing people to use them sparingly. This was why Capital Crystals were so valuable. Not only were they enormous, but they also had an ability to generate mana within them over time and link with smaller crystals across vast distances to recharge them.

Capital Crystals were national treasures and were always kept close to a nation's seat of power. That usually meant the capital of a country or province—hence the name.

Celia placed a tentative hand on the surface of the Capital Crystal, her hand tingling at the point of contact. There was so much power there, enough for a whole country. Shaking her head, she pulled her hand back; she had a more immediate and personal problem to address.

She made her way carefully down the path, back toward the entrance—stopping abruptly when she saw a naked human male on the floor. He was surrounded and covered in his own dried blood. Celia rubbed her nose; she was no stranger to dead bodies, and from the hanging smell of decay, this one had been here for a while, at least a day.

Since she did not recognize this person, he must have come in after her, meaning Celia had been unconscious for at least that long. How was that even possible? Could the forging of the link be the reason? Celia bit her lower lip, her focus returning to the corpse. His injuries gave the impression that something large had stepped on the poor man, squashing him like an insect. Grimacing at the thought, she moved on.

Closer to the doorway, she noticed a familiar-looking contraption discarded on the ground. She recognized it as one of the more common Magitech devices the adventurer guilds used to Detect Magic on their new applicants, but this one had been burned to a crisp.

There was also another human at the edge of her vision, a woman this time. She was slumped against the chamber wall and looked in rough shape. Celia moved closer, looking for signs of breathing. To her surprise, the girl was still alive.

She instinctively tried to Inspect her—the girl was unconscious and in a hostile place, and therefore not likely to complain to anyone. But the same notification appeared again:

You have successfully Inspected your target.

Error logged. An overseer has been alerted.

Celia sighed, and with no other options available, she examined the girl without magic. A white shield-shaped insignia with a red rose at its center was woven directly onto the girl's armor, identifying her as a soldier of the Maivian Army.

"Well, you got here quick," Celia remarked. They must have taken few to no rest stops to reach all the way here from their capital in such a short time. The girl's appearance provided no more clues, so Celia decided it would be best to question her directly.

Celia leaned in closer and whispered into the girl's ear, "Hey, wake up."

The girl did not respond.

Celia scratched her cheek as she went through her options. Steeling herself, she slapped the soldier hard across the face. The resulting *whack* echoed through the chamber, but she again got no response.

What had happened to this girl? She was out cold. Celia stood, looking down at the unconscious soldier before letting out a defeated sigh. She then turned and gazed at the doorway.

It was time to meet whatever that golden egg was, but the signs of recent battle and the squashed human man were not helping to calm her nerves.

Cautiously, she exited the crystal chamber and moved back along the hallway toward the library. Echoes of things being shuffled and heavy objects being dropped came from that direction. A curiosity bordering on compulsion cut through Celia's anxiety as she followed in the direction of the link.

At the library's open doorway, she peered inside. The once dusty but neatly organized library was now a total mess. Books and scrolls were piled and thrown about everywhere.

What in the dark Abyss? She thought, as she stepped into the large, circular room. It was as if a strong wind had swept through the place.

Carefully, she walked up and down the aisles looking for who or what was responsible, while trying to avoid stepping on the books and scrolls on the ground. Although the link between her and the mysterious being showed her what general direction to go in, they were now too close for it to be of any use.

This had to be the largest collection of knowledge on the continent. Her brief glances at the shelves revealed that the books here covered all kinds of subjects. Given their age, who knew what kind of secrets and lost understandings she could find in here? If she took the time to look.

Just then, she walked into a large open circular area marking what she assumed was the library's center. In the middle of this space sat a lone humanoid figure, cross-legged on the ground, surrounded by piled-up books and scrolls. The area around and above him was dimly illuminated by small gray orbs, hovering in the air.

He was facing away from her, but she could see he wore a red robe and had black hair and white skin. The book he was reading seemed to completely absorb him; he was quickly flipping pages as he scanned its contents.

Celia stared at his back from the edge of the circular area. Was that the being she was linked with? It seemed to be. But then, what had happened to the strange egg? She could feel a strange sense of closeness, as if every piece of her wanted to meld and become one with him.

She tiptoed closer, fearful of how he would react to her presence. He was an Ascended, after all—at least, if her theory was correct. And no one in their right mind would want to startle an Ascended...

"He-hello...?" she said meekly, her voice as light as a whisper.

The man's head shot up, causing her to flinch backward. Without turning to face her, he said in a deep, but pleasant voice, "Ah, you have finally awakened. I was beginning to fear you would never do so." He closed the book he was reading and placed it on top of a pile to his right. "I was planning to read about the circumstances of prolonged sleep next," he continued, placing his hand on the cover of another book with a chuckle.

He then stood and turned to face her.

The man was taller than she expected, towering several heads above her, and he looked human, in every detail except one. It was his eyes; they marked him as something different. They were light gray and shone brightly, like two full moons. Celia stared into them and couldn't help but admit how attractive he was. And from the way his eyes kept flicking down toward her body, she figured the feeling was mutual. Celia gulped as a familiar yearning began to spread within her.

The clothes he wore did not match the pretty face, however. They were smeared with blood, reminding her of the naked, mutilated corpse in the other chamber. As she looked, he raised one hand toward her. Before she could say anything, he smiled, and the link between them expanded and was flooded with mana—all of it headed into her.

She let out a soft moan, not expecting this turn of events, but then quickly realized what was happening. "Oh… oh! No! Stop!" she screamed as her legs buckled and she blinked rapidly, trying to keep herself upright while enduring the waves of pleasure spreading across her body.

At her cries, the flood of mana abruptly stopped. The man stared at her, his head tilted slightly to one side and his expression displaying utter confusion.

"P-please, my lord… warn me before you do something like that," she gasped, trying to control her breathing. *My lord?* What was she saying? A hint of panic invaded her mind.

"Does my reward not please you?" he asked with a slight frown. "I wished to thank you for the gift you have given me. I have read that giving something in return is proper etiquette."

Gift? Reward? What was he talking about? Celia's mind ran through the entire series of events that led her here, trying to make sense of his words.

"I don't understand… I didn't give you anything for you to reward me…" she said, rubbing the back of her neck nervously.

"Did you not bestow upon me the ability to read these texts through our link?" he asked.

He must have received his answer from her expression, since he continued without giving her a chance to reply. "Mm... interesting. Perhaps you didn't do it consciously? Or is it something that comes naturally with the link? I don't know much about how it works, and I'll admit I was slightly concerned at first. I also have found no text that speaks of it yet... unfortunately." He glanced toward the bookshelves to their left before turning back to her. "No matter, this changes nothing. I have still received a gift and must repay you for it."

Celia opened her mouth to respond, but before she could say anything he suddenly frowned and turned to face the direction of the library's entrance. His eyes narrowed and his body tensed, but a few moments later he seemed to relax. Shrugging, he turned back to face her again.

"So, what would you request as a reward?" he asked with a gentle smile.

"I... I don't know," she said as she looked away from his glowing eyes to take a quick glance toward the library's entrance.

What did he see back there? This whole situation was bizarre. She couldn't remember the last time she spoke to another person without some ulterior motive behind it, usually of the Siphoning kind. She also never thought an Ascended could be so... *normal* in his behavior. She wasn't sure what she had expected, but in her mind, this Ascended would have tried to kill or dominate her, not reward her.

Also, what could she ask for from an Ascended without being too presumptuous? Should she ask for some of his crystals? Perhaps some mana? Or maybe she should ask him to break the link? While she went through her options in her head, she used this opportunity to learn more about him; for the moment, they were linked together, after all.

She nervously bit her lower lip before swallowing her fears. "My lord... would you be willing to perhaps... answer a few questions for me?"

He was still standing in front of her, waiting patiently for her to answer his previous question.

"Questions?" he asked, as an eyebrow slowly rose in response to her request. "Certainly, it's only fair."

"Wha—" she squeaked, then coughed to clear her throat and tried again. "I... I suppose I should start with: what is your name?"

He stared at her, his face absent of any expression or emotion. "Ah, yes, how could have I forgotten my manners already?" he said, then took a few steps toward her. She flinched backward again, but he reached out and gently took her right hand in his, bending over it to kiss it briefly before straightening.

"My name is Aziel," he said confidently with a smile. "Would the beautiful lady before me honor me with her own?"

Celia felt her face and body heat up. She was caught completely off guard—and the fact that his touch was infused with mana didn't help. She could feel the tingling where their skin touched, and it even lingered at the location of his kiss.

"Aziel..." Celia repeated the name softly to herself, testing how it sounded. It was a name she had never heard of before now, but she found that she liked it. It took her a few moments to break out of her inner thoughts, but when she did, she smiled back at him. "I'm Celia," she replied before quickly adding, "and I'm not a lady or anything... that's just for nobles."

"It's a pleasure to meet you la—I mean, Celia," he replied, before letting go of her hand and scratching his right cheek lightly. "The gulde mentioned nothing about nobles..." he murmured to himself. "Is there anything else you wish to ask?"

Celia again took a second to examine him, remembering the golden misty egg she had found in the chamber when she first entered.

"Lord Aziel, forgive me for being blunt, but... what are you, exactly? I only ask because I'm fairly sure you're not a human." This time, she mustered the courage to look directly into his eyes.

What she saw surprised her. He looked away, breaking eye contact, his face expressing embarrassment—maybe even sadness—at her enquiry. She felt a slight pain radiate from her core at the sight, as if she shared in his worries.

Not wanting to upset him any further, she immediately added, "You don't have to answer; I was just curious! I didn't know it was a sensitive topic."

Aziel shook his head. "It's all right, the truth is I don't know what or even who I am, or at least I don't remember," he answered, his voice taking on a more solemn tone. "I have looked through these texts and the information you provided in search of answers, but have found nothing satisfactory." He again looked directly at her and added, "But you are correct. Although I seem to resemble them, I do not believe I am human."

Celia hesitated. "I think I have an idea of what you might be, but it is just a guess, based on what little I know..."

His eyes narrowed as he studied her for a moment. "Well, it would please me to hear—"

He was suddenly interrupted by a loud, piercing scream, which echoed through the hallway and into the large library. He again turned to face the entrance.

"That must be Elsie," he said flatly, his face devoid of emotion. "Perhaps she ran into some trouble?"

Celia's muscles had tensed, and she rubbed her suddenly sweaty palms on her ruined dress. That scream—the memory of her mother's bloodied face flashed through her mind. A chill ran down Celia's spine.

"Elsie? Who is Elsie?" she asked.

His gaze drifted back to her. "Elsie is a human girl who arrived here shortly after I was freed. She accompanied another... but he is dead now. She's been asleep almost as long as you were."

His gaze returned to the library's distant doorway. "I sensed her leaving, but thought it would be rude to pursue her before our conversation concluded. But... I now believe it would be wise to check up on her, given the circumstances."

Celia slowly nodded and followed him out of the library and back along the rock-hewn passage, toward the entrance. Despite another horrifying scream rending the air, Aziel did not appear to be in a hurry. In fact, he seemed to be taking his time, and she could have sworn he stumbled a few times as they walked.

As they neared the main entrance, he stopped suddenly. Not expecting this, Celia bumped into him and bounced back a step. It was like crashing into a wall… he didn't move or react at all.

"S-sorry," she mumbled, rubbing her head.

"She is not alone," he said ominously, ignoring her apology, but then he grinned. "Let us meet our new guest, shall we? This is turning into an interesting day indeed." He then stepped through the gap between the bent gates and into the light.

Celia didn't quite share in his joy. To her, the period since entering this place had been a series of dramatic ups and downs, and she didn't know what fate had in store for her next. But there was a need within her, almost forceful in its attempt at keeping her close to Aziel.

Shielding her eyes from the sudden assault of sunlight, she squinted and found herself in a familiar clearing. Aziel stood just a few steps in front of her. His head panned back and forth, a wide grin plastered on his face. It reminded her of children discovering Jannatin sweetcakes for the first time. She thought it was kind of endearing, but she couldn't entertain those thoughts due to the scene unfolding in front of them.

By the tree line stood two figures. The first, Elsie, was wrapped in vines which hung down from the trees. They were restraining her limbs and covering her mouth, silencing her. A single root as thick as her arm jutted out of the earth and appeared to have stabbed her clean through on her left side. She whimpered in pain, but glared defiantly at the second figure standing beside her, who now placed a hand on her cheek.

This second woman was shorter than Celia. Her skin had a light green tinge, her dark green hair reached just above her shoulders, and her large oval brown eyes gave them a sideways glance.

She might as well have been wearing no clothing, as all she was dressed in were a few strategically-placed leaves and thick green vines that wrapped around her hands and legs. Her body and the way she moved exuded a sexuality that even made Celia gawk, and a twinge of jealousy crept into her, which she immediately squashed. The plant lady leaned closer and licked a tear off Elsie's cheek. Her whole body shuddered as if experiencing pleasure from the act.

"Shh, child... see, I told you they would come." Her voice was soft but had a dangerous undertone. Ignoring Elsie's muffled cries of pain, she turned to face them. "Took you long enough. When I cleared the way for you to check what was inside that hole, I didn't realize it would take you two full days to reappear. I noticed this one fleeing and made use of her."

Celia blinked. It took her a moment to realize she was the one being addressed. "Two days? Clear the way? What are you talking about?" she replied, but then remembered the lack of creatures she had encountered. "Wait, that was you?"

The stranger nodded. "So you noticed... Yes, it was I who kept the Wilds away from you." She took two steps forward toward them.

"Why would you do that?" Celia asked, somewhat confused.

The plant girl narrowed her eyes, then shrugged. "I suppose there is no point in hiding this kind of information from you," she replied in a dismissive tone. "You see, powerful mana sources are often accompanied by something equally powerful and dangerous, so I needed someone to... hmm, how do I put this... test the waters?" She then covered her mouth with her right hand and giggled. "Just when I thought I would have to go into that maelstrom myself, you stumbled into my domain. I must say your timing was quite impeccable." She smiled. "So, I cleared a path to expedite your journey. Just under a day later, two humans followed you in. I could have stopped them, but I thought you might have perished in there."

Celia balled her fists as her annoyance boiled over. "Who are you and what do you want?" she growled.

Before the creature could answer, Aziel spoke. "A dryad," he murmured, as if talking to himself. "They were mentioned briefly in one of the books I read in the library. She should have a tree somewhere close by… or perhaps she is a member of a grove? Seeing a grove would be interesting." He looked around as if trying to find something.

The dryad glared at him, the disdain clear in her tone. "Be silent, human, I don't know how you sneaked in there without me noticing, but your betters are speaking—even if this one is just a Lesser succubus. I will deal with you later, like I've done with your friend here."

Celia cringed inwardly, hoping Aziel would not react negatively to the dryad's words. She did not want to be around an upset or insulted Ascended. The dryad seemed to have dismissed him as just another human.

Her worries proved unfounded however. After tilting his head for a few seconds in puzzlement, he turned to look at Celia and asked, "Lesser succubus?"

In those few seconds that she looked at him, she noticed his eyes had stopped glowing. They were normal light gray eyes now.

"Imbecile…" the dryad said, then refocused her attention on Celia. "Where were we before we were so rudely interrupted? Ah yes, I am Amber, a Stem of the Rosa Grove. The surrounding area was assigned to me as my domain." She spread her arms wide to indicate the forest around them. "Which means everything within that mountain is mine, too. And since so much of that delicious mana seems to have gone, it can only mean that you have taken it. So tell me, what did you find?"

Celia hesitated for a moment. Should she tell this creature about Aziel? Would she even believe her if she did? "What I found is mine to keep," she declared. "And I'd be damned if I let some naked plant lady take what is rightfully mine."

She wasn't really sure if she could take on a dryad; she had never encountered one before. She again lamented not being able to use her Inspection skill, as perhaps it would have given her something to work with, her level at the very least. But that didn't change the fact that this creature was getting on her nerves with her high-and-mighty attitude. And for some odd reason, she felt miffed at how the dryad had brushed Aziel off.

The bridge of the dryad's nose scrunched as she shook her head. "My dear," she replied in a calm voice, "as a fellow Enlightened I would have thought you were smarter than this. But then again, you are a demon. Perhaps I put too much stock in your kind." She shrugged and took a few steps back to stand beside Elsie again. "I should get rid of the distractions first. Then we can have a more... *direct* conversation."

The dryad raised her arm and dark-green mana flowed from her fingers. Elsie's eyes opened wide at the sight and renewed her struggle against her restraints. Aziel simply stared at the mana, grinning at this new development.

"That must be nature mana," he said. He took a few steps toward the dryad, but then stopped mid-stride, staring down at his open hands with a stern expression.

Amber didn't appear to pay any attention to Aziel's movement. She continued to weave her spell, symbols forming within the cloud of mana she had unleashed. As they collected into one larger symbol, she turned to the struggling soldier and leaned closer to her.

"Goodbye, my dear. You have been... somewhat useful."

Elsie's muffled voice grew more frantic as the dark green symbol glowed brightly, then shot into the ground beside her. A light rumbling sounded from the earth, followed by a loud crack as two branches similar to the one already impaling the struggling girl broke through the soil. Their sharp tips plunged into Elsie's body, one through her lower abdomen and the other through her heart.

Elsie gasped, then coughed once, vomiting blood as she did. Her face contorted as Celia witnessed her struggle to take in air before her eyes dulled, her body falling limp. The vines gradually loosened their grip around her and pulled back into the trees, leaving Elsie hanging in the air, impaled on the three thick wooden pikes.

Celia watched as Amber stroked the dead girl's cheek one last time, then turned to face them. "I wonder; why did you not kill these two? I would have thought Siphoning them would have been quite a treat, for someone with your... special needs. But I suppose it doesn't really matter now." Her eyes narrowed as a pair of branches manifested around her. They locked on Aziel, and she smiled innocently.

Celia looked at Elsie's violated body, and a hint of sadness crept into her heart. She didn't know this girl, but she didn't deserve to be tortured and then killed. Celia's hatred for this dryad only increased with every passing second. But then, the dryad's branches shot forward toward Aziel. Panic exploded within Celia as her hands reflexively reached out. She quickly unleashed her fire mana, the red mist coalescing into symbols in the air in front of her.

She completed her spell just in time as bolts of newly-formed fire flew toward the pair of branches, exploding on contact. Aziel didn't seem to notice any of this, however. He just stood where he was, unmoving, staring at his hands.

Amber scowled at the unexpected interruption, glaring at Celia. "Have you stooped so low, demon, that you would aid these humans!" she roared before weaving more branches, but this time targeting Celia herself.

Celia rolled to one side to avoid them, but to her surprise, the branches simply twisted and followed her. She quickly wove another spell as she dashed away, before turning and tossing a glowing red symbol on the ground in front of her. The symbol struck the ground and exploded into a horizontal curtain of flame, high and wide enough to provide her with cover. The branches shot into it, but immediately whipped back to avoid being burned. Celia used the moments afforded to her to take in a deep breath to try to calm her nerves. She hadn't been in an actual fight in years.

The dryad, on the other hand, hissed in fury. "Just accept your fate, demon. You have no chance against me," she declared, then started weaving a different spell, this time using brown earth mana. She crouched low, slamming the newly-formed symbols into the ground. A large crack formed in the soil, accompanied by a loud rumbling. Celia inhaled sharply as the crack exploded forward and quickly made its way toward her.

Celia again rolled aside to avoid the incoming spell, but as she scrambled to her feet, she was yanked back by her ankles and slammed into the ground hard, face first. Even with her eyes closed, she could see and read the runes of the notifications clearly:

Warning, you have sustained a minor injury!
Error logged. An overseer has been alerted.

She groaned, opened her eyes, and tried to pull herself up, only to find that she could not move her limbs. It was then she realized her grave mistake.

She had been so focused on avoiding the spells the dryad was throwing at her that she hadn't noticed how close to the tree line she had moved. And now, several vines had dropped down from the tall trees to wrap around her limbs, immobilizing her.

Warning, you have sustained a minor injury!
Error logged. An overseer has been alerted.

Amber laughed mockingly as more vines dropped from the trees and wrapped around Celia, slowly pulling her up off the ground. The last vine wrapped around her neck, and she struggled futilely as it began to squeeze.

Warning, you have sustained a minor injury!
Error logged. An overseer has been alerted.

"You're even weaker than I expected," the dryad commented, walking leisurely toward Celia. She had a smug grin plastered on her face as she began to weave another spell. Several sharp branches broke through the earth and began to coil around her. "I wonder… how many will you be able to take before you die? I hope you can endure more than the human," she cooed.

Celia tried to reply but couldn't—the vine around her neck continued to squeeze. She glared at the dryad, trying to figure a way out of this mess, but there was nothing she could do. Was this really the end? After all she had been through all these years, surviving on her own, would she die here? And for what?

A thunderous bang followed by a strong gust of wind caused Celia's muscles to stiffen as she dangled in the air. She looked around for the source and her eyes opened wide at what she saw.

Aziel was still standing in the same spot, staring at his hands seemingly oblivious to the violence forming around him. The soil and rock below his feet cracked. The air churned and mixed with a thick gray mist, picking up debris from the ground and hurling it around. It was as if a small storm had appeared before them and Aziel was its eye.

"My mana…" he said ominously. He glanced back at the entrance to the mountain behind him, and his hands clenched tightly. Slowly, he turned toward the dryad and Celia. His whole body was trembling. Celia could practically feel his rage, his frustration through the link, and she noticed his eyes were glowing again.

"Release her at once," he commanded, his voice as cold as ice. His eyes held a glint that promised violence.

Celia gaped at the sight. The person before her was nothing like the mysterious and somewhat carefree person she had spoken to in the library. Aziel looked like a force of nature now, and it was absolutely terrifying to behold.

Amber, however, did not seem cowed. Looking at the massive display of mana, she began to laugh hysterically. "So it was you all along! All this mana… with it I can finally evolve and create my own grove, away from mother and that harlot she calls a sister!" She swept her hands sideways, the distraction causing the vine around Celia's neck to loosen enough for her to take in a much-needed breath. But the sense of relief didn't last long. Celia's heart skipped a beat as she watched the sharp-tipped branches originally meant for her twist toward Aziel.

Her worries were unfounded, however. Aziel's eyes glowed even brighter, and the small storm around him grew in intensity. He raised his right hand toward the dryad's rapidly approaching branches, and as they got within a few feet of him, they slammed into a translucent shield. A thundering noise rang from the contact, leaving only splinters behind.

Amber stared at him in shock, her eyes wide in the face of this unexpected turn of events. Aziel did not pause to hear her response; gray mana churned around him as he dragged his outstretched hand slowly to one side. The dryad took a step back, and for the first time, fear—real terror—could be seen in her eyes.

Under Aziel's direction, the gray mana began coalescing around her. Several large translucent walls appeared and shot toward her, slamming into her from all sides. As they did, the edges merged with one another and quickly morphed into a shimmering translucent sphere, with her trapped within.

Aziel raised his hand, and the sphere followed its movement. He glared at the helpless and terrified dryad held inside it, and their eyes met for a moment. Then he slowly clenched his fist. Celia could see his hand tremble, as if pressing against a resisting force—and as his hand closed, the sphere shrank in response, beginning to crush its sole occupant.

Amber pushed back against the constricting walls and screamed. Celia noticed the dryad attempting to weave a spell to help her escape, but her mana seemed to evaporate as soon as it was released.

"Please stop! I'll do anything!" Amber begged; her cries fell on deaf ears, however. Aziel kept clenching his hand, and soon the sound of her screams died away, replaced by loud cracks and snaps of bones.

Celia watched, unable to tear her eyes from the gruesome scene. Nausea crept into her. Where once there had been a dryad, now only a small red sphere remained. Aziel kept his fist fully clenched as he stared at the aftermath of his work, and Celia could only watch him numbly for a few seconds before the vines restraining her suddenly loosened. She yelped in surprise before hitting the ground, hard.

Wincing from the pain, she looked up to see Aziel slowly take in a deep breath. Soon after, the winds around him died down, and he finally lowered his arm and released his tight grip.

The sphere dissolved, allowing gravity to take back control of its contents. The red, gooey remains fell to the ground with a loud splat. Celia scrambled backward to avoid some pieces which came too close for her liking. She glanced back at Aziel, only to see him already making his way back toward the entrance to the mountain.

Celia slowly rose from her crouched position, a mix of fear and an odd feeling of respect churned within her as she watched Aziel move further away from her and the gory scene left in his wake.

"Well, that was a mess," she said, to no one in particular. She staggered forward and began searching the bloodied clearing. To her disappointment, the dryad had not left a crystal behind after her death, but she decided it wasn't her place to complain about that. Amber had been Aziel's kill, after all, meaning Celia would have been stealing had she found one.

She then carefully moved toward the impaled girl. And there, behind her, was another corpse she had not noticed before; it was the crushed naked man from the crystal chamber. Celia's gaze drifted to Elsie. The poor girl had dragged the man all the way out here—to bury him perhaps? No, they were from Maiv, so burning his body was far more likely.

Celia examined the branches which suspended Elsie's body in

the air. She knew they were conjurations, made of mana. In time those branches would simply breakdown into mist again. It would take magnitudes more power—far more than what she saw the dryad using—to actually create something permanent with weaving, even if it was just a pointy branch. That however didn't change what Celia needed to do. It took all her strength, but eventually she snapped then pulled the three large branches out of the girl's body, before gently laying her down in the shade of a nearby tree, beside the man.

"I would burn you, but the smoke would be a problem and burying you would just be a waste of time and effort, the beasts around here would just dig you out," she whispered, smiling sadly as her hands moved to close Elsie's eyes. "So, you will just have to settle for not being impaled." She then turned and followed Aziel back into the mountain.

CHAPTER 6

AZIEL FOUND HIMSELF sitting on the curved rock at the far end of the crystal chamber. He buried his face in his hands in an attempt to hide his frustration as he thought about his most recent discovery. He had noticed this problem before, but had only just realized the scope and full implications of it.

When he had first been freed from his prison and had moved away from this chamber to the nearby library, he had noticed a small drain on his mana. It was such a minute drain, however, that he had simply ignored it.

But as soon as he exited the mountain, that minute drain had turned into a torrent. The change was so drastic and surprising, it had actually frozen him in place as he tried to wrest back control.

But here in this crystal chamber, he felt calm again. That same drain disappeared completely.

He had escaped one prison only to fall into another, he realized. This only increased the resentment building in his heart. He pressed his fists harder against his face as dark thoughts churned in his mind.

Just as when he killed Silus, killing the dryad had rewarded him with a portion of her mana—along with the same error message he had now grown used to. But that wasn't his main concern. The mana he received, though only a small amount, had revitalized him. Did his experience mean he had to kill in order to survive? Given the amount of mana he was getting back from each kill, he would have to kill many, many creatures simply to maintain himself.

These genocidal thoughts were interrupted when a meek but familiar voice echoed through the chamber.

"Aziel…? Are you all right?"

"Celia…" he whispered. Looking up, he saw her peering out at him from behind a crystal column. Again, a strange sensation reverberated from his link with this woman. Somehow knowing she was close brought about a sense of calm to his troubled heart. Aziel took a moment to examine her. Her skin looked paler than usual, making the red, deeply bruised skin around her neck seem even more pronounced.

Concerned, Aziel stood—but his sudden movement caused her to flinch backward. Not wanting to scare her away, he slowly sat back down, keeping one careful eye on her. "Do not fear Celia… I will not harm you," he said. He gestured toward his neck, and Celia's eyes widened as she quickly tried to cover her own with her hands. "Are you all right?"

"I'm fine," she told him, and for a long moment they simply stared at each other.

Aziel did not know what to say. His situation essentially demanded he kill every being he came across. It was a solution he rejected with every fiber of himself, but what else could he do? And why was he so different from the rest of the people here? Celia, the humans, even that dryad—none of them seemed to have any problems moving around, and he had not escaped from that listless world just to kill everything in this one.

Aziel desperately wanted to know who he was, who the lady in white from his visions was, and what had happened in the past to lead to his imprisonment. More importantly, he wanted to live the life he had been denied all this time.

Celia didn't move from where she hid, but she smiled at him

tentatively. "Care to explain what's got you all twisted out of shape?" she asked, the cheery tone not fully concealing her nervousness.

"I... I discovered a problem and am not sure how to resolve it," he replied. Slowly, he relaxed his shoulders and leaned back against the curved rock. He thought a change of topic might lighten the mood, and recalled the dryad's words. "So, you're a succubus," he said.

"Wha—I mean yes, I am," she replied, somewhat defensively. "Is that the problem?"

Aziel interlaced his fingers, watching Celia's half-hidden form. "It depends. What is a succubus?" he asked curiously. Even with the information he collected from his extensive reading within the library, there were still such enormous gaps in his knowledge.

Celia looked down and bit her inner cheek. "Well, succubi are a demon race," she said glumly. "Pleasure... or sex demons, to be exact."

Aziel tilted his head to one side. "What do you mean? Is your purpose to bear demon children?"

Celia's eyes opened wide at that. "What?" she cried, startling him. "No! My purpose isn't to bear demon children! I Siphon through sex! That's why we're called sex demons!"

Aziel dug through his memories of the books he had read when Celia was unconscious. He was certain sex was an activity creatures performed to bring about children, but Celia's reaction seemed to suggest otherwise. He wanted to continue asking more, but it was clear she didn't appear to like this topic of conversation at all. She was still glaring at him, so he again tried to change the subject.

"Tell me, Celia, why are you still here? You have an entire world of possibilities out there waiting, yet you remain in this place."

Celia's face turned a shade crimson. For a moment, Aziel thought she might flee. Instead, she looked down and shifted her weight from one leg to another.

"U-uh, I..." she mumbled, unable to get the words out.

Aziel waited patiently for her. Finally, Celia sighed in defeat.

"I came here for a reason," she admitted.

She stepped out from behind the pillar and leaned one shoulder against it, facing him.

"I thought if I Siphoned you, it would free me from my dependence on demonic mana for a good while." She paused. "Instead, you linked me to yourself and continue to provide me some of your mana through it. Which is, oddly, achieving the same result." She let out a self-deprecating laugh. "I was worried about it at first, but it honestly feels nice not to have to think about my next meal all the time. You also saved my life, just now." Her finger slowly traced the bruising around her neck. "So it seems like I owe you for quite a few things... even if you ignore the whole Siphoning bit," she added, a bit guiltily.

A moment of silence followed, as Aziel considered her reply. He wasn't really sure if she was indebted to him... all this time he had been trying to figure out a way to repay her for helping *him* escape. Saving her life was just another part of that, and he had to admit, his actions with the dryad had been mostly due to rage. Her attempt to Siphon his mana for herself had opened the door for his escape, even if she had not intended to do so.

Then there was the link; its creation was very much an accident, so was it really that big of a deal? Yes, he was unconsciously funneling mana to her through it, but the amount was minimal at best. He had no real idea of how it worked or what it did exactly.

Aziel didn't feel compelled to argue with her, however. If she wished to stay, then he would enjoy her company and use this time to learn all he could from her. He turned his thoughts to their most recent battle.

"That dryad... Amber. She called you a Lesser succubus... a 'fellow Enlightened.' What did she mean by that?"

Celia looked at him, her eyebrows raised. "How is it you know none of these things?"

Aziel frowned. His ignorance was an aspect of himself he did *not* appreciate having pointed out quite so bluntly. "I have been… imprisoned for a long time," he told her, "and I don't remember why, or much from the time before that."

Celia pursed her lips. "You remember nothing?"

"I remember a few things, but nothing that would help with answering my question."

Celia nodded, then lowered herself down to sit cross-legged on the ground, her back resting against the crystal column. "Then I guess we should start with the basics, hmm?"

Her smile was contagious; Aziel couldn't help smiling back. Then her expression turned serious.

"Well, the Enlightened are one of the ranks recognized by the World Seed. It goes something like this: at the lowest rank you have Critters. These are usually harmless animals, insects, and some smaller monsters. A riding horse, a boar, or a horned rabbit are all considered Critters, for example." Celia took a deep breath before continuing. "The next rank are the Variants. The vast majority of what the civilized races would call monsters fall within this rank. As their name implies, they can come in various shapes, sizes, races, and types. This rank includes creatures such monstrous bears, harpies, elementals, zombies, goblins… the list goes on and on."

She paused for a moment, looking directly at him.

"The next rank, of which I am a part, is called Enlightened. And this is where things get a bit more interesting—at least, to me it does. When a Variant evolves upward into the Enlightened ranks, the transformations are usually far more extreme. For one, they typically take a more humanoid form, if they hadn't had one before. But more importantly, they become more sapient and less instinct-driven."

Aziel nodded. "So they change from simple beasts only striving to survive, into individuals with ambitions and dreams… Intriguing. But a question before you continue, if I may? What is this World Seed you mentioned?"

Celia paused for a moment, then rubbed one cheek. "That's… I'm not sure. All I know is that the World Seed governs magic and the natural order of our world, by connecting all life with one another."

Her words sounded as if she was quoting something word for word from a book, or a memory. It was obvious she did not know much more. Not wanting to push her on a topic she wasn't sure of, Aziel moved on. "What did you look like before you become an Enlightened?" he asked.

Celia blinked in what he interpreted to be surprise. "Um, well. I never was a Variant, I was human…" she mumbled, and looked away. Aziel, however, scarcely noticed this change in behavior, as he had found her answer so confusing.

"So, humans can't be Variants?" he asked, his brow creasing again.

Celia seemed almost relieved at the question. "No, they can't. All humans are born Enlightened… but we will get back to that later. Where was I? Ah, right. The rank of Enlightened is split into three levels. The lowest or first level is called *Lesser*. So, in my case, Lesser succubus. The second level is known as *Greater,* and the highest level is referred to as *Elder*."

Aziel took a second to arrange everything in his head, then nodded. "So when Amber called you a Lesser succubus, she wasn't being unkind, but accurate?" he asked, still a little skeptical.

"Yes," Celia replied. "Given how arrogant she was, I would guess she was a Greater dryad—or close to becoming one."

Aziel tilted his head. "So… all Enlightened must evolve from Variants, but humans don't?"

"No," Celia replied flatly. "While that's true for most, there are quite a few races that are born Enlightened. It's also very likely a child born of two Enlightened would also be Enlightened, but that's not a universal truth, and fertility usually drops the higher up the rankings you go. But even that differs from one race to another. Humans, for example, see no real drop in fertility, while elves experience a rather large one." She shrugged.

"What are these other races?"

"Hmm, there are a few. The most well-known are humans, along with the many races of elves since they make up the so-called 'civilized' races. It's a self-made distinction, really," she said, dismissively. She must have noticed Aziel's questioning look, as she then added, "Other than a way to look down on others, what makes the civilized races unique is that they are born and as far as anyone knows, cannot be anything other than Enlightened. They also don't drop a crystal when they die for some unknown reason. Greedy even after death." She let out a small chuckle. "In my case, since I was human, when I inadvertently absorbed demonic mana, it transformed me into an Enlightened-ranked demon, a succubus."

She let out a small breath. Aziel nodded to show his understanding, and Celia smiled before continuing her lecture.

"The last rank after Enlightened are the Ascended." Aziel noticed her eyes narrow at that. She leaned back against the crystal column. "I know little about the Ascended, unfortunately, just the bare minimum."

Aziel smiled appreciatively. "That's alright. But how do you know any of this?"

Celia fidgeted nervously. "I went to a mage school and spent a lot of time taking advantage of the books and documents held there when I was younger." She then looked to one side, hiding her face from his view. Aziel thought it best to move on.

"I have another question, if I may?"

Celia looked back at him, which he assumed meant that she accepted.

"You have spoken about the ranks, but what exactly do they represent?"

Celia winced. "Ah, I should have started with that… never had to explain things to anyone before." She looked thoughtful for a few seconds, then took a deep breath before speaking. "It's actually a very difficult question to answer, as no one really understands why or how things work when it comes to these things. The distinctions were just taken from the World Seed, I believe, but in general, they represent milestones indicating the power a creature has."

"So, the more power a creature possesses, the higher rank it will be?"

"It's an overly simplistic way of putting it... but yes, that's basically it. The World Seed tracks what you do and rewards you for working hard and achieving special feats. Once you achieve enough, you level up. Each subsequent level requires more than the last to achieve, and once you reach a certain level you 'evolve,' as most call it. The amount and difficulty differs from one race to another, as far as I know." She paused, frowning. "The exact level required to rank up for each race isn't well known, either, but I know that for humans the first rank up is usually around level twenty-five. The main point is that once a creature's power reaches a certain critical point, it will evolve toward the next rank, and so on."

Aziel shifted on his seat. "I see... thank you for explaining." The World Seed seemed to play an integral role in how things worked in this world, and who knew what these levels Celia was talking about were referring to. Aziel held back from asking about that, and instead asked a question he was far more interested in.

"So, does that make me an Enlightened?"

Celia frowned, and her eyes narrowed again before she answered. "I don't believe so."

"Oh?" Aziel replied, a little surprised, but then he registered Celia's guarded demeanor. "Then what is it you believe I am?"

She hesitated for a few moments, then blurted out: "I think you're an Ascended."

"An Ascended?" Aziel asked, blinking in surprise. Based on her explanation, he had expected to perhaps be an Elder Enlightened. "What makes you say that?"

Celia shrugged. "I'm not really an expert on this sort of thing, but as far as I know, only Ascended can create mana links and give their mana to others. And you have been doing that ever since we've met. Also, I've felt the size of your mana vessel, and if you're not an Ascended, then the Ascended are even more terrifying than I thought." Her gaze then turned inquisitive for a moment. "Why don't you just bring up your log and confirm it?"

"My log?" Aziel asked.

"Yeah... you know, your log," she said in a matter-of-fact way.

Aziel's expression must have given him away, as her shoulders slumped slightly. "Your parents really didn't do you any favors, did they?" she muttered, before standing and approaching him. "May I?" she asked, as she gestured to his right arm.

Aziel slowly nodded and offered her his arm. Carefully, she pulled the sleeves of his robe up and squinted as if looking for something. She then pointed at a diamond-shaped mark on his wrist he had never seen before.

"That's it. I've never seen one so faded, but that's the Seed's mark. Focus or place your left hand on it and try to think about viewing your personal log, and the World Seed should provide all the information related to you."

Aziel stared at her as if she had lost her mind—but then again, he hadn't been in this world for very long, so who was he to question how things worked and what this World Seed did? So he did as she asked.

The mark immediately began to heat up, before odd gray runes again appeared before him.

Error logged. An overseer has been alerted.

Aziel shook his head; he should have known something like that would happen. He told Celia about the message, and she frowned, but said nothing for a while.

"I've been getting the same notification. I don't get it, what's going on? And who or what is this 'overseer' that keeps getting alerted?" She covered her mouth to stifle a yawn and turned to look back at the doorway at the far end of the chamber.

"I suppose there's no point worrying about it if we don't even know where to start... Any chance there are any bedrooms in this place?" she asked, hopefully. "I'd really like to avoid sleeping on the floor again, if possible..."

Aziel wasn't paying her much attention; everything she had said about logs, an overseer, and the World Seed simply constituted different levels of nonsense to him. What he wanted to understand was what being an Ascended actually *meant*, and whether he really was one.

When he had first awakened in that world he called a prison, he had been but a child. Certainly, he grew bigger as time passed, but he had never "evolved" or transformed into a more humanoid form. So, did that mean he had been an Ascended from the very beginning?

"Azi—I mean Lord Aziel?" Celia asked.

"No, I didn't see any bedrooms," he replied, distracted. "But there is a door at the other end of the library I have not checked."

"You found a door and didn't look inside?" she inquired, with a raised eyebrow.

"No," Aziel said. "It gave me an unpleasant feeling, so I continued reading instead."

Celia stared at him for a few seconds. "Well, let's go see what's in there, then." She turned and waited for him to follow suit. When he didn't, she looked back over her shoulder at him. "Come on, maybe exploring will distract you from what's going on in that pretty head of yours." She then blushed, adding rather quickly, "Um, I didn't... what I meant..." Her face grew redder and redder. "Let's just go!" she blurted, before quickly making her way down the path toward the passage beyond.

Aziel grinned before following after her. He didn't understand what kept making her so flustered, but he found it enjoyable nonetheless.

CHAPTER 7

"So... where is this door again?" Celia asked, a little irritably. After passing through the large circular space at the center of the library, they had entered the maze-like aisles. Aziel really didn't want to go back to that door—just walking past it made him uncomfortable, though he wasn't sure why.

"It's on the other side of those shelves," he said.

Aziel kept a single misty sphere of gray mana suspended in the air above them, its dim glow lighting their way. They both moved to the end of the aisle and turned a corner. What greeted them was a massive door made of some type of metal, intricate designs and symbols were carved into it.

"Look at this thing," Celia whispered. She moved closer, tracing the carvings with her fingers. "Enchantments, but whatever crystals were powering them are probably dust by now..." She took a few more seconds to examine the large metal door, then turned to face Aziel, a wide grin plastered across her face.

"This must be a vault! A real Caelian vault!" she exclaimed. "I can't wait—let's open it up." Her hands moved forward to grip the large metal handle. Before Aziel could stop her, she pulled, but the door didn't even seem to register her attempt. Celia grunted, her expression twisting out of shape with the exertion as she leaned backward to make use of the weight of her whole body. But again, the door didn't even make a sound to protest her efforts.

"Stop!" Aziel commanded, his voice harsher than he had intended. Celia quickly let go of the gate, surprised.

"To begin with, what is a Caelian vault?" he asked. "Also, I told you... this place, it gives me an unpleasant feeling."

Celia stared at him. "Wait, you're *serious*?" she blurted out. "How long have you been trapped for you to not know about the Caelian Empire?"

Aziel frowned, causing the succubus to take a nervous step back.

"Ah... right, sorry. Well, the Caelian Empire was a faction which once controlled practically all of the Eastern Peninsula. It was powerful and scientifically advanced, to the extent that many of its magical and technological achievements have not been replicated since." She paused, as if trying to order her thoughts. "It fell a thousand years ago. The country was ripped apart almost overnight, at least from what little we know of that time. What followed was a period of complete anarchy. In time, new nations rose from the ashes, including the country of my birth."

Aziel glanced at the solid metal gate. "So, you think you will find something Caelian in there?"

"Yes!" Celia beamed. "Do you realize how rare it is to find anything from that period? Just this library *alone* is probably worth more than its weight in gold."

Aziel also felt the books in this library were valuable—he had learned a lot from them already, and would learn much more in the future. If what Celia was saying was true, then further explorations might be worth the effort. But that didn't change the feeling he was getting from whatever lay on the other side of this gate.

Celia must have noticed his hesitation. "What could possibly be worrying you so much?" she asked. "The chances of anything dangerous still being alive in this place are, well... small, to say the least. And there is something valuable behind this gate, I can *feel* it," she said, placing one hand stubbornly on her hip. Her brows furrowed, and she turned toward the gate again. "If only we can find a way to open it…"

Aziel sighed. Celia seemed to have a one-track mind when there was something she wanted involved. "So be it. Let me try." He moved past her and gripped the handle firmly, pulling on it with all his strength.

The gate was heavier than he expected. Aziel pressed his feet into the ground as the muscles in his arms began to bulge and tremble. A deafening screech sounded from the gate, accompanied by a loud *crack* as the mountain rock around one of its hinges broke apart under the stress. The door dragged across the rocky ground, scraping it as it went.

Celia cringed, covering her ears with her hands, but Aziel kept pulling until the opening was wide enough for them to comfortably pass through. A gust of air escaped from within.

"Ugh! What is that smell?" Celia complained. Her nose had wrinkled, and she shook her head from side to side as if trying to shake something off.

"It is peculiar," he agreed.

Celia narrowed her eyes at him. "Peculiar? It smells worse than a goblin waste pit in here! And trust me, I would know."

Aziel tilted his head, but before he could ask, Celia interrupted tiredly. "Let's just take a look around."

Without another word, he slowly entered the darkness, Celia pinching her nostrils closed as she followed closely behind.

Inside was a square room, tiny in comparison to the crystal chamber and library. Each wall held a doorway similar in size to the one they just entered. Celia made straight for the left-hand opening, which was the only one not sealed behind a similar metal gate. Aziel watched her disappear through it, and then he heard her voice echo back through the open doorway.

Her voice had a nasal quality to it which made him smile. "This place used to be a barracks of some sort… All the furniture in here is so rotten they break apart at the slightest touch." There was a short pause before she asked, "What about the others?"

He walked up to the door on the right, and placed his hand on it. When he drew it across it, the engraved lines on it glowed a dim white. "This one has mana coursing through it."

Celia came up beside him, her face still scrunched in disgust. "Agh, the *smell*…" she complained, then leaned forward and toward the gate to examine the engravings herself. Aziel couldn't help but stare as she moved and readjusted her body, trying to get a better angle on each engraving. He could tell she noticed him staring, but she did not seem perturbed by it.

"Yeah, the carvings look similar to the first door, but the enchantments on this one are still active… Best to not mess with it—I've never seen some of these symbols before, so we don't know what the function is." Stepping back, she turned her gaze toward the last door. "What about that one?"

Aziel frowned. "The source of that feeling I spoke of, it's coming from in there. I can now tell it's a different type of mana. I just don't know what exactly it is."

"I can't feel anything. Maybe it's because that horrid smell is blocking the rest of my senses," Celia complained. "But the enchantments on it aren't glowing. We should be able to open it up and see what's going on in there."

Aziel still had his reservations, but since he was trapped in this place, ensuring it was safe seemed worth the effort.

"So be it," he declared, and moved to the last door. It also complained loudly as he pulled it open, its weight resisting any movement. In the end, however, it gave way and came loose entirely from the surrounding rock, swinging open with a screech before falling to the ground with a loud and echoing bang.

Again, there was a gush of wind from within, but this time it was accompanied by a thick black mist which rushed by them.

What followed was a series of retching noises, as Celia knelt and vomited beside him.

"Ugh, I should have expected that," she grunted, wiping her mouth.

The smell here was the same, just more intense. Aziel didn't know what it was exactly, but he was sure now it was a type of mana, given the mist. "Are you done?" he asked. "Because there is something alive in there."

Celia stared up at him, her eyes reddened. "A-alive...?"

"Yes—at least, I think so. I can sense some of my mana in there." He found he had to actively tear himself away from staring at the swells of Celia's breasts—which was difficult given his viewing angle. Aziel didn't know what to make of this new, almost compulsive interest he was experiencing with regard to the succubus.

Celia pulled herself up and grabbed the back of his robes unsteadily. "Okay. Just stay close, okay?" Her voice was quivering, and he could feel her trembling against him. Not understanding what had caused such a change in her behavior, Aziel slowly slipped into the room beyond.

The room was several feet wide and at least five times as long. Aziel noticed scratch-marks all across the wall, from floor to ceiling. Some were more worn away than others. He moved closer, and his hands traced the lines he realized were notes and letters to loved ones. Most of them were barely legible, but those that were all followed the same basic storyline of being helpless and trapped, while trying their best to survive and escape.

Aziel glanced back at the last metal door they had passed through. More than a dozen dents and what looked like old char marks marred its surface and the mountain rock surrounding it. A soft crackling noise brought him out of his thoughts, and he squinted to see what had caused it. A grin spread across his face when he zeroed in on the source.

"So, it was necrotic mana all along," he said.

"N—necrotic...?" Celia shuddered and pulled herself closer to him.

"Yes," he confirmed. He felt an odd enjoyment from having Celia practically stick herself to his side.

The crackling grew louder, and there was the sound of something dragging itself across rock. Aziel glanced to one side. Four human skeletons slowly came shuffling toward them.

Their bones were yellowed, their eyes empty voids. In the middle of their bony ribcages, where their hearts used to be, small black balls of mist flickered and glowed ominously.

"What... are those?" Celia breathed, sounding truly terrified.

Now that Aziel knew what that bad feeling was and where it was coming from, he found the situation interesting again. These skeletons were moving, but they did not contain any trace of his mana. It seemed they used pure necrotic mana. Did that mean they were dead? Or were they just another form of life?

He would consider that more later, because right now there was something else in here that had his mana in it. Quite a lot of it, in fact, compared to the people he'd met so far.

Before the four skeletons could come any closer, he swiped his hand from left to right, creating a wave of gray mist. With a flick of his hand, it crashed into the skeletons, knocking them first into each other and then back against the wall. Loud cracks and snaps followed, and slowly the black mist within them puffed out of existence.

Taking a few steps forward, Aziel's eyes glowed brighter. Small gray spheres shot out of his hands to further illuminate the room in front of him. "Are you going to show yourself, or will you waste more of my time?"

A darkened figure slowly rose from behind a stone desk at the far end of the room, and they heard a dark, throaty chuckle. A black cowl covered its skeletal face, decayed skin stretched tightly across it. Bones showed through the wreck of its cheeks and forehead, and a long, unkempt beard fell from its rotting chin. Blue, ethereal light shone from its eyes and flashed when they met his own.

Beside him, Celia whimpered.

Aziel examined the figure more closely. Its body was wrapped in multiple layers of what he imagined were once regal, obsidian-black robes, but now they were in tatters. The creature's right hand gripped a long staff of ashen wood, a black spherical crystal mounted on the crown, while its left arm hung limply from the socket.

"It is finally open," the creature croaked, its voice throaty and dry.

Celia tugged on Aziel's sleeve, and he glanced down at her wide-open eyes and quivering lips. "K-kill it! Kill it now!" she stuttered.

Aziel, confused, asked, "Why?"

"That's a lich, and I—look at it! It looks like the end of the world incarnate! Kill it before it does anything!"

The lich chuckled darkly again. "A colorful description... I rather like it. But alas, I don't seek the end of the world. That would be quite the workload, don't you think?"

Aziel stared at the darkened form, examining its sizable vessel. "Then what is it you want?"

"Until a few minutes ago, I wanted my freedom. And now..." His eyes drifted toward the open door. "...I have it."

"But why were you trapped in here in the first place?" Aziel asked, his eyes narrowing.

The lich's free hand stroked its long beard. "I do not know... my colleagues and I came in here willingly, but our... *my* loyalty was met with betrayal." His eyes flashed again, and he slammed the bottom of his staff against the rocky floor, causing an echo to reverberate through the long room.

"I'm guessing those are your colleagues, then?" Aziel gestured toward the now inanimate pile of bones near the wall.

The lich grinned. "Yes... we were fourteen at the start, not including myself. But that is all that was left of them."

"What happened?"

"I killed them. Out of necessity, of course," the lich replied, still grinning horribly.

Aziel glared at the creature, and gray mist began to form around him as he prepared himself for what might follow. The lich's own eyes narrowed at sight of this.

"Tell me who you are, and what is this place?" Aziel demanded.

"And why would I do that? I believe I have been more than generous with information already," the undead replied flatly, with a shrug of his bony shoulders.

"Because if you don't, I will kill you... in a more permanent fashion. Out of necessity, of course." Aziel eyes hardened and his lips pressed together.

The lich chuckled loudly, its voice echoing through the long room. "Confidence or arrogance? I have been trapped in here for too long not to enjoy a test, to find out which of them apply." It raised its right arm, and the temperature in the room dropped noticeably. "Let us see how you cope when death's chill comes calling."

Aziel felt something odd, as if tiny insects were crawling all across his skin. He looked up to see the lich frown for a split second, before it grinned again.

Aziel's whole body tingled, and another strange feeling crept into him—his muscles tightened, and his palms started to sweat. For reasons he could not fathom, he felt uncertain about the coming battle. Trying to overcome this sensation, he closed his eyes and focused his will. Gray mist materialized around him.

Opening his eyes again, he noticed the skeleton's grin grow wider as it took in the mana forming around Aziel. Not waiting for it to make the first move, Aziel directed the thick mist toward it. But instead of crushing the lich under its weight as it did with the skeletons, the mist simply parted like water against a rock as it struck him.

Aziel stared at this in shock. He again directed his mana toward the creature, this time concentrating it into a thick tendril. But the lich simply raised his staff, and a large wall of bones erupted from the ground to block the attack.

"I believe it is my turn now," it said, then released a blue mist of mana from its hand which quickly formed into a series of symbols. The lich's eyes flashed, causing the many symbols to merge together, before he said with a hint of finality in his tone, "Flash Freeze."

A cold wind swept across the room, and Aziel's body immediately constricted as ice crystals formed in the air around him and against his skin. Behind him, Celia screamed as she tried to pull herself free. His entire body shivered against the power of the biting cold, the sudden and unfamiliar violent chill affecting his ability to think clearly.

Warning, you have sustained a severe injury!
Error logged. An overseer has been alerted.

Aziel lost control and for a moment his mind went blank, mana streamed out of his body, and the heavy gray mist expanded to engulf everything around him. The ice quickly melted under the churning mist, releasing him from its grip.

Fearing his mana would harm Celia, Aziel again directed the torrent toward the lich, before collapsing to one knee, his breathing labored.

This time, Aziel saw and felt his mana work hard and fast to heal the damage caused by the ice. What troubled him most, however, was that he had used more mana to escape the ice than he had done in the entire period since entering the world. And as far as he could tell, it was for nothing. A throaty voice cut through his thoughts.

"Arrogance, then…"

Aziel looked up just in time to see the creature dismiss another elaborate symbol he seemed just about to unleash.

"But you do feel familiar." The undead creature took a long, hard look at Aziel, then grinned so widely the skin on either side of its mouth ripped open. He began to laugh. "I knew it! I was right all along, that was no artifact."

The lich drifted around the stone desk, then bowed. "It is an honor and a pleasure to finally see you awakened. I am Vhal'nuel Novaul, keeper of the grand library and lead researcher of the Facility. Please, call me Vhal. I most humbly greet you and thank you for freeing me from my long confinement."

Aziel hesitated. Was the lich playing some sort of game with him? But then again, he was under no illusion that this Vhal'nuel could have ended both him and Celia just now. "My name is Aziel. As you said, I have awakened a short time ago and found myself in this place."

With all trace of hostility gone from the lich's manner, Aziel stood. He tried to move closer, but Celia pulled him back and shook her head vigorously. "Don't…" she begged.

Looking back at Vhal, Aziel asked, "Are you causing this?"

Vhal chuckled. "Yes, the demon is under the effect of my Aura. It causes beings around me to experience a deep sense of fear and anxiety. The effect is stronger on weaker creatures."

"Can you stop it then?" Aziel hissed; this Aura, he realized, must have been the origin of the sensation from before. If it had such an effect on him, he could only imagine how bad it would be for Celia.

"Of course I can. But why? It is rather enjoyable when they squirm, don't you think?" The lich's grin grew wider, but Aziel just glared back.

"All right, all right," Vhal acquiesced, sighing.

The effect was immediate: Celia blinked a few times, then blushed when she realized how closely she had clung to Aziel. Pushing herself away from him, she stuttered, "Wha-what is going on?"

In the most soothing voice he could muster, Aziel said, "Look at me and relax, Celia… there is nothing to fear, you were under the effects of his Aura." He indicated Vhal with his head.

Celia's eyes went wide. "Stay away from me, lich!" she spat.

"Ah, you wound me, demon. I have feelings like any other, you know," Vhal replied with mock hurt. "And I am an Elder lich, not *just* a lich."

"An Elder lich…? Doesn't that mean—" But Vhal interrupted her before she could finish.

"Yes, I am an Elder Enlightened. I suppose being trapped in here for so long did have a few benefits…"

"And just how long have you been trapped in here?" Aziel interrupted.

Vhal ran his decaying gray fingers through his beard as he glanced at the scratches that covered the surrounding walls. "Well… I ran out of wall after about nine hundred and thirty years, by my estimate. It was dreadfully boring, mostly, but I must admit I found the first few months to be the most difficult. Killing and absorbing my colleagues to fuel my transformation was… unpleasant. I liked, even loved, some of them. But time heals all wounds, or so they say."

Celia scoffed at this, then turned to Aziel. "We can't trust him, he's an undead. All they care about is killing the living."

Aziel glanced at her, then back at Vhal. While he didn't trust the lich either, he wanted to know more about this place, and the lich had the answers.

"So, you weren't always a lich?" he asked.

"Of course not!" Vhal exclaimed. "I was an elf. When I realized no one would come to help us, I came up with a plan. I knew we would never break through that aranite steel gate or the enchanted walls, no matter how many spells we threw at it. So we gave up trying, and I instead made use of the tools I happened to have at the time. I killed them, then used them to fuel a ritual I learned from a book, leading to my transformation… immortality opens doors otherwise closed to us, after all. At least this way one of us survived… in one form or another."

Celia was staring at the gate he had mentioned, entranced. "Aranite… so much of it," she whispered, her words dripping with desire.

Aziel shook his head at that, then turned on his heel and walked out. Startled, Celia followed after him.

"Where are you going?" she asked.

"To the library," he replied. "I tire of this room, and all the necrotic mana annoys me."

Vhal chuckled as he followed the pair out into the main chamber. "Yes... necrotic mana can be quite problematic to those with no affinity for it."

"I still don't feel anything... other than the smell, of course." Celia looked down at her body as she stepped through the broken doorway, as if she might see some physical manifestation of it.

"That smell is how your body is reacting to the necrotic mana, demon," Vhal explained.

Celia turned to glare at him. "My name is Celia, *lich*," she snapped, practically spitting out the last word.

"Ooh, a feisty demon. Perhaps another dose of my Aura would do you some good?" His wide grin returned in full force.

"That's enough," Aziel announced.

Grimacing, Celia strode on ahead, into the high-ceilinged space of the library. As Aziel and Vhal followed her, the lich gazed around at the shelves, and his blue eyes flashed.

"Ah, it's good to see the great library still whole... if a little messy," he said joyfully, as he picked up a book from where it had fallen.

Aziel looked at the lich, a thousand thoughts rushing through his head. "What is this place? You said you were the lead researcher, so what was it you researched?"

Vhal turned away from the shelves to look at him. "Isn't it obvious? I studied you, of course."

CHAPTER 8

AZIEL STARED AT the lich in confusion.

"To be more specific," Vhal continued, "we studied your mana. As for what this place is, or was… they called it the Facility, and it has quite a long history."

"I would like to hear it," Aziel said.

"Lord Aziel, you can't trust anything he says!" Celia protested. "He's a lich—you never know what he could be planning."

"I understand learning something new would be asking too much of you, Celia. Perhaps you should go play with yourself in the hall. I believe your kind love to do that sort of thing in their spare time… yes?"

Celia reddened, then glared at the lich, her golden eyes glowing brighter. Vhal merely chuckled. "Do you really believe your pathetic Charm will work on me?"

"Enough," Aziel interrupted. "Vhal, tell me what you know about me and this place."

Vhal smirked at Celia, which only made her scowl deepen, but then turned back to Aziel.

"The Facility was built by the ruler of what was the Kingdom of Cael at the time, after the discovery of a so-called artifact among some ruins in the Wilds." Vhal paused. "At least, that's the story we were told. The purpose of the Facility was to study the artifact's unique mana and harness it to empower the Kingdom, then the Empire, both militarily and economically."

Vhal stroked his long beard before he continued. Despite the ravaged condition of his face, the lich wore a somewhat wistful expression.

"As you can imagine, this research project continued for many years. Utmost secrecy was always maintained; once assigned a post here, you were not allowed to leave unless given permission by the Emperor himself—which to my knowledge never happened. In the pursuit to learn more about your mana, methods were developed which detected and mapped the very structure of mana, the many parts that made it what it was. What was discovered redefined practically everything we knew about how mana and magic worked."

Aziel was listening carefully. Even Celia had settled herself cross-legged on the floor and seemed interested now.

"We first started by mapping the structures of the elemental manas: fire, water, earth, and air. As expected, we discovered several minor differences between them but nothing too surprising. So we moved on to the advanced manas: light, dark, nature, and necrotic… again, differences were discovered, though these were generally more complex." Vhal paused and made eye contact with Aziel. "When your mana was mapped, instead of discovering something new, we found the exact foundational structure that every other mana type shared."

"I don't understand…" Celia frowned. "His mana is like every other mana?" Aziel was thankful he wasn't the only one confused.

Vhal nodded. "In a way, you are correct. To be more precise, what they discovered was that while mana, in the most general sense, does not change…" The lich's grin grew wider as he pointed at Aziel. "*His* mana does. It is always in a state of flux—ready to morph into something else under the right conditions."

Aziel shook his head. "I don't see how this makes any difference to me."

"Yes, I still don't get the point," Celia agreed.

Vhal grinned. "Let me try explaining in a different way then. Celia, can I ask you something?"

"What?" she replied, almost aggressively.

"When you utilize a skill such as your Charm, does it use some of your mana?"

Celia narrowed her eyes at the grinning lich, as if expecting some sort of trap. "Of course it does, my skills use mana, as do most others. What's your point?"

"And what type of mana do you use?" Vhal persisted.

Celia tilted her head slightly as she contemplated the question. "I don't know; it's just listed as mana on my log… it's probably fire mana, right? That's the only mana I have an affinity for—other than demonic, of course."

Vhal shook his head, but his grin remained. "That's where you're wrong—where we were all wrong. It's a fundamental part of mana theory no one ever asked about because there was no clear reason to do so… until we found you," he added, looking directly at Aziel again. "The mana you use is so common it's literally within every living thing. We all use it to varying degrees to fuel our non-weaving related skills, whether it be Celia's Charm or my Fear Aura. But here is where things get truly interesting. Before you came along, no one had ever seen your mana before. It only exists and is created within the vessel of a living creature, or for a fraction of a second within Capital Crystals when new mana is created within them."

Aziel looked down at his open palm and released a small stream of gray mist. "So my mana is not unique? It's just some sort of bridge that connects the different mana types?" he asked, a tinge of disappointment leaking through.

Vhal chuckled. "That is true, your mana is not unique by definition. But the way you use it and the amount of control you have over it *is*."

Aziel looked up at the grinning undead. "Explain."

"As far as we could tell, unless in large quantities, your mana doesn't exist for long outside of a living creature or crystal." Vhal absently touched the books on a nearby shelf as he continued. "As I mentioned, your mana is always in a state of flux. If a certain ratio of your mana to another is reached, then a chain reaction occurs where it will all change to match the mana it was mixed with."

With some care, Vhal began to rearrange the books.

"My predecessors," he continued slowly, "encased what they thought was an artifact in glass and funneled the rather incredible amount of mana which it generated into eight identical chambers. Each held a sufficient amount of a single mana type. The mana would then change to match the dominate mana type in the room, which the Empire could use in any way it saw fit." Vhal chuckled, "It was as if the Empire had a never-ending well of all eight primary mana types. It wouldn't be a stretch to say that finding you gave them the edge to become as powerful as they did."

Aziel felt strangely uncomfortable knowing what had happened to him while he was essentially asleep. Celia, on the other hand, seemed fascinated.

She stretched her arms and let out a small satisfied moan. "What did the Empire use the mana they collected for exactly?" she asked.

Vhal shrugged. He bent to pick up a small stack of books on the floor by his feet, using his staff for balance, and began placing them back on the shelves. "I wasn't involved in that side of things."

Aziel glanced at his hand again and the little mana he had let flow out of it. "So, I would need to mix my mana with another, then wait for it to accumulate for it to be useful...?"

Vhal shook his head. "We had no real control over your mana. All we could do was provide the conditions it needed and wait for it to do what it did naturally. Anything requiring any sort of manipulation was outside our capabilities at the time. A good example was our experiments with crystals. Theoretically, your mana should be able to recharge any mana crystal, but while crystals of other mana types reacted to being exposed to your mana, they didn't absorb it as hoped." Vhal shelved the last book in his hand and turned to point at Aziel with a single bony finger. "You, on the other hand, are different, you can do what we could not. You can manipulate it freely—and directly."

The lich wore a thoughtful look for a few moments before continuing.

"Look at it this way," he said, "like you mentioned, your mana acts like a bridge which connects all the other manas together. I believe that with just a little manipulation on your part, then perhaps you could force a change in your mana to act like the others while still keeping the transformed mana within your control."

"Wait!" Celia said, with a hint of awe in her voice. "Are you suggesting he is proficient in *all* mana types?"

Vhal shook his head. "No. But, in theory, he should be able to mimic the effects of other manas as *if* he were proficient in them."

Celia frowned. "I don't understand the difference."

"It makes a huge difference." He glanced over to Aziel, their eyes connecting for a brief moment. "Being proficient means you can absorb, manifest, and weave that mana type. In a way, we are all somewhat proficient in his mana, as we all use it to activate many of our non-weaving related skills and can absorb it into our vessels. But we can't manifest it like he does."

It was a confirmation of something Aziel had already known and made use of. The existence of his mana within people was the reason he could so easily sense their presence when they came close enough to him. "How would one get this proficiency you two keep referring to?" Aziel interrupted.

The question caused the lich to look at Aziel oddly. "Other than from birth, there is only one other way for someone to gain a proficiency," he said carefully. "You can gain the trait by ranking up—I, for example, was born with Necrotic Weaving, a common trait in my family. I then gained the trait Water Weaving when I became an Elder lich."

Aziel thought about this, but before he could respond, the lich spoke again.

"Returning to your question, Celia, the major difference is the absorption part. As an Ascended, Aziel has a limit in what he can absorb from the environment around him and cannot absorb any mana type other than what he was most proficient in at the time of his evolution. It is one of the conditions set by the World Seed. In a way, it is very similar to what demons such as yourself have to deal with. You might be skilled in using other mana types, but you can only directly absorb demonic mana."

Celia looked at Aziel, realization dawning. "Is that what you meant when you said you had a problem you didn't know how to solve?"

Aziel looked into her striking golden eyes, and for a moment forgot about his surroundings, losing himself in their beauty until Celia looked away, her cheeks slightly flushed. Realizing he might have stared at her for a bit too long and remembering that he had been asked a question, Aziel quickly responded. "Yes, it is." He then looked at Vhal, his head tilted slightly. "Why do you assume I'm an Ascended?"

Celia blinked, then quirked a brow.

"I would think it was obvious," Vhal replied, his blue ethereal eyes switching between Aziel and Celia, studying them.

Aziel frowned. "What makes you say that?"

"Several things," Vhal said, his hands moving up to stroke his beard again. "Your probable age, and the quantity of mana you were throwing around back there is a good place to start. But mainly, it's the rate of mana leaving your body all these years we studied you. An Ascended is the only thing you can be."

"I don't understand," Celia said. "Why would losing mana be a sign of an Ascended?"

"Hmm…" Vhal pondered her question, bending to pick up a few more books. "Have you ever wondered why there aren't many Ascended? Granted, I do not know the situation today, but historically speaking."

"I just assumed it was very difficult to become powerful enough to reach that point." Celia replied.

"You aren't wrong—very few reach the level required to evolve into an Ascended. But there is a more prominent reason." Vhal's gaze returned to Aziel. "Such an evolution brings major changes and consequences, the biggest of which is how unstable your mana vessel becomes."

"Unstable?" Celia frowned. "That sounds bad."

Aziel kept silent as he listened to the exchange.

"It isn't pleasant," Vhal continued. "Mana vessels normally regenerate a bit of mana over time. Ascended, however, lose this ability completely: their mana vessel has a hard time properly containing all the mana circulating within their bodies. As time goes on, more and more of their mana radiates out of them. If left unchecked for long enough, the Ascended in question would essentially waste away… The closest thing I can think of is what occurs when you Siphon someone, Celia, just slower."

"Why would anyone want to be an Ascended, then?" she blurted. Aziel himself was growing a little worried about his prospects.

Vhal chuckled again, which Aziel realized was the lich's reaction to everything— probably a side-effect of being isolated for so long.

"It has nothing to do with wanting it or not, you don't have a choice in your evolutions. But to answer your question, there are many reasons," Vhal replied. He began shelving books again as he spoke. "For one, the Ascended gain one of the most useful and powerful skills available, which is to imbue other beings and objects with their mana. And being an Ascended is not a death sentence. There have been Ascended since before people began recording history. It simply requires some preparation. They usually claim a place of power, for example, which helps counteract the loss."

"Place of power?" Aziel asked. "What's that?"

"It's a location with a naturally high concentration of a specific mana type. A fire-based Ascended would probably use a volcano, while a nature-based Ascended would use an old forest." Vhal paused, thinking. "The best sign of one, other than a great deal of atmospheric mana, is a higher than normal concentration of mana crystals."

Celia's eyes opened wide, but before she could speak, Aziel glanced at her and shook his head slightly. Even though he had no personal reason not to trust Vhal, her earlier warning still had him on his guard.

Celia must have understood his signal, since she nodded slightly before glancing back at Vhal. "The solution is simple, then," she said. "Just find a place with a lot of his mana and he should be able to get all he needs... right?"

Vhal scratched his chin, causing some of the rotten skin to flake off. Celia gagged at this, trying to stop herself from vomiting again.

The lich grinned at that, then asked, "Tell me succubus, do you know of such a place? Have you ever seen or even heard of his mana before you met him? Of course not. Before we found him, we didn't know his mana even existed." He paused, placing a finger thoughtfully on an earth crystal embedded in the nearby shelf. "The only exception we ever found were the mana crystals, which we only found around him. But these were small and few. They stubbornly reflected and resisted anything that tried to Analyze or modify them." He looked at Aziel. "But I think even that would change if he tried it."

Celia stood. "So what? We give up? Wait!" She pointed at Aziel. "Didn't you say you felt a bit of your mana in the room we found the damned lich in? Maybe it's still in there!"

"No, it's not." Aziel smiled at her theatrics, which he guessed were for Vhal's benefit. "It was simply inside him and inside you—I sensed my mana in every living person I've met so far." His gaze shifted toward the Elder lich, who for the first time since meeting them was not grinning.

"Vhal?" Celia asked hesitantly, stepping forward. "What's wrong?"

The lich's blue eyes flashed, and Celia jumped back in surprise. "Hey! Don't do that!"

"My apologies, Celia," Vhal said, lowering his head slightly to show his sincerity. "I just got a little overexcited."

Celia studied him for a second, then rested her weight provocatively on one hip, smirking. "What got you so excited? And is that how you show it: glowing eyes?"

Aziel forced himself not to stare—it was something he kept having to actively remind himself not to do when it came to Celia. What made it worse was that he wasn't too sure whether Celia enjoyed this effect she had on him or resented it.

Noticing his gaze now, she blushed then twisted her body slightly in a failed attempt to hide as it only resulted in a more alluring pose.

Vhal was watching this, and his grin grew wicked. "With a succubus as beautiful as you around, it is hard not to get excited. It is unfortunate that I am no longer capable of the pleasures of the flesh."

The tension evaporated immediately as Celia stared at the lich, her mouth dropping open. "Ugh… gross!" she spat, her whole body seeming to shudder at the thought.

Aziel mentally thanked the lich for saving them from that moment of awkwardness. "Can we get back on topic? Vhal, it looked like you had something to say?"

"Ah, yes… Soul mana," he replied, his eyes flashing brightly again.

"Soul mana? What's that?" Aziel asked.

"That was one name proposed for your mana. It was based on the idea that the mana vessel itself actually being made of your mana rather than just storing a bit of it. The more rebellious researchers actually just started referring to that mana vessel *as* the soul." He shook his head, a more solemn smile taking root before it disappeared just as quickly as it appeared. "Tell me, what else did you feel or notice?"

Aziel tilted his head, thinking. "Well... the amount of my mana in every person differs... you have a lot more of it than Celia does, for example." Just then, a detail he had almost forgotten came to mind. "Also, if I kill someone, a portion of their mana transfers to me... I have not yet seen a natural death, and so do not know what happens in those situations."

Vhal nodded slowly. "That makes perfect sense. As an Elder lich, my mana vessel will be many times larger than that of a Lesser succubus. And killing is the fastest way to increase the size of your vessel, so directly absorbing a portion of someone else's makes sense."

"Why's that?" Celia blurted out, curious.

"Well, as we all know, the vessel naturally grows with time. This is why age usually means power, and is the reason why I am an Elder, despite being trapped in a room. But as you might imagine, it's a slow process. Killing, while gruesome, is a tested and proven alternative. It expands the vessel much quicker, but the reasons why were never understood. Now we do. If all of our vessels are made of soul mana, then absorbing a portion of the killed party's original vessel would have an instantaneous effect." Vhal stroked his beard. "I suspect the amount taken is a tiny percentage, however."

Aziel eyes hardened at this. He glared at the little mana he had let leak out of his fingers. "So it's true... the only way for me to replenish my mana is to kill and take it from others."

Celia's face paled at this.

Vhal chuckled. "Indeed, killing will help you, Lord Aziel, at least in the short term. But sooner or later there will be no one else to kill, and you will waste away." Vhal grinned, his eyes flashing. "In any case, while I'm sure the feeling of your... victims' mana coursing through you would be exhilarating, with the size of your vessel, I suspect you would need to slaughter a whole town of people to even notice any real change."

Aziel thought about that, before slowly nodding. In a more hopeful voice, he asked, "Then there is another way?"

Vhal nodded. "It's simple, really... you need to act like the Ascended you are."

Both Celia and Aziel stared, waiting for him to continue. The lich only stared back with the same grin he always wore.

"Are you mocking me, Vhal?" Aziel asked, his gray eyes glowing brighter as he struggled to keep in his frustrations.

"Of course not, Lord Aziel. I would do no such thing."

"Then would you care to explain what you mean?"

"Mmm... I suppose you wouldn't know about that either, would you?" Vhal mumbled, as if to himself.

Aziel took a deep breath, reminding himself that Vhal probably didn't even realize when he was insulting someone. He also did not believe he had a chance against the lich in a straight-up fight.

"As I mentioned," Vhal continued, "Ascended lose mana over time. So they need to find a place of power to help regulate and halt that loss. But simply stopping the drain is not enough is it? You need to find a way to actually regenerate your mana."

Celia frowned at that. "What could give him mana, other than a place with high concentrations of it?"

Vhal's everlasting grin grew even wider. "You weren't entirely wrong when you suggested taking it from others. A more accurate way of putting it would be to *convince* others to give it to you."

Both Aziel and Celia raised their eyebrows at that.

"Ascended usually have organizations built around them," Vhal explained. "Guilds, cults, religions, armies. Regardless of the form, their aim is always to recruit followers for their Ascended. The more powerful the Ascended, the larger the organization usually has to be to support him... or her."

Celia laughed. "You can't be serious. How would we get people to follow Aziel? And how would that even help?"

Vhal shrugged. "I don't know how, but it is a fact that when people or creatures become sworn followers of an Ascended, that act somehow channels mana to them. The more numerous and powerful the followers, the more mana they receive. It's really the only practical way for an Ascended to regenerate their mana."

Celia again opened her mouth to protest, but Aziel raised a hand to stop her.

"So all I need to do is convince people to become my followers?" he asked.

Vhal nodded. "Yes. If you get enough followers, the mana issues you are experiencing should dissolve."

"But how would I find these followers? How do the other Ascended do it?"

Vhal began to pace back and forth, leaning heavily on his staff. "Well… an Ascended with a vessel as large as yours would likely need to become a faction's divinity, with all its members required to become sworn followers."

"Hmm," Celia said. "Now that you mention it, every year, a man used to come to our village and gather any new settlers or children who had recently come of age for a swearing-in ceremony. I was too young at the time, so I did none of that." She looked down for a few moments, as if considering something else. "When I was in Maiv, the towns had shrines to the fire divinity Adara, and the larger settlements had a representative from the Order of Flames."

Vhal nodded. "Shrines are special structures imbued by a divinity's power and are used to mark its domain. They can also be used by people to swear themselves as followers and voluntarily offer up additional mana. The Order of Flames you speak of is most likely led by this Adara."

Aziel shook his head in frustration. The more he learned, the more complicated it all seemed. "Vhal, you still have not said why people would agree to follow an Ascended. Why would these kingdoms, empires, or factions as you call them, ask—or even compel—their peoples to do such a thing?"

"Ah, yes. My apologies, Lord Aziel," Vhal said, with a slight bow. "There are many reasons. But the most important are Capital

Crystals. As populations grew larger, the mana taken from these crystals quickly outgrew their regenerative abilities. Ascended are the only beings who can channel mana directly into other objects. So, nations would negotiate a deal with a chosen Ascended, naming them as their divinity, and in return, the Ascended would maintain their Capital Crystals. But none of this matters unless Lord Aziel first finds a place of power."

At that, Aziel simply grinned. "I believe I already have one."

CHAPTER 9

AZIEL STRODE INTO the main chamber, where he seated himself on his familiar rock. Celia wore an amused expression as Vhal looked around in a daze.

"When I'm here, I feel a sense of calm unlike any other," Aziel said.

"I... I don't know what to say... this is incredible..." Vhal mumbled.

"Hey! Snap out of it, bones! You need to focus! Is this a place of power you were talking about or not?" Celia smirked, leaning against a crystal column.

"This is certainly *a* place of power, but not a natural one," Vhal said quietly, his eyes taking in each of the eight pillars. "These were the large glass feeds that funneled your mana off-site to be converted... something must have blocked them, causing your mana to accumulate within to the point that they solidified into Capital Crystals."

Aziel let out a soft sigh of relief at his words. At least something was working in his favor.

Vhal placed his hand reverently on a pillar. "This is the result of you releasing so much mana when you were held here, Lord Aziel, to the extent that it's now self-sustaining. I don't know how you could possibly have done this, but it is humbling, to say the very least..."

"Yeah, all these Capital Crystals in one place. I'm just glad I'm on his side," Celia said with a smile.

Vhal nodded in agreement then frowned, his gaze traveling around the cavern walls. "None of the Magitech we used to monitor the mana remain..." he mumbled softly to himself. He wore a grim expression for a few moments, before he again turned to face them, his grin back in place.

"No matter. What this means is that Lord Aziel has a lot to offer. Rarely—if ever—does an Ascended have his own Capital Crystal... never mind eight of them."

Aziel looked at Vhal questioningly, not knowing what to make of his strange behavior. He was fairly certain Vhal didn't mean for the first part to be heard, and Aziel only heard it due to his proximity. He wanted to ask about these Magitech he mentioned but thought it best to keep his curiosity to himself and focus on what really mattered, at least for the moment. "So what is the first step to gaining these followers?"

"Not yet, Lord Aziel," Vhal replied. "This place grants you time, but converting followers will paint a large target on you. Even with your enormous mana reserves, you will most likely get yourself killed."

"Killed?" Celia said.

"Yes. My information might be out of date, but I can't imagine any rival Ascended will simply allow you to convert their followers to your side. And you are not yet ready for that sort of confrontation."

Aziel remembered how easily Vhal had defeated him in their first encounter. "I need to learn how to weave... that is what you are alluding to."

"Indeed," the lich replied. "You also need to learn the structure of the other manas, so that you may replicate them."

Aziel sighed. "So be it. Celia, could you please bring me some mana crystals from the library? I will need to examine them."

Celia glared at Vhal, as if warning him against doing anything stupid, then left to do as he asked. Aziel couldn't help but smile as he watched her go. Having the succubus be this protective was growing on him.

When she was out of sight, Vhal turned to Aziel. "Lord Aziel… may I ask what you have planned for the succubus?"

"Planned?" Aziel replied. "What do you mean?"

"You keep her around, but I cannot fathom for what purpose. It does not appear you are using her to satisfy your carnal desires, and as a Lesser succubus, she cannot serve you effectively in any real way." His hand rose to his beard, before he added, "Not that I'm saying you should get rid of her, of course."

Aziel's eyes hardened. It seemed to him the lich was saying exactly that. "She helped free me and helped me understand the world around me. For that, I will forever be grateful to her. She is also linked to me and wishes to stay by my side. Until such a time as that changes, I will allow her to do so," he concluded sharply.

Vhal bowed slightly. "My apologies, Lord Aziel, I—wait, you say you're linked? What do you mean?"

"When she tried to Siphon me, I used the connection to create a link between us."

"She did *what*?" Vhal yelled, just as Celia re-entered the chamber holding three small crystals, a little breathless, as if she had run to the library and back.

"What's the matter?" she asked when she noticed them staring. "You look like someone stole food off your plate."

"You used a basic Siphon on an Ascended?" Vhal hissed, as tiny ice crystals formed around his hand.

Celia blanched and took a step back. "Uh, I—I didn't know he was an Ascended at the time!" She eyed the blue mana flowing from the lich's hand warily. "You didn't know either!"

"He created *eight* Capital Crystals just from the excess mana he was releasing whilst essentially asleep!" Vhal's voice grew angrier as he spoke. "And you thought unleashing even a fraction of that in the form of demonic mana was a *good idea*? We might have not known he was an Ascended, but we had him for a long time and not once did any of us even *suggest* doing something as idiotic as directly Siphoning mana out of him!"

Celia's eyes were wide. "I didn't know! I just needed the mana… using my racial Siphon wasn't an option either, he was just a large golden egg."

"Fool! You could have destroyed everything for hundreds—if not thousands—of miles in every direction! Apocalyptic would have been the best-case scenario!" Vhal's eyes flashed as yet more ice crystals formed on his hands.

"That's enough," Aziel announced. "I am fine, and I am sure Celia will be more careful in the future. May I remind you, Vhal, the only reason I am awake is due to her actions."

Vhal glared at the succubus. Without breaking eye contact, he said tightly, "You are right, of course, Lord Aziel. I do apologize for my outburst." He slowly turned to face Aziel, and continued in a calmer manner, "You said you linked her to yourself. Does that mean you provide her with your mana?"

"I suppose, yes. The amount involved is insignificant, however. I forget about it most of the time."

Vhal sighed. "You do realize what you're saying is abnormal? Permanent mana links require a large amount of mana to create and maintain… that is why only the strongest and oldest Ascended even attempt to create them." He glanced back at the succubus, who still looked miserable from her scolding. "The recipient of such a blessing is usually named that Ascended's champion."

Celia looked up. "Cha—champion?" she asked, in surprise.

"Yes. You should feel honored, succubus. A truly unique and powerful Ascended has chosen you to enact his will, after all." Vhal treated her to a wide grin, obviously enjoying the panicked expression on her face.

Celia glanced at Aziel, speechless. Seeing this made him feel a pang of protectiveness he did not expect. He wondered if Celia had felt the same things he did.

Just as he was about to stand to interfere, Aziel saw the world around him suddenly stop. Celia and Vhal remained as they were, but they stood frozen like statues. Aziel grunted as a new sensation began to spread through him, and his entire body felt as if he was falling. The sound of air being sucked in reached his ear then it all went black. He blinked—and found himself somewhere else altogether.

* * *

Aziel immediately hunched over and retched as his organs tried their best to vacate his body. He let out a pained breath and looked around as he swallowed the foul taste which remained in his mouth. Instead of the familiar crystal chamber, Aziel now stood alone, stark naked in a small, empty room. It was perfectly square in shape, with bright white walls. Behind him and at the center of the room sat an odd-looking white chair made of a material he did not recognize. In front of him was a large window looking out into a dark void.

He looked around, confused. Then he slowly approached the window, his eyes opening wide at what he was witnessing.

Below him was a planet. Wherever he was, he seemed to be orbiting around it at a tremendous speed. He looked at the land-masses below, and it did not take long for him to recognize a few landmarks he had seen on the many maps within the library.

That was Kadora, but it was so much larger than he realized. The peninsula containing the Central Wilds and all the other places he had read about made up a small portion on the eastern side of a rather massive continent. Many islands of different sizes peppered the ocean which covered more than half the planet, and the only other features visible to him were the two large ice caps at the poles.

Although seeing the planet was a shock, it was the objects hovering around it that consumed Aziel's attention.

His eyes tracked several massive metallic fortresses as they orbited the planet at different angles. Even from his perceived distance, they looked likely to rival mountains in size.

As one of them drifted closer to him, Aziel saw a flurry of activity across its surface. Tiny metallic bees flew in and out of the fortress through holes on its middle and bottom, each carrying boxes of different colors and sizes. It reminded him of a hive which had been recently disturbed. He noticed markings on the fortress's side. Aziel squinted as he tried to read what was written there, surprisingly, it was written in the same type of runes as those error messages he kept receiving.

W.S.: Kadora 23

Aziel remained silent as the metallic fortress passed by his window and continued along its orbit around the planet. *W. S....?* *World Seed?* he asked himself, not sure of his own answer.

But how could a metallic fortress in the sky do what the World Seed supposedly did on the ground? It was too much to grasp. He again glanced down at the planet below just in time to witness a thin beam of red light streak down through space toward the planet. The clouds parted to give way, and it struck one of the smaller isolated islands on the western side of the continent below.

Aziel was stunned, the amount of energy that beam of light contained was staggering. Although the whole event had been completely silent from inside his sealed room, he had felt it... the violence it had packed within. His eyes tracked the now diminishing streak of bright red light until he settled on its source, another fortress exactly the same as the one he'd just had a closer look at; It was all he could do to try to keep his fears in check.

"What is this place..." he whispered under his breath. He looked away from the window and scanned the white walls of the room, seeking a way out. But there was none. There was only the white chair.

"Where am I?" he said, hoping to get an answer, but he was met with silence.

Aziel took a step toward the chair, and the floor suddenly lit unexpectedly before dimming again. A feminine yet detached voice sounded within the room, as if coming from everywhere at once.

"Isolation of unregistered living asset completed," it said. "Local Time Dilation successful. Use of controlled mana type observed. Estimated nexus realm contamination level: high. Overseer Assembly majority reached. Recommendation logged. Unregistered asset disposal procedure initiated."

Aziel glanced around, his eyes frantic. Unregistered asset? Disposal? What was she talking about?

"Who are you!" he called out, but the only response he received was an increasingly loud humming and thumping from behind the walls, before another identical wall slid across the large window behind him and locked into place, blocking his view of the heavens outside.

"Where am I? Release me at once!" Aziel shouted again, his heart beginning to beat faster and faster. He ran up and punched one of the white tiles making up the walls, then yelled out in agony as the full force behind his punch bounced back into his hands and arm, his bones cracking as a result. The material had no give at all; not even the aranite gates were this dense. Clasping his shattered hand, he instinctively tried to weave a protective dome around himself, but nothing happened. There was no mist… nothing.

The sense of helplessness was overwhelming. Aziel looked to his left, then his right, waiting for something to happen.

And then it did.

The once-white walls turned bright red with heat, and the whole room's temperature rose sharply. Aziel inhaled at the sudden change, then coughed violently as the super-heated air burned his lungs. He collapsed to the ground as even the sweat on his skin began to sizzle.

"Stop…" he said, his voice hoarse and full of pain. The inside of his throat felt seared. He closed his eyes in an attempt to protect them, as his vision began to turn white.

"Archivist key logged; authorization approved. Emergency override activated," the female voice said.

The room temperature suddenly dropped and cool air brushed across Aziel's burned skin. He opened his eyes as he heard a soft gushing noise and saw a green mist, the color of forest leaves, manifest from the floor. As it flowed over him, he began to heal, chunks of blackened skin falling off him as if he was shedding it. He could feel his ravaged innards healing too, as he breathed in this nectar of life.

He pushed himself to his knees and glanced around in a daze. The room had reverted to its original pristine white. Even the pieces of burned skin seemed to have melted into the floor.

"Why are you doing this? Release me!" he again demanded, but there was no force behind it now. He felt so weak, so tired. The female voice paid him no mind, continuing to speak of things he didn't understand.

"Warning, living asset integration protocols may have unintended consequences. Do you still wish to proceed?"

There was a pause.

"Archivist key logged; authorization approved. Integration protocols initiated."

There was another pause.

"Overseer Assembly majority reached. Recommendation logged. Error, Overseer Assembly recommendation in direct conflict with authorized Archivist key. Recommendation denied."

Aziel was only half listening, still out of breath from his ordeal. He tried to swallow a lump in his throat, but it felt so dry, and his every muscle ached.

"New living asset designation: Aziel," the voice continued.

Aziel felt the ground below him shift. Fearful of another surprise, he recoiled backward only to fall into the chair behind him. Immediately, a white viscous liquid seeped from its surface and washed over his wrist before solidifying, restraining him. Aziel tried to push himself off the chair only to discover the same had occurred to his feet.

"Living asset Aziel, for your own safety, please remain still during integration," the female voice said.

Aziel struggled, trying to free himself. "Release me, now!" he hissed, but then something pricked his right arm, and a moment later, his whole body went limp. He grunted as he struggled to move in vain. While he could still move his eyes and at the very least make noises, he could no longer move his body.

Panic flooded him. First this place had tried to kill him and now it was going to trap him. Was he going to be imprisoned like before, but this time without even the illusion of movement?

Just as he was about to yell out again, he gasped as a sharp, piercing pain exploded from his chest. He wanted to move, to curl up in a ball, but his body wouldn't listen to him. Then everything turned black—he couldn't tell if it was he who was blind, or if the room had changed color again.

The pain radiated out and spread from his core until it rang through every part of him, before starting its cruel and rhythmic pulsing. Several notifications appeared, one after the other, and it took everything he had just to focus on the runes.

New living asset integration initiated.

Language imprint detected… bypassing…

There was a brief break in the pain and Aziel tried to clear his mind. Language imprint? He thought of the infusion of information received the moment he established a link with Celia, but what did this mean? Did Celia not have anything to do with it, then?

He yelled out as another wave of sharp pain shot through him, accompanied by more notifications.

Generating new asset log…

Race undetermined… allocating… race category identified.

Warning, race category is protected. Race status set to: Hidden.

Identifying attributes…

Identifying skills…

Warning, you have exceeded the limit of available free skill points. All free skill points exceeding the limit will be lost.

Assembling traits…

Error, Class S sealed trait identified. Archivist key is required to proceed.

Archivist key logged; authorization approved. Asset's Trait: Soul Weaving unsealed.

New living asset log generation completed.

Living asset integration successful.

Warning, Faction creation may cause unintended consequences to nexus realm historical record: in-depth Archivist review recommended.

Archivist key logged; authorization approved. New faction established: The Fallen.

Faction leader designated: Ascended Aziel.

Faction leader? was all Aziel could ask himself as the pain kept escalating; it felt like a billion ravenous worms were eating him alive. A terrible thought surfaced in his mind: was this process just another way of killing him? Was cooking him alive simply not enough for whoever was behind this?

Another wave of searing pain spread through him before concentrating on his right wrist—followed by an immediate sense of relief as it all melted away. Aziel stared forward, still unable to move and in a state of shock as a single notification stared back at him.

Realm designated. Welcome to Kadora.

Aziel stared at the now fading runes until he felt the pressure around his body increase and the sound of air being sucked in reached his ears. The same feeling of falling overcame him, as his consciousness went black.

* * *

Aziel blinked and found himself again seated on his familiar rock. Celia and Vhal faced him, but both had a glazed look to their eyes, which he guessed meant they were reviewing their own notifications.

He looked around then down at himself. Nothing appeared different, but he could feel that things had changed. For a start, he felt far more powerful and could tell he had regained control of his mana again. He also felt a familiar burning sensation on his right wrist, glancing down at it, he noticed the diamond-shaped mark was no longer faded. Beneath it also lay another mark, similar in size, but in the shape of a hollow circle. He instinctively knew that he had many notifications pending his review, and that the new mark was something called a faction log. Before he could check on them, however, his two companions blinked. Both were staring at him now with a mixture of interest and shock.

"What did you do?" Vhal asked, his eyes flashing curiously.

Celia took a step closer, still holding the crystals she had brought from the library. "I can access my log again..." she whispered.

"I didn't do anything," Aziel replied, confused. As far as he could tell, it was not a lie. That strange encounter... had it all just been some terrible dream? He had felt like it had taken forever, but now here he was, and no time at all seemed to have passed. None of it made sense.

Celia shook her head. "Check your notifications, Maste—" she stopped and blinked once before continuing. "You did *something*, that's for sure. Or else something has gone awfully wrong somewhere. I received a notification congratulating me on joining a faction."

"A faction?" Vhal interrupted. "I find the timing of this suspicious. Your eyes glazed over for a moment before all this happened."

The fact those two were agreeing with one another gave Aziel a strange sense of unease. He swallowed as he pressed his left hand against his wrist, and gray runes appeared before him.

Kadora Announcement: Beware. A new faction rises, the Fallen.

Aziel frowned. So it wasn't all a dream. He looked at Vhal, somewhat perplexed. "Does the World Seed announce all new factions in this way?"

Vhal grinned. "Why do you ask—does this faction concern you?"

"Yes, it does," Aziel replied. "I lead it."

He had surprised himself by how confidently he spoke of it, as if this was how things were meant to be.

"You what?" Celia cried out, almost dropping the crystals she was holding. "What do you mean you lead it? How?" Vhal, however, merely grinned and laughed.

Aziel was about to explain what had just occurred and ask the questions burning in his mind. Questions like who or what was this Archivist who had saved him from the World Seed and this unknown Overseer Assembly, and why was he given a faction? But at that moment, another searing pain shot through his head, along with a vision of that red beam striking the planet. He felt his hands beginning to sweat.

Had that been a warning? Was he meant to keep his experience a secret? Aziel looked at Celia, his mouth and throat feeling dry, and she looked back at him with clear concern. He was doing an awful job of hiding the turmoil within. He did not like the idea of lying to her, but being struck by that beam was infinitely worse.

"I was given the role by the World Seed," he said. "I didn't have much of a choice in the matter."

Celia looked at him suspiciously, and Vhal's expression suddenly turned serious. A flicker of black flashed through the lich's eyes, and Aziel felt something change within him. It only lasted for a split moment, but he was certain Vhal's vessel had expanded before reverting back again.

Not knowing what to make of this, Aziel let it go for now. At least the lich seemed to understand that Aziel could not or did not want to elaborate further on the topic of the World Seed.

Vhal turned to the succubus, "Don't you think it's rude to question your faction's lord?" he asked, bringing his face close to hers.

Celia's face contorted as she struggled to control her displeasure. "Vhal... if you don't get your face out of my sight, I might just take it away permanently," she growled, and Aziel watched in fascination as her fingernails elongated into claws to emphasize the threat.

Hoping to avoid a fight, Aziel cleared his throat loudly to regain their attention. "Perhaps we should get back to the topic of mana. Celia?"

Caught off guard, Celia hesitated. "W-What? Oh, right... of course." She moved quickly past Vhal, offering Aziel the three crystals in her hands.

Aziel watched them glow dimly in their respective colors, then picked up the red one. "So, I should just try to examine its structure?" he asked.

"Yes," Vhal replied excitedly. "Try to examine the building blocks of the mana, its behavior, its essence. It should give you an idea of what is required to re-create it." The lich leaned forward to get a better look at what Aziel was about to do.

Aziel stared at the crystal, uncertain of what to expect. He closed his eyes and took a deep breath as he focused on the small crystal in his hand. Aziel could feel the mana in there but could not see it clearly. It was as if it lay hidden under a thin sheet of cloth. Opening his eyes again, he sighed and tried with the other two crystals, but the results were the same.

Disappointed, Aziel looked at Vhal.

"Perhaps the difficulty is due to the mana being crystallized... maybe using raw mana would work? Here, try examining my own." Vhal lifted his hand and let a steady stream of blue mana manifest from it.

Aziel again closed his eyes and tried to focus on the blue mist in front of him. This was much clearer. Unlike his own mana, water mana felt cool and fluid, its component parts mixing and dissolving into one another. But the mana dispersed into its surroundings too quickly. It would be impossible to get what he needed this way.

Frustrated, Aziel abruptly stood. "This will not work, I need raw mana that is trapped, isolated, and unmoving. Otherwise, I won't be able to examine it long enough to get what I need."

Vhal frowned as he stopped the stream of blue mist. "That presents a problem. Other than in crystals, mana is free-flowing."

"It's no use then," Aziel said, flatly. A silence followed.

"Maybe…" Celia said, causing Aziel and Vhal to glance over at her questioningly. "Soul mana requires a little of another mana type to help it transform, right?"

Vhal nodded.

"Then there has to be a way for the soul mana within us to interact with another to do that. Otherwise, a mana weaver wouldn't be able to use the mana he is proficient in. I mean, how could I release fire mana like this?" In illustration, she released a tendril of fire mana from her palm.

Vhal considered this. "A logical conclusion, I'll give you that."

Celia grasped Aziel's hand and placed it on her chest, right on top of her heart. "Here… I can use fire mana, see what you can find." She swallowed hard, and Aziel noticed her cheeks grow redder.

As he gazed at her, Aziel felt her heartbeat quicken—not unlike his own. What was this feeling that kept resurfacing between them? On the one hand, he felt this need to be near her, to touch her as he was now. On the other hand, he also felt a deep sense of anxiety about her closeness and how it affected him. He simply didn't understand it.

Vhal sighed. "Could your intentions be any more blatant… succubus?"

"No one asked for your input, Vhal," Celia hissed back. She then gently pressed Aziel's hand against her chest again. "Go ahead, Master, take a look," she said quietly.

Aziel looked at her, trying to keep his face devoid of emotion. Celia didn't even seem to notice she was now calling him *master*, so he simply nodded and closed his eyes.

This close, he could sense her vessel clearly. It was made of soul mana, just as Vhal theorized. Its oval shape overlapped her heart, and tiny streams of soul and demonic mana flowed out of its gray shell, coursing through her body alongside her veins.

He reached out to the shell of the vessel, and it parted slightly to let him glimpse its interior. Unsurprisingly, inside was a pool of soul mana, surrounded by what he could only describe as a raging storm of demonic mana. Interestingly, he also could see the soul mana he was providing through their link pour into her vessel.

Even more surprising, however, was the tiny speck of concentrated fire mana hovering just above the pool, like a small candle suspended from a thread.

It appeared Celia's logic was correct. Aziel quickly got to work, studying the red mana as Vhal had instructed. Unlike water mana, fire mana was violence and rage. Its component parts felt as if in constant battle to devour each other. Slowly, the fundamental pieces, their shape, and their very essence began to make sense. He could see the tiny differences which made it special, and what he would need to manipulate within his own mana to force the change to occur. But before he could commit this completely to memory, something grabbed his shoulder and pulled, shattering his focus.

"Lord Aziel," he heard Vhal say, "you must stop!"

"What are you doing?" Aziel hissed, spinning around to glare at him. "I was almost done!"

"My apologies, but perhaps the cost would have been too high for you to accept…" The lich pointed.

Turning, Aziel saw Celia on the ground in a fetal position. She was grasping her chest as she struggled to breathe. Tears streamed down her cheeks.

"Celia?" he asked, dumbfounded. How did this happen? He didn't even notice the moment his hand was no longer in direct contact with her.

"I just… need… a minute," she gasped, struggling with every word.

Rushing to her side, he knelt and placed his hand on her trembling shoulder. "What happened? I was just looking. I didn't attack her."

That deep sense of anxiety he had felt only increased. What was wrong? What had he done?

Vhal moved closer, looking over his shoulder. "I'm not sure, but perhaps having your vessel examined so intimately causes some kind of heavy strain or violent feedback? I unfortunately know little on this subject. I wouldn't advise doing that again to her, though... or me while we're at it," he added.

Aziel instinctively channeled more of his mana into Celia through their link, and she twitched in response, then relaxed and let out a breath. "Th-thank you. That feels nice..." she whispered, with a ghost of a smile.

Seeing that smile brought calm back to Aziel's heart, and he let out an overdue breath. "Relax for a bit, Celia, we shall talk later." Satisfied she would recover, Aziel sat her up against the nearest Capital Crystal before he made his way back to the curved rock and sat down himself. He closed his eyes and sighed in frustration. "Failure. Again," he muttered.

"I wouldn't put it that way, Lord Aziel," Vhal interjected. "We now know you can learn what you need from studying the mana within someone. All you need is a more... *disposable* subject." He grinned widely.

Still frustrated, Aziel shook his head. "Why are you still here, Vhal?" he said sharply. "While I am thankful for your help, for someone who's been trapped in this place for so long, you don't seem to be in any hurry to leave."

"I was wondering when this question would come up," Vhal replied, leaning on his staff. "I don't intend to leave... I swore an oath to serve the master of this place, and as far as I'm concerned that is you, Lord Aziel. I also wouldn't miss the chance to study and witness how things here develop! Do you realize how irregular it is for you to have your own faction?"

Aziel shook his head.

"The answer is *very*. Factions usually require many conditions in order to officially form. A more or less stable government, laws, lands, and subjects... and even then, it is rare. I feel we are in the midst of some great change, and you are an important part of it all." Vhal then knelt, bowing his head in a gesture which caught Aziel off guard. In a low and respectful voice, he added, "Since my former masters have betrayed me and I am no longer part of their faction, I believe I am free to swear fealty to you, Lord Aziel, if you would accept my humble service as head researcher for the Fallen. In return, I ask only that you grant me a single wish without question, at a time of my choosing."

Aziel hesitated, considering this. Why would the lich do such a thing? He couldn't deny how useful Vhal had been in the short time since they'd met, but the lich's sudden actions brought up the question of what Aziel was supposed to do with this faction he had been given without explanation. He didn't even know what a faction actually was—not really. Was he supposed to work toward strengthening it? If so, then Vhal would contribute greatly on that front, and Aziel couldn't help but think it would be unwise to waste such talent.

There was the minor yet worrying detail of the unexplained momentary change in Vhal's vessel. But then again, the suspicious event happened so quickly, Aziel could have imagined the whole incident—stranger things had occurred recently after all.

And what about the single wish? From the way he had phrased it, Vhal would not tell Aziel what this wish was until he actually asked for it... was it wise to place himself under such a promise?

Taking a deep breath, Aziel stood and placed his hand on the lich's head. In the end, there was only one choice: Vhal was invaluable, and any future wish he might have was more than likely a price worth paying for his services.

"As Lord of the Fallen, I accept your terms and fealty, Vhal'nuel, Keeper of the Grand Library. I also appoint you as my head researcher. Serve me and our faction well, and I will ensure you are properly rewarded," Aziel declared confidently. The words came to him as if he had known them all his life.

Vhal looked up at his new lord, his ethereal blue eyes flashing.

"I will," he replied. Aziel felt a now-familiar heat on his right wrist, but this time, it originated from his new mark. He looked down to see the mark flash for a moment, just as a smaller one appeared from under Vhal's sleeve.

Aziel removed his hand, allowing Vhal to stand. As he did, the lich pulled up the sleeve of his black robes, allowing Aziel to see his right wrist which now bore a mark of a hollow circle, just like Aziel's. A notification then appeared in Aziel's view, followed immediately by another:

Faction officer position: Head Researcher has been assigned.

You have received a world quest: **Rise of the Fallen**
Fate has chosen you to be a catalyst for great change in Kadora. You have taken the first steps in growing your faction, but old and new races alike stir and call out for greater purpose. Gather allies, increase the strength and influence of your faction.
Quest objective: Raise your faction level to 5
Reward: Variable

Aziel felt mana pour into his vessel as Vhal's contribution came into effect. Although it was orders of magnitude higher than Celia's contribution, which was almost unnoticeable, the amount was still small. The only reason he even felt it, he decided, was due to them being in his place of power. Anywhere else and he guessed it wouldn't be enough to counteract the drain, but it felt good nonetheless.

But what was this so-called world quest? Its revelation brought about a feeling of urgency, as if his very existence depended on fulfilling it, but why? And *how*?

The notification also reminded him that he had not looked

through his new personal log since his so-called integration, but just then, Vhal spoke again.

"If you will allow it, my lord, I have a suggestion that will likely help you in your rise to prominence."

Intrigued, Aziel nodded. "Already? What do you have in mind?"

Vhal's grin grew wider, then he turned to look at the peacefully napping Celia. "Perhaps it is time to invest in your champion." He then chuckled in a way which made Aziel question his newest follower's motives.

"Invest?" he asked warily. "What exactly do you mean by that?"

Vhal pointed at Celia with a bony finger. "As a Lesser succubus, Celia is actually quite weak compared to other races of the same rank... she's just a small step up from a low-level human mage. Which is to be expected, since succubi specialize in more infiltration-based skill sets rather than raw power. But as they evolve further, their rate of growth and potential is far higher than most."

Understanding dawning, Aziel knelt beside Celia. Carefully, he brushed a few strands of her blonde hair away from her face. "You want me to force her evolution," he said softly, not wanting to wake the girl.

"Yes, my lord. Even with your massive mana reserves, you should use it wisely. Empowering your champion at a time when you yourself are limited in the way of movement is as wise as it comes," he added, with a slight shrug.

Aziel did not reply. Perhaps sensing his hesitation, Vhal continued: "You need a champion to enforce your will on the outside world. To pave the way for you to gain the followers you need and protect your interests, while you stay here and work on your weaving."

"Does Celia have to be this champion?" Aziel asked.

"You made her your champion the moment you created a link with her, my lord."

Aziel sighed. He could not really deny the truth of that. "She was never given a choice. I established the link without realizing what it was or meant."

"I suspect she won't mind helping you, though." Vhal smirked.

"Perhaps…" Aziel's gaze again drifted toward the peacefully sleeping succubus.

"Or perhaps I could find another champion?"

"Severing a link can be traumatic, my lord," Vhal replied quickly. "I advise against it, as it will most likely cause irreparable harm to Celia's vessel, assuming it doesn't kill her outright."

"Severing?" Aziel asked. "I was not aware that was even possible… but that was not my intention. I was thinking of creating a new link."

Vhal pondered this for a moment, then shook his head again. "Creating and maintaining mana links represent a drain on your reserves. Especially at a time when your mana levels are stagnant, I think it would be best to use what resources you already have."

A low groan from Celia interrupted Aziel's next thought. Her face contorted slightly with pain as she struggled to pull herself up from the ground. "Did you get what you need?" she asked, in a strained voice.

"No, I did not," Aziel replied, as he helped Celia slowly sit up straight and lean back on the crystal column. "Vhal has proposed a plan that might help, but only if you agree to it."

Celia glanced at the lich warily, then turned back to Aziel. "Do you agree with it?" she asked, a little groggily.

Taking a moment to think it over, Aziel looked directly into her golden eyes and nodded once.

Celia gazed back, their eyes connected, and Aziel could see the moment she came to a decision within them. "What do I have to do?" she asked.

"The first step is for you to grow stronger, so relax while our lord blesses you with his mana," Vhal exclaimed.

"What do you mea—?" Celia tried to ask, but was silenced

by Aziel fully opening their link and increasing his flow of mana to her. She shivered and moaned, then grabbed Aziel and hugged him tightly against herself, her nails dug into his back as if she was holding on to a stray piece of flotsam in the middle of the ocean.

"Wait... I feel..." Her words trailed off, but Aziel kept going. After a few seconds, Celia closed her eyes and went limp as she fell back into unconsciousness, her whole body glowing a faint gray.

Not knowing when to stop or what to look out for, Aziel leaned her against the crystal column and kept pushing his mana into her as notification after notification appeared in front of him.

You have channeled 163 mana using Soul Link.
You have channeled 185 mana using Soul Link.
You have channeled 202 mana using Soul Link.

Slowly, minor aspects of Celia's appearance began to change. First, her horns grew larger, then her hair grew longer. At this point, Aziel was channeling a raging river of mana into her and he began to feel the drain.

"I don't know how long I can keep this going... it's taking more than I expected," he said in a strained voice, as sweat began to run down his brow.

Vhal stared at the succubus in what looked to be a state of shock.

Aziel clenched his jaw, every muscle burning as more and more sweat dripped from his forehead and body. His body was practically overheating from the strain. "Vhal!" he ground out. "How much longer?"

The lich continued to stare at Celia, his mouth slightly parted. "Keep going... just a little longer."

Aziel groaned and pushed as much mana as he could through their link. The room shook, and all the surrounding crystals dimmed noticeably. Celia's body also began to shake, as she kept glowing brighter and brighter—until Aziel had to avert his gaze from the brilliance.

Aziel winced as he felt his vessel tremble within him. Each time it did, a sharp pain was sent all over his body. But Aziel tried his best to ignore that—his focus was entirely on sending as much mana as possible to Celia, until he heard Vhal cry out.

"My lord! That's enough!"

Hearing the panic in his follower's voice, Aziel sealed his side of the link. Breathing heavily, he planted his hands on the crystal column in front of him for support, barely avoiding collapsing on top of the unconscious succubus. His whole body ached and for the first time since he had been freed, he felt a sizable gap within his mana vessel… it was an odd and uncomfortable sensation.

"My lord, are you all right?" Vhal asked, concern evident in his tone.

"Ye—Yes… I will be fine… Did we succeed?" he asked, with some difficulty.

Vhal chuckled softly. "My lord… even with some idea of the depth of your power, I never thought what I witnessed today was possible."

"What do you mean?" he asked wearily. Had he again done something bad to Celia without realizing it?

"When I recommended you expedite Celia's evolution, I was thinking along the lines of a rank two Enlightened—a Greater succubus, in her case. But you did that within the first few seconds of the transfer, an impressive feat on its own." The lich then hesitated, as if not believing what he was about to say. "You didn't even seem to notice or exhibit any strain at that point. So I thought perhaps you could go further… What you did in a few minutes here took me hundreds of years to achieve on my own. You pushed her up to a rank one Enlightened, the greatest rank a living being can achieve, short of being an Ascended… an Elder."

Aziel looked at Vhal, then back at Celia. He could tell something had changed, something more than just her rank. As if she could sense his gaze, he saw her lips spread into a small smile as she slept.

CHAPTER 10

Slowly, Celia opened her eyes. Her head was spinning; she could hear some muffled voices coming from somewhere nearby. Her wrist was practically on fire due to the veritable mountain of notifications that angrily demanded her attention.

Looking up, she saw Aziel seated on his curved rock, only a few feet in front of her. He was discussing something with Vhal, and all she could feel was a deep hunger. She licked her lips, and slowly crawled toward him, stalking her prey. When she got closer, he somehow sensed her presence and his gaze shifted, his bright gray eyes connecting with hers.

"Ah, Celia, you're awake," he smiled, the relief clear in his voice. "I'm glad to see—"

Celia leapt up and straddled him, interrupting whatever he was going to say. Her whole body tingled with need, and he was all she could think about. She slowly wrapped her arms around his neck and leaned forward to nibble on his earlobe.

"Master…" she whispered. Even as she molded her body to his, slowly grinding herself against him, Celia wondered why calling him master felt so right. She grinned as she pressed herself harder against him, it didn't matter why, all that mattered was satisfying the ocean of desire which threatened to drown her.

"I can't say I'm surprised…" Vhal commented from somewhere behind her, but Celia's focus was entirely on her master. Unable to hold back any longer, she pulled his head forward and kissed him hungrily. A moan escaped her lips, as the first traces of demonic mana started to pour into her.

She couldn't help it as she felt her Siphon pierce her master's vessel over and over again, and for a moment, a deep sadness mixed with her endless lust. Like everyone else she made love to, she was killing him. She tried to stop herself, to pull herself away, but her body wanted this. No, it *needed* it.

Celia pressed her body against his, she wanted to feel his warmth against her skin, even if it was just for a short while. To her absolute shock and amazement, Aziel didn't fight her; instead, he reciprocated. One hand slid under her ear to wrap around the back of her neck as his lips pressed into hers, while the other ran down her back. She shuddered as his mana-infused touch sent shockwaves of pleasure into her. Her Siphon didn't seem to be bothering him at all—at this point her victims would have been wheezing and grunting in pain. Vhal, who had reached out to grab and stop her from killing Aziel, stopped as he no doubt noticed the same thing.

Celia focused in and watched in amazement as the holes her Siphon was poking into her master's vessel closed as if they'd never existed in the first place. Her master's vessel had healed itself from a Siphon… She didn't even know such a thing was possible. She smiled against his lips, her mind completely consumed with relief and deep yearning for more, as she wrapped her tail around his right leg possessively.

Tail…? The unfamiliar sensation of an extra appendage brought her out of the moment, giving Aziel a chance to breathe.

"Celia…" he whispered, in a daze.

His words refocused her attentions, and she grinned as she rocked herself on his lap, slowly, rhythmically. The whole experience was electrifying—her body felt several times more sensitive than she was used to. More than anything, however, she was enjoying the fact that her actions were having a visible effect on Aziel… an Ascended. And yet, he somehow appeared to be immune to the deadly effects of her Siphon.

He managed to muster enough strength of will to resist her advances for a split second, which he used to grip her shoulders and gently push her back.

"Stop," he panted, but she could feel his arousal and practically see the conflict in his eyes. He wanted this, but was fighting it—for what reason, she was not certain.

She let out a deep breath, then slowly and deliberately took her time sliding off him, ensuring he got to see as much of her as possible in the process.

"We can continue this later," she purred, giving him a wink. She unwrapped her tail from around his leg and drew her hands along its length. Her thoughts had clarified the moment she got what she wanted—or at least a taste of it—so she took a moment to examine her new and improved self.

The most drastic change was her tail, which protruded from her tailbone. It was black, thick, and satisfyingly flexible. Long enough to easily wrap around her waist, its tip ended in a shape that reminded her of a blunt arrowhead.

Her skin color had also changed to a shade of gray, while her once-blonde hair had turned platinum white. It had grown in length, spilling over her shoulders and down her back. She could also feel the unfamiliar weight of her newly-enlarged black horns. They curled noticeably, their normally smooth surface now ridged.

The final thing Celia noted were the changes to her body shape and height. She could have sworn she had grown taller, and her body was much leaner and curvier. Her much-abused dress seemed to agree with her observations.

Completing her self-inspection, she faced Aziel again. A devilish grin spread across her face while she gazed into his eyes. He was still breathing a little heavily, which had her worried for a second—until a realization struck her.

Was Aziel a virgin? He had mentioned being imprisoned for a long time and that he had lost his memories, but how far in the past did that extend? If he was a virgin, then it would explain how vulnerable and blindsided he had been when she straddled him.

Getting that sort of attention for the first time from a succubus was bound to be overwhelming. But then again, a person usually wouldn't survive that sort of attention. She grinned as she remembered how his vessel had healed—it was incredible.

"Like what you see, Master?" she purred, as she spun slowly in place to give him a clear view of her from behind—maintaining eye contact all the while by peeking over her shoulder. She could see his gaze drift across her, and her body began to heat up in response to the attention.

Vhal sighed loudly. "Celia, while I am just as eager to find out more about our lord's apparent resistance to your Siphon, perhaps you could keep yourself in check while we are discussing important matters?"

Celia groaned at the interference. "Bones, my master and I have some serious things to discuss, in private…" She glanced at Aziel and bit her lower lip in a way that made her intentions crystal clear to even the most naïve of persons, before she gave Vhal another haughty look. "Would you leave us for a while?" she asked, in an overly sweet tone. She wanted to test this resistance.

"As entertaining as it is to see you like this, no, I cannot. There are more pressing issues than your sexual appetite," he replied curtly.

"Enough!" Aziel declared, glaring at the pair. It looked like he had recovered from the experience of being mounted. "Celia, do you feel any different after your evolution?" He continued in a much calmer tone.

Still annoyed by the lich, Celia sighed, then faced Aziel with a smile. "Hmm, other than the physical changes? I feel more powerful, but I will have to test things to see to what degree," she said thoughtfully, then held up her hand and allowed a bit of her fire mana to leak out.

"Why not check your log?" Vhal asked.

Celia's smile widened. "I would rather do that in private, to really delve into it."

"Go ahead, try to weave something," Aziel suggested. "Perhaps something you found difficult before?"

Still smiling, Celia bowed low enough to give Aziel a clear view of her full breasts. "As you wish, Master."

She began forming red symbols in the air in front of her. Instead of the methodical step-by-step process she was used to when weaving, the symbols practically snapped into existence. It happened so fast, in fact, that at one point she almost lost control of the spell.

She grinned, aware of Vhal studying her every move. Just as the symbols joined into a single glyph, his eyes flashed, and he quickly drew his staff forward, "Bone shield!" he cried out before slamming the base into the ground.

A large wall of bones materialized between himself and Celia, just as she yelled, "Focused Flame!" and turned to toss the spell toward the lich. The temperature around them rose sharply as the red symbols burst into flames then quickly concentrated themselves into a large lance of fire. The lance flew through the short distance between them and exploded with a loud bang as it struck the wall of bones, shattering it into tiny pieces.

Vhal's surprisingly quick reactions helped him to avoid the majority of the damage, but the powerful spell still pushed him back a few feet. Not wasting any time, he again lifted his staff to begin weaving another spell. Celia, however, was not going to give him the chance. She tossed a second lance of flames at the lich, forcing him to abandon whatever he had been planning and to again raise his staff to summon another Bone Shield. This time, the force of the blast threw him back into the far wall.

Celia was amazed at how easy it was. Before her evolution, she might have been able to weave a single spell at this level before needing time to recover. Right now, she was shooting them off like normal Fire Bolts. Vhal—who had seemed impossible to touch before—could only barely defend himself against her onslaught, and she wasn't even trying that hard. Thinking she could take it up a notch, she continued weaving another Focused Flame, while also attempting to weave another spell in unison.

It was far more difficult than she imagined, and she could tell she was pushing against her limit of the number of symbols she could keep up at the same time, but she just about managed it.

"Let's see what you can do against something like this," she yelled. "Phoenix Fire!"

The new symbol expanded rapidly, before bursting into flames as it took the form of a large bird. It flapped its wings once and roared before diving forward toward the lich who glared at it in defiance. Black symbols instantly formed in front of him, their speed catching Celia off guard. Opening his arms wide he yelled back, "Banshee's Wail!"

The symbol grew larger, then collapsed and morphed into a ghostly feminine face which shot up to the chamber's ceiling. Celia covered her ears as a loud shriek emanated from it, instantly snuffing out all the flames she had woven.

Vhal then moved his hand and the feminine apparition followed his movements. He directed it closer to her, and Celia dropped to one knee, panting, as the simple act of breathing became more difficult. It felt like her organs were being ripped apart by the vibrations the scream was pushing into her.

Vhal took a few steps toward her, wearing the same grin he always had plastered to his rotted face. "Admirable effort, but it is time to teach you a lesson."

He began to chuckle darkly. Celia glanced to one side and saw Aziel leaning forward, watching them with interest. She did not want to admit defeat in front of her master. Her face twisted from pain as she forced herself to her feet and charged forward, a slight bony crack sounded as her horns slammed into Vhal's side. The unexpected move caused the lich to lose control of his spell, which thankfully silenced the horrid scream.

"What are you d—!" he tried to protest, just as Celia placed both her hands on his chest and grinned. If Vhal could go pale—or paler than he already was—then she was certain he would have at that moment. Red mist flowed from her hands, before she yelled, "Burst!"

The red mist exploded, blasting the lich and slamming him against the far wall. The force of the explosion caused the large chamber to shake and bits of rock to fall from the ceiling. Vhal groaned and shook his head before he quickly pushed himself up and on his feet.

He glared at her, his annoyance clear, and his blue ethereal eyes flashed once again. He let go of his staff, but instead of falling, it simply hovered where he had left it as black mana streamed from both his hands. Celia was just happy she had finally been able to wipe that damn grin off his face.

"Let's get serious," Vhal said ominously, his voice deeper than usual, and she felt a shiver run down her spine. The cloud of mana he had released was quickly forming into symbols, some of which she had never seen before. What was more alarming was the sheer number of them. Had Vhal gone mad? A spell using that many symbols was likely to blow the whole cavern up.

Celia raised her hands and got to work. "Heat Shield," she muttered, and the air around her rose in temperature, enough that the rock below her feet began to glow a bright red.

Vhal chuckled, which quickly turned into hysterical laughter. His complicated series of symbols pulsated with black energy, and even with the intense heat of her shield around her, Celia's blood went cold.

She didn't know exactly what that spell was, but she knew it would end her if she didn't do something. She had underestimated Vhal and overplayed her hand. Even though she was many times stronger than before her evolution, she was still practically a newborn compared to Vhal's experience and knowledge. She maintained her Heat Shield and started weaving another Focused Flame in the hopes of intercepting Vhal's spell and possibly weakening or even blocking it.

Vhal's laughter began to quieten, but he still grinned at her menacingly. Before he could unleash his spell, however, a voice came from behind her.

"I believe you two have shown me enough."

Vhal's frown was immediate, but he stopped what he was doing. The symbol he had so painstakingly worked on puffed away into black mist, and his eyes flashed a few times. His body sagged a little, as if something had just drained him of mana. Celia also ended her spells, before turning and kneeling in one smooth movement.

"Master," she said, and let out a small sigh of relief. "I hope my demonstration pleased you."

"It did," Aziel said, then looked beyond her. "Vhal?"

"I am fine, my lord," the lich replied as he moved and knelt beside her. It was true, he looked completely unharmed from the duel. "She caught me off guard, but her power is noteworthy nonetheless. She will require some training to utilize her full potential as an Elder, however."

Celia frowned, but then nodded in agreement.

Vhal grinned at her. "You are lucky, succubus. Things would have progressed quite differently if our lord had not stopped us."

"Sure," she replied, dismissively. Then her expression turned serious as she addressed Aziel. Her master had spent a great deal of mana on her so that she might complete a mission—a mission she had yet been informed of. "Master, what is it you ask of me?"

Aziel leaned forward, interlacing his fingers together. He stared at her for a few long moments before he began to speak. "Celia, I need you to find and bring me weavers... preferably several of each mana proficiency, so that I may study the mana within their vessels." His tone made it clear he expected no excuses, and for some reason that made her body tingle with desire.

At that moment, her mark began to heat up, and a block of runes appeared before her.

Your Faction leader has offered you a faction quest:
Knowledge of Mana.
Your Faction Leader has tasked you with gathering mana weavers so that he may increase his knowledge and understanding of mana. Quest objective: Collect weavers of different specializations and deliver them to your Faction Leader. Reward: Variable.

Celia grinned. This was the first time she had been tasked with an actual quest. Unlike everyday requests, quests were tasks recognized by the World Seed. If a task was challenging or important enough, then the World Seed itself granted a reward in the form of skill points, attributes, and in rare cases, items. She had heard that adventurers and high-level professions were more likely to receive quests due to the nature of their work, and it was well known that completing them was the quickest way to gain power.

"As you will, Master," she replied courteously, then stood to leave only to be stopped by his voice.

"Wait… not yet," Aziel said. "There is something we should do before that, and I wish you to be around when we do it." He only gave her enough time to raise a questioning eyebrow, before he turned his attention to the lich beside her.

"Vhal, what is behind the last gate?" he asked.

The enchanted gate they had left behind. Celia couldn't help but feel a jolt of excitement. Their discovery of Vhal had distracted them from exploring it.

Vhal, however, wore a confused look. "Gate, my lord?"

"Yes, beside the room we found you in was another," Aziel explained. "It remains sealed by another of those aranite gates. We didn't interfere with it, as it still had active enchantments placed on it."

"Hmm," Vhal said, as he stroked his beard thoughtfully. "If my memory doesn't fail me... that would be the Imperial Wing of the Facility. I have never been in there; no one was allowed in, other than the emperor, his immediate family... and perhaps some invited guests."

"There is a place called the Imperial Wing here? This was still a Wilds even when the Caelian Empire was at the height of its power," Celia said, more than a little skeptically. "The location makes sense for a secret research base, but an Imperial Wing?"

"We can answer those question when we get into the wing itself," Aziel said. He then addressed Vhal again. "So? Can you open the gate?"

Vhal remained silent for a few seconds. "I don't know if I can. When we were sealed in that room, someone changed the words that would have unlocked the gate which trapped us. If the same was done to the rest of the gates, then there would be no way to open it other than force... which I would advise against."

"Is there any reason we should not try?" Aziel asked.

"I suppose not..." Vhal replied, hesitantly. Celia noticed him finger the hem of his sleeve, which looked somewhat singed, though it was difficult to tell as his robes were black.

"Then shall we?" Aziel asked.

Celia nodded, but couldn't help feeling a little anxious. Although she was interested in—even excited—about the thought of entering an Imperial Wing in a Caelian facility, that place had smelled terrible. And the last sealed room they had opened had given them Vhal. She wasn't sure she could handle another Vhal... With that nightmarish thought, she followed her master down the path toward the passageway beyond.

As they made their way to the library, Aziel updated her about what had occurred while she was unconscious. She wasn't sure about how she felt about Vhal swearing fealty, but having him appointed as head researcher was interesting, especially if it led to ancient Caelian technology. That single wish had her worried, though... very worried.

When they reached the sealed gate, they all stopped in unison. Vhal looked upon the gate and the glowing encryption with something like trepidation.

Celia, however, let out a sigh of relief when she discovered that the horrid smell seemed to have lessened. It now resembled something akin to bad mold, which was nowhere near as terrible. Noticing Vhal's hesitation, she asked, "Something wrong?"

The lich glanced at her for a moment, before focusing back on the dimly glowing gate. "I never opened this gate... I was never allowed to," he replied solemnly.

"But you can though... right?" she asked.

"As the appointed lead researcher of the Facility I was given the method of doing so..." he agreed.

Aziel took a few steps closer and gestured to Vhal to get started, which he did.

He slowly placed his hand on the center of the gate, and it hummed in response. He then took a deep breath and closed his eyes.

"Aslan Da Caelian," he whispered, and visibly tensed as if expecting something horrible to happen.

A moment of silence followed, but then the symbols glowed brighter and a loud click emanated from somewhere deep within the gate. It slowly began to swing open, as whatever mana was left within it struggled with the weight involved.

Celia was just able to restrain herself enough to not cry out with excitement. Vhal took a step back, allowing Aziel to grip the handle and pull the gate wider.

"It's much lighter than the other two…" he said, puzzled.

"The enchantments lighten the load when activated, allowing anyone to use it," Vhal replied, his voice distant.

Celia glanced at the lich again with concern, noticing his slumped shoulders.

"Bones?" she asked.

Vhal quickly straightened and smiled. "My apologies. I was lost in thought, that's all." Celia noticed his hand go to the right side of his robes, but he didn't remove anything from what she assumed was an inner pocket there.

"Riiight…" she said, narrowing her eyes. As Aziel worked on the gate, she moved closer to the lich. "Listen, you're insufferable when happy, so I can't imagine how much worse it would be with you being all gloomy and depressed. And since we're stuck together… spit it out."

Vhal chuckled softly. "If I didn't know any better, Celia, I would think that you're actually worried about me." His grin returned as he withdrew his hand from his robes, still empty.

"On second thought, just keep it to yourself," she huffed, walking back toward the open gate.

"I was hoping the password wouldn't work," he admitted, causing her to stop in her tracks.

He sighed before continuing.

"The password I used worked for all the gates here… at least, it used to." He pointed at the gate Aziel had pried open earlier, and which had imprisoned him for so long. "When my colleagues and I entered that storeroom… the same password didn't work. So we were trapped."

"Someone changed the password to that specific gate…" Celia mused. "But who could have done that?"

"Only someone with imperial authority, and they would have had to be here in person to do it," Vhal replied, solemnly. "But I don't know why the emperor or princess would go through all that trouble to get rid of us... all they had to do was order us to be killed. Whatever the reason, I was right... we were betrayed."

"Maybe we will find a clue in there, then," Celia said, indicating the doorway, which Aziel was pulling open even wider. "Plus, whatever the reason was, it happened a long time ago... the Caelian Empire no longer exists, and the Imperial Family are long gone. So at this point, maybe it doesn't really matter why they did it. Also, the final years of the Caelian Empire were known to be turbulent, and not a lot of records survived from that time. Discovering what exactly happened could prove difficult."

Vhal gave his beard another long stroke, before saying, "Perhaps you are right." But Celia could tell he didn't mean it.

"Shall we?" Aziel asked, now holding the door wide open.

Together, the three took their first steps into the Imperial Wing. Celia glanced around and noted the rocky walls and V shape of the room they had entered, which led to yet another door. This one was made of some type of dark wood and was not enchanted.

"Well, this is underwhelming," she commented.

"This looks like a security room," Vhal replied, pointing at the slanted walls. "It is shaped in a way to force any attackers who get past the gate into a chokepoint."

Aziel stepped forward and pushed open the next door. Immediately, the darkened room they were in shone brightly as light crystals sprang to life. Celia followed him in and stood staring open-mouthed at what she saw laid out before them.

This room was long and wide, with a high, arched ceiling. The walls and floors of mountain rock were covered by polished white stones. Multiple pairs of tall obsidian pillars stood on either side of the room, connected by overhead arches. Between each pair of pillars hung large black silk banners, with golden embroidered borders that reached all the way to the ground. The imperial silver phoenix of the Caelian Empire decorated each of their faces.

In the center lay a long black carpet, with silver and gold threads woven in intricate designs all along its surface. The symbols shone as they reflected the golden light emitted from the large chandeliers and small light crystals that hung from the ceiling. The carpet stretched from one end of the room all the way to the other, marking the path forward.

As they neared the end of the great hall, the walls shifted inward to focus on the central point. The carpet they were walking on also expanded to cover the whole area in front of them, including a raised dais.

They stared at the throne at the center of the raised platform. It had a wide seat, large armrests, and a tall, imposing back which ended in a rounded top. It was made primarily of a marble, but also had what looked like obsidian worked along the outside of the throne.

"I'm not the only one seeing this… right?" Celia asked, breaking the silence that had engulfed them ever since they entered the chamber. The sheer wealth on display here was staggering.

"No," Vhal replied. "I always thought the Imperial Family used this place as some sort of vacation home, a place away to escape the capital and its politics for a short while. But, this place looks exactly like the audience chamber in the Imperial Palace."

"I thought you said this place was a secret," Celia said, glancing at the lich who she saw was deep in thought. "Can't really hold court In secret, can you?"

Vhal crossed his hands, his ethereal eyes focusing on the throne and the massive Caelian banner hanging behind it. "I don't know… I don't even know how they got all this material in here without any of the researchers noticing."

Aziel had his eyes closed, but now opened them again. "I don't sense anyone nearby," he said. "No one with any soul mana, in any case."

Celia let out a long breath. "Good to know we can look around without anything trying to kill us." She glared pointedly at Vhal, who simply ignored her.

They all looked about themselves for a few moments, then shifted their gaze to a large set of wooden double doors to the left of the throne.

Celia moved first, pushing the doors open. They were met by a hallway beyond. Light crystals again sprang to life in the ceiling, illuminating the area. The walls and floors were of the same white stone as the throne room, but the hallway was otherwise empty.

They proceeded cautiously along it until they reached a medium-sized rectangular room containing eight slightly raised circular platforms arranged in a row along the middle. Each platform also held a thin rectangular dark stone jutting upward out of their centers. Celia stepped closer to one of the platforms, then looked over her shoulder at Vhal questioningly.

Vhal smiled and moved toward another platform. He stepped onto it, and a long strand of symbols along the platform's edge instantly lit up. The whole thing began to hum lightly.

"What are you doing?" Celia asked, taking a few steps back. She didn't trust the lich, and now he was playing around with things she didn't understand.

"Calm down, Celia, it's just a simple levitation platform," Vhal said, in a matter-of-fact way.

"Levitation platform?" Aziel asked. "As in… it will rise?"

All three of them glanced upward. The ceiling was gone, and now all they could see was a darkness staring back at them. Even with her Dark Vision, Celia couldn't see far enough into it to discern where the ceiling actually was.

Vhal grinned. "Shall we, my lord?" he asked.

Slowly, Aziel stepped up to join him, Celia following hesitantly a moment later.

Vhal placed his hand on top of the thin rock at the center of the circle, then turned back to face them. "There are apparently two floors above us," he said.

"Two floors?" Celia said incredulously. "They dug through a mountain both horizontally and vertically? How can you be so nonchalant about this? This levitation platform is Magitech no one else has... well, maybe the Ejani do, but they wouldn't tell us if they did."

Vhal's eyes flashed. "The Ejani Empire is still around?" he asked, staring at Celia.

"Well... yeah. Why?"

"I'm surprised such an expansionist nation survived for this long," Vhal replied. "My guess was that they either would have been stopped by another at some point or would have taken everyone over by now."

"Expansionist?" Celia replied, with a raised eyebrow. "They might have been during your time, but today's Ejani are peacekeepers."

"Peacekeepers?" Vhal echoed mockingly, then chuckled.

"While this is all interesting, can we proceed with what matters at the present moment?" Aziel interrupted, pointing upward.

"Of course, my lord," Vhal replied, and swiped his finger along the surface of the thin rock in the center of the platform. Celia watched as three separate symbols which seemed to illustrate floor numbers lit up, with one flashing more brightly than the others.

The platform reacted and shook lightly before it began to rise. As it did, the tunnel above them started to brighten as light crystals came to life around them. The platform rose and rose, and then came to a rest before a wide stone path leading to another set of double doors, similar to the one they had passed through below.

They made their way toward it and Celia pushed the doors open. A long, curved hallway stretched out in both directions, seeming to form a large circle. Celia glanced up and down it, noting the many doors on each side of the hall.

They split up to explore, painstakingly checking every room, until they met at the opposite end of the long circular hallway.

"Well I'm impressed," Celia said. "There seems to be a room for everything here."

"Studies, meeting room, dining rooms, several types of training rooms, a rather large bath house and a massive compartmentalized storage room," Vhal said, then pulled out a small clear bag with some sort of brown paste within it. "Too bad most of the normal food had gone bad, but we are left with a rather large stock of emergency rations. They were made to last. Of course, sacrifices had to be made to reach that result."

Celia tried her best to hide her disgust at the sight of the thick brown paste. "Did you notice the crystals embedded into the furniture? What's with this place and using crystals to preserve things? I get the books, but furniture?" she added incredulously. "Guess the imperial family always got the best."

"With every passing generation, the imperial family used this place to escape their responsibilities in the capital more and more… I just didn't realize just how much they had invested in it," Vhal replied, while brushing his hand over a piece of fine purple silk cloth that covered a table, an expensive-looking vase resting on top of it.

Aziel pointed to the last door before them. "So what's left that could be in there?"

"I really hope its bedrooms," Celia said. "We haven't found any of those."

Vhal grabbed the door handle. "Let's find out."

They slowly shuffled in and were met by another large ornate room. A carpet just like the one in the throne room shimmered under the light crystal chandeliers, while detailed paintings depicting exotic landscapes covered the walls. Several seating arrangements consisting of plush chairs and couches were laid out with one corner even containing a fireplace powered by fire crystals. A total of twelve doors connected to this large common room, with five identical single doors on either side and one double door at the opposite end of the doorway they had just entered from.

Celia peeked through the first door to their right, then let out a squeal of delight. She dashed in and jumped onto the large bed in the center of the richly furnished and decorated room, sinking into the soft feather-filled mattress.

"Ahh," she moaned. "This is just great! I can't even remember the last time I lay down on an actual bed… never mind one this luxurious."

"Celia, get up, we can rest later," Aziel commanded from the doorway. She grinned mischievously at the sight of him.

"You know, Master… this bed has more than enough space for two," she said, her tone full of promises before she began stretching provocatively. Aziel's mouth opened wider, he then quickly looked away to avoid eye contact. Celia giggled inwardly as she slid off the bed and stepped closer to him, curling her tail loosely around his leg.

At that same moment, Vhal entered from behind Aziel and sighed. "All these rooms are copies of one another," he said. "Except for that one, which is locked. Nothing magical, though." He gestured toward the double doors.

Celia scowled at the lich for interrupting, but she had to admit she was interested enough in the locked room to postpone her enjoyment for now. She unwrapped herself from her master—but not before giving him a soft kiss on the cheek—and strode toward the last door.

She pushed the handles down, but it was indeed locked, just as Vhal said. She knelt in front of the lock, grinning when she noticed Aziel staring at her from behind. She concentrated for a moment on elongating her nails, then slowly started fiddling with the locking mechanism.

"You know how to pick locks?" Vhal asked, with a raised eyebrow.

"Yeah, had to learn a few things when I was trying to survive on my own. Plus, it was good practice for my Demon Claws skill." Her last word coincided with a click, and the doors swung open slightly.

"There we go," she said, then looked over her shoulder and

grinned at Aziel before asking, "Seen enough? I could give you a better angle," she teased, waiting just long enough to catch his embarrassment before she pushed herself up on her feet and giggled knowingly as she stepped into the room.

The room was rather spacious, and full of large wooden boxes stacked on top of each other, along with several large glass-topped display cases. Celia took a few steps forward to look into one of them.

"Uhh, I think you two should take a look at this," she called out.

The case contained a selection of fine, expensive-looking daggers. Glancing around, Celia could tell that all of these cases contained different types of weapons, ranging from standard swords and spears to weapons of exotic shapes and styles she had never seen before. There must have been dozens of them, and all of them looked to be master-crafted. She again cursed not having the Analyze and Detect Magic skills—these weapons were obviously magical, and both skills would have listed their properties, which she reckoned would have been an interesting read.

"Well?" she asked turning to Vhal. "Any ideas?"

The lich picked up one of the daggers and examined it closely before placing it back down.

"These are definitely the imperial family's prized weapons. But they were supposed to be in the palace, not a secret research facility stashed away from prying eyes," Vhal replied.

Celia and Vhal were so focused on the expensive and powerful-looking weapons that they did not notice Aziel move toward one of the larger wooden boxes, until he called out to them.

"These boxes contain clothes and armor. They also seem to be enchanted somehow, but I can't tell in what way," he said as he pulled out a few sets of leather armor and tossed them on the ground.

Celia picked up a leather tunic to examine it, taking note of its quality. Just as Aziel said, these armor pieces had mana running through them, so she tried to find the enchantment runes. It took her a few moments, but she found what she was looking for on the inside of the leather.

"Those are longevity, physical resistance and weight runes," a hoarse voice came from over her shoulder. She turned slightly and saw Vhal standing right behind her, examining the same armor. "They are powered by these earth crystal threads." His fingers traced the brown threads on the armor.

Celia couldn't help but stare. Crystal threads? What in the Abyss were those? She had never heard of anything like it. Enchanted armor usually had crystals embedded in them, but somehow, the Caelians had been able to convert crystals into threads and use them in their design. It was astounding.

"Yeah, I know," she said in an attempt at indifference, before dropping the armor back to the ground. She continued through the maze of boxes. This was by far the largest storeroom they had found, and if all these boxes contained enchanted armor and weapons, then they could equip a small army. It would be one of the most well-equipped armies in history, as far as she knew.

Toward the back of the room, she found three large wooden cabinets. They stood out from the rest due to their highly decorative surfaces. Curiosity getting the better of her, she unclasped the hook that locked the first, and the double doors swung open on their own. She took a quick step back just in time to avoid being hit by them as her eyes scanned the interior.

There hung a set of black leather armor, along with a black, regal, high-collared jacket with gold lining. A cape of a similar design hung from the shoulders, along with what looked like a gold scarf with an intricate artistic impression woven into it. On the side shelves sat a pair of black gloves and metal shoulder pauldrons, one much larger than the other, with a neck guard as part of the design. There were other armored pieces, including a thick metal belt and a heavy metal gauntlet.

The sound of footsteps brought her out of her reverie. She turned just in time to see Vhal gasp at the sight in front of him.

"Vhal?" Celia asked cautiously.

"This makes no sense," he whispered. "What happened in the years I was trapped...?"

"Uhhh, Vhal? What's wrong?" Celia asked again, as Aziel joined them with a questioning look.

"Those belonged to the emperor... every emperor," he said, leaning on his staff. "The emperor would have worn it wherever he went, and yet it's hanging here in a storage room."

"There is mana coursing through this fabric," Aziel said, brushing his hand across the jacket sleeve. "A lot of it."

"Yes, it was enchanted by the very best the empire had to offer and infused with mana by the empire's divinities," Vhal replied.

"I don't see any crystals," Celia said questioningly, before adding, "or crystal threads."

"There aren't any. Ascended can bestow mana upon anything—not just people, but objects as well. Some materials can take in more mana than others, and with the right enchantments, they can even have their own mana vessels. Just like this one." Vhal's eyes slowly scanned the set of regal clothing.

"What about the others?" Aziel asked, pointing toward the other two cabinets.

"Only one way to find out," Celia said excitedly, and proceeded to open them.

The next one boasted a collection of smaller, highly decorated boxes, which contained a few pouches and bags of various sizes, but it was the dress displayed in the last cabinet that claimed Celia's attention. She stroked her hand slowly across the soft fabric, mesmerized by it.

Aziel stepped beside her and placed his hand on her shoulder. "Those bags and this dress are all infused with mana, a sizable amount of it." He then reached in and pulled the garment out of the large crate and presented it to her.

"Try it on," he said with a smile.

Celia nodded slowly, then grabbed the dress and gave Aziel the most dazzling smile she could muster. She slowly undressed, enjoying her master's gaze as she finally freed herself from the worn-out dress she had been wearing. Making a show of putting on the new garment and armor, she took great care to twirl and bend at opportune moments, in the hopes of teasing a reaction out of him. Aziel, however, sheepishly shifted his gaze away from her, and so to her disappointment and disgust, all she got in return was a grin from Vhal.

Taking a moment for herself, she looked down to examine her new attire. The dress she wore looked to be the female equivalent of the emperor's suit hanging in the first cabinet. It was a tight-fitting sleeveless black dress with intricate gold lining, one part dress, another part armor. The upper portion was form-fitting, feeling almost like a second skin, before opening up and flaring outward by the time it reached the ground.

The cut included a plunging V-neck, exposing a generous portion of her breasts and also included a slit up the right side, starting at the bottom and reaching all the way to her upper thigh. The dress flowed around her in a way that emphasized her form and was somehow both elegant and over the top, which Celia couldn't help but appreciate.

The dress also came with several armored pieces, such as shoulder pads and greaves, which blended seamlessly into the overall design of the dress. They were made out of true silver, a metal only one step down from the legendary aranite when it came to toughness and magical capacity. Celia stroked her hands slowly down the fabric as she felt the mana within it get to work, expanding and shrinking it to fit her body perfectly. It even morphed to accommodate her tail.

"You look beautiful," Aziel said with a smile. "It suits you perfectly." His eyes slowly drifted up and down her body.

Celia reveled in his attention, and took a step closer to him, placing a delicate hand on his chest.

"Do you really think so?" she asked, softly. "I have never worn something like this…"

"I'm sure you haven't," Vhal interjected breaking her out of the moment, "Especially something like that. That's the Empress's ceremonial dress, after all."

Celia dropped her head and sighed, before she turned to face the lich with a deadpan expression. "Do you get off on interrupting us, Vhal?"

"Not particularly, but I do enjoy your irritated expressions." He grinned.

Celia took a deep breath and let it out slowly, then brushed a hand along the fabric again. "It does feel weird, though… almost like it's alive."

"That's probably the mana coursing through it," Vhal explained.

She turned her body from side to side, and again examined her outfit in a more practical way. "It does have some glaring flaws… protection-wise," she said, indicating the exposed back, neck, arms, and right thigh.

Vhal chuckled again. "When it comes to enchanted or magical armor, such things have little impact. But then again, the dress is ceremonial, and was never meant to be used in battle."

Celia didn't respond, as she was engrossed in moving her tail around, making sure it had freedom of movement. She noticed Vhal glance back at the first cabinet.

"Perhaps you should don the emperor's suit, my lord," he suggested.

Aziel tilted his head. "But I am not the emperor," he said. Celia smiled as she noticed how his gaze kept drifting back toward her.

"And she isn't the empress," Vhal replied.

"None of that matters now, Master," Celia interjected. "As I said, there is no Caelian Empire anymore, and by extension, no emperor or empress. Plus, you need to get rid of those bloody robes," she said, pointing at his clothes.

Aziel examined himself in surprise, as if only just now noticing the state of his attire. He stalked back toward the first cabinet, where he pulled out the emperor's jacket and began to undress.

Celia stared at him shamelessly, licking her lips as she took in the scene. He was even more delicious than she imagined. Her eyes took in every curve and bulge of his fit and toned body, all whilst ignoring Vhal's tired and disapproving glare.

Aziel adjusted the belt and attached a long, sheathed blade to it, which Celia assumed must have been hidden at the back of the cabinet. Finished dressing, he turned and presented himself to them. Celia took a long and appraising look at the result and couldn't help but appreciate how good the outfit looked on him.

"You look majestic, my lord," Vhal commented, and Celia nodded in agreement before stepping in close again and gluing herself to his side, her tail wrapping around his waist.

"You know, Master, as your empress I have certain… *responsibilities* I am duty-bound to perform," she whispered in his ear as she proceeded to plant light kisses down his neck.

"I see," Aziel replied nervously, then pulled on his collar slightly and cleared his throat. "And what are those duties, exactly?"

"She wants to have sex with you," Vhal interrupted, bored.

Celia turned and glared at him. But before she could say anything, Aziel wrapped his hand around her waist and pulled her in close. Their lips met and what began as a gentle kiss quickly devolved into a passionate embrace.

Celia couldn't help herself—she craved the intimacy. Her whole body was wrapped in that familiar tingling only her master's mana-infused touch could bring.

He was an inexperienced kisser… but his mana-infused kiss felt good, addicting even, as did the small amount of demonic mana that she reflexively Siphoned. Technique could be taught later.

Aziel slowly pulled away from her and took a deep breath. "I think that's enough for now," he said with a smile.

Celia nodded dreamily, still recovering from the experience of getting spiked by mana. She couldn't even begin to understand how that worked, but she craved more of it—and she could practically smell the arousal coming off Aziel, too.

"Celia, you should prepare for your quest. I need you to bring me weavers," Aziel said, firmly, but she could hear an undercurrent of uncertainty there as well. She grinned at that—her master was torn between wanting her to go on this important quest and wanting her to stay close to him. Her succubus instincts went wild with need at the thought, but she fought against her nature and held herself back. She would take her time, she decided. Her smile grew mischievous, as she thought of all the things she wanted to do with Aziel—and oh, how fun the future looked!

Vhal must have been able to read her thoughts, as he had to lean on his staff for support as he sighed his rotten lungs out. Celia really didn't care. She leaned forward to whisper into Aziel's ear while drawing a finger lightly down his chest. "As you wish, Master, but we will continue this when I get back."

"A-alright," Aziel said, a hint of nervousness in his voice. "I will await your return... Meanwhile, Vhal will teach me how to weave."

"I am proud to serve my lord," Vhal replied with a low bow.

"Kiss-ass," Celia muttered as she walked by him.

The lich only chuckled again.

"The closest settlement I know of within the Central Wilds is Whiteridge. I have never been there, but I have heard about it from one of the men I Siphoned. Since it's in the Wilds, I'm assuming it's a small frontier village... but I should be able get my hands on a weaver or two there." Celia paused and looked up at the ceiling for a moment as she tried to calculate the distance before adding, "It should be a few days' trek from here."

"Try to keep a low profile," Vhal said, his tone serious. "Our lord may be powerful, but he is still unfamiliar in the ways of the world and needs time to learn and gather followers. Be especially wary of any forces that might belong to another Ascended."

"I know, I know, I'll be quiet and try to keep the noise to a minimum," Celia replied dismissively.

"Before you go, take this," Vhal said, tossing her one of the small sacks from the middle cabinet.

She caught it easily, surprised at how fast her reflexes were. "What's this?" she asked, examining its rather drab design. It looked like any other brown leather pouch, which was in itself notable, given the luxury of everything else they had found in here.

"That is probably the most useful and valuable object in this storage room, Celia. I am actually surprised the empire even has this many of them... but like most things I have discovered here today, it seems the imperial family had more than they let on." Vhal tossed another pouch to Aziel and placed a third in the inner pocket of his robes.

"Alright... if you say so, but what is it? I'm assuming it's not just a pouch," Celia said.

"No, that is a dimensional bag. It allows you to store pretty much anything that fits through its opening, and you can retrieve anything from it by just thinking of it while your hand is within. If the object you are thinking about is there, it will simply manifest in your hand," Vhal said with a wide grin.

Celia examined the unassuming-looking pouch again. She had to wonder if Vhal was just making things up. "How would that be even possible, Vhal?" she asked skeptically.

"I couldn't even begin to explain it," he said with a shrug. "This type of enchantment uses dark mana, which I know very little about. I am certain those bags came from Ishna Noan, the home of the dark elves. They are secretive by nature and forbid the sharing of their knowledge on principle."

If what he said was true, then what she was holding could be amazingly useful. Celia glanced at Aziel, who seemed to be engrossed by his bag, too. When he sensed her gaze, he looked up at her, and she smiled and winked at him. "See you soon... Master," she teased, then glided out of the room, pulling one of the daggers from the display case as she went.

CHAPTER 11

AZIEL STOOD IN the largest study within the Imperial Wing, gazing around. After Celia's departure, he and Vhal had continued their exploration to the second floor. This floor was very different to the first: instead of a circular hallway, there was an enormous open, rectangular space with a large working fountain at its center and a single double door set into each side. The door immediately across from the entrance led to a massive living complex full of bedrooms, kitchens, baths, and anything else anyone could ever ask for to live comfortably.

The other two doors, however, led into what Vhal described as an administration zone. They were large spaces, each containing fully furnished offices, meeting, and storage rooms as well as a much larger office which overlooked the others.

"These types of administration zones are usually found in cities, not remote locations such as this…" Vhal commented as he scanned the larger office. "Unless…"

"Something bothering you, Vhal?" Aziel asked.

"Perhaps, but I need to confirm it before I say anything. Also, I will be taking this half for my own use and future research."

The lich didn't seem to be asking, so Aziel simply shrugged. The area Vhal claimed could easily accommodate a few hundred people, but Aziel didn't have any use for the space, not at the moment anyways.

There were hundreds of rooms in total on the second floor alone—a truly impressive achievement given how it was all built within a mountain. But, of the rooms they had discovered so far, it was the large study on the first floor that Aziel found the most interesting. The reason being that it contained even more books.

"Tactics, geography, politics... Most of these books are instructional, some are even penned by different generations of the imperial family themselves," Vhal commented as he perused the shelves.

"Good, then they will be most helpful," Aziel replied, opening a small cabinet and pulling out a thick black-bound book.

Vhal glanced toward the book briefly—then his eyes flashed as he moved to snatch it from Aziel's fingers. "Impossible!" he gasped, holding the book with shaky hands.

"Vhal?" Aziel asked, surprised by this reaction.

"This is a grimoire..." Vhal said, his voice hoarse. "It's what the mage guilds use to record all their spells for future use and education."

Aziel pointed to the open cabinet. "Well, there are five more in here."

Vhal peered into the cabinet, and his jaw fell wide open. "Six grimoires...! What was the imperial family doing with such things? The mage guilds would have never surrendered them willingly."

"Perhaps they didn't," Aziel replied flatly.

Vhal pulled a red-covered book from inside and examined its contents carefully. "These two belonged to a Caelian mage guild, but what about the other four?"

"If these are as valuable as you are suggesting, then perhaps the imperial family came here to hide from the retribution that followed," Aziel suggested.

"It would explain why all their valuables have been stored here..." Vhal said slowly. "But it doesn't explain why there is no sign of the family themselves. None of these rooms look lived in. I also have doubts that the mage guilds, even united, could have forced the imperial family into hiding." Vhal stroked his beard a few times, thinking. "Perhaps I should spend some time investigating the Facility for more clues. But for now, we can enjoy their hard work in collecting these."

"What do you intend to do with them?" Aziel asked.

"Study them, of course!" Vhal replied, excitedly. "From the book covers, it would seem each book is dedicated to a single mana type." He pulled the rest of the books out of the cabinet and laid them on the large wooden desk in the middle of the room. "We have fire, earth, air, light, nature, and necrotic," he said, pointing to each corresponding book. "Quite a treasure trove, I must say."

Aziel pulled out a chair and sat down across from the books. He picked up the closest grimoire, which happened be the brown one representing earth magic. Opening it to a random page, he was met by a series of symbols arranged in ways he could not understand. Some had simple designs while others were layered in their complexities. He looked up at Vhal with a questioning look.

"I'm guessing you're finding some difficulty understanding what's written, my lord," Vhal said with a smile. "It's encrypted. Discovering and developing new symbols is a difficult and time-consuming task, which is why these are so valuable. It's also why measures are taken to protect them from unauthorized eyes."

The lich collected the books together eagerly. "I'll put these in my new office, for now. I'm sure I can decrypt them, given enough time. We will begin with your lesson once I return."

Aziel watched the lich as he left the room, instinctively tracking the soul mana within his vessel as it moved further away. Then he sighed, as he realized this was the first time he had been alone since meeting Celia. He gripped his right arm with his left hand to stop the tremor which ran through it, as his mind went through the events which had occurred in that white room—the memory of his skin and flesh sizzling and burning, his inability to scream as the heat scorched through his innards.

The World Seed was something people of this world seemed to consider almost as a force of nature, like gravity or the wind. But Aziel had seen another side to it. The World Seed was not a natural phenomenon. It did what it did to him after a recommendation from the mysterious Overseer Assembly, whose authority was again overshadowed by whoever or whatever the Archivist was which had apparently saved his life and bestowed upon him the faction he now controlled.

Aziel honestly didn't know what to make of it, but all these thoughts reminded him of his pending notifications and his new personal and faction logs. Although he didn't understand the World Seed, or why the others associated with it did what they did, learning how to utilize these tools would be important to his survival—and the survival of his fledgling faction. Somehow, he knew them both to be one and the same. The world quest he had been given only gave more emphasis to that.

He willed his notifications to appear and decided to start with the ones which felt inherently negative.

Warning, you have lost one point of Vessel.

Warning, you have gained a new condition, Weary Vessel. Mana cost of all spells and skills increased by 20%. Condition will remain until Vessel has been given sufficient time to rest.

Warning you have lost one point of Vessel.

Warning, your condition Weary Vessel has deteriorated to Vessel Fatigue. Mana cost of all spells and skills increased by 40%. Condition will remain until Vessel has been given sufficient time to rest.

These concerning notifications coincided with when he had channeled his mana into Celia to hasten her evolution. It seemed that using such a large amount of mana in such a short time caused his vessel itself to tire. That would have been fine if it were the only consequence, but that wasn't the case—his vessel had actually shrunk. Counting all the notifications revealed he had lost a total of forty-eight points of Vessel.

Aziel did not know if that was a small or large amount, but he remembered the weakness and awful hollow feeling he had felt immediately after he was done with the channeling. Shaking his head slightly, he continued reading, but this time looked for the more positive notifications.

You have gained a new trait, Soul Weaving.

You have gained a new trait, Ascended's Bane.

You have gained a new trait, Faction Leader.

Ascended's Bane and Faction Leader have combined into a new trait, Ascended's Domain.

You have gained a new trait, Mark of the Succubi.

His focus lingered on the last notification. What could that be? Remembering Celia's instructions, he focused on the diamond-shaped mark on his wrist and pulled up his personal log. Unlike last time, however, a rather large number of runes formed before him, containing a confusing amount of figures and text.

Name: Aziel
Race: Hidden
Rank: Ascended
Mana: 5,630/10,300
Level: 91

Attributes:
Strength: 28
Reflex: 25
Mind: 35
Vessel: 206

Skills:
Soul Rejuvenation (Level 10)
All-Seeing Eye (Level 10)
Long Blades (Level 10)
Soul Link
20 Skill points available to spend

Traits:
Soul Weaving
Ancient Being
Soul Infused
Ascended's Domain
Mark of the Succubi

Aziel scanned his log, and to his surprise found he could interact with it. He could mentally focus on a rune, and more details would appear.

Aziel glanced at the door to make sure he was still alone. Then he began exploring.

The first section, which contained his name, mana, and other personal information, had only a single article with which he could interact with. This was his race, listed as *Hidden*.

Even with access to his personal log, he still didn't know what his race was. Aziel had no idea as to why it was hidden or by whom exactly, but it was done on purpose—the World Seed practically admitted it by stating it was a "protected race category." Aziel shook his head in annoyance. Was he supposed to just accept that? He knew there wasn't anything he could do about it, but that only made it all the more frustrating. Aziel focused on his race, and the runes flashed slightly then expanded, allowing more to form to one side.

Race: Hidden
+15 All attributes.
+Vessel per level.
Unlock one free skill point every two levels.

Aziel stared at this, trying to make sense of what it said. But he simply couldn't; he knew too little. So, he moved on to the attribute section in the hopes it would shed some light on what it meant.

Some of the attributes listed seemed straightforward, but he didn't want to assume anything, so he focused on each one and read their descriptions carefully. Strength and Reflex were exactly what he expected them to be, but Mind was an attribute he thought integral to his success, as it was directly associated with magic and magical-based skills. It reflected his ability to focus, which Aziel assumed helped with those strange symbols Vhal and Celia created when they weaved their spells. He could imagine that maintaining multiple symbols at the same time would be difficult.

The last attribute, and the one of greatest importance to him personally, was Vessel. It determined the maximum amount of mana his body could contain within it and its passive regeneration.

Here, he made a shocking realization. He had lost over twenty percent of his maximum mana permanently when he empowered Celia, and that was not even taking into account the simple mana expenditure.

Aziel stared at his log as regret and resentment crept into him. Why would Vhal suggest he do such a costly thing? Aziel shook his head. No, he didn't know if the lich knew of the cost or not, but one thing was for sure: he wouldn't be doing anything like that again.

Aziel quickly calmed himself. He had to look at the benefits of the action—as Vhal said, it had been an investment. He had no doubt Celia would make this personal sacrifice worth it in the end.

Putting that issue out of his mind for the moment, he moved down to his skills.

Soul Rejuvenation
Skill Set: Utility
Skill Level: 10
The soul mana coursing through you protects your body and vessel from harm.

Passive healing is increased by 500%.
Soul Link Affix: Skill effect may be directed and shared through a permanent Soul Link.

Well, that explained what had been healing him. But the affix was curious—was this skill the reason why Celia had recovered when he channeled his mana into her after his examination of her Vessel? Still uncertain, he moved onto the next skill.

All-Seeing Eye was a combination of the Inspection, Detect Magic, and Analyze skills, together they allowed him to view an almost complete description when it came to other creatures or objects. Curious, he tried it on a random book on the shelf in front of him, and he felt his mark heat up before a notification appeared before him.

You have successfully Analyzed your target.

Fair Trade Practices
Type: Document

Author: Forlin Da Caelian
Comprehensive view of how international trade should be conducted, and the best practices involved.

Well, that was interesting, not to mention useful. He tried it on other items within the study and kept receiving the same breakdown of information.

It was at this point an idea came to him. It was such an obvious course of action that he was frustrated he had only now thought of it. Aziel looked down at his gloved hand, and again activated his All-Seeing Eye.

You have successfully Analyzed your target.
You have successfully Detected the magic within your target.

Emperor's Ceremonial Suit
Type: Armor Set
Quality: Mastercraft
Mana: 2,800/2,800

Passive Enchantments:
Magic Nullification: Nullifies the harmful effects of low-level spells.
Greater Magic Enhancement: Empowers the effects of wearer's spells by 30%.
Greater Magic Efficiency: Reduces the mana cost of wearer's spells by 30%.
Self-repair: Armor will self-repair any damage inflicted upon it over time.

Passive Regeneration: Armor will slowly regen-
erate its mana over time

Aziel stared at the window before him. Given Vhal's description of the suit, he had expected it to be impressive—but this was something else. No wonder the emperor didn't go anywhere without it. Aziel wondered if Celia's dress was the same. With a smirk of appreciation, he moved onto the next skill.

Long Blades
Type: Martial
Skill Set: Martial
Skill Level: 10
Determines your overall proficiency in the use of long bladed weapons.

This was a curious one. Aziel did not remember ever using a sword—but the sword he now carried felt right to him, as if he had been using it for years, and this skill could explain why.

He touched the sword now, as he thought. Its blade was long and had a decorated black hilt and an air crystal for a pommel. He again activated his All-Seeing Eye.

You have successfully Analyzed your target.
You have successfully Detected the magic within your target.

Air Splitter
Type: Long Blade
Quality: Mastercraft
Mana: 2,300/2,300

Passive Enchantments:

Sharpness: Cutting potential increased by 20%.

Self-repair: The weapon will self-repair any damage inflicted upon it over time.

Passive Regeneration: Weapon will slowly regenerate its mana over time.

Active Enchantments:

High Frequency Vibrations: When activated, the blade will vibrate at a high frequency, increasing its cutting potential by up to 500%.

Aziel read through the long list of enchantments. The active enchantment sounded particularly interesting, so he quickly willed it to activate.

The sword's ornate central grove, which stretched from the hilt to two-thirds of the way down the blade, began to glow white. Aziel stared at it and felt the mana within the blade begin to drain as time went by. He pressed the tip into the hardwood floor of the study, and the blade sank into it with no effort at all. The hard floor gave way just as easily as water would have.

Aziel deactivated the enchantment and grinned. This blade was going to be entertaining to use, but now was not the time for games. He quickly sheathed it and returned to viewing his skills.

The last skill on the list was Soul Link. From what Vhal and Celia had been telling him, this was the skill that made the Ascended special, since it allowed him to channel mana into others. But it seemed his ability to use soul mana had enhanced his version of the normal Mana Link.

Soul Link
Skill Set: Ascended

Forge a mana link between two mana vessels allowing the Ascended to channel mana through it and into the connected vessel directly.
Soul Affix: Reduces a permanent link's mana upkeep by 90%.

That explained why he didn't feel any strain from his link with Celia, despite Vhal's doubts. But just like Soul Rejuvenation, why did it specifically indicate permanent links? Did that mean he could create a temporary one? Since he entered this world, Aziel had not tried channeling his mana into anything or anyone other than Celia, so this was something which required further examination.

With the exploration of his skills complete, he was about to start going over his traits when he noticed something. The section which listed the unspent skill points could be interacted with.

He focused on it and runes flashed before expanding into an even larger string; they appeared to be a list of skills arranged under three categories: Ascended, Martial, and Utility. Each had a few faded-out skills under them, while others were clear and bright. It was easy to work out that these were the skills he already had in his log.

He focused on the first category, Ascended, and was disappointed to find there were only two listed here—including Soul Link, which he already had. He quickly went over the other.

Ascended's Haven
Skill Set: Ascended

A permanent bond is created between an Ascended and a single place of power, restoring a portion of its Vessel's passive regeneration when within it.
25% passive mana regeneration restored when in a bonded place of power.
Warning: Losing bonded place of power may lead to dire consequences.

Requirement: 10 skill points

Aziel could only stare at the skill description in wonder. Was this the answer to his troubles? At present, his place of power only stopped the drain. But with this he could actually *regenerate*.

He didn't know what to make of the warning, but even if he ignored it, there was another glaring issue: the cost. Ten skill points were half of all he had, and he didn't know if he could get more. Instead of rushing into a decision, he decided to save them for now and seek Vhal's advice.

With that settled, he quickly went over the other two skill categories. Martial skills comprised of an assortment of specialized abilities which required a weapon proficiency such as Long Blades to be at a certain level to unlock. They generally strengthened certain actions and enhanced his capability in using them.

A person didn't need to be a weaver to use these skills, he realized, as they all appeared to use the soul mana everyone already had coursing through their bodies. Power Strike, a skill he had encountered when he'd fought off the pair of humans after he first awakened, used soul mana to empower Elsie's arm muscles enough to almost break through his shield.

Utility, on the other hand, contained skills such as Soul Rejuvenation and All-Seeing Eye. What was intriguing, however, were the numerous skills under this category which were simply listed as locked.

Having nothing else to cover, Aziel finally moved onto the last section of his log: traits. These seemed to provide passive bonuses, access to additional skill categories, and other more specialized effects. The Soul Weaving trait simply stated he had an affinity for soul mana, and could now absorb, manifest, and manipulate it. The others, however, were more interesting.

Soul Infused
Class: General
Every fiber of your being is infused by highly concentrated soul mana.

Attacks and skills using soul mana will cause additional soul damage.

Aziel didn't know what to make of this "soul damage," as he had no point of reference for what that actually meant. So, he moved onto the next trait, which was thought-provoking to say the least.

Ancient Being
Class: General

Through time and experience, your vessel has succeeded in becoming more efficient in its storage of mana.

═══════════════════════════════

Maximum mana is doubled.

═══════════════════════════════

Did this trait literally refer to his age? He didn't know how to feel about being referred to as ancient. Vhal had mentioned that age usually meant power, and perhaps this was one of the reasons why. Doubling the total mana his vessel was able to store was an advantage even someone as ignorant as he could appreciate.

The next two traits had far more reach when it came to his personal daily life, however.

═══════════════════════════════

Mark of the Succubi
Class: General
You have been marked by a powerful member of the Succubi race, and she has bestowed upon you her gift.

═══════════════════════════════

Enhances others' existing attraction to you

═══════════════════════════════

This trait was obviously due to his relationship with Celia; there was no other explanation. He wondered how and when she had "marked" him. Had he gained this trait immediately after the link was forged, or when Celia became an Elder? He supposed it didn't matter at this point—what did, was its effect.

While the description made it clear that the trait did not create an attraction but rather enhanced an existing one, Aziel was still somewhat uncomfortable. How much of Celia's attraction to him was due to this trait? Or was she immune to it due to the fact she was a succubus herself?

The trait made no mention of its strength, or whether he could turn it off. Would this literally affect anyone who had any slight attraction to him? Would a short glance be enough? Aziel considered the possible adverse effects if this were the case, then shook his head, before moving on to the last—and probably most important—trait.

It was the ball and chain that kept the Ascended from simply taking over with their overwhelming power, instead making them join or form groups and communities around them to support their needs.

Ascended's Domain
Class: Rank specific
An Ascended's high concentration of mana causes a disequilibrium within themselves, resulting in an unstable Vessel.

Total loss of ability to passively regenerate and absorb mana.
Mana is drained over time.
Mana drain is intensified with distance from a high source of mana of a relevant type.
Sworn followers provide a portion of their excess mana regeneration to the Ascended.
Faction Leader Affix: Mana drain is reduced by 80% when in faction-controlled locations.

It seemed being a Faction Leader had reduced the drain, at least when he was within so-called faction-controlled locations.

The trait mentioned that his followers would provide him with a portion of their excess mana regeneration, meaning the larger the vessel, the more mana he would get from a particular follower.

After her evolution, Aziel had felt Celia's contribution add to Vhal's. Both of them together provided him with enough mana regeneration to counteract the drain when he was within the mountain. But from his short experience on the outside, he knew they would not be able to offset that drain.

Aziel glanced down at the circular mark on his wrist and was just about to activate it, when he heard the familiar sound of Vhal's staff striking the floor of the corridor outside. He turned to see the lich re-enter the study and grin.

"Well, my lord, are you ready for your lesson in weaving?" he asked happily.

Aziel quickly dropped his hand. "Of course." Getting a look at his faction log would have to wait for now.

CHAPTER 12

CELIA EXHALED HEAVILY. It had been some days since she left the Facility, and the trek had been uneventful. It seemed that the creatures of the Wilds could sense her new power and bolted at the sight of her... even while she was asleep, no less. At least the journey had given her the time to review her new—and much improved—log.

Her notifications should have prepared her for the absolutely ridiculous power up she had just experienced. But even with the thirty-five level up notifications, trait gains, and attribute increases, Celia could only stare in shock at what she found.

Name: Celia
Race: Demon, Succubus
Rank: Elder Enlightened
Mana: 600/600
Level: 48

Attributes:
Strength: 9
Reflex: 13

Mind: 10
Vessel: 12

Skills:
Charm (Level 6)
Demon Claws (Level 6)
Small Blades (Level 3)
Inspection (Level 3)
Mana Siphon
Dark Vision
20 Skill points available

Traits:
Fire Weaving
Air Weaving
Succubus Allure
Soul Linked

Her previous level, 7, had been higher than average for someone her age. If she had been an adventurer or a very active soldier, she might conceivably have attained level 8 or perhaps 9.

But she was now at level 48, an absolute powerhouse. She wasn't sure there was a single human, elf, or any member of the civilized races who surpassed level 40, and even those people were probably very old and had worked exceptionally hard to reach that level. She, on the other hand, had simply agreed to her master's proposal and woken up like this.

Her expedited leveling came with other benefits. All of her skills had leveled up—some more than others, for reasons unclear to her, but that wasn't really something she was going to complain about.

Then there were the new traits. She had actually acquired a

new affinity for air mana, in the form of the Air Weaving trait. This opened up a whole new world of magic for her to explore; it also made her a dual mana weaver—quite a rarity.

But as impressive as that was on its own, there were still two traits which proved more eye-catching. The first was a racial trait.

Succubus Allure
Class: Racial

Effects:
Enhances others' existing attraction to the Succubus.
Effects may be enhanced further by marking a specific being.
Marking is permanent, and only one being can be marked at any given time.
Current mark: Aziel

It was an interesting read indeed. She didn't know if this was an ability she had acquired as a Greater or Elder succubus, but it made luring prey for Siphoning that much easier. She had hardly met a single person who had absolutely no attraction to her, and this made her job even easier.

But it was the marking that left her puzzled. How did it work? Was it a mental trigger, or did she actively have to do something to point out a target? Was the fact that her attentions had been trained solely on Aziel the reason he was marked? Celia let out a small chuckle at the thought before moving on.

The second trait was arguably even more remarkable and had

major implications for her life. It also shed some light on her drastic behavior changes since her master had ranked her up.

Soul Linked
Class: Magical
A permanent mana link has been forged between your vessel and an Ascended, enabling the Ascended to channel mana through it regardless of distance.

Effects:
+1 All attributes.
Racial Affix: The powerful connection binds you. You are bound by contract.

Her link with her master had increased all her attributes by one, which made her physically and mentally stronger. Gaining attributes usually required a long time and hard work. But it was the affix that had her emotions in turmoil.

Following her transformation, Celia had spent a considerable time reading and learning all she could about herself and demons in general. It was then she had learned of a ritual called Demonic Binding.

Demons were considered dangerous by everyone in Kadora due to their ability to create demonic mana, and that mana's ability to infect and transform others into demons themselves. But some people did make use of them through Demonic Binding. These warlocks, as they were known, used the powerful ritual to bind a demon to them and place terms on their service. Those terms constituted an unbreakable magical contract that the demon was compelled to obey.

As expected, these contracts were always one-sided. As demons never actually wanted to be bound to another being, they essentially became slaves.

Ever since learning of the ritual's existence, being caught and bound had been a constant fear of Celia's. It was the main reason why she had never traveled farther west to the Princedoms of Odana, where slavery was a major trade. She would be chained, sold, then ritually bound to serve whoever bought her. A succubus such as herself was a valuable commodity, and succubi were only used for one type of service…

Terms such as to never harm herself or her master and to never disobey would be included in the contract, and she would be magically compelled to never be able to break them. She would be used, and the contract would stop her from Siphoning whoever bound her… she honestly did not know if she was strong enough mentally to survive something like that. She hated the fact it even existed.

Now her Soul Link with Aziel stated she had been bound by him—the link was so powerful it had taken on the effects of a fully completed Demonic Binding ritual. Celia did not understand why the affix had suddenly come into effect, but it coincided with the moment she had regained access to her log… or more specifically, when those unexplained overseer notifications had stopped appearing.

Her being bound explained why she had begun to call him master. That was one of the aspects of the ritual even warlocks could not change.

But what were the actual terms of this contract? What had her master included in it? Celia let out a sigh of defeat… but then she remembered her first encounter with Aziel after her evolution. While still in his place of power, she had essentially attacked and Siphoned him. A term such as "do not harm your master," always the first term in a contract, would have stopped her immediately, even if her master could heal himself afterward. So then… was it possible her master had not placed any terms at all on her?

The edges of Celia's mouth slowly inched upward. She was becoming more and more indebted to Aziel, and she was not sure he even realized what he was doing. If he had not placed any terms in her contract, then he had effectively freed her from her fear of being bound. A demon could not be bound twice, after all.

There was an unnatural element in their relationship, but Celia had never felt this way about another being before. Her father had been strict when it came to boys, even though her mother had tried her best to give her as much room as she could. After her enrollment in the mage guild's classes, Celia had found herself even more isolated from other children and had never had any real relationships. The thought of her parents brought about a pang of sadness to her heart, which she tried her best to ignore.

After her transformation into a demon, any chances of an actual relationship with someone were dashed. The act of love was a death sentence for whomever she laid with. She simply couldn't control her Siphon at that level.

But this did not seem to be true when it came to Aziel.

She had Siphoned him multiple times since they had met, and he was still alive. He might literally be the only person in the world who she could possibly have a genuine relationship with.

Her mind wandered to how he had kissed her… it had been completely unexpected, and just the memory of that moment had her heart fluttering.

She had always viewed the people she had Siphoned before as food; it was the only way she could cope with what she was. Aziel, however, was different.

To begin with, there was no doubt in her mind that she was attracted to him. She loved it when his gaze drifted across her, and her body heated up instantly at the sight of his obvious desire for her. But her insecurity had kept her away… at least until after her evolution. A tinge of red colored her cheeks as she thought about how she had kept on propositioning him. She really couldn't help herself around him anymore.

Celia let out a deep breath and closed her eyes for a moment, trying to control her arousal. Thinking about her master while alone and deep in the forests of the Central Wilds was not a clever move. Instead, she tried to focus on her skills. Leveling up and becoming an Elder must have opened up many new ones to explore, including some in her succubus racial skill set.

The first skill was Create Illusion, a skill open to her previously, but she hadn't had the skill points to spend on it. It essentially allowed her to attach illusions to herself and others, tricking people into seeing something that was not there—a powerful ability for someone who would like to stay hidden. Celia would have immediately assigned all her points to it, if not for the other options now open to her.

The first newly unlocked skill that caught her eye was not actually a skill but an affix to her existing Charm. It required her to spend a single skill point to acquire it, which seemed a fair exchange given that it would allow her to apply her Charm on multiple targets at once.

This was a no-brainer really—she selected it and received a notification shortly after, confirming that it had been added.

Her focus then shifted to the last skill in the succubus skill tree.

Shapeshift
Type: Magical, Activated
Skill Set: Succubus
Level: 1
Allows the succubus to morph her shape into any biological she has come in contact with.

> *Shapeshifting also generates a fake log which protects the shifter from Inspection.*

Requirements:
Elder Enlightened
1 skill point per level

It was an amazing skill, there was no doubt. With a skill like this, she could simply take on the identity of someone else and walk around Whiteridge, or anywhere else, without worry. It would be invaluable for a mission which required her to abduct weavers from settlements.

Comfortable and confident in her decision, she immediately assigned the required skill points, leveling the skill up to 10. Celia closed her eyes as the mark on her wrist grew hotter while an uncomfortable tingling began to spread throughout her body. It was the same sensations she always went through when spending skill points, but this one was more intense and lasted a while longer than usual, no doubt due to the number of skill points she was spending in such a short time. Now at its maximum level, Shapeshift could even be applied to articles of clothing her target wore, making the already powerful skill that much more valuable.

She smirked, then assigned four skill points to Charm and another four to Demonic Claws, expanding her ability to harden nails to her tail. With the three most important skills available to her at their highest possible potential, she decided to assign her last remaining skill point to Inspection.

At level 4, assuming her target did not have any protection against it, Inspection would allow her to inspect a creature up to level 40—which had to be the vast majority of all beings living in Kadora, she reckoned.

Her train of thought was suddenly shattered by a high-pitched scream from ahead, followed by a loud series of clanks and the sounds of other heavy objects bashing into one another. This was accompanied by a hissing noise, the likes of which she had never heard before.

Celia dashed between the trees and tall brush toward the sound. Sensing she was getting close, she stopped, growing wary, and looked around until she found a tree that suited her plans. She then elongated her nails, which were far harder and sharper than before, and without a second thought jumped up and stabbed them into the tree's broad trunk. Her nails easily penetrated the hard bark, which helped her climb toward the canopy above.

When she reached the high, thick branches at the top, she pulled herself onto one and dashed across it, then leapt from one to the other. She was amazed by how easy it was to balance—she would have never been able to do this just a few days before. Without slowing down, she leapt across the gap between two trees landing safely on the other side. Tree by tree, she continued forward toward the ongoing commotion.

By the time she arrived at the scene, whatever battle was being fought seemed to have ended. She crouched down on her branch, peering between the leaves to spy on what was occurring far below. What she saw surprised her.

In the small clearing were four human bodies—at least, she thought there were four, but since they had been cut to pieces it was hard to tell. To one side knelt two more humans, a man and a woman, wearing expensive-looking clothes. Their arms looked to be tied behind their backs, but Celia could not confirm that from her vantage point. The woman was crying and begging, while the man kept shouting and glaring at something just outside of Celia's field of view.

Taking a few steps along the branch, she again peered down to see what the couple were looking at. Her eyes went wide at what she saw: a young, blonde-haired girl, perhaps between twelve and fourteen years of age was being pulled from a rather large and elegant carriage before being shoved toward who she now assumed were her parents. Her tears caused her freckled skin to shine under the light breaking through the thick canopy above. They were surrounded by perhaps a dozen bipedal insect-like creatures, the likes of which Celia had never seen before.

She had to stop herself from Inspecting them, as they would more than likely feel it and be alerted to a presence in the area. Instead, she had to content herself with examining them from afar.

They had roughly humanoid forms, but an additional set of limbs protruded from their backs, ending in sharp, boney scythes. Their other set of hands ended in five-fingered claws. Two large black eyes were set into each bulbous head, and a pair of small black antennae sprouted from the top. Finally, two wickedly sharp mandibles jutted from their mouths, stretching their cheeks wide.

The insects wore only a ragged loincloth over their crotches—which made it easy to distinguish their genders given the exposed breasts of the only female Celia could see amongst them. Unlike the males, who very much looked like the insects they were, the female's features were softer and far closer to what Celia would consider human.

The only weapons Celia could see on the males were simple, sharpened, stone-tipped spears, attached to long branches. The female, however, held a wooden shield in one hand and a much higher quality metal-tipped spear in the other. Celia couldn't be certain, but from the deference the males were giving the sole female, she seemed in charge.

Given their lack of armor, these creatures must have depended on their chitin exoskeletons for protection. Their color ranged from black to a light brown, which Celia imagined allowed them to blend in quite easily with the shadows of trees and in long grass or shrub.

While the male insectoids fully focused on the three humans, the one female seemed absorbed by something out of sight. Hoping to see what the female found so interesting, Celia again moved forward onto the branch. She took slow deliberate steps to ensure she remained silent, and as she reached the edge, her gaze returned to the scene below. Once more, her eyes opened wide at what she witnessed.

There was another female insectoid very much like the first, but this one was secured to a tree by a set of ropes wrapped around her torso and legs. There must have been a dozen arrows embedded into her flesh, and two stumps were all that remained of her scythe arms which lay on the ground. Beside her were the corpses of two other male insectoids who appeared to have been subjected to the same treatment. Celia's attention was fixated on the bound female, she was still alive… barely.

She was covered in her own blood and Celia couldn't help but notice that none of those arrows were aimed at her vitals. This creature was tortured, toyed with, and was now slowly bleeding to death from her many wounds.

The first female took a step closer and leaned her head against the injured one. Celia stared as the wounded female struggled and failed to raise her own head. She let out pitiful noises, and it almost sounded like she was weeping.

The two females stayed like that for a few moments, their foreheads together. Then the first female pulled away and stabbed her spear through the injured one's heart and twisted, killing her instantly. A mercy killing. The female pulled out her spear then plucked out every arrow before cutting the ropes and carrying the dead female off the tree and laying her on the ground before moving on to do the same with the other two males.

She stood there, staring at the three corpses as they lay there beside each other, only the desperate cries of the three humans broke the silence of the solemn atmosphere. With a loud snap of her mandibles, the female turned on her heels, her scythe arms rising high in the air. She glared at the three humans, a low hiss escaping her lips.

The hiss slowly grew in volume as the surrounding males joined in and moved. Following the movement, Celia's watched as four male insectoids grabbed the little girl who screamed and cried, her arms flailing toward her parents as they pulled her away from them, only to be viciously stabbed in both her legs. This brought her to the ground, gasping.

The couple screamed and tried to move toward the girl, only to be shoved back by another of the male insectoids, hissing as it did so.

The four males picked up the child and laid her on her back, presenting her to the one female, who clacked her mandibles at the sight. She slowly knelt beside the girl, allowing some of her saliva to drip onto the poor, sobbing child. She stayed that way for a few moments, then blinked before lunging forward and clamping her mandible around the girl's small arm, severing it completely from the elbow down.

The movement was so abrupt, it took a second for both Celia and the child to realize what had happened. Blood spurted from the gruesome open wound, in time to the child's rapid heartbeat, painting the surrounding forest soil a bright red. She wept and struggled weakly against the four male insectoids who held her down, but the sight of the female insect biting, chewing, and salivating on her severed hand and fingers must have been too much to bear, since she passed out shortly after. Celia wasn't entirely sure if it was the shock or the blood loss that had overwhelmed her—probably both.

Not giving the wailing cries of the two humans any thought, the female insectoid gorged herself on the arm. When she was done, she simply moved onto the other one and repeated the process. The hissing had stopped by now. The father had positioned himself in front of his wife, seemingly to spare her the sight of watching her daughter being eaten alive.

Celia watched in silence as the female insect stood, licked her fingers clean, then wiped her mouth with the child's once-white clothes. She had consumed all four limbs and a large part of the girl's torso. She even took a bite of her face and nose.

Seemingly satisfied with her meal, she turned her attentions from this gruesome scene to the parents and made two clicking sounds with her mandibles. The dozen males reacted to the signal immediately. They ran around the small clearing and collected then packed the weapons and armor left behind by the four dismembered humans into several large leather sacks. They then proceeded to encircle the sobbing pair, glancing expectantly at their leader.

The female didn't respond as she made her way back to the dead female insectoid and sat beside her. She pulled her up and rested her head on her lap, a hand combed through her long brown hair as her other hand rested on her bloody chest, over the wound she had inflicted. She then looked up and nodded.

A loud hissing followed as the dozen males lunged forward, ripping into the couple. Celia could only stare at the scene as pieces of cloth were pulled apart and tossed aside, while the sound of mandibles clicking loudly was followed by breaking bones and ripping flesh.

A strange numbness took over Celia as she witnessed the horrific scene unfold below, as if her mind was attempting to disconnect her emotions from what she had seen. She couldn't help but reflect on how much she had changed. Just a few days ago, she had cringed at the sight of Elsie being impaled and had felt angry enough to take drastic action.

But now, even though it was not pleasant, she had been able to stand by as a family was brutally eaten alive by insects. Turning into an Elder succubus had changed more than just her physical body and power. The voice of her former human self was silent, as if it had never existed in the first place. Celia wondered: had she lost her humanity in the process?

She could have intervened—these insectoids would hardly

have given her new and improved self any trouble, especially if she ambushed them from above. Celia shook her head, despite how they looked, these insects were intelligent, and these humans might have even deserved it. She did not need to insert herself into something like this.

There was also the question of what to do if she did save them. Unlike before, her appearance would never be mistaken for a human, and her Shapeshift skill only worked after she came into contact with someone. Instead, she would have a group of scared humans who would only see her as the demon she was, and probably try to kill her the moment they had the chance. No, this had nothing to do with the mission her master had assigned to her. Intervening would have only complicated things.

Glancing at the carriage, she noted the fine wood and curtains, along with the travel crates secured to its roof. These people were of means, perhaps merchants or a part of some noble family, but why would they be so deep in the Wilds? She watched the insects finish off their meal, then enter the carriage and bring out a few small bags and what looked like a large cheese-wheel. They then gathered around the female and picked up their dead as well as the large leather sacks they had packed. The female inspected the clearing one last time, her antennae twitching slightly, before they all marched off into the forest.

Celia rubbed both sides of her neck and stretched. She had been in this position for a while now, and her body was feeling a bit stiff. Carefully, she climbed down the tree and took her time canvassing the surrounding area, looking for anything they might have left behind.

In her search, she found another abandoned carriage several yards away from the now-gory scene. This one was of a far lower quality, and the roof was already breaking apart. Whatever had pulled it was also long gone, but it didn't look like it had been attacked. She guessed the occupants must have fled when they heard the nearby scuffle.

Pulling herself up into the old carriage, she checked the bags and chests for anything useful. Whoever these people were, they had been dirt poor. There were mostly only old clothes and tools inside, but she did find something useful in one of the smaller boxes: a rough, old, hand-drawn map of the local area, which depicted where Whiteridge was.

The map also had two large red circles drawn around the entire north and east of the town. Probably a way for the mapmaker to warn them to avoid traveling through there—which these people had, of course, ignored.

Celia folded up the map and placed it inside her dimensional pouch. She then jumped out of the abandoned carriage, landing lightly, and made her way back to the more elegant, well-built carriage. Its rich interior confirming that these people were not simple travelers.

The inside was luxuriously decorated with shiny wooden surfaces and drawers. One of the couches was even adjustable, enabling it to turn into a small bed. It was the type of carriage she had read about in stories of noble balls—if she ignored all the muddy prints from the insects who had raided it.

Celia was baffled when she found jewelry, fine clothes, and other valuable items still inside. The only thing she did not find was food, not even a single ration or water-skin. Those insects had robbed a guarded carriage full of valuables, and only took the snacks? It was all simply unbelievable.

There was no reason to let this go to waste, she reasoned, so she began stuffing her pouch with all the jewels, gold, and other valuable objects she could find. To her amazement, her pouch did not seem to gain any weight.

As she was leaving the carriage, her tail banged against a wooden panel which looked like just another part of the decoration. To her surprise, it slid open. Curious, she bent to peer inside.

There she found more gold coins, as well as a stack of letters and official-looking documents. What made them especially interesting was that they were stamped by the Royal House of Maiv. Reading through them, Celia discovered that this family were indeed nobles. They had been tasked by the kingdom and their king to govern the town of Whiteridge.

Celia could not believe this. Whiteridge was a Maivian colony? But how? None of the surrounding countries would have even entertained the thought. The Central Wilds was a neutral territory bordering two other nations other than the Kingdom of Maiv. All of them benefited from the resources they collected from here, as well as from the uninterrupted trade roads that crossed its southern edge. These countries' relations were fairly hostile already, and all three had made claims on the Central Wilds, which only made the region's neutrality that much stronger. Even she knew that building a town here could lead to a war.

Celia could not understand what the Maivians had been thinking. Provoking the Jannatin Empire or the Princedom seemed foolhardy, even to someone like her, who admittedly knew little of the geopolitics of the region. But to provoke both at the same time? The kingdom would be crushed!

She shook her head, then noticed another document. It was an entry pass to Whiteridge. Celia read over the first two names, which she identified as those of the dead nobles. *Yonden and Jewel Tiaus*, she read, and below that the name of their unfortunate daughter: *Miley Tiaus*. There was also another pass attached to the first, which listed what Celia assumed were the names of the four house guards who had died protecting these nobles.

Celia had never heard of House Tiaus, but she grinned as an idea began to take form in her head. If she was reading the map correctly, Whiteridge was only a few hours' hike from her current position. Quickly, she placed the documents back inside the hidden compartment and slid the lid back into place. She then jumped out and took her time picking up the human remains scattered all over the forest floor, piling them together beside the carriage. But not before she placed a hand on the now-mangled remains of the child. She had not been certain her Shapeshifting ability would have registered a target so *damaged*, but it seemed the skill's high level helped in that regard.

Celia then wove a Fire Bolt and threw it at the heap of torn-up and mostly eaten flesh. She watched as it burst into flames, quickly spreading to consume the carriage too. If her plan had any hope of working, no evidence or identifiable bodies could be left behind. She waited patiently until only ash, charcoal, and embers remained. With her cover secured, Celia turned and continued on toward the town.

* * *

She arrived at her destination by late afternoon. Crouching at the edge of the tree line, she examined the clearing and town in front of her. Whiteridge was far larger than she had imagined, but it was the fortifications on display that gave her pause.

She had seen settlements before in the Wilds, but they were in the southern plains, and along or close to the old road that cut through it, not this deep into the valley. Whiteridge was surrounded by a tall wooden palisade and a deep trench. It even had a few manned towers for scanning the surrounding area.

On the western side stood a half-built keep made of stone, perched on the edge of a white-stone ridge, which presumably had given the settlement its name.

Knowing it was a colony made far more sense now that she had seen the place. Thankfully, she had anticipated something like this. The fact that nobles needed an entry pass meant immigration controls would be strict. Celia couldn't imagine how the Maivians kept something like this secret, but then again, the town's existence wasn't the secret, only the fact it was Maivian was. Also, locating it this deep into the Wilds and keeping track of who came and went probably helped. One thing was for sure though: a town of this size would certainly have some weavers.

Staying put, she gazed at the palisade, trying to refine a plan for how to infiltrate the place. The clearing between herself and the wall was around three hundred feet long, probably cleared by the residents to give them an unobstructed view of their immediate surroundings. This would allow them to easily detect and target threats with their bows. Pursing her lips, Celia took a few steps back into the forest. It was time to see how her new abilities stacked up.

First, she raised her hands above her head, then slowly drew them back down again. Her golden eyes glowed brighter as she activated her Shapeshift, and slowly, following the movement of her hands, her appearance began to shift. Within a few seconds, she had changed from a beautiful, seductive succubus into an exact copy of the blonde-haired, freckled little girl who had been eaten alive just a few hours before.

"This is amazing," she whispered to herself and was taken aback when she realized even her voice had changed. She stroked her hands across the white dress and then her white skin. Not only did she now match the young girl's appearance, but the Empress's dress had shifted as well. Her clothes, hair, and skin felt real.

The dagger had stayed the same, however. She quickly unbuckled it and dropped it into her pouch. Which raised another problem she had not yet considered… what to do with the pouch? It would be too suspicious for a little girl to have something so unique on her person, even if she was of the nobility. Celia could imagine the guards asking to check it, only to find the bag had no visible bottom and stored anything within it in another dimension—one now containing a dead noble family's treasures.

With an annoyed sigh, Celia drew out a handful of coins from the loot she had obtained, then wrapped the pouch in a cloth and buried it beside a marked tree. She did all she could to remove any sign of the soil being disturbed, hoping it would be enough to hide this expensive and unique item until she was done with her task.

Celia then lay down and rolled on the ground to dirty herself and her clothes. She had a story to tell, after all. Examining herself carefully, she nodded approvingly, before inching toward the tree line again. There, she knelt and focused her gaze at the far gate.

"Alright, Celia, you've got this," she told herself. Rolling her shoulders, she took a deep breath then bolted toward the gate, screaming loudly, trying to put as much fear into her voice as she could.

As she neared the halfway point, she could hear shouts from the palisades in front of her. She didn't want to chance a guard shooting her out of panic, so she dived and fell, rolling on the ground, crying and screaming.

Not long after, three men in leather armor stood before her. Two of them practically glared at the forest behind her, as if daring the trees to cough something up, while the third knelt by her side.

"Hello, child, what are you doing out here all alone?" he asked. His voice was rough, but she could tell he was making an effort to be soothing, which she found amusing. She sobbed and grabbed his leather vest, pushing herself into his comforting bulk.

"It's alright, child, you're safe now," he said, gently, while rubbing her back. "Let's get you inside where we can talk, alright?"

She nodded, her face still buried in his chest.

"All clear, sir, nothing to report," one of the men said from behind her.

"Well something happened out there, look at the poor girl," he said, lifting Celia off the ground. "No matter. We will discuss this when we have more information to work with—let's head back, boys."

"Yes sir!" they both replied, beating their fists against their chests in a salute, before all three turned back toward the gate.

Celia couldn't help but smile as she hid her face from the soldier. Her disguise was perfect! She had half expected it to fail with all the touching that was going on, but it held. It was incredible—she would make sure to properly thank her master when she got back.

The man holding her, who she realized was the captain, kept her head secured against his chest, which meant she couldn't get a very good look around. He carried her through the gate, up an incline, into a building, up some stairs, and finally into a large room before seating her on a bed.

The room was made of wood planks and was furnished with several identical beds, a small cabinet set between each of them. The whole room reeked of sweat, which led Celia to believe it was some sort of break room for the guards.

"There you go, little one. Just relax while I go get you some help and some clean clothes," he said, turning to leave.

Celia panicked for a moment—what would happen if she took off her clothes? Would the Empress dress revert back to its original form? Not wanting to risk it, she reached out and grabbed his belt, making sure to adjust her strength to that of a child. When he turned back to look at her, she shook her head vigorously, allowing tears to streak down her cheeks.

The captain knelt before her again. "It's alright, child, I won't leave you alone… alright?"

She nodded as she feigned struggling to swallow a lump in her throat. The older man smiled and placed his hand on her head to gently comb her messy blonde hair with his fingers.

"What is your name?" he asked.

Celia looked up at him, ensuring her face was flushed and her eyes teary. "Miley… Tiaus," she mumbled softly.

The man's entire body stiffened for a moment when she mentioned the noble name, but then he relaxed again. "Miley… a beautiful name," he said softly.

Celia buried her head in his chest and whimpered. In response, the captain wrapped his hands around her and gently stroked her back.

"It's okay, you will be okay, Miley," he said, rubbing her back. "My name is Alistair and I am the captain here. Do you know what that means?"

She shook her head no.

"It means I am in charge of protecting the people of this town."

She again looked up at him. "P-protect?" she said.

"Yes. But I cannot do that if I don't know what's out there. So, when you're ready, do you think you can be brave and tell me your story?" he asked, with a disarming smile.

Before she could reply, the door swung open and a middle-aged lady walked in. She had her brown hair tied into a bun and wore a white apron over her clothes. She glanced at Alistair, who looked back at her with a raised eyebrow.

"Is that her?" the woman asked. Her voice was warm and full of concern. "Daniel told me what happened."

Alistair sighed. "That boy could never keep his mouth shut," he grunted, but then turned back to look at Celia. "She was spotted running toward the east gate. Rook was on watch and raised the alarm, thinking the poor girl was being pursued. But whatever has her so shaken didn't follow her out of the trees."

The woman pursed her lips and knelt beside Alistair. "How's she doing?"

"She's still shaking, Marth..." he said, as he kept stroking Celia's back.

"Here let me have her," she replied, slowly pulling Celia toward her. "Come on lass, Alistair needs to go back to work. I'll make sure you're taken care of."

Celia resisted at first, but let go of the captain when he tried to gently pry her hands off him. "Are you leaving?" she asked, bringing herself to the verge of tears again.

"Of course not, Miley. I'll be close to protect you," he replied, with a soft smile. He turned to Marth and whispered something into her ear. Marth's eyes opened wide, and she glanced at Celia for a second, before turning back to Alistair and nodding.

Alistair patted Celia's head warmly, but she could tell the captain was lost in his thoughts as he looked at her. He had a solemn air about him for a moment before he blinked as if awakening from a dream. He let out a throaty cough. "Be a good girl and let Marth take care of you," he said and hurriedly exited the room, leaving her alone with the middle-aged woman. Celia had no idea what that was about, but she supposed it didn't really matter.

"Okay, let's go somewhere more comfortable, deary," Marth said, before taking hold of Celia's hands and pulling her gently out of the room and down some stairs.

Celia glanced behind her, trying to get a last peek at the captain, and Marth smiled when she noticed that. "He's a good man, is he not?" she asked.

Confused by the question, Celia looked back at her and blinked rapidly, causing the middle-aged women to let out a chuckle.

"We're going to my tavern, where I'll set you up with a room and a bath so you can get yourself cleaned up."

Celia nodded again and followed the lady quietly.

As they walked back out the front door, Celia took note of the many guards who were loitering around the building. This was obviously a barracks. Marth gently pulled on her hand, causing Celia to stop looking and follow her lead.

They walked side by side along the packed dirt that formed the streets of Whiteridge. It was late evening now, and many of the stores were starting to close their shutters. The buildings here were well built, mainly two stories in height, which was definitely not the norm within the Central Wilds. The streets were laid out in a grid pattern, the level of organization further proving that Whiteridge was indeed a planned settlement. The half-built stone fort also looked far more imposing from this position, as it loomed over the town from the higher ridge.

A lot of time and gold had been spent to develop this town. As far as Celia could tell, it was only a few years old, and yet it had already been built up to this extent. But where was it all coming from? Celia could not see how the kingdom could afford to build, garrison, and supply this base, not with the current state of their economy.

As they drew closer to the town center, Celia scrunched up her nose: an overwhelming smell of alcohol mixed with the stench of vomit and other bodily fluids hung in the air. A cursory glance around made it abundantly clear that this place was where the bars and taverns were. She also noticed a few stares and side glances directed toward her. To avoid any unnecessary attention, she sought safety in Marth by pulling herself closer. This caused Marth to smile, and she gripped Celia's hand tighter in response.

"They're just staring at your beautiful face, deary," she said. "Jealous lot we have here."

Celia made herself blush at the compliment, prompting another chuckle from the older woman.

"Here we are," she said, pointing toward a three-story wooden building. "The Gilded Cask, my pride and joy."

Celia glanced up at the tavern. It looked older than the other buildings they had walked past, probably one of the first structures built here. She had spent a lot of time in taverns in her time within the Kingdom of Maiv—though granted most of it had been spent in the stables and often without the knowledge of the owners.

Marth pushed open the main door, and a bell chimed just above them, followed by a rush of sound—people talking and mugs slamming into tables. Celia jumped and pulled her hand back, causing Marth to visibly wince.

"Sorry about that. I should have warned you it would be a bit loud," she said, offering Celia her hand again.

Slowly, Celia placed her hand in the older woman's and followed her in. The ground floor of the tavern was large, easily seating sixty people, and it was at that moment more than half full. Men and a few women laughed and exchanged stories, while chugging down mugs of assorted alcohols. Celia looked up to see a red fire crystal fixed to the ceiling, which provided enough warm light for the whole room on its own.

"Marth!" a rough voice yelled out. "Who's the new lass?"

Celia looked up to see a modestly built, brown-haired drunkard watching her closely from his seat at the bar, a glint of lust in his eyes. She was particularly sensitive to detecting that sort of thing.

Marth scowled, seemingly noticing the same thing, and turned to face the man. "You're a pig, Landin. She's not even a woman yet."

"I could help with that," the man said before grabbing his mug and chugging it down in one go, slamming it back down on the table when he finished.

"Ooh, no, I'm not having any of that in my establishment," she growled. Then she turned toward the bar. "Danny, throw the pig out! And maybe give him a kick in the balls for good measure."

"Yes, ma'am," a voice came from somewhere behind the bar, followed by heavy footsteps.

"Come along, Miley, let's get you into a room and away from the rabble," Marth said, leading Celia up the stairs and into one of the rooms.

"You just take a seat while I go draw some warm water for you, okay?"

Celia silently took the few steps from the door to the bed and sat down, then stared at the floor. Marth must have taken that as an affirmative, since she grunted and slowly closed the door behind her.

Finding herself alone, Celia sighed in relief. That had gone far better than she could ever have hoped to expect.

She stood and glanced around, taking in her surroundings. Marth had given her a corner room with two windows. One looked out at the main street, and the other at the alley between the tavern and the next building. The room only had the bare necessities in terms of furniture: a bed, a trunk, a desk and chair, as well as a few candles for lighting.

Celia walked toward the first window and pulled the curtains apart slightly to peer out into the main street. She saw men with torches lighting up several braziers strategically placed to chase off the darkness. It seemed that most people returned safely indoors by nightfall—apart from some two-man guard patrols, she could only see a handful of people walking around, most of them obviously drunk.

Sensing someone come close to her door, she quickly sat back down on the bed. A few seconds later, Marth entered, along with a large man she had noticed by the bar earlier. They were carrying a wooden tub between them, which they placed at the center of the room.

Marth wiped the sweat off her forehead using her apron, then breathed out a sigh of relief. "Tell you what, I'm getting a bit too old for this type of work," she said.

"Nonsense," said the larger man. "I couldn't think of anyone better to run a tavern, Marth."

"Aw, that's sweet of you to say, Kaeden..." she replied with a smile then pushed herself up on her tiptoes to give him a quick peck on his lips. "Alright, go grab the water pitchers. Miley should get cleaned up before bed."

The larger man turned to Celia and gave her a wide, toothy grin. "Hello, Miley." He then dragged in two large pitchers from the hallway and poured one of them into the tub. "We got it nice and warm for yah," he announced.

Celia remained silent, but nodded and gave him a slight smile. He seemed to enjoy this.

"Okay, that's enough, let's give the girl some privacy," Marth said, from somewhere behind Kaeden's large body. She peered around him to look at Celia. "Will you need some help?"

"N-no… I'll be fine…" Celia mumbled.

"Good girl. Just leave the tub where it is when you're done. I'll pick it up in the mornin'." She elbowed Kaeden's side and he grunted in agreement.

"Try to get some sleep. I'll be down by the bar if you need anything," he said, then they both left, closing the door behind them.

Celia stood and quickly locked the door after them. She glanced back at the steam coming off the tub. Ever since her self-exile, she had had to settle for bathing in cold rivers and streams. There had been a large bathhouse in the Imperial Wing, but even then, she'd had no chance to partake in it. What stood before her was a luxury she had yearned for.

She slowly undressed and noticed gladly that the Shapeshift persisted on the garment, even after it was no longer attached to her.

That was good to know, she thought, as she tested the temperature of the water with her toe. Dipping it in slightly, she grinned and slid herself entirely into the tub, sighing happily.

"Mmm…" she moaned softly. "I've missed this."

Picking up the second pitcher from where it stood beside the bath, she slowly poured it over her head, washing the grime and mud from her hair and face. It was amazing how real her form felt. Turning into an Elder had empowered her immensely, which made her wonder what else Vhal could do.

The thought of Vhal made her frown. While she no longer hated the lich, she still did not trust him. He was an undead, after all, and the undead did not help anyone other than themselves. Who knew what other agenda he had in keeping close to Aziel? Whatever it was, it couldn't be good. She sighed, then leaned back and soaked in the warm water, allowing her thoughts to wander as she enjoyed this rare experience… until two knocks brought her out of her trance.

"Miley? Sorry to bother you, but I realized you probably don't have a change of clothes, so I'll put some right outside your door," said Marth, her voice slightly muffled by the door between them.

Celia stood and unlocked the door, just before the tavern owner could leave. She stared at Celia's naked form with wide eyes.

"Miley!" Marth gasped, before pushing her gently back into the room and closing the door behind her. "You can't open the door naked, deary..." she continued with a sigh. "Here you go..." she passed some folded clothes to her.

"Th-Thank you," Celia said, allowing a light blush to spread across her face.

"Don't worry about it," Marth replied, warmly. "Now get dressed and jump into bed, alright?" She smiled at Celia before exiting the room.

Locking the door again behind her, Celia examined the clothes provided. There was a white shirt with frills on the cuffs and a long brown skirt. They were identical to the set Marth wore under her apron, only a few sizes smaller. Shrugging, she stuffed them into the hay-filled mattress and grabbed her Empress dress.

She really didn't want to go anywhere without it. Celia had been in contact with the tavern owner, so she imagined herself Shapeshifting into Marth, focusing solely on her clothes. The skill activated and did exactly as she intended: the Empress's dress morphed until it perfectly matched the provided clothes, and she quickly put these on.

Thoughts of her master appeared in her mind as she prepared to slip into bed. She yearned to be by his side, to be close to him. The feeling had only grown as the distance between them increased. A loud bang rang out from the outside, breaking her out of her thoughts. It was as if something had struck the side of the building with a metal drum.

She again moved to the windows to peer outside, and grinned mischievously at what she discovered. With her Dark Vision, she could clearly see into the unlit alleyway below.

A familiar man was having some difficulty keeping his balance. Every time he pulled himself to his feet, he would simply slump down again and slam into something, letting out a string of curses.

Celia pulled the window up and looked both ways to ensure no one else was around. Then she jumped out, landing lightly in the street below. The sound startled the man, causing him to turn around, only to trip and drop to the ground again.

"Ah…" he groaned, before looking up at Celia.

"Hello there." She waved at him, wearing a wide, innocent smile. "Landin, was it?"

Landin blinked a few times as if trying to clear his vision. "Wh- who are you?" he slurred.

"Oh, you're hurting my feelings now, Landin." Celia pouted. "You were looking at me with such hungry eyes not too long ago, and now you don't even remember me."

She took a few steps forward then knelt before him, giving him a clearer view of her face.

"How about now?"

Landin squinted then laughed. "Ooh! You're the pretty lass Marth brought in." He sat up and tried to reach out to her with his hands.

Celia grabbed them, tsking. "Now come on, Landin, where are your manners? You're supposed to woo a girl before touching, you know."

He frowned and pulled his hand back. "Woo you? You should be grateful, lass. I'm going to turn you into a woman right here, and when I'm done you're going to thank me for it," he slurred, a bout of hiccups interrupting this declaration.

He stood, then threw himself unsteadily forward with both arms outstretched, in a clumsy attempt to grab her. Celia simply ducked under them and kicked his legs out from under him, causing him to fall flat on his face with a yelp of pain.

"Oh, no, are you alright?" she asked, in mock concern.

"You bitch, I'm going to make you scream for that!" Landin barked. Celia waited patiently for him to struggle back to his feet. When he finally did, he turned and glared at her.

"Tell me, Landin, are little girls your thing?" Celia asked innocently.

"My thing?" he replied. "What are you on about?"

Celia sighed. A moment of self-reflection coming to the forefront of her mind. This was very unlike her. She didn't usually play around like this, but she couldn't deny how much fun she was having bullying the pervert. She wondered if this was another side effect of her evolution into an Elder succubus. Without another word, she smiled and lifted her frilly skirt, exposing her upper thighs.

Landin's eyes drifted downward to stare, only for Celia to slap him hard across the face. She didn't hold back, and the force of the slap threw him off his feet and slammed him hard against the wooden wall behind, before he slid down it, curling defensively into a ball.

Celia was surprised by the power behind that slap—she had expected it to drop him to the ground, not throw him clean backward. She supposed that was what her newfound strength looked like.

She strode toward the downed and groaning man, and planted one foot into his side, causing him to wheeze.

"I'm sorry, Landin, I'm the type of girl who likes some rough play," she said before kicking him, hard.

He yelped again, then dragged himself over to the wall and leaned against it, one hand clutching his side.

"What the hell are you?" he gasped.

Celia thought about showing him the truth. Seeing his reaction to her change could be interesting... but why go to all that trouble? She grinned and bent closer, enjoying how he drew back his legs and practically plastered himself against the wall in response.

"Stay away from me, please," he begged.

"What's wrong, Landin?" she asked with an innocent smile. "Isn't this what you wanted? To be all alone with a young girl in a dark alley?"

"N-no," he replied.

Celia moved even closer and he whimpered. Ever since her link with her master and the continuous stream of mana he had been providing her, she had not felt that familiar hunger and yearning for demonic mana. But then again, her thoughts of her master had her in a wanting mood. There was no rule against taking in more than she needed, men like him didn't deserve to live, in any case. While she felt sick at the thought of having sex with this man, given his overall condition she could probably use a Basic Siphon on him.

She pointed a finger toward Landin, thinking about this, and he stiffened reflexively. Celia giggled at that.

"Stop worrying so much. It will all be over soon, I promise."

It took no time at all to weave the Basic Siphon. At the sight of the light-green mana emanating from her finger, Landon's eyes went wide.

"D-demon!" he gasped, just before the beam hit his chest. His body began to wither and shrink. Celia closed her eyes and let out a soft sigh as she began absorbing as much of the demonic mana leaking from him as she could.

It only took a few seconds. When she opened her eyes, Landin's skin was wrinkled and gray.

Celia frowned at the sight. It was the same with anything she Siphoned, but when she saw humans this way, it always took her back to her first.

At that moment a realization came to mind and Celia cursed at her oversight. Why hadn't she asked Landin if there were any weavers in town?

Scowling, she picked the dead man up and threw him into the corner of the alley, then stacked rubbish from the tavern's back door on top of him. They would discover him eventually, but this way, she might buy herself a day—perhaps two.

That done, Celia elongated her nails and used them to climb the walls of the inn, taking care not to create deep grooves or holes into the wood. When she reached her window, she jumped easily into the room, before glancing back down to ensure she had left nothing behind that might incriminate her. Satisfied that her cover was still intact, she shut the window and pulled the curtains tightly across it.

Celia snuffed out the candle and slipped into bed, under the warm, woolen blanket Marth had provided. A rush she didn't realize she was riding waned off. She thought about what she had just done. Why did she kill that man? Why did she even confront him in the first place? She didn't need to. Her master provided her with all the mana she needed, and as far as she knew, Landin didn't play any part with regards to her objective in being here. Was it really just because he ogled her in the tavern? And yet... she enjoyed it, the control, the absolute power she had over him, listening to him beg for mercy. How much had she really changed?

With that worrying thought in the back of her mind, she distracted herself with a luxury she hadn't experienced in a long while: A chance to sleep on a real bed. Her slowing thoughts turned to her objective and what she would need to do tomorrow... before she closed her eyes and drifted off to sleep.

CHAPTER 13

"BEFORE YOU ACTUALLY start weaving spells," Vhal said, propping his staff against the desk between them, "you will need to understand some of the basic concepts and what weaving truly is."

"I'm listening," Aziel replied tiredly. They had been shut up together in this study for some days now without a single spell being cast. The lich had thought it prudent to first go over the entire history of mana and every detail of weaving discoveries. Aziel was beginning to grow impatient.

Vhal raised one rotting finger. "The first thing you should know is that raw mana is generally passive and, for the most part, harmless. Demonic is the only real exception to this rule. When encountered in high enough concentrations, it actively attacks the person in an attempt to infiltrate its vessel and corrupt it. If successful, the mana would force a transformation into a demon."

Vhal let a little water mana leak from his fingers.

"All mana is invisible, but it takes the form of a thick fog when in a high enough concentration. The only aspect distinguishing them from each other is their color."

Aziel looked at the drifting and dissipating mana, considering this.

"The act known as weaving," Vhal continued, "is about

channeling mana in specific ways, allowing it to take on different properties. Each completed channel is called a symbol, and the final result is called a spell."

Aziel tilted his head slightly as he remembered Vhal's duel with Celia. "I noticed that when you weaved that screaming woman, you drew multiple symbols."

"Yes, I was just about to get to that. Weaving is split into three parts." Vhal proceeded to draw a symbol on a piece of paper from his notebook. "The first is called *activation,* the core of every spell, and the symbol for this is the same across all known spells."

Aziel looked closely at the complex symbol. It was made up of two circles, one within the other, with a series of runes in between. The runes looked remarkably close to the ones depicted in his log, but he couldn't read these. He recognized the symbol as a whole though.

"As the name suggests," Vhal continued, "this symbol activates the mana. With that said, on its own, activation only has a visible effect on the elemental ones. You should check if your soul mana activates, just to be certain."

Aziel released a small cloud of mana and willed it to take the form of the symbol Vhal had showed him. It was easier than he expected—but then again, it was only a single symbol. As soon as he relaxed his focus, the mana dispersed. Had it worked or not? He glanced at the lich expectantly.

"I suppose soul mana also has no activation…" Vhal said in a strange tone, watching the rapidly disappearing gray mana. "Weaving an activation symbol on your first try is impressive… unheard of, actually."

"Thank you," Aziel replied, uncertainly.

Vhal's grin grew wider. "It usually takes approximately a week of training and study for a new mage apprentice to weave their first symbol. But no matter—let me demonstrate what activation does to the elemental manas. Simply so that you have an idea."

The lich stood, allowing himself a few feet of separation from everything around him.

"Observe," he said, and Aziel leaned forward in his chair to see exactly what he was doing.

Vhal let out a little water mana, which quickly shifted to form the same activation symbol. He then pushed on it gently, causing the symbol to let out a faint blue glow… before it collapsed into itself, re-forming into a ball of water, which fell to the ground with a splash.

"As you can see, elemental manas activate into their respective elements. If Celia were here and only activated her fire mana, it would simply burst into flames, then die out shortly after."

Aziel was mesmerized by Vhal's demonstration. *He* wanted to be able to do that. "Why is it that the advanced manas, like my soul mana, don't activate?" he asked, disappointed.

"That is not strictly true, my lord," Vhal replied. "They do activate; they just need a little more guidance to actually manifest into something… which leads us to the second part of weaving. This is called *function*."

The lich bent forward over the table and started to draw several symbols on another sheet of paper, ranging from simple lines to extremely complex curves and rings.

"These are just a few examples of the function symbols used in spells," he said, pushing the sheet toward Aziel for inspection. "They give direction and purpose to the activated mana you are using. Allow me to demonstrate."

Vhal again released a cloud of water mana which quickly coalesced into the now familiar activation symbol. But then another symbol began to form, and as soon as it was completed, Vhal manipulated it and both symbols morphed into one. The lich grinned at Aziel before announcing, "Water Bolt."

The symbol glowed brighter before collapsing into a sphere of water just like before, but this time, instead of simply falling to the ground, it shot forward over Aziel's head to strike the far wall. The force of the impact stripped off a small portion of the paint.

Aziel stared at the wall with interest. "As you can see," Vhal said, "by adding a function symbol—in this case bolt—I gave the activated mana a command as to how it should act."

Aziel's finger traced the many symbols on the paper in front of him.

"It is important to note that while the symbols you see might be universal," Vhal continued, "each mana manifests differently and boasts different properties. Learning the properties of each and how a specific function will manifest is essential to weaving effectively—and, more importantly, safely."

Aziel nodded to show his understanding. "And the third part?" he asked.

"Ah, now things get a bit more complex," Vhal said. "The third part of weaving is called *expansion,* and it does exactly as its name implies—it allows the weaver to expand the effects of an already functional spell. Thankfully, there are only two expansion symbols: empower and multiply."

Vhal must have noticed Aziel's confusion, because he paused here.

"Each spell has a power rank determined by the number of symbols it is made up of, and also represents the spell's overall mana cost and strength. If a spell uses an activation symbol plus one functional symbol, like that Water Bolt, then it is a rank one spell. A total of ten functional and expansion symbols would be classified as a rank ten spell, and so on."

Aziel frowned slightly. Weaving so many symbols into a single spell sounded difficult… but again he gestured for Vhal to continue.

"The vast majority of unexpanded functional spells are between rank one and four, but they can be empowered into the higher ranks. Let us use the simple bolt spell again, as an example."

The lich lifted his hands and again went through the motions of weaving the Water Bolt spell.

"As discussed, this is a level one spell. But what happens if the same spell is empowered?" Vhal released more water mana from his hand and formed a third symbol out of it, which he connected to the others. "Now, with the addition of the empower symbol, this spell has a total of three symbols, but still has the same function. Put simply, it is now a rank two bolt spell, which in this case is called Water Jet."

As he spoke, Vhal pushed the symbol forward. Just like the previous spell, it glowed brightly before it turned into a sphere of water, then a thin column of water exploded forward and slammed into the same patch of wall the Water Bolt had struck. The sound of rushing water filled the room, and Aziel could see fragments of rock begin to flake off before Vhal dismissed the spell and silence fell again.

There was now a small, shallow hole in the wall. "Can any spell be expanded in the same way?" he asked, intrigued.

"In theory, yes," Vhal replied. "But in practice… nothing is that simple. Some spells' functions simply cannot be expanded due to the nature of their base effects." He frowned, examining the hole he had just created. "It looks like the earth crystals which strengthened the walls have been dusted…" he murmured.

Aziel cleared his throat, and the lich blinked, returning to his lesson.

"In any case, you should note that with each increase in spell rank, the mana cost increases exponentially. There will be a limit to the number of symbols you can safely weave… Given the massive implications of high-ranked spells, perhaps that is a good thing. I do not believe this world would have survived until now otherwise. In the long history of the Caelian Empire, I have never heard of anyone weaving more than a rank five spell without some sort of aid."

Aziel wondered what those high-ranked spells would look like.

Perhaps he would have the chance to find out in the future, when he gained enough followers for him to safely try one. "What about multiply?" he asked.

"Ah, yes. Multiplying is a little different. Instead of strengthening a spell, it simply multiplies its current effect by a factor of two. So instead of weaving a Water Jet, it would weave two Water Bolts. Add another multiply symbol and it would weave four... and so on." Vhal's ethereal eyes flashed slightly as he retook his seat opposite Aziel. "You need to be careful, however. Weaving is a powerful tool, but there are dangers to overusing your mana."

"Dangers?" Aziel asked, somewhat alarmed. "What dangers?"

Vhal leaned forward in his chair. "We are all creatures of flesh, bone, and mana. If our mana drops to critically low levels, our vessel will not be able to maintain itself and will collapse—leading to a painful death. This is the reason why a demon's Mana Siphon is so dangerous—its ability to puncture the vessel is a death sentence no matter how powerful the victim... except for you, it seems. Powerful weavers can accidentally kill themselves, as they sometimes forget to regulate their mana use. At a certain level, it becomes easy to keep expanding a spell, and by the time you notice the cost is higher than what you can safely supply, it is too late. The end result, as I said, is deadly."

Aziel remembered how drained Vhal had looked immediately after he had refrained from using his last spell against Celia. "Is that what happened when I stopped you during the duel?"

Vhal hesitated, then nodded. "I wasn't in any danger of dying, but I still had to pay the full price of that spell, even though I didn't unleash it."

"Ah," Aziel said. The whole system was actually simpler than he expected. He desperately wanted to start testing things out. But before he could begin, Vhal spoke again.

"I suppose you should know that acting alone, most weavers can only weave up to level two spells. Perhaps the strongest amongst them might be able to execute a level three or four spell. Elders, such as I, should be able to push into level five."

Aziel then remembered he had yet to ask Vhal for some advice. He quickly explained all he had learned from exploring his log, including his new attributes and the skills open to him. The only thing he omitted was his race, as the fact it was Hidden would raise questions he couldn't answer.

Vhal looked thoughtful for a minute after he was done, and his bony finger tapped the tabletop slowly a few times. Aziel waited patiently for his follower to gather his thoughts.

"It is easy to tell you are powerful, my lord," Vhal began, "but your attributes and skills have exceeded my most optimistic estimates. To have such a large vessel is... remarkable, even for an Ascended. I think you will be hard pressed to find anything that could stand in your way, if you learn to apply your power correctly."

The lich then let out a self-deprecating laugh.

"Your reservations regarding Ascended's Domain are understandable. Ten skill points is quite a heavy price to pay, even taking into account the short-term solution it provides for your mana problems." Vhal pursed his lips for a moment before continuing. "At this stage, the only situation where such a cost would be worthwhile is if you were at the brink and had not yet gained the followers you need."

Aziel agreed with this assessment, but it was good to hear another's opinion on the matter. Vhal went back to tapping the table, maintaining his thoughtful demeanor.

"But let's get back to weaving. As I mentioned, the real limitation for weavers is the mana cost. The only realistic way of weaving higher-ranked spells is to use a sufficiently sized enchanted crystal... and those require expensive reagents, which are hard to come by."

Aziel scanned the symbols on the pages in front of him, then remembered the mana tendrils and the translucent screen he had used while battling the dryad. "Vhal, I have weaved some spells before without weaving any symbols."

"Of course," Vhal replied excitedly. "You've witnessed me do it, too, when I weaved Bone Shield to protect myself from Celia's cowardly ambush."

Aziel had in fact completely forgotten that.

"Snap weaving, as it is referred to, allows you to bypass the weaving part of the spell and go straight to the effect. Only those with great control over their mana can achieve this, and it becomes more difficult the more complex the spell is."

Aziel did not remember having any difficulty weaving his spells. He hadn't even had any difficulty weaving multiples of them at the same time. It was hard not to allow his imagination to run wild with all the possibilities. "I hope Celia returns soon," he said. "I am eager to try weaving different mana types."

"Are you sure that's all you're looking forward to?" Vhal asked, as his grin grew wider.

Aziel felt his face heat up, remembering Celia's promise to continue their *activities* when she returned. His desire for her to return only increased with that thought. Just the idea of her being close to him made it that much more difficult to focus.

Vhal must have taken his silence as an indication to move on.

"I should also mention that weaving, while the most understood and widespread use of magic, is not the only method. There is also ritual magic..."

Aziel waited expectantly for him to continue, but Vhal simply stared back at him.

"Are you really waiting for me to ask, Vhal?" he said, irritated.

"I meant no disrespect, my lord. It is just nice to have a conversation, after so long... I am enjoying teaching again. I have been alone for so long, after all... but you are right. Let us get back to it."

Vhal shifted slightly in his seat and coughed to clear his throat.

"In addition to mana, rituals often use other components and sometimes blood or a being's life to fuel them. Rituals usually have more complex and subtle effects than regular weaving. Enchanting is a type of ritual, though it's not usually referred to as such."

Aziel noticed Vhal's skeletal jaw tighten and he seemed to go into an internal debate with himself for a bit before giving Aziel his attention again. "Perhaps it would be best to leave any in-depth discussion of rituals for another time and focus on weaving. For now, I think it's enough to simply know that such a thing exists."

Aziel agreed wholeheartedly, letting out a tired breath in response. Although his interest was certainly piqued by the notion of rituals and what they could entail, the several days long lesson on the history of magic and weaving had put a toll on his mental capacity. Knowing what he knew of Vhal so far, the lich enjoyed teaching far too much to not find the time to instruct Aziel about rituals later.

"Good," Vhal declared, more happily, "it will take Celia some time to return from her mission. We will utilize this time to experiment with your mana and determine the symbols required for each of your spells in the training hall. We might even learn a few new ones."

They both stood, and Aziel picked up the sheets of paper with the symbols written on them. "You should get some rest first," Vhal counseled. "It would be a waste of mana to experiment with a Fatigued Vessel condition. I will use this time to see if I can find any clues about this place and the final days of the empire…"

Aziel nodded in agreement, then left to make his way to one of the bedrooms. He was in fact feeling quite tired, a new feeling to him. He had never slept before in the world he had been trapped in. But even that did not dampen his anticipation of all the new ways he could soon try weaving his mana, or his excitement at the thought of Celia's return.

CHAPTER 14

THE NEXT MORNING, Celia awoke to a loud knock on her door.

"Miley!" Kaeden called. "Breakfast is ready downstairs."

It took a moment for Celia to realize that she was in fact Miley. "Okay," she mumbled, groggily.

Celia reluctantly slid out of bed and brushed her golden hair back with her fingers. She did her best to smooth the wrinkles on her clothes before unlocking the door and making her way downstairs to the already busy bar.

"Good morning, Miley," Marth said, coming out of a door behind the long bar counter. She was holding a steaming pot. Kaeden, following behind her, held a tray stacked high with bread.

"Pull out a stool, and dig in," Marth said, as she placed a bowl of hot soup and half a loaf of bread on the bar counter.

Celia did as she asked, gazing down at the hot meal. As a demon, she could go for days without eating or drinking as long as she had some demonic mana. She wasn't sure she would have survived for so long on her own if that hadn't been the case. Hot food or a proper cooked meal had been a rare occurrence over the past few years. She could not, in fact, remember the last time she had tasted actual bread.

Thanking them, she tore off a piece of the loaf and dunked it into the soup before taking a large bite. The taste of garlic mixed with other spices filled her mouth, and she let out a soft moan. She noticed Kaeden smile as he saw her eat, with what almost looked like fatherly affection, before he and Marth began serving the rest of their patrons.

When she had finished her meal, Celia jumped down off the stool and was just about to make her way back to her room when she was stopped by Marth.

"Miley, Captain Alistair came by last night, but I told him you were resting. If you're feeling up to it, go give him a visit, okay?"

Celia nodded and turned to walk out the front door.

"Do you remember the way?" Marth yelled out.

"Yes, lady Marth!"

"Oh, dear—I'm not a lady, not at all… just call me Marth," the kindly woman said, waving her fingers in embarrassment.

Celia blushed slightly and made herself stare meekly at the ground, causing the tavern owner to chuckle.

"Here, take this," she said, placing a few copper coins in Celia's small hands. "Buy yourself something tasty on your way back." She gave Celia a warm smile and patted her head to smooth out her bed hair. "Now go along. Don't keep him waiting."

Smiling slightly, Celia dashed out of the tavern and into the streets of Whiteridge. The town was much busier in the morning. People were milling about, while vendors called out for them to peruse the wares on offer. The smell of baked goods and the burning of oil in the numerous smiths was in the air. Celia made her way down the same streets she and Marth had walked along last night. She took her time, however, taking note of the people and storefronts along the way, hoping to find something that might lead her toward a weaver.

While she didn't notice any weavers per se, she did realize that practically everyone in the town was armed, even the street vendors. She also didn't fail to notice how there was a distinct lack of children and older folk. Celia pondered why that would be, as she continued on her way toward the barracks.

Beside the unfinished stone keep, there were two other, smaller military installations, which housed a rather sizable garrison. One was located beside each gate, on the eastern and western entrances to the town.

It took Celia just under half an hour to reach the eastern gate's barracks. It was a large building, she could see now, protected by a wooden wall which connected to the main palisade surrounding the town.

On either side of the wooden gate in front of her, two guards—clad in leather armor and wielding spears—were deep in conversation. Their voices only interrupted by the loud grunts and the sound of wood hitting wood coming from inside the compound.

"Halt!" one yelled when she approached, while the other straightened up from where he had been leaning against the wall. "What business have you?"

"I am he—" Celia began, before being interrupted by the other guard.

"Calm down, will yah? The captain told me about this one." He elbowed his partner lightly. "Go right ahead, missy. Captain Alistair is expecting yah in his office on the first floor."

Nodding, Celia shuffled between them and made her way into the courtyard beyond. Several guards were patrolling here, and a group had gathered in one corner. They were training and sparring with each other, using an assortment of wooden practice weapons and shields.

Not stopping to watch, Celia moved straight for the double doors of the central barracks building. This was the same one she had been taken to yesterday. She inhaled deeply, pulled one of the doors open, and stepped inside.

"Can I help you?" a familiar voice called out.

Looking up, she saw another male guard standing on the stairs.

It took a few seconds, but she realized he had been one of the two guards who had run out to meet her when she had first approached the town, along with the captain.

"Ah! Lady Miley, you're here. Come on up, the Cap is waiting for you," he said with a smile, which brought his rather deteriorating teeth into view.

Celia made her way up the stairs after him. On the landing above, he escorted her to a door at the far end of the hallway.

"There are a few other people in there. They came into town a short time before you did," he cautioned, before knocking twice and opening the door. Gesturing for her to step inside, he called out, "She's here, Cap!"

Alistair stood and bowed slightly to Celia, before frowning at his subordinate. "It's *Captain*. How many times will I have to repeat myself, Daniel?"

"Sorry, Captain," Daniel replied sheepishly. "I'm just used to it, that's all."

Sighing, Alistair turned his gaze back upon Celia and treated her to a warm smile. "Please, come in, Lady Miley. Do have a seat."

Celia took a few steps inside, then stared at the three strangers already seated inside the room. A man, a woman, and a boy sat around the long table, staring back at her. They wore ragged clothes, and each had deep, sunken bags under their eyes.

Noticing her gaze, Alistair explained, "These three say they have some information regarding what might have happened yesterday. I asked them to join us."

Celia nodded, then pulled herself up to sit on a tall chair facing the strangers. She kept a neutral expression as she watched them. They were likely the owners of that broken-down carriage she had found, but she hadn't seen them, or even sensed their presence at the time, so what could they have seen? Things were going to become awkward if they had witnessed her looting the carriage or burning the bodies.

"Alright, now that everyone is here, I would like to know what happened out there. Anyone care to start?" Alistair asked, glancing between Celia and the strangers.

The man grunted, then leaned forward, placing his hands on the table. "We were makin' our way here from the capital. We were told by dem military folks that there would be jobs for a blacksmith out here in the Wilds. I didn't believe 'em at first, but the coin they gave us was real enough. Still had to sell almost everything we had to buy the carriage, but we decided to make this trip as a family, and so we did."

The man scratched the beginnings of his unkempt beard, then continued.

"We were given a map and a pass with our names on it to hand in when we arrived. Once we were packed and ready, a guard told us not to speak of our destination to anyone on the way here—on pain of death, no less," he added, with a sigh. "Everything was going well until two days ago... our son got feverish and started coughin' up blood all of a sudden, so we took a shortcut though the forest."

Celia noticed the lady, who she now knew was the man's wife, rub the hand of the boy she was holding in her lap.

"That was not wise..." Alistair commented, leaning back on his chair.

"Yeah, well... it's easy to say that in hindsight, ain't it!" the man barked, slamming one hand against the table and causing his son and wife to jump in surprise. "Tina and I thought we were losin' our only son if we didn't get him to a healer soon."

"I suppose. Please continue," Alistair instructed flatly, undisturbed by the outburst.

"It was uneventful going at first. But then we started hearing this awful hissing."

Celia twitched, and she noticed Alistair's eyes narrow. He leaned forward, displaying an intensity of interest she had not seen before. "What kind of hissing?" he asked.

The man hesitated, then tried to imitate the sound. Recognizing the hissing he was making, Celia decided it was time to play her part.

Quickly, she covered her ears and began to scream, shaking her head vigorously to either side.

Daniel burst into the room brandishing his sword, his eyes darting left and right, on the alert for threats. Alistair stood and grabbed Celia by her shoulders, then hugged her tightly.

"Shhh, it's okay little one," he whispered. "Those monsters are not here." He nodded to Daniel to sheathe his sword and shut the door, but this time the guard remained inside the room.

"Did I say something wrong?" the man asked, concern in his eyes.

Easing Celia away from him a little, Alistair looked into her teary eyes. "Are you okay, my lady?" he asked.

"I'm sorry..." Celia mumbled, rubbing her right eye with one hand.

"Don't be, I understand," he said, before turning to face the man again. "No, you didn't say anything wrong. But we now know what she was running from yesterday."

"Poor child," the woman said, looking at Celia with pity. Clearly, her acting efforts had worked.

Retaking his seat, Alistair glanced over at Daniel, who wore a grim expression, then back at Celia.

"Miley, do you need a break?" he asked.

Celia wiped at her eyes with her sleeve, then shook her head. "I'm fine," she mumbled. "It just reminded me o-of-of—"

"It's alright, you don't need to say anything yet," Alistair soothed. He indicated for the man to continue.

The older man looked at Celia, then back at Alistair, before coughing to clear his throat. "Right... well, later on I heard some men laughin'. I thought they might have been bandits, so I told my wife to hide in the carriage and tend to our son while I checked what was going on." He paused. "I stayed low and quiet when I approached the clearing the noises were coming from. There I saw four soldier types playing around. They were passing a bow between 'em and shooting off arrows at this creature they must have caught and tied to a tree. It was a thing of nightmares I tell ya. Even as they kept sticking it with their arrows, it kept on hissing at 'em."

The man glanced at his wife then back down at the table. Celia could practically see the color escape his face as he slowly looked up at the captain. "It happened so fast," he said, a dark look in his eyes. "More of them bugs just appeared from the forest across the clearing from me, like ghosts I tell ya. They came chargin' in with that horrific hissin'. The poor lads tried to fight 'em off, but I could tell they weren't doing so well, they were outnumbered. There must have been at least a dozen of the monstrosities." He clasped both hands on the table, shaking his head slowly.

Alistair had a grim look on his face as he listened.

"They were protectin' an expensive-looking carriage," the man continued. "But I couldn't see who was in it... I ain't no fighter, so I ran back to my family and told 'em to abandon our carriage as it would attract too much attention. I freed the horse and we ran as fast as we could. By Adara's guiding flame, the town was just a few hours away at that point. I don't really know what happened to those men after we left," he concluded, grimly.

"They're dead," Celia mumbled, hoping she had a convincingly haunted look in her eyes. She was in fact relieved by what she had heard. This man had left before she arrived at the scene—and more importantly, had not seen Miley getting killed—so her cover was still intact.

Alistair sighed. "I thought as much."

"They were our house guards... they tried to protect us..." she whispered, her eyes low.

"Can you tell us what happened exactly?" Alistair asked, softly.

Celia stayed silent for a few moments, then said hesitantly, "Mom and Dad told me to hide when the others were fighting...

so I hid. But, then… then…" Celia sniffed, making her voice crack as she continued. "They didn't have a chance! Those things started biting them, and—"

"That's enough," Alistair interrupted. His eyes burned with fury, but his voice was still soft. "Thank you, Miley," he added, before letting out a long breath. "The creatures you described are called Grauda. They are a colony-building insectoid race we encountered when we first settled here. Until this moment, we thought that we had exterminated them… Daniel!" he yelled.

"Yes, Captain?" the guard replied.

"Report to Rook and tell him to inform the adventurers guild: the garrison will be posting a call to arms with an eight-gold reward for any information leading to the discovery of the Grauda lair."

"Right away." Daniel saluted smartly and marched out of the room.

"Thank you for reporting this. I assure you we will hunt down these creatures." Celia noticed Alistair's eyes soften as his gaze drifted toward her hunched and shaking form. "Marth will take good care of you, Miley, so don't worry. Perhaps it's best if you head back for now."

Celia nodded once, then slid from her chair and left the room. As she made her way back to the Gilded Cask, she reviewed what she had just learned.

It seemed the settlers here did indeed have a history with those Grauda. But, more importantly, there was an adventurers guild here in town. That was a surprise.

As far as her understanding went, most factions had their own adventurers guild. With that said, however, the guild's presence was puzzling. Such guilds might not have been a single entity, but all of them shared the same set of laws and values in the form of an adventurer's code, which made it easier for members to move around when they needed to.

For a start, they were famous for their policy of non-involvement when it came to the politics of the nations they operated in. They only accepted contracts that involved gathering materials or hunting monsters. Celia knew that any member who deviated from this policy would immediately be kicked out of the guild and sometimes even banned from using its services. That was what had happened to her father in the end… Celia's expression darkened as the memory came to her. It had been the loss of his job as an adventurer that drove him to drinking.

Celia forced herself to smile as she reached the tavern door. With an eight-gold reward, adventurer parties would be jumping over themselves to find that lair, and adventurer parties usually meant weavers. Even better, out here in the Wilds, a disappearance would not be out of the ordinary, especially in their line of work. All she had to do now was find a way to participate in the coming search.

Getting back into character, Celia pushed open the door of the tavern and entered. The bar was far less busy than it had been at night, and she saw Kaeden wiping the tables with a wet cloth.

"Ah, Miley!" he said as he stopped what he was doing to smile at her. "You're back."

"Hello, Mr. Kaeden," she said politely.

"Ah, just call me Kaeden, missy. So how did your chat with the captain go?" he asked.

"He said he would talk to the adventurers guild about the Gra… Grauda?" she said, intentionally stumbling over the word.

"Grauda?" Marth's surprised voice came from the back-room kitchen. "Did I hear you right?" she asked, appearing in the doorway, wiping her hands on her apron.

Celia nodded.

"Adara's flame have mercy…" she muttered. "To think those things are still out there after all this time."

"Tell me about it," Kaeden agreed, with a shake of his head. "You would think after all the time we spent fighting them, they would have the decency of staying dead."

Celia stared at Kaeden before asking, "You fought them?"

He looked down at her for a moment, clearly not expecting the question. "Yeah, Marth and I were amongst the first to settle here. Marth was actually the captain back then, the first woman to ever make captain in the kingdom no less," he said, looking proud.

Marth scoffed at that, "Captain of what? We were a bunch of idiots walking around like headless Odanian red chickens."

Kaeden bellowed a laugh. "Well, now we do have a proper garrison, and I'm sure the adventurers guild will take care of it. There can't be too many of the bastards left," Kaeden added. Marth nodded in agreement.

Celia was still not sure what she was hearing. She stared at the pair, curious. "You two were soldiers?"

They both looked down at her as if she had asked something particularly idiotic, before Marth answered. "Well of course, deary. Only soldiers and chosen specialists are allowed to move here. Until recently, not even families were allowed to come. Didn't your father tell you?" She immediately winced. "Oh, I'm sorry, Miley. I didn't mean to bring him up."

Celia was so busy thinking through this new information that she hardly noticed. So everyone in Whiteridge was a soldier or specifically chosen by the crown. Now that she thought about it, it made perfect sense. How else would you keep something like this a secret?

Her thoughts were interrupted by Marth placing a hand on her shoulder. "Miley, are you alright?"

Celia stared at her blankly, then collected herself and nodded.

Kaeden wore a somewhat worried expression. "So, little one, any plans for the day?" he asked, in an obvious attempt to change the topic.

"I want to explore the town, if I'm allowed to," she asked, gazing up into his eyes and clutching the hem of her shirt with both hands.

"Of course you can," he said. "Right, Marth?"

Marth nodded. "Just don't be too late, alright? And if you get lost, just ask any of the guards for directions, they all know the way here," she added.

"Tha-thank you, Marth," Celia replied.

"You're very welcome. Now, go on," she said, making a shooing motion with her hands.

Smiling, Celia ran out the door and back into the central plaza. There was much to see out here, but she was only interested in one thing now.

"Excuse me," she called to a man who was passing by. "Can you please tell me where I might find the adventurers guild?"

Stopping, the man glanced down, grunted, then took a moment to examine her. "Are they letting kids back in here now?" he asked with a raised eyebrow.

Celia forced herself to fidget in place, but then looked up at him with pleading eyes. "Adv-adventurers guild?" she asked.

"Adara have mercy," he said then let out a deep sigh and pointed toward a building on the other side of the plaza they were standing in. "See that building with the red roof?" he asked. "That's the adventurers guild."

"Thank you." Celia curtsied quickly, before bolting toward it.

Over the doorway hung a sign which had a knight's helmet painted on it, resting between two crossed blades. It was the same insignia the adventurers guild in the Jannatin Empire used. A small bell rang when Celia pulled open the door, and she was greeted by a large hall.

On one side stood many wooden tables and chairs, which were mostly occupied by men and women talking busily amongst themselves. Unlike most militaries, the adventurers guild didn't usually care about gender. They were all armored and armed to varying degrees, the weapons ranging from small throwing knives, bows, and short swords to large two-handed mauls. On the other side of the hall was an administration area, marked by a large board with documents pinned to it, and four desks, each manned by a single scribe.

Celia had been in an adventurers guild branch before. Her parents had taken her along with them when they wanted to post or pick up a job in the town closest to her home village. But this place was at least twice as large and seemed to have a much larger number of adventurers on standby.

She shuffled toward the one reception desk that was free, but to her annoyance found that she was too short to look over the top. Standing on tiptoes, she called out to the busy scribe, "He-hello?"

"Hmm? Why, hello there—oh, it's a *child*..." she said, her voice losing all interest. "Listen here, are your parents about?" the scribe asked, taking a quick glance at Celia. She had brown eyes and hair which she kept cut short, and she wore a pair of spectacles that she fiddled with as she spoke. She was dressed in a neat suit, which Celia assumed was the guild's uniform.

"No..." Celia replied meekly.

"Oh? Then how may I help you?" she said with a forced smile, leaning forward to have a better look at Celia.

"I... I want to hire a party..." she mumbled.

The scribe raised an eyebrow at this, then tapped the desk in front of her with her quill. "And for what purpose?"

"Hunting?" Celia replied, trying to give the impression of being unsure of what she desired.

Scratching her head, the scribe stood and walked around the desk to kneel in front of Celia. "What's your name?"

"Miley..."

"Miley. Why would a child your age want to hire a hunting party?"

Celia allowed her eyes to tear up.

"Oh, no, no! Don't cry, I didn't mean to upset you." The scribe awkwardly patted Celia's shoulder, glancing around worriedly.

"I want to kill the Grauda!" Celia yelled, as tears began falling down her cheeks.

"Wha..." the scribe gasped, her eyes wide.

A male voice sounded from somewhere behind them. "What's going on here?"

The scribe let out a breath of relief. "Guild Master, thank Adara you're here."

"Sarah, I knew you hated children, but I never thought it went as far as *bullying* them," the large, armored man quipped with a grin.

Sarah pouted, before standing up and returning to her desk. "Then maybe you should take care of this. She wants a hunting party and said something about killing Grauda."

Celia sniffed, then looked up at the man. Light brown eyes gazed down at her kindly. He had brown hair, a long beard styled into a single braid, and a large scar on the right side of his face that stretched from his forehead all the way down his cheek. She wondered what sort of creature could have caused such an injury.

"Ah, yes, the garrison told us about them." He leaned down, causing his heavy red cape to heave more to one side, revealing a one-bladed axe strapped to his leather belt. "You know hunting parties can be expensive, right?"

Celia again nodded, reached into her pocket, and pulled out ten gold coins and fifteen slivers. The guild master gawked at her.

In the Jannatin Empire, the average pay for a guard or soldier was approximately fifty silvers a month. Celia guessed they were probably paid even less here, in the middle of the Wilds, so she couldn't help but giggle inwardly when she saw this man's reaction.

Scratching the root of his beard, the man sighed. "I still need to speak to your parents to let you issue a contract."

Celia looked down at the floor between her feet, her shoulders shaking. "My parents are dead… the Grauda ate them on the way here,"

The guild master placed his right hand on her head and rubbed it gently. "I'm sorry to hear that child. But that doesn't change things, I can't let you issue a hunting contract. You're too young."

Celia took a step forward and pulled the man's left hand toward her. He didn't fight her and leaned down until his much larger figure hid her whole body from the room. She looked up and her eyes connected with his. He looked genuinely confused, but Celia acted quickly and activated her ability. His eyes grew cloudy as her Charm started to take effect, and a few moments later, Celia took a step back.

"Please, I have to do this!" Celia begged.

The guild master looked at her for a few moments, and Celia's heart began to beat faster as she wondered whether or not her Charm had worked on the experienced warrior.

The guild master then turned and took a small book and a piece of paper from Sarah's desk. He glanced at Celia, hesitating for a moment, before sighing again and passing it to her.

"Here you go. You know your letters?" he asked, and Celia nodded, hoping her overwhelming sense of relief wasn't getting through her acting. "Good. Fill in the details on this form and pick the parties you want to send the offer to if you wish for privacy. Otherwise, it would be best to have it be an open contract. You'll find all the information you need in this guide, and all registered adventurers parties in Whiteridge are listed in that book over there."

He pointed at a large red book sitting on Sarah's desk.

"For that amount, you will probably have the bronze ranks begging you for the contract, but you should be able to get a silver rank if you offer enough."

Celia thanked the guild master and took the book, guide, and forms to an empty table. She took her time reading through the documents, as they contained information which would likely be useful in the future.

For a start, adventurer parties required a minimum of four members, but had no hard upper limit in place.

Each adventurer would be given a badge made of a particular metal, representing their rank within the guild. They started at bronze, before making their way up to silver, gold, platinum, and finally true silver.

To move up a rank required passing a test, overseen by a guild master. Adventurer parties were also ranked and tested using the same method and scale.

The benefits of becoming a high-ranking adventurer or a member of a high-ranking party were, of course, immense. Not taking into account the fame and glory higher designations were always accompanied by, this also opened up more lucrative contracts to which only certain ranks had access to.

Her father had once told her of a platinum contract posted by one of the princes of Odana, it promised to award a title and lands to the adventurers that fulfilled it.

Celia quickly filled in the form, which asked for details on the nature of the job as well as the timeframe. Taking one last glance over it, she signed Miley's name at the bottom.

Now for the important part: she began perusing the book she had been given. There were twenty-one parties on standby in Whiteridge, making a grand total of two hundred forty adventurers. Other than two silver parties, who all had an out-on-job mark against them, the rest were all of bronze rank, but that did not really matter to her. She was here to find weavers for her master, after all, not actually kill the Grauda.

One party did grab her attention, however. It was a newly-formed bronze party consisting of four members, two of whom were weavers. They were listed as earth and fire weavers. Marking them on her form, she took out six gold coins and made her way to the guild master. She guessed hiring a bronze party for a job like this would usually be worth four gold coins, maximum, but she was asking them for something extra, and did not want to spend time negotiating prices. There was also the small detail of possible rumors spreading of the contract the longer it took to finalize the deal—attention she did not want.

The guild master placed the coins in a pouch and started reading over her form, his brows slowly creeping upward as he did.

"You want them to escort you while they hunt a specific group of Grauda?" he asked.

Celia nodded.

"Why? I'm sure they will be able to complete your task, but having you with them will only make their task more difficult, as they would need to protect you as well."

"I can take care of myself," she huffed, placing her hands on her hips. The guild master stared at her, unconvinced. Celia couldn't help but think that he was not looking at her as much as through her. But just as she began to suspect that he was going to Inspect her, he shrugged.

"Right. Well, you're paying above the usual, so I'm sure they'll still take on your contract." He then glanced at the scribe for a few seconds and must have carried on some sort of silent conversation with her before nodding. "Many of the adventurers are heading out in the next three days to try to locate that Grauda nest. I'll inform the party to meet you by the eastern gate on the third day."

Celia smiled up at him, then again nodded.

"Let me be clear," he warned, "whether or not you show up, the guild will not refund a contract once it is taken up by its members in good faith."

"I'll be there," she said.

"Then your contract is accepted, Miley. I wish you good hunting and a safe return to Whiteridge."

Celia left the guild most satisfied. Three days from now she would go out into the Wilds with these adventurers to do what had to be done.

Adventuring was a dangerous job, after all. No one would think twice about a bronze party going missing during a hunt. The faster she completed her task, the sooner she could go back to her master. Celia grinned as she again made her way back toward the tavern.

CHAPTER 15

CELIA SPENT THE next two days helping Marth and Kaeden with various tasks about the tavern, as well as exploring the town further in an attempt to find out more about the kingdom's agenda in the Central Wilds.

People here were either exceptionally tight-lipped or simply didn't know much, because as far as she could tell no one spoke about such things, even in private. She did find something else, however.

It was a stone statue of Adara, placed at the center of a smaller plaza on the eastern side of town. The statue was about eight feet tall and had long hair and a slender build. Her arms were spread out to either side as if preparing to embrace whoever stood before her, while flames blazed at her back.

Every now and then, someone would kneel before the shrine and close their eyes for a few seconds before standing and returning to their activities. A few minutes later another person would do the same.

It was safe to assume these followers of Adara were offering additional mana to her through her shrine. But she had always imagined the direct transfer of mana to a divinity would be more...

exciting than this. If she hadn't known better, she would have said that absolutely nothing was going on at that shrine.

Although her master had not explicitly ordered her to find followers for him, Celia had hoped she would have a chance to do so during this mission. She knew how much he wanted to be able to leave the Facility. She remembered his downcast and defeated expression when he had first discovered how trapped he was. But this shrine confirmed that Whiteridge was very much loyal to Adara. She wouldn't be finding any followers here.

By the time the third morning arrived, she could hardly contain her anticipation.

"Are you going to explore the town again today?" asked Kaeden, over her breakfast of boiled eggs and ham.

Celia nodded. She didn't enjoy lying to the pair. She had discovered she actually liked this kind, caring couple, who had—as far as they knew—taken in a traumatized orphan and had asked for nothing in return. She did not know if her status as a noble had anything to do with this; if it did, they hadn't mentioned it once.

But she knew being honest with them would be a bad idea. If they knew what she was planning to do this morning, they would probably lock her in her room to prevent her from leaving.

"Just try to get back here before evening, alright? Marth mentioned she wanted to teach you a bit of cooking," Kaeden said.

"Okay!" she replied cheerfully, before running out the front door. It was a good thing she wouldn't be coming back, she reflected. Cooking was most definitely not for her.

As she made her way toward the meeting place by the eastern gate, she again noticed the groups of armored men and women walking about. It had been like this for the last two days. She knew the eight-gold reward had probably attracted a good number of adventurers, but it looked like every adventurer in town was participating in the call to arms.

Arriving at the gate, she looked around, trying to spot her party.

The growing crowd and her short-bodied disguise was making it difficult. She rose up on her tiptoes to see over one man, only to be shoved by another as he ran past. He yelled out an apology as he disappeared into the sea of bodies.

Scowling, Celia leaned against the palisade and waited.

It didn't take long. Within moments, a pair of young women approached her and looked at her curiously, before one of them cheered and smiled widely.

"Yea! That must be her!" yelled the girl, who wore her hair tied back in a band. She had light brown skin and was quite short. She wore a high-collared shirt with simple leather armor over it, designed to maintain the wearer's maneuverability rather than to provide serious protection. But that wasn't what made her stand out in Celia's eyes.

This girl was a beastkin—the only beastkin Celia had seen in Whiteridge so far. A pair of furry ears showed on either side of her head, and a furry tail swished excitedly behind her. Her light brown eyes and their catlike pupils turned into vertical slits as they focused on her. Celia had the unnerving sense that this girl wanted to pounce on her for some reason.

The second girl was taller, with white skin, long raven-black hair, and a beautiful face. Her black eyes narrowed slightly as she examined Celia. She was dressed in simple red robes cinched with a leather belt, a dagger, and a small sack strapped to it.

"She does resemble the description we were given," the black-haired girl said flatly, again adjusting her spectacles as she looked down at the familiar contract form in her hand.

"Kim!" exclaimed the beastkin girl. "She's right in front of you! Stop reading and let's introduce ourselves." She was hopping excitedly from one foot to the other, her gaze turning slightly predatory as it landed on Celia.

Noticing this, the black-haired beauty quickly grabbed her

shoulder, as if to restrain her. The beastkin frowned slightly, but kept her distance.

The taller girl let out an irritated sigh before refocusing her attentions on Celia. "I'm Kim, fire weaver and member of the bronze-ranked party White Streaks." She pointed at a black cloth patch on her upper right arm, which was shaped like a shield with a white stripe running diagonally through it.

"And I'm Melody," the beastkin girl said. She pointed with her thumb toward the bow that hung from her back. "I specialize in scouting and long-range combat."

Celia blinked a few times, a little overwhelmed. "I'm—"

"You are Miley," a masculine voice interrupted, causing the group to turn as one.

Behind them stood two men. The first had an almost childlike appearance, enhanced by his blue eyes and short blond hair. He wore a simple brown leather tunic over normal civilian clothes, and held an ordinary-looking wooden staff.

The other was a much larger man. He wore a thick white gambeson with a chainmail shirt over it. He wielded a metal faced buckler with his left hand and a sword was strapped to his side.

"I'm Griff, frontline defender," said the large man. "And he is Alexander, earth weaver."

"Hi," Alexander said, meekly.

Celia nodded in greeting—but before she could say anything, she was tackled and embraced tightly.

"I can't... she's too cute!" It was difficult to see who was squeezing her, but Celia recognized the two furry ears.

"Melody, stop assaulting our client!" Griff commanded.

"Aww!" the beastkin girl said with a frown. "Just a few more seconds..."

"Melody!" Kim said sternly.

Melody abruptly released Celia, who had to take a second to

catch her breath. "You guys are no fun sometimes," the beastkin muttered under her breath.

"I'm sorry about, Melody." Griff sighed. "She's easily excitable and can't control herself when she finds something—or I suppose *someone*—she likes." He gave the short girl a stern look, and Melody looked away nervously, her ears flattening back against her head.

The dejected and pouty look on the beastkin brought a pang of protectiveness Celia did not expect, and she couldn't help but pity her. "It's okay... I don't mind," Celia said as she raised her right hand to pat Melody's head a few times.

Kim stepped forward, pulling Melody away. "Please don't encourage her. And let's get back on topic. It is my understanding that you want us to hunt a specific group of Grauda," she said. "Anything we need to know about them?"

Celia hesitated, trying to decide what to tell them, while Melody gazed at her lovingly from behind Kim. Noticing this, Griff gave his colleague a sharp slap on the back of her head. "Let's go somewhere quieter to talk," he announced. "Melody will stay here, in case anything important happens."

"What!" the girl cried, her furry ears drooping again. "But I want to be close to Miley!"

"You can walk with her when we move out. For now, just keep an eye on things while we discuss the contract with our client." Griff's tone made it clear there was no debating this.

Melody looked at Kim pleadingly, but the black-haired girl only shook her head in response. Exhaling in defeat, Melody pouted and pawed her drooping right ear. "Fine..."

When they had all withdrawn to an empty plot of ground a few yards away, Kim again asked her question. "So, anything specific?"

"There were thirteen of them, I think..." Celia responded. "One of them looked different from the rest."

"That's probably the female," Alexander said. His whole face turned red when he realized everyone's attention had shifted to him, and he took a half step behind Griff.

"Alex, if you have something to say, just say it," Kim said, her eyes narrowing in obvious irritation.

"Don't pressure him," Griff retorted, pushing Alexander back to the front. "You know how he is."

"At some point, you're going to have to stop coddling him, you know," Kim scoffed, "otherwise he'll break down when things get dangerous."

Alexander flinched visibly at this. Sighing, Griff looked down at him. "Come on, Alex. Tell us what you know."

The young man fidgeted before finally beginning to speak. "The Grauda are a matriarchal race. The males outnumber the females by a large margin, but all the power is concentrated with the few females."

"The one female was like a squad leader, then?" Kim asked with interest.

"Y-yes..." Alex replied.

"So Grauda are what... pack monsters?" Griff asked. "I must admit, I've never heard of them before. From what little I could gather from the guild, they are only found in the Central Wilds."

"Anything else we should know?" Kim persisted.

"Th—they ate my parents," Celia added, quietly. She saw all the color drain from Alexander's face at her words.

"Hmph, guess that's not at all surprising," Kim said nonchalantly. "It explains the reaction from the garrison and guild. There wouldn't be such a large mobilization for some plant eaters, would there?"

"I suppose not. But Kim, maybe you should be a little more considerate toward our client, don't you think?" Griff glanced at Celia, concerned.

"Hmm? Oh, sorry for your loss," the girl said, as an afterthought.

Griff squeezed Alexander's shoulder encouragingly. "Alex, what about their ranks and levels? I heard they were humanoids. We aren't dealing with a bunch of Enlightened, are we?"

"No… the males are all Variants, I'd say level five to seven. The female leaders are probably Lesser Enlightened and could maybe reach around level thirteen, but I'm not sure. The queen will be a Greater Enlightened, however, but I don't think we will be meeting her unless we enter their actual colony. Plus, if the guild expected some major confrontation with Enlightened ranked monsters, they wouldn't have allowed a bronze party like ours to take this contract on."

"Yea… I suppose you're right. This 'colony' you mentioned—it's the same nest the call to arms is about, right?" Griff asked.

"Yes, but the Grauda are closely related to ants, so it's more accurate to call it a colony than a nest."

"Do you think the group we're looking for will be in that colony?" Kim asked, nervously.

"Probably…" Alex said. "But if they were out hunting, then they might still be out looking for more food."

Kim crossed her arms across her chest and glanced at Celia. "Anything about their fighting style?"

Celia thought about that. "I didn't see much… but they had spears and sharp claws and long sword hands." Griff nodded at this before Alex continued speaking.

"The males are drones; they don't really think for themselves and follow whatever the female orders them to do. They very rarely show any sign of self-preservation and will do anything to protect the females from harm. I think it's fair to say that they will be relentless and organized."

"So they're perfect soldiers. What if we kill the female first?" Griff asked.

"I don't know… they would probably just go into a frenzy and start attacking everything around them…" Alex's voice trailed off, as his confidence in the information he was providing seemed to dwindle.

"Depending on how effective the female is in organizing them, a frenzied mob would probably be easier to manage," Kim added, before fixing her gaze on Alex. "How do you know all this stuff, anyway?"

This was an answer Celia was also interested in, given how young he looked.

Alex flushed at the attention and looked ready to escape, but Griff stood behind him, his sheer bulk keeping the younger man in place.

"I… like to read. My uncle was a scholar and had a lot of old exotic books sitting around his house," he answered reluctantly, before he was interrupted by a shout.

They all turned to see Melody running toward them. "Guys! You gotta hear this!" she screamed, her tail swaying from side to side.

Celia noticed how agile the girl was on her feet as she dodged and sidestepped the people in her way. When she reached them, she seemed barely out of breath from her sprint.

"The captain, Alis-something, he was just speaking to the crowd… and listen to this! He said that an additional five silvers would be awarded for every Grauda head we bring back!"

At that, the mouths of everyone in the party opened slightly in surprise. That was a rather large bonus to add to an already sizable reward.

"Are the Grauda that much of a threat?" Griff asked, breaking the stunned silence.

"I don't know, but it's obvious this isn't the first time the captain has dealt with them," Kim replied. "I overheard him speaking to some of the guard before meeting Miley. He seems to think that they represent an existential threat to Whiteridge."

"That doesn't matter to us," Melody said dismissively, but shied back when Kim glared at her. When she spoke again, the beastkin's tone lacked the usual confidence and cheeriness Celia had grown used to from her. "I mean, we have a private contract to fulfill, and this just means we get some extra silver."

Kim turned back to face Celia. "Miley, this might be a silly question, seeing as you're so young, but I must ask it anyway. Do you have any skills or abilities that might be useful to the party?"

"Other than your cuteness, of course," Melody added quickly, with a giggle. Kim scowled at her, and Melody took a step back, her fluffy tail tucked slightly between her legs. "Sorry," she mumbled.

"No…" Celia replied, trying to ignore this peculiar dynamic. There was something wrong here, though she couldn't figure out what exactly. "But I know where they were hunting a few days ago," she continued, more confidently. "Maybe they'll still be nearby?"

"Hmm, that might be a good place to start," Griff replied, running a hand through his hair.

"Great!" Melody exclaimed. "Let's go!" She grabbed Celia and squeezed her close, already leading her toward the gate. Celia could hear some disgruntled voices and the occasional laugh from the others as they followed.

* * *

Outside the town, Celia soon found herself in a familiar clearing. As they drew closer to the tree line, she called out for the party to stop.

"Can you wait a bit?" she asked. "I need to get something."

"What?" Kim asked.

"I… I hid something before coming into town. It belonged to my father," Celia added.

"I see," Kim said, a little more sympathetically. "Where is it?"

Celia pointed toward a thicket of trees.

"Alright. Melody, go with her and make sure she gets back safely."

Melody nodded, accepting the order without reaction or complaint. Celia gave Kim a grateful look, then started toward the marked tree she had buried her dimensional bag beneath.

But when they arrived, she noticed that the dirt there had been disturbed slightly. Panic-stricken, she dropped to her knees and started digging furiously, startling her companion.

The pouch, however, was still there. As Celia grabbed it and held it close to her chest, she let out a breath she didn't realize she was holding. She didn't know who or what had disturbed the ground. Whatever it was, she was just glad she hadn't lost something so valuable.

She checked through the pouch's contents, making sure not to pull any of the gold out for Melody to see. Everything was still there. She pulled the dagger out last, deciding that if she was headed into a possible fight, she would need it.

"Wow, that's a neat dagger you have there, Miley," Melody commented, her eyes wide with surprise.

"It belonged to my father," she replied, holding it tighter.

"Can I have a look?"

Turning away slightly, Celia glared at the beastkin distrustfully. She hoped she wasn't overplaying her role, but Melody took a step back, holding up both her hands in a placatory gesture.

"I'm not going to take it! I just wanted to see it, that's all."

Still glaring, Celia nodded slowly. Reluctantly, she extended her hand, offering the sheathed dagger. Melody smiled as she took it, then carefully examined the sheath. She drew the dagger halfway out, an action accompanied by a sizzling sound before she sheathed it again.

"That's some dagger your father had. I'd say it's better than the really good stuff they sell in some auctions." She looked at Celia. "Who was your father again?" she asked, offering the dagger back. Celia grabbed it from her and hugged it tightly to her chest.

"He is... *was*... the head of House Tiaus," she said.

"I see." Melody's eyes narrowed visibly, her tail stiffening, before she relaxed back to her usual cheery self. "Alright, let's get back to the others," she announced, but before Celia could take a step, Melody grabbed her and turned to face her.

"Wha—"

"Don't show that to the others, Miley," Melody warned, her

expression the most serious Celia had ever seen. "I wouldn't trust them with something as valuable as a true silver weapon, especially one as enchanted as yours." Then Melody's bright smile returned, and she released her.

Nodding feebly, Celia tried to make sense of what had just happened. With trembling hands, she wrapped the dagger's belt around her upper thigh, where it wouldn't be visible under her clothing. Then she removed the sack she had been using and replaced it with her dimensional bag, before following Melody back to the others.

When they reached the others, Celia informed them, haltingly, that her father's things had been missing from where she had hidden them.

"It's true," Melody said. The rest of the party expressed their sympathy. Griff even offered to help track her stolen belongings down.

"If someone did take them, then they're most likely somewhere in Whiteridge. There aren't any other settlements close by."

"Thank you. I'd appreciate that," Celia mumbled. "Maybe when we return."

* * *

The hike back to the location of her attack was conducted mostly in silence—if Melody's fawning over her was to be ignored, along with the chidings this drew from Griff and Kim. But Celia did have the chance to learn a few things about her adventurer party.

With the exception of Melody, the group had been childhood friends. Griff was the eldest while Alex, as Celia had guessed, was the youngest. All three had been born and raised in the same town within the Kingdom of Maiv. From a young age, they had decided to become adventurers and trained hard together toward that dream. The discovery that Kim and Alexander both had weaving traits came as a surprise, but only strengthened their resolve.

Details about Melody were more difficult to unearth. It seemed that the party was reluctant to talk about her, and Melody herself would fall quiet the moment Kim glanced at her. But even so, Celia was able to pry some information from the group.

The beastkin girl had joined them shortly before they passed their party forming exam. Unlike the others, she came from the Free State of Tijar. Like the Kingdom of Maiv, it was a country which had declared its independence from the Jannatins. But unlike the kingdom, which had both economic and political issues, Tijar was in fact doing immensely well for itself at present. It was the country that minted, enchanted, and regulated the coin most factions now used, and it had become a hub of trade and commerce for the entire Eastern Peninsula.

If Tijar hadn't been completely surrounded by the Jannatin Empire on all sides—except for the east, which faced the stormy Silver Channel—Celia might have ventured there instead to Maiv. She had heard that the Tijarii didn't care about race, just commerce. As long as you didn't create any trouble that interfered with business, they left you alone.

The newly formed White Streaks had taken on some minor contracts that barely paid for their expenses. But that was when the guild master of a town they had just finished a contract for told them of Whiteridge and its need for adventurers.

They had to agree not to speak of it to anyone, and to spend a minimum of eight years there. He also made it clear that they would be expelled from the guild if they broke these rules, and might even be arrested by the kingdom. With his recommendation in mind, however, they had set out for the town, arriving just over a week ago. And to their surprise, they had received a highly lucrative hunting contract soon after.

Kim was just explaining this to Celia, when Melody stopped abruptly ahead of them. Her whole body had stiffened, and her tail curled inwards. Noticing this, Griff raised a closed fist in the air, and the group halted behind him.

"What is it?" Kim asked in a whisper.

"Melody?" Griff grunted.

Closing her eyes, the beastkin sniffed the air a few times, then scrunched up her nose. "Can't you guys smell that?"

Celia imitated her, sniffing deeply. She did smell something faint but couldn't tell what it was.

"I can't smell anything," Alexander said, meekly.

"Blood," Melody said. "It smells of blood."

Griff instantly pulled out his blade, then nodded at her. Melody surprised Celia again by giving her a tight hug. "I'll be back in a second," she whispered into her ear, before bolting into the thick forest.

"That girl…" Kim complained, eliciting a laugh from the others.

"What's going on?" Celia asked, confused.

"Ah," Griff replied. "Well, Melody is going to scout ahead and let us know what exactly we're facing. It shouldn't take too long, so we'll just sit tight until she returns."

Celia frowned. "Won't she be in trouble if caught alone?"

This only provoked another laugh from him.

"If whatever is out there is able to catch her, then we're screwed anyways," Kim said.

Troubled, Celia took a seat on the ground while the others kept guard around her, waiting for their scout's return. It didn't take long—in what seemed only like minutes, Melody jumped down beside them from somewhere high up in the trees, startling her.

"Hi!" she waved, before diving against Celia and holding her tight.

"Me-Melody!" Celia squealed. "You're back."

"Yea! Missed you too," she replied joyfully, as she rubbed her cheek against Celia's.

"Ahem," a loud grunt sounded from behind. Melody froze, before turning around slowly to face Griff. "Well?" he asked.

"Oh right… scouting," Melody mumbled, getting up and tugging on her armor to straighten it. "There's another adventurer party a few miles out—it's pretty bad. As far as I can tell, only one of them has survived whatever happened."

Sighing heavily, Kim stomped up to her companion and slapped her hard on the back of her head.

"Ow! What was that for?!" Melody protested.

"For wasting time, idiot," Kim replied sternly. "Let's get moving. We might be able to help."

Grunting, Griff sheathed his sword and started out in the direction Melody had taken earlier. The others followed shortly after, Melody still rubbing the back of her head while scowling in the direction of her black-haired companion.

Although something still felt odd about how Melody and Kim interacted, Celia couldn't help but smile at her traveling companions. She had always wondered what her life would have been like if the whole turning-into-a-demon thing hadn't happened. Would she have had friends like them? But thinking that way only made what she was planning to do with them that much harder to contemplate.

Celia felt a sudden heaviness pull at her heart as she glanced between the adventurers before shaking herself. She refocused on the task ahead—she must do this for her master's sake. She just needed to find a more isolated spot first.

A short while later, the group found the other party. Just as Melody reported, only one was still alive—out of what had once possibly been a party of six, given what remained of the other bodies scattered around.

The injuries on display ranged from severed limbs to rough puncture wounds. But it was obvious that all of the bodies had been mutilated even after death, with some even missing large chunks of flesh.

Kim walked slowly up to the only survivor. He sat slumped on the ground, his eyes glazed, and his pack clutched tightly against his chest. He was young, probably only twenty years of age, his black hair plastered to his forehead. When Kim placed a hand gently on his shoulder, the man visibly tensed, but otherwise didn't react to her presence.

"You're safe now," she whispered. "Can you hear me?"

The man didn't respond.

"He's in shock," Alexander said, looking at the bodies lying around. "I don't see any traces of what attacked them."

Griff ran his fingers through his hair. "These guys were ambushed—some of them didn't even get a chance to pull their weapons out." He crouched beside a heavily armored man with several puncture wounds in his chest and legs, before picking up a short sword from near the body. "But they did fight back," he added, studying the green blood that coated the sharp edge of the blade.

"Hmm… these puncture wounds were made with spears. Pretty jagged tips, I would say." Alexander rubbed his chin, apparently deep in thought. "I suppose it's fair to assume this was the work of the Grauda, given what we know of them. But all signs point to this being a fairly one-sided engagement. And if they had any wounded or dead, they had the time to evacuate them, so…"

"So why did they leave one alive?" Kim finished.

The party's focus shifted back toward the silent survivor again, suddenly tense.

Celia, however, already knew the answer to that question. And she was pretty sure Melody did too, based on the quick glances she kept taking at the surrounding forest, her hands tightly gripping her bow and arrows. Celia made her way over to the girl and knelt, as if she had found something interesting on the ground.

"It's a trap, isn't it?" she asked softly, making no attempt to appear childish. At this point, keeping up appearances was a secondary consideration.

Melody looked down at her with one raised eyebrow, then nodded. "I can sense five, but there are probably more," she whispered back. "I need to warn the others, but they will probably strike if I do."

"I'll go tell Kim," Celia replied. "They probably don't see me as a threat, so moving around won't trigger them."

Melody pressed her lips together in frustration, before nodding. "Be careful and don't act suspicious."

Without another word, Celia stood and walked as calmly as she could toward Kim. The other girl was a few steps away, but as Celia got closer she could sense more and more Grauda around them. By the time she reached Kim's side, she counted at least fourteen.

How had she not noticed so many on their way in? She was certainly impressed by their stealth abilities.

"Kim," she whispered, drawing the black-haired beauty's attention away from her examination of the survivor. "We're surrounded."

"What?" Kim replied, her voice as quiet as Celia's. "How?"

"I don't know, but Melody said she sensed at least five."

"Grauda?" she asked, her lips pressing together.

Celia nodded.

Kim looked conflicted for a few seconds, before pushing her hands into her pack and pulling out a fingertip-sized yellow crystal with tiny symbols written on it.

"I don't think they'll let you walk around to warn the others too … so we're going to have to make the first move. When I count to three, close your eyes," she commanded.

Celia knew what an enchanted crystal looked like—the fact that this was a light crystal meant it was quite expensive, even at that size. But she had no time to examine the symbols to determine what the function of the enchantment might be. Nodding slowly, she maintained eye contact with the taller girl.

"One… two… three!" Kim hissed, then yelled, "close your eyes!" at that moment, she straightened and tossed the yellow crystal into the air above them.

Celia covered her eyes with her hands, just before hearing Kim cry out, "Activate, Flash!"

What followed was a soft sizzling sound, before a wave of warm air bathed Celia from above. Celia waited a moment or two longer before opening her eyes to witness a rapidly fading ball of yellow light. Still illuminated by it, writhed at least a dozen familiar male insects, splayed on the ground, hissing and covering their eyes. The bright light must have dazed them, forcing them out from their hiding spots.

Seizing this opportunity, Celia sprinted toward the edge of what she knew would soon become a battlefield. She quickly took note of everyone's positions, catching a brief glimpse of Melody's swiftly climbing form in a nearby tree. Celia knelt behind another tree, peering out just in time to see an arrow streak down from above and plunge itself deep into the eye of one of the creatures still lying prone on the ground, rendering it motionless.

The rest of the party was also starting to move, with the exception of Alexander, who it seemed hadn't reacted fast enough to Kim's warning. He whimpered as he rolled on the ground in a fetal position, covering his face with his hands.

Blinking rapidly and shaking his head to clear his vision, Griff stood and let out a battle cry, before charging into the few Grauda who had been able to recover.

He engaged them with his blade, and the insectoids responded by attempting to stab him with their spears. Griff deflected their thrusts with his buckler, jumping in closer to take away the advantage of their weapons' long reach, only for them to slash at him with their sharp scythe-shaped arms.

Using his buckler, Griff again deflected their blows while taking every opportunity to slash at them. Celia saw him score several hits, even amputating the antennae of one Grauda when it tried to duck under his horizontal blow. But as more and more of them recovered from their daze, they gradually began to overwhelm him and push him back.

"Flame Curtain," Kim yelled and tossed two red symbols to either side of the conflict zone. Almost in unison, two parallel lines of flames erupted upward from where the symbols had landed, their arrangement halting the Grauda's attempts at flanking Griff. Two Grauda who were too close to the spell were set alight, and they rolled on the ground to douse themselves as pained shrieks filled the air. The sudden appearance of flames also gave Griff a chance to recover, while also providing some easy targets for Melody in her elevated position among the trees.

Celia was genuinely impressed by their coordination. This party was practically novice, after all, and yet they were holding back a force many times their number—all while missing one of their weavers. She was sure that with Alexander's earth weaving, things would have gone much smoother.

Unfortunately for them, however, it didn't seem he would be joining them any time soon. Whatever that Flash spell had done to his eyes, it appeared far more effective on humans than it was on the Grauda.

Their attackers had also begun to adapt and change tactics. A few now hung back, and Celia thought they might have been retreating until a wave of spears sailed through the air, one piercing Griff's left shoulder, almost causing him to drop his shield.

Celia gripped the tree she was behind, her nails digging into the bark as she watched Griff struggle to keep his footing. He stumbled then gripped the long pole embedded in his shoulder. With a guttural grunt he pulled it free. Griff took in heavy breaths as blood poured out of the gaping wound, but then he yelled, "Second Wind!" and within moments his wound stitched itself together.

Another spear had been aimed directly at the last surviving adventurer of the ill-fated party. It went straight through his neck then embedded itself in the ground, the force of the strike arching his body forward and propping him up where he sat. Blood bubbled from his mouth and neck as his hands weakly gripped the spear jutting out of his throat.

Celia chewed on her lower lip as the back line of Grauda picked up additional spears that were hidden behind bushes and trees. They raised their spears up and above their shoulders as they readied themselves for another volley. Celia shook her head knowingly. The writing was on the wall—the group might be able to hold on for a little while, but not much longer.

The Grauda had essentially prepared a killing field and were far more tenacious than she had thought. She would have preferred to do this a bit farther into the forest to reduce the chances of someone bumping into them, but it was now only a matter of time before her targets were all killed, and that was unacceptable. She needed Kim and Alexander alive if they were to be of any use to her master.

Cracking her neck and rolling her shoulders, Celia pulled out her dagger. The blade sizzled as she unsheathed it fully for the first time, and its edges began turning bright orange from the heat.

She strode forward, gaining the attention of one of the Grauda. It turned and charged at her, its spear held low. Celia heard Melody's voice calling out something from above, but her focus was entirely on the charging insect and just how slow he seemed to be.

The moment her mind anticipated combat, everything slowed down around her. It was a bizarre feeling—she couldn't tell if it was her senses working hyper-fast, or if the world had actually slowed down. Either way, the end result was the same.

Even with the child body she now inhabited, it was easy to dodge and duck under the Grauda's attacks. Celia grinned as she saw the obvious frustration in the bug's glittering eyes, its mandibles clacking furiously as it tried its hardest to stab her.

Deciding it was probably best to move on before she lost one of her targets, Celia sidestepped a last thrust of the insect's spear and dashed forward, thrusting the dagger deep into his skull. It went in so easily that it took her a second for her to realize she hadn't missed.

"Huh... well that's something," she muttered in astonishment, pulling the dagger out again. The insect fell to the ground, and her blade sizzled as the green blood that coated it began to boil.

Celia recoiled from the stench, then quickly scanned her surroundings again. She was still at the edge of the combat zone, but in the few moments it had taken to dispatch her foe, things had become quite dire for the rest of her party. Griff and Kim had fallen back and were now trying their best to protect Alexander, who still lay prone on the ground, while Melody kept peppering the Grauda with arrows in an attempt to pin them down.

Celia really didn't want to weave anything and risk revealing her power. But given the situation unfolding in front of her, she decided it would probably be best to act instead of risking failing in her mission and upsetting her master.

She raised one hand slowly, as an unfamiliar, almost transparent white mist leaked from it. She then began weaving the mist into multiple symbols in rapid succession.

Kim, as the only other able-bodied weaver still on the battlefield, whirled around immediately. She had noticed the spike in mana coming from behind her, and now stared in shock as Celia completed her spell.

The white symbols glowed ominously in front of her and the air around them had become visibly turbulent. Kim had just enough time to yell Griff's name before Celia grinned sadistically and clapped her hands together hard, crushing the symbol between them.

The resulting thunderclap shook the ground and rattled the trees in a vast arc in front of her. Every human and insect in the way collapsed to the ground, screaming and hissing as they instinctively covered their ears. Celia noticed blood begin to drip from the ears of the Grauda closest to her, their eardrums punctured.

What followed was an eerie silence, that was almost immediately broken by Melody falling off whatever perch she had claimed up in the trees and slamming hard into the ground below. The beastkin yelped in pain as she struggled to get back on her feet, before she grew terribly still.

Celia darted to the prone beastkin and let out a sigh of relief when she noticed Melody's breathing, heavy as it was. She had only fallen unconscious. But one cursory glance at her lower body made Celia wince. Melody had fallen at a bad angle and had broken her right leg, Celia could see white where a bone protruded. Thankfully the bone also seemed to block the wound, preventing a huge loss of blood. While seeing Melody in such a state dampened her mood, it didn't completely eclipse her excitement at using a new spell.

Celia marveled at her new ability to use air mana. The level two spell had worked better than she could ever have hoped, and using it had felt *great!* She mentally thanked her magic instructor who attended her morning classes many years before for teaching her the few symbols she knew.

Still in Miley's form, she ran a hand through her blonde hair as she stood and strode forward toward the remaining party members.

She watched Griff's attempt to stand with some pity—he looked like a drunkard. He kept losing his balance and fell back down again.

"Well, I can't say I'm not glad the charade is over," she said, glancing down at Kim's confused expression.

"Wh-Who are you?" the girl asked.

"Don't really know why you would think I'd answer that," Celia replied with a raised eyebrow. "Anyway, time for you guys to go to sleep. Seeing Griff fall over and over again is fun and all, but if I have to listen to Alexander weep for another minute, I might just kill him myself... which would be tragic, since he's one of the reasons I'm here in the first place."

Her eyes began to glow as she activated her Charm skill, and within a few seconds, both Kim's and Alexander's eyes clouded over and their bodies grew still. Only the slight movement of their chests gave any indication they were still alive.

Celia sidestepped to dodge a sloppy stab from Griff, who had pushed his entire body toward her, only to fall over when he missed.

"You know, this is kind of sad," she said, with a grim smile.

"Damn you!" he grunted. "Whatever it is you're doing, it won't work!"

"Oh? And why's that?" she asked.

"The guild won't allow it!"

"Right… the guild is going to investigate the disappearance of a bronze party, one of probably many lost during this particular call to arms? I don't think so. While I do regret things having to come to this, by the end of the day, you'll all be no more than a statistic in some report," she said, matter-of-factly.

Griff screamed, his anger boiling over. He finally managed to pull himself upright and swing his sword at Celia—only to stare dumbfounded as it was cut clean in half when it struck her red-hot dagger.

Celia grinned wickedly, twirling the dagger a few times in the air before catching its grip again. "I mean, I have to say this thing is truly remarkable," she commented, just before she kicked Griff in the stomach hard enough to land him flat on his back again.

During this time, the surrounding Grauda had recovered, but remained silent and wisely kept their distance as they watched the scene unfold in front of them. It was a little creepy having so many just staring at her, but it was better than them trying to poke her with their sticks or slash her with their scythes, so she wasn't going to complain.

Seeing Griff once again having trouble getting his balance in order, she dragged both Charmed weavers across the clearing and placed them side by side.

"I really didn't think this through, did I?" she sighed. "I guess I can just drag these two all the way back…"

She paced back and forth as she tried to work out a solution to her dilemma, before a loud snap brought her out of her thoughts. Glancing toward its source, her eyes widened slightly at the sight of a familiar female Grauda taking a few tentative steps toward her.

"Why, hello there! Took you long enough to show yourself," Celia said brightly, sheathing her dagger in an attempt to show that she meant no harm. "You wouldn't happen to know how to speak, would you?" she added, hopefully. Fighting this many of them at such close quarters would be difficult, even for her improved self.

The female glanced around the remains of the battle, taking a few long seconds to stare at Griff and Melody, before focusing back on Celia.

"Who...?" she rasped in a strange, high-pitched voice, catching Celia by surprise.

"Oh," Celia mumbled, before quickly regaining her composure. "Right. Well, who I am isn't as important as what I..." her words trailed off, as an idea came to her. Grinning, she took a step closer to the female, causing the male Grauda around them to start hissing, but a snap from the female's mandibles silenced them. "I have a proposition for you. My name is Celia, and I am an Ascended's champion. It's his will that I meet your leader."

The female Grauda glared at her, which was followed by the return of the awful hissing her males seemed to like so much. "Queen... Protect... Kill!" she hissed.

Raising her hands, Celia quickly replied, "I won't harm your queen. You have my word and that of my Ascended."

The hissing stopped as the female seemed to consider this; her antennae twitched several times before she asked, "Ascended?"

"Yes, an Ascended, but I will only speak to your queen about him." Celia smiled even wider.

The insectoid blinked once before looking over at Griff. The large man was still glaring at Celia with absolute rage and hatred in his eyes.

The female stared for a few seconds, then snapped her mandibles, causing the surrounding males to shuffle forward to grab Melody's limp body and carry her off to one side. Celia's eyes tracked them as her emotions roiled within. Should she stop them? Remembering what had happened to the real Miley, the Grauda could want the beastkin for only one reason.

Keeping herself from intervening was proving difficult, especially since she had come to know and like the cheerful beastkin. But she had known from the start that bringing these people out here could only end with their deaths. Antagonizing the Grauda right now would not be a good idea.

While Melody peacefully slept through the whole moving process, Griff actively resisted the Grauda advances, swiping his half-broken blade frantically in their faces.

"Are you even *trying*?" Celia scoffed loudly. If she was willing to let things get to this point, then perhaps taking the role of the monster he thought she was would be easier, even if just for her own state of mind.

"Shut up!" he yelled, as he continued to struggle.

The momentary distraction allowed the Grauda to stab their spears into both his legs, eliciting a long scream of pain from him. Griff twisted and stabbed his broken blade into the thigh of the closest Grauda. The male hissed as the others twisted their spears to widen the wounds, causing Griff to gasp, drop his blade and beg them to stop.

Of course, they did no such thing.

Celia winced as she watched them coldly begin inflicting stab wounds all across his body, before his screams finally fell silent.

This grisly task completed, the female approached Celia, who was still looking at Griff as the males carried his unmoving body over to place him beside Melody.

"Killed four Grauda… suffer," she squeaked.

Celia didn't react and kept her reservations to herself, but the female pointed behind her. Celia glanced at what she was pointing to, which turned out to be the two weavers she had collected.

"No, they belong to me," Celia said shortly. "But I wouldn't mind some help carrying them."

The female's antennae twitched slightly, then she snapped her mandibles again. Immediately, a few other males lifted the two unconscious weavers, before forming themselves into neat ranks in front of their leader. Celia also noticed them pick up their dead and whatever pieces of human flesh they could get their hands on, leaving as little evidence behind as possible.

"You... follow," the female Grauda commanded in her high-pitched voice, before turning and walking off to the west. The remaining males fell into marching step behind her.

Celia followed the convoy of insects deeper into the forest, wondering what she was about to get herself into.

CHAPTER 16

It took just over four hours of heavy marching to reach their destination. Unlike Griff, Melody had been kept alive for now. During their march, she even briefly regained consciousness, only to lose it again when her Grauda minder ruthlessly struck the back of her head. Celia didn't know why, but she was certain it wasn't for some merciful reason.

The location the convoy led them to was what could only be described as a large hole in the ground. The female Grauda pointed toward it, indicating that Celia follow her in. Reluctantly, she did.

The ground the tunnel had been carved from seemed to be mostly loose soil. The whole colony, Celia discovered, was just a maze of tunnels which opened into larger open spaces from time to time. She did notice some interesting things as they descended, however.

The first was how much smaller the males within the colony were than those she had fought against on the surface.

The second was the sheer number of male Grauda who worked on the inside. Whether digging or tending to white slimy eggs or a strange-looking fungus, it was the males who did all the work with a few females supervising. There was even a section dedicated to Alchemy. Celia watched as a Grauda male gathered several herbs and what looked to be some animal's dried out innards before tossing them into a large pot. Celia gagged as a whiff of whatever he was making reached her nose.

Her explorations were abruptly interrupted when the female she had been following stopped in front of a set of rather ordinary-looking wooden double doors. It was the first door Celia had seen in this whole colony.

The female turned and looked her straight in the eye. "Queen," she said, before knocking on the door.

The double doors swung open to reveal a large chamber containing more than a dozen female Grauda, some of whom looked pregnant. They were milling about, carrying clay plates and other assorted items. But as soon as Celia made her presence known by stepping inside, they all spun to look at her.

There was a moment of tense silence before the females rushed toward the walls, where they stood in a row like statues. Their eyes followed Celia's movements as she slowly made her way toward a throne made of hardened clay at the far end of the chamber.

The throne had two females standing to attention on either side, each were very similar in appearance to the one who had guided Celia here, but these two actually wore armor made of an assortment of hides, and wielded metal-tipped spears and a small shield.

It was the queen herself that was the biggest surprise. Celia had imagined her to be a huge egg layer, just like their Critter-ranked ant equivalents. But the creature before her looked remarkably human— a Greater Enlightened, she figured.

Curly black hair tumbled all the way down her chest and back, falling over golden brown skin that sparkled in the light of the braziers, like armor.

It took a few moments, but as she got closer and got a better look, the reason finally dawned on her. The queen's skin was actually a type of soft chitin that mimicked normal skin in appearance.

The queen also had her own pair of black antennae sprouting

from her head, which twitched from time to time, as well as a pair of the boney, scythe-like arms which were a hallmark of her race.

She sat on her throne with one leg crossed over the other, wearing nothing but few loose pieces of cloth. The first was a long strip of material, half-white and half-brown, which crisscrossed over her chest, before wrapping around her shoulders for support. The others—an assortment of red, white, and brown fabrics—hung loosely from two belts around her waist, one of which was no more than a string.

Finally, she wore an assortment of bronze and gold jewelry around her neck and arms. The whole outfit left her arms, legs, and midriff exposed, bringing further attention to her well-muscled and toned body.

The queen studied Celia without expression as she approached. But once Celia arrived at the slightly raised dirt dais of the throne, the queen's nose twitched, and a small frown formed on her exotically beautiful face. This change in mood was instantly reflected by the rest of the females around her, causing them to hiss softly. The guards on either side of her visibly tensed, their clawed hands tightening around their weapons

"You hide your true self," she said, glaring at Celia. Her voice was surprisingly pleasant, but her tone was decidedly not.

"Oh?" Celia replied with interest. "What makes you say that?"

"Do not play games with me," the queen retorted. "Do away with your tricks or leave us in peace."

Smiling, Celia maintained eye contact with the queen as she raised her hands above her head. As she lowered them again, her appearance and her dress gradually reverted to their original form.

The queen narrowed her eyes, her distaste growing with every passing second.

"Demon," she spat, her brow and nose furrowed. Celia could practically feel the tension rise in the room.

"Yes, I am a succubus," Celia said, before politely bowing slightly forward from the waist, one hand on her heart.

"Your kind is not welcome here, demon, and neither are your lies!" the queen yelled.

"We haven't even spoken yet." Confused, Celia glanced at the agitated Grauda around her.

"I have already been informed of your supposed *Ascended*," the queen said. "You are no different from the rest of your kind, playing with the hopes of others to reach whatever end suits you."

Celia shook her head. "I didn't lie to you. I am an Ascended's champion, and I am here to talk to you about him."

The queen glared at her, her piercing honey-colored eyes attempting to burn holes into Celia. Finally, her features relaxed, though she remained cautious.

"Say your piece, then. Who is this Ascended you speak of, and what does he want?" Celia noticed a flicker of need in her eyes as the queen spoke.

"Before we get to that, I would like to know how you saw through my Shapeshift," Celia asked curiously. She knew very little of her new abilities, and if they had any weaknesses, it would be immensely helpful to find out.

Sighing, the queen leaned back on her thrones and re-crossed her legs before sniffing the air.

"Your smell," she stated flatly. "Or more specifically, your lack of one. I have experience with humans, and their smell is quite distinct. I couldn't tell what you were, whatever you did masked your scent quite well. Too well, perhaps."

This was interesting. Celia had never considered whether her Shapeshifting extended to the sense of smell. She wondered if Melody had noticed her lack of scent—as a beastkin, she more than likely also had an enhanced sense of smell.

"Your Ascended?" the queen prompted impatiently, forcing Celia out of her thoughts.

"He is an Ascended in the Central Wilds. He is looking for followers," Celia answered quickly.

Her plan was as simple as it was brilliant. Why not recruit the Grauda as followers for her master? They were intelligent enough to speak and to work together. More importantly, however, from what she had seen, she was fairly confident they were open on the Ascended front.

"So, he is a new Ascended," the queen sighed, a hint of disappointment in her voice. Celia chuckled at this, causing the queen to frown. "Do you find something humorous, demon?"

"I'm sorry, it's just that you are both right and wrong about Lord Aziel…" she replied with a grin.

The queen leaned forward, uncrossing her legs, her eyes boring into hers. "Explain," she demanded, her sudden intensity startling Celia.

Celia hesitated. "My Ascended is new… but, saying he is also old is an understatement. He doesn't talk about it much."

"For an Ascended to live a long time and not have any followers is impossible," the queen replied shortly. "He would have wasted away long ago."

"That's why I am here," Celia smiled. "I think my master will be willing to take you as his followers."

The queen stared at her for a few long seconds, her antennae twitching. "Is that right?" she asked sardonically, as a single clawed finger tapped her exposed thigh. "Quite gracious of him… or is it perhaps that he is the one in need?"

Celia grinned. This queen was a sharp one. "That's something you should talk to him about. If I'm being honest, I'm just here for the muscle, but then I saw an opportunity we both might benefit from."

The queen's antennae twitched again. "Muscle?" she asked.

"Yeah. I'm not going to carry those two weavers if I don't have to, so when I saw your people carry them—it hit me." Celia smiled. "You can help carry them to my master and meet him at the same time! It's perfect!"

The queen's rage flared again. She scowled ferociously, her bony scythe arms rising. "You seek to treat the Grauda as pack mules?" she spat, causing Celia to flinch slightly.

"No, that's not what I meant! I just meant that we could both benefit from this." She probably could have handled this better, Celia reflected.

"And how would *we* benefit from gaining the favor of failing Ascended?" the queen roared.

"You've got some nerve saying that in front of his *champion*," Celia roared back, anger consuming her. They both glared at each other and the rest of the Grauda in the room took a step back, as if afraid of what might erupt.

The queen stood and strode toward Celia, stopping less than an arm's length from her. "We Grauda might not be what we once were," she growled, "but we still have our pride. We will not follow an Ascended that will not last long enough to fulfill his duty to his followers."

"That's one way of looking at it," Celia replied as calmly as she could. "From where I'm standing, you're living on borrowed time, and the only thing that might save you is if *my* master decides to protect you. I give you three—maybe four—weeks before Whiteridge's adventurers and garrison start walking all over your little hole in the ground."

At this, the queen took a step back and her eyes opened wide. The other females in the room expressed different reactions to the news, ranging from shock to rage. The hissing returned in force shortly after, but Celia's attention remained fully on the queen.

Like the rest of her colony, the Grauda queen's expression showed hate... but also fear. Her lips quivered as she ground her teeth, but Celia could tell that she was fighting back something. Could it be tears? This was the complete opposite of what she'd expected from the arrogant queen.

"So, they return to finish the job," the queen whispered

solemnly. Sensing her mood, the rest of the females stopped hissing and lowered their heads. The queen turned around and walked back to her throne, where she sank down on it. "I suppose it was always just a matter of time."

Celia looked around awkwardly as she tried to take in the sudden shift from high tension to this sense of depression. She glanced back at the queen's gloomy form and sighed. "You must have known they would react if you started attacking them," she said.

The queen looked up at her, as if just remembering Celia's presence. "We did no such thing; we went out of our way to avoid the vile creatures. We only protected our own. Those humans strayed from the paths they usually take and caught my sister's hunting party off guard. And what was their first instinct? To play and laugh as they gave her and the males they captured a slow and painful death. They kill everything around them—and what they don't, they drive away. We need to hunt for food, our fungal crops are too young to support even the few of us that are left." She began chewing on her claws morosely. "I knew this day would come, but it being a reality is proving... hard to swallow."

"Well, at least it will take a while for them to find you," Celia said encouragingly. "And the adventurers are all bronze ranked, as far as I know."

The queen's brown eyes studied Celia carefully "A minor comfort at best," she said. "Once they find our colony, they will trap us and starve us—a simple case of history repeating itself."

Celia frowned. "What happened, back then? The humans couldn't have had such a large force when they first arrived. So how did you get to this point?"

The queen looked down, as if deciding whether to tell the story. Reluctantly, she started to speak.

"The humans arrived here about eight years ago. Back then, my sisters and I—" she gestured around the room, "—were still young and under the care of the queen mother... my mother."

Her voice grew soft, and her antennae drooped slightly.

"When the presence of intruders in our territory was reported, our queen made the disastrous decision to pursue a more peaceful approach with the humans. She sent them a warning to leave. It was a warning the humans took very seriously, but instead of retreating, they dug in and requested reinforcements. More and more started arriving, and as their numbers grew, so did their attacks." The queen's expression turned sour. "The war that followed was bloody and cruel, and we had no weavers to counter the humans, so they gained ground. But unlike the colony we stand in today, our original home was strong and large. We were too numerous, and they could not breach our defenses. Instead, they surrounded us in the hopes that we might starve."

The queen balled her clawed fist, before slamming it on the arm rest, startling Celia.

"When that didn't work, they started mutilating our fallen bodies, wearing our skin and attaching our body parts to their shields." She lowered her eyes again and whispered softly, "We watched as they taunted us with the corpses of our fallen brothers and sisters."

Celia nodded. She didn't mention that the humans were probably only using their chitin exoskeletons as armor—the idea of psychological warfare had probably never even occurred to them.

"Then a group of stronger humans arrived," the queen continued. "And with their help, they stormed our homes, killed our helpless males, and burned our eggs and farms."

The surrounding Grauda hissed softly at that. It was not the aggressive hiss Celia had become accustomed to, however; it was almost like they were weeping. The queen remained silent for a few moments before she continued her tale.

"We fought bravely to hold them back, but the queen mother knew it was not enough. She bestowed upon me the title of queen earlier than planned and tasked me with leading my sisters in a secret escape, thereby preserving the Grauda race. And now it will happen again, but this time we have no female brood to escape with... it will be the end of the Grauda for good." The queen sank even deeper into her throne, an expression of utter hopelessness on her face.

Celia, however, was thinking about what she had just been told. While Whiteridge was indeed deep within the Central Wilds and therefore well hidden, Celia couldn't fathom how the kingdom had moved so many people—especially a group powerful enough to do what the queen had said—without anyone noticing.

Then again, Celia had been living in the Central Wilds during that time, and she hadn't noticed anything, either.

Whatever the case, the result for the Grauda was the same. Celia was surprised to feel pity for them. Those that stood around her were essentially refugees, and the soldiers and adventurers of Whiteridge were hunting them down with the intent to completely annihilate their race.

"The offer still stands... to meet my master, that is," she said, causing the queen to look up at her again. "What have you got to lose at this point?"

The queen pondered for a moment before answering. "This Ascended of yours, Aziel... is he a demon too?"

"No," Celia stated, a knowing grin forming on her face. "But that's something for you to discuss with him. I will say, however, you won't be disappointed on that front."

The queen looked at the two armed guards standing beside her, and their antennae twitched. Then she shifted her gaze back to Celia.

A few moments of silence followed as the queen stared into Celia's eyes, as if looking for signs of deception. But then she blinked.

"I will see this Ascended you're so boastful about," she said, her tone still suspicious.

"Great!" Celia exclaimed, relieved. "You're still going to arrange for those two to be carried, right?" she added hopefully, putting on the most endearing look she could muster.

The queen let out a deep sigh. "Fine." She turned again to her armed guards. "Pull back all the hunting squads and ration whatever food we have left. If the humans are looking for us, then we will reduce our presence and make their job as difficult as possible. With any luck, this will give us more time to plan."

She then turned back to Celia.

"I will take a few of my sisters and brothers to meet this Ascended," she said, confidently, sounding much closer to how she had when Celia first entered the chamber. "Perhaps, for once in history, the involvement of a demon will actually be a positive one."

"You know, that's quite rude..." Celia retorted.

The queen ignored her and—to Celia's surprise—a pair of mandibles slowly grew from her mouth. She turned to face one waiting female, then another, snapping at them as she did.

Celia shuddered at the sight, at how the mandibles had stretched the queen's cheeks and kept her mouth slightly ajar.

What followed was a flurry of activity, as the surrounding females went about enacting whatever orders the queen must have given them. Celia, meanwhile, simply stared at the queen's face, unable to hide her shock. When the queen noticed, she raised a questioning eyebrow.

"That's quite... something," Celia commented.

"I suppose it would be," the queen replied, her words slightly distorted. Shaking her head, she slowly retracted the mandibles until there was no longer any trace of them.

Celia shuddered. "Are they in there... in your mouth, right now?"

"They retract into my jaw," the queen replied with a grin, obviously enjoying Celia's discomfort. "They just feel like a set of teeth."

"Right, so why did you not just, you know... *tell* them to do whatever it is they're doing?" Celia asked, turning one finger in the air to indicate the flurry of activity around her.

"Although we understand words, we usually use our mandibles and antennae to communicate. If you haven't noticed, the males of our race do not think for themselves," she said, dismissively. "They instead depend on signals from us females—but of course, as queen, they would listen to my orders before any of the others."

"That sounds tedious," Celia replied.

"I would think that everything is tedious to you. You don't even want to carry your own spoils," the queen quipped, a sinister smile gracing her face.

At least this was better than the scowling and glaring, Celia thought to herself. "So what's the plan?"

"We leave in a few hours," the queen replied. She turned away only to turn back again, a question on her face. "How far do we need to travel?"

"It's a few days north from here, toward the mountains," Celia said.

The queen looked thoughtful for a moment. "This Aziel, does he have a special type of mana?" she asked.

Celia was able to hide her surprise, but only barely. That was a strange question to ask, unless the queen knew something. "Maybe that's another question you can ask him, hmm?" she replied, her expression neutral.

The queen glared back at Celia, making it clear that she was displeased. "My sisters will lead you out and collect your spoils to be transported with us. I will meet you there as soon as I am ready," With that, she strode away down a corridor that led deeper into the colony.

Celia didn't really know what to make of the queen—at least, not yet. But this seemed like a win-win situation for both the Grauda and her master… assuming things went as planned, of course.

She really didn't know how Aziel would react to her decision to recruit an entire race to be his followers without his knowledge. She didn't even want to think about what would happen if the Grauda did something stupid should things not go their way.

"She's got some nerve!" Celia hissed, and the Grauda around her had the good sense to look embarrassed. "How long is she going to take?"

Celia sat on a rock, beside where the Grauda had placed Kim's and Alexander's sleeping forms. Apparently, while she was busy speaking to the queen, they had both awoken from the Charm she had applied on them. But one of the females had explained that they were given an alchemic concoction that put them back to sleep. Whatever it was, it seemed very effective.

But now it was getting dark and the queen had yet to emerge from the colony. Celia, along with what must have been the whole escort, had been forced to wait. She was beginning to lose her patience.

Just as she was about to storm back into the hole in the ground, the queen swept out and looked over the assembled ranks.

"Good, everyone is here," she said, nodding toward one of the female guards.

Celia glared at her. "Glad you could join us, Your Majesty," she said, her voice dripping with spite.

The queen looked back at her, expressionless. "Yes. I had a few things that needed tending to, but we are set to leave. You don't mind traveling in the dark, do you? We prefer it."

"I have Dark Sight, so there won't be a problem." Bottling up her annoyance, Celia turned and began pushing her way through the brush, back toward the Facility.

The thought of returning had her whole body tingling in antici-pation. She couldn't wait to get back and rejoin her master. She was certain some of these feelings were a result of the link somehow, but she was long past fighting or even questioning them. All she wanted was to be close to him, to feel his mana infused touch, his warmth. She smiled as she hastened her pace, causing the rest of the convoy to follow suit.

They made good time on their travels, taking few rest stops, during which the Grauda made sure to re-administer their potion to the captives, to ensure they remained unconscious whilst also taking the opportunity to pour some water down their throats. Though her reasons may have been different, the queen also appeared to want to get there as quickly as possible.

Just as when she had made her way to Whiteridge, the wildlife actively avoided Celia. The Grauda had to run quite far to hunt for food, in fact. Even so, Celia started to notice something off about her traveling companions.

The closer they got to the Facility, the more protective the Grauda became. It started with the addition of a few more scouts, then they began keeping their weapons at the ready at all times. By the third day, they insisted on keeping the convoy's formation as tight as possible.

At first, Celia just thought it was another quirk of the Grauda, but as time went on, it became obvious they were worried about something. Her curiosity getting the better of her, she sought out the queen.

"Maybe it's time you let me in on what's got you so worried?" she asked.

The queen glanced at Celia, then back to her female guards. There were four now instead of the two she had started the journey with. Just like the rest of the Grauda, the queen had pulled in some of the rear guard to be beside her at all times.

"We are in Arachne territory," she whispered, her eyes drifting toward the dense canopy above. "Even if we are just walking along the border, it would be unwise to underestimate them."

"Arachne?" Celia asked, a cold chill running down her spine. "As in spiders?"

The queen nodded. "I'm surprised they have let us pass without a confrontation for this long... they are usually very protective of their territory. We are quite fortunate."

Celia couldn't help but think that good fortune had nothing to do with this. On the way to Whiteridge, she had gone far deeper into their territory then they were now. So perhaps it would be more accurate to say that the Arachne were avoiding a confrontation with her specifically.

Celia shook away any more thoughts of creepy-crawlers, and focused on forging ahead with the rest, keeping much closer to her travel companions than before.

It took another full day of rapid travel to arrive at the debris-riddled clearing at the foot of the mountain. The last day's progress had outpaced the others by a good margin, as the convoy had practically sprinted to get to their destination as soon as possible.

"Hmm," the queen said, pointing at the broken gate and small entrance before them. "Is that where your Ascended resides?"

"That's it," Celia replied. She quirked a brow as her eyes scanned the browning grass and vines which surrounded the bent gates. With her master freed, there was no longer a torrent of mana rushing out of from the mountain, any and all unnatural growth which existed because of it was starting to die off. Things were returning to normal.

The queen frowned as she looked to the east then west, a hint of worry crossing her face. "This place is right on the border between the Arachne and Dryad Groves. I'm surprised they haven't simply gotten rid of you already."

"Well, my master did squish a dryad," Celia said, "but I never saw any trace of the Arachne."

"Squish?" the queen asked.

"It's a long story," Celia replied with a shrug.

The queen looked thoughtful at this. "I must say I am looking forward to meeting him. I hope he won't disappoint."

"Only one way to find out," Celia said, then led the group through the entrance.

No one spoke or made a sound as they made their way down the dark stone hallway, but as they entered the crystal-filled chamber, the Grauda stopped and stared at the massive crystal columns in shock. Even the queen looked awed. Celia didn't hurry them along—she understood the feeling.

It took a few moments for them to recover, but when they did, the queen glared at the succubus.

"You have kept too much to yourself, demon," she hissed. "You should have told me that your Ascended holds so much."

"Don't you think it's about time you started calling me by my name?" Celia replied. "It is sort of annoying, you know."

"Says the demon who didn't even bother to ask for mine," the queen replied, with a scowl.

Celia scowled back. "You're supposed to introduce yourself, not wait for someone to ask!"

The queen glared a moment longer, then refocused her attention on the crystal pillars around them. Realizing the queen was not going to respond, Celia let out a frustrated breath and closed her eyes. She focused on her link, feeling out her master's location, before opening them again.

"Well, he's not in here right now… but you might as well wait for him there." She pointed toward the curved rock at the far end of the room.

Without acknowledging her in any way, the queen walked forward, her entourage following close behind. But as soon as they arrived at the final pair of crystal columns, the demeanor of the group suddenly changed. Frantic chittering sounded from the group as the males and females surrounded their queen. They crouched low, holding their spears outwards, ready to lunge and strike at anything close by. The queen herself glanced around the room, her brow furrowed, her scythe arms held high. Celia felt it too, a creeping sensation of danger and a nagging need to get away. She didn't understand what was happening—not until a dark figure emerged from behind the curved rock, a book in one hand and a staff in the other.

"My, my… what have we here?" it said in a throaty voice, causing Celia to wince in understanding.

"Vhal! Don't be a creep—turn off your Aura," she yelled, prompting an amused chuckle from the lich. It appeared being an Elder had not eliminated Vhal's Aura's effect on her, but had significantly reduced it.

"Ah, welcome back, Celia. I see you have brought guests." He examined the Grauda before him with interest, before giving a small nod. The group relaxed.

The queen, however, stood silently. She stared at Vhal, her face going through multiple expressions as each one battled for prominence.

"Your Ascended is undead…" she whispered, the sheer disappointment in her voice giving Celia pause before she started to laugh.

"Me? Serve Vhal? I'd rather be buried alive," Celia said, then waved at the lich in question dismissively.

"I'm sure that can be arranged," Vhal replied curtly.

Celia glared at him, "He's another of my master's followers."

Vhal smiled his signature toothy grin, and refocused his attention on the queen before shutting the book he was reading with one hand. "Welcome to Soul's Rest. It's a pleasure and honor to meet you," he said, with a slight bow of his head.

The queen hesitated for a second, then nodded in acknowledgement.

"Soul's Rest?" Celia asked, confused.

"I discussed it briefly with our lord after you left. I think it reflects this place far better than 'the Facility,' don't you agree?"

Celia couldn't argue with that, so she simply leaned against a nearby crystal column.

The queen took a few steps forward to stand in front of her group before glancing at Celia, then back at the lich. "I am here by invitation of your Ascended and his champion to discuss terms," she declared confidently.

"Terms, you say… odd. As far as I'm aware, my lord issued no such invitation, nor has he given his champion permission to do so." Vhal turned his head to glare at Celia with his ethereal blue eyes. She tried to look away from them, only to notice the queen was doing the same thing.

"Stop it!" she complained. "You both know this is a good thing. Master needs followers, and she needs his protection…"

Shrugging, Vhal placed the book into an inner pocket of his robes. "I will inform my lord of your presence and request, but you might not be as welcome as you think. As I said, he knows nothing of this… arrangement." Vhal then strode forward past them, the sound of his staff striking the rocky floor echoed through the large chamber.

Celia winced at his words. She really hoped things wouldn't unravel. The queen had taken a leap of faith by coming here, and Celia hoped she wasn't naïve enough to think she could force her way if things went badly—even with her entourage.

Hoping for the best, Celia gave the queen a reassuring smile before turning to the entrance of the crystal cavern, awaiting her master's arrival.

CHAPTER 17

AZIEL SIGHED AS he flopped back onto a cushioned chair in the corner of the training hall. In the past few days, he had spent practically all his time here. He had spent these hours trying out every combination of the symbols Vhal had given him. He had tried hundreds of combinations, with limited results.

Aziel was able to work out the symbols associated with the spell he had now dubbed Soul Tendril, which was the equivalent of the simple bolt spell for other mana types. He had also discovered that Soul Screen, his barrier spell, was quite powerful. Rivaling light-based barriers, which according to Vhal, were the most effective.

Other than its ability to physically block things, it also had a nullification aspect to it. Simply put, it would dispel any lower-level spell that came into contact with it. This was the reason why that dryad's branches had shredded upon contact, and why she couldn't weave anything when she had been surrounded by it.

In all his time experimenting, however, he had only discovered a single new spell. He named the spell Soul Wisp—and its existence gave him hope of discovering more spells in the future. Soul Wisp conjured a number of small, floating creatures made purely from soul mana, which did his bidding. When expanded, he gained the ability to actually see through the wisps' eyes and even communicate through them. The spell allowed him a level of flexibility, which was invaluable in his currently constrained situation.

On the second day Vhal had recommended they duel again so that Aziel could experience weaving under pressure. The outcome had been very different this time.

Aziel had been worried given the first time he faced the lich, and therefore didn't hold back. His power utterly overwhelmed Vhal. An onslaught of empowered Soul Tendril was all that was needed.

And that was when they discovered what soul damage actually was.

Unlike spells using other mana types, which usually did damage to their targets' physical bodies, soul mana also inflicted damage to the opponent's mana vessel. This discovery had resulted in Vhal insisting against additional duels. Recovering from even minor damage to the vessel, he had said, would take considerable time. Aziel wondered if this was the reason why it took Celia and the female human Elsie so long to awaken after being exposed to his mana. Celia through the forging of the link and Elsie through several Soul Tendrils to the chest.

The lich had also been quick to explain the ramification of such an ability—rather gleefully, Aziel thought. Vhal had observed that there was no defense against Aziel's soul-based spells, other than completely nullifying or avoiding them. The fact that his attacks shaved off mana and damaged the vessel meant that non-magical creatures would die almost instantly, while magic-based creatures would have the very basis of their power drained. This soul damage also extended to his summoned wisps, which turned them into small guided assassins for the mana-weak.

While all that was good news, Aziel's experimenting did have a downside. While the few spells Aziel knew came with relatively tiny mana costs, even when weaved at higher levels. The continuous practicing had caused a strain on his mana reserves—nothing like when he had ranked Celia up, but still noticeable. He was now below one-third of his total mana, according to his log, and he felt a weakness in his muscles and a mental fatigue he had never before experienced.

Aziel slammed his fist down on the armrest in frustration. The force of the blow cracked it, making him wince. He had recovered some mana when he sat in his place of power due to Vhal and Celia's contributions, but the amount was so tiny it was almost not worth considering. Though securing the Ascended's Haven skill would solve his problem, he didn't want to spend the skill points required. But the longer he waited, the more he felt he needed it.

"I must be missing something." He sighed. There must be a quicker way of securing the mana he needed, and Soul Weaving couldn't be limited to three spells, could it? It made no sense for the World Seed to go so far as to seal Soul Weaving as a trait if that was the case. There had to be something else which led soul mana to be a "controlled" mana type. But what?

He raised his hand, and a gray translucent sphere hovered in front of him. As he watched, the sphere morphed into a cube, then into other shapes, before returning to a spherical form. His time spent practicing his barrier spell had brought this aspect of his powers to light—he had done this before when he had enclosed the dryad in a sphere, but he hadn't really noticed it then.

The exercise had a calming effect, so he kept doing it until he felt the frustration in his heart subside a little. He then released the spell, allowing it to burst like a bubble back into mist and disperse.

Aziel sat up, remembering his faction log. He had been so busy with Vhal's lessons and practicing that he hadn't checked it yet. He focused on the second symbol on his arm, and runes began to appear before his eyes.

The Fallen
Faction Level: 1

Military: 1
Civil: 1
Economy: 1

He didn't understand what any of this meant, but it didn't take a lot of thought to conclude that his faction was weak. In fact, if faction levels worked at all like normal log levels, then his faction's power practically didn't exist.

The log also listed all faction-claimed locations. This was important to Aziel, as they were places which reduced the mana drain on him. Unsurprisingly, the only location it listed was Soul's Rest.

Aziel's gaze shifted to a blinking heading in his log with the title of "claims". He quickly read over the information provided and smiled before pressing on it.

The Fallen have met the required prerequisites to lay claim to an adjacent region.

Would you like to proceed with laying claim to the region known as the Central Wilds?

Do you accept? Yes or no.

The requirements for claiming a region seemed simple: the region had to be adjacent to a faction-controlled location, and his faction had to pacify the region and maintain a presence there. Since Soul's Rest was already under the control of the Fallen, Aziel could therefore lay claim to the Central Wilds. Seeing no reason why he shouldn't, Aziel quickly focused on yes, but another more concerning notification appeared immediately after.

Warning, the region known as the Central Wilds is claimed by several factions.

Proceeding will notify all existing claimants of your claim.

Are you certain you with to proceed? Yes or no.

Aziel focused on the existing claimants. The runes glowed momentarily, then expanded, and he frowned as he read over the new information.

The Kingdom of Maiv, The Jannatin Empire, and the United Princedoms of Odana had all laid claim to the Central Wilds. If he claimed the region for himself as well, then the World Seed would notify all of them of it—exposing his general whereabouts in the process, something he absolutely could not afford at this time.

Regretfully, he chose to reject the claim for now and focused on the other ways he could assert control.

The log explained that one way he could go about strengthening his claim was by building up his faction's presence within the region. If his presence exceeded all other claimants' combined, then the World Seed would simply award it to his faction. Aziel had no idea what was meant by "presence" exactly, but he assumed it meant people, and perhaps buildings and infrastructure to increase the power and influence his faction had over the region.

The only other way to gain control was to secure a majority claim. This would mean convincing the majority of the other claimants to support his faction's claim over their own.

Aziel sighed again. Building a big enough presence to exceed all three nations would take years, if it was even possible… but getting one of them to give up their claim in favor of his? That was even more improbable. It would seem gaining that eighty percent drain reduction within the Central Wilds was still a distant goal.

The faction log also included information regarding appointments, which dealt with the officer positions for his faction and were split into minor and major roles. Of these, only the minor position of head researcher was currently filled.

Other than faction leader, Aziel focused on the first major officer position listed, and additional runes appeared to one side.

Head of the Guard
Class: Title
Faction appointment whose responsibilities are to coordinate efforts to secure the safety and protection of key personnel and locations in regards to their faction.

Effects:
Access to faction log set: Head of the Guard

The other major positions were: high commander, who would be in charge of all things military; the interior minister, whose responsibility included enforcing laws, resolving internal disputes and espionage; the economic minister who would take care of trade and the treasury; and finally, the viceroy, who had administrative authority only second to the faction leader.

There were other, more specialized roles which required certain conditions to be fulfilled before appointing people to them. One such role was divinity, which require the faction to be at level 3 and could only be filled by an Ascended. Aziel thought about appointing himself as one when the time came, he had every intention of fulfilling the role and its responsibilities anyways.

As the faction level increased, so did the ability for major officer positions to appoint and expand their organizations below them. As faction leader, Aziel had the ability to issue faction associated guild charters. He imagined the mage guild classes Celia attended before her transformation was an example of these, but the current amount of guild charters he could issue was zero—these would only become available when his faction reached certain levels.

Reaching the end of the Appointments tab, Aziel frowned as he read over a warning notification.

Warning, major appointments remain unfilled. All relevant rating increases will not be accounted for until relevant officer roles are occupied.

In other words, Aziel could have the largest military in Kadora, but their contribution to his faction's military level would remain at zero until a head commander was appointed to lead them.

The Fallen had very little going for it at the moment. As head researcher, Vhal didn't appear to contribute anything to the faction's level. Reaching level five and fulfilling the requirements of his quest seemed like a far-off possibility at the moment.

Deciding to take a much-needed break, Aziel closed his eyes and tried to relax. He had discovered, to his annoyance, that he did require sleep. It wasn't anything like what other creatures experienced, however. A few hours every few days would suffice. It was a simple case of efficiency. If he did not go to sleep, his body would simply use mana to keep itself going. In his current situation, that was not acceptable.

Just as he began to doze off, he sensed a familiar vessel approach through the main hallway of the Imperial Wing. Taking a second to study it, he recognized it as Vhal's.

Aziel had not actually seen or interacted with the lich in some time. Vhal seemed content to leave him to his practice, while he explored and looked for clues regarding who might have imprisoned him for all that time. His presence now indicated that something had changed.

A moment later, three knocks resounded on the wooden door of the hall.

"My lord," Vhal said, entering respectfully with a bow. "How goes your experimentation?"

"Not so well, I would say," Aziel replied. "What's the matter?"

Vhal grinned. "Celia has returned."

"She has?" Aziel leaned forward, failing miserably to hide his excitement at the news. He had been too busy to check on the link to track her whereabouts recently. He still found it strange how much he was looking forward to seeing her.

Vhal nodded, his grin growing wider. "She has not come alone, however. She has brought… guests."

Aziel's eyes narrowed slightly, concerned. "What do you mean, *guests?*"

"Apparently, she decided to invite a race of insects to be your followers." Vhal scoffed, shaking his head. "I don't know how she found them, but I suppose we should be thankful she didn't actually promise them anything… at least, as far as I know."

Aziel tilted his head. "Isn't this a good thing? Especially given the state of my mana reserves."

"Perhaps. I warned you against trying to convert followers claimed by other Ascended, but these insects don't seem to be following another." Vhal stroked his beard. "It might be best to speak to them directly before making any decisions on the matter."

Aziel nodded. "And they *want* to be my followers?"

"Not exactly, my lord," Vhal said. "Their queen is here to negotiate terms."

"So… it's a type of contract?"

Vhal shrugged. "This is a bit beyond my expertise. All I can say is that she seemed somewhat… desperate."

Aziel looked at the lich, his brows raised. "Oh? What makes you say that?"

"Celia indicated as much. Also, when the queen mistakenly identified me as you, she seemed quite… defeated. As if all hope was lost," Vhal added thoughtfully, then grinned.

"So you think I should go through with this?" Aziel asked, standing.

Vhal looked down and seemed deep in thought for a moment.

"I don't know anything about this race. With that said, the queen seemed intelligent. When I spoke of followers, I must admit that I pictured humans or elves, or the other civilized races. It never occurred to me to gather followers from amongst the monster races."

Vhal leaned on his staff, still thinking.

"If the terms are not too outlandish, then I think you should pursue it," he said at last. "You do have a massive mana reserve, considering, but you have also been using much of it in a very short period. Even if their numbers are few and their contribution low, it should provide you with some relief... perhaps even let you walk out of here for a short while."

Aziel couldn't argue with that. Even a small amount of additional mana would offer some peace of mind. The idea of recruiting followers from populations other than the so-called civilized ones sounded interesting, and would avoid antagonizing another Ascended.

"I trust your judgement, Vhal," Aziel said. "And I admit I don't even know where to start with any negotiation of terms. I would appreciate if you stood by me and volunteered your advice."

Vhal bowed deeply at that. "I have sworn to serve you, my lord. You honor me with your trust."

"Then let us meet our guests," Aziel replied with a smile. "And let's welcome Celia back as well."

* * *

As they entered the large crystal chamber, Aziel saw a familiar figure approach him.

Celia stopped just a step away, one hand on her hip. She took her time, her golden eyes connecting with his own. She let out a small breath before she gently bit her bottom lip.

"Welcome back." Aziel smiled.

"It's good to be back... Master," she purred, moving closer to trail a finger down his chest.

Aziel took a deep breath and tried to calm himself. Just as before, his body reacted instantly to her touch and his thoughts were in turmoil. He was glad the chamber was large enough for this interaction to take place out of sight of his guests, who awaited him by his seat.

Celia took another step toward him, her body practically melding itself to his as her tail wrapped around his leg. She looked up at him and licked her lips.

Aziel's heart was beating so hard he could hear it in his ears. He had been looking forward to this, but now that it was happening... he wasn't sure what he was supposed to do or how to proceed. The last time he had kissed her, his body had acted on instinct. Should he kiss her now? His thoughts were interrupted by a light pat on his shoulder.

"Lord Aziel?" Vhal asked, with a deep sigh. "Perhaps you two can continue this at a later time?"

"Ah..." Aziel muttered, trying to get his head back in order. Celia kept herself glued to him but turned her head to glare at the lich.

"Oh, *you're* back," she said, her voice dripping with derision.

Vhal bowed slightly. "Of course! My place is at our lord's side, Champion." He was enjoying Celia's irritation.

Aziel shook his head then separated himself from Celia's embrace. She pouted at that, but let him go without any fuss.

"We can talk once we are done with our guests," he promised her, then leaned forward and gave her a light kiss, before turning away and striding toward the far end of the chamber. He could feel her eyes on his back the whole way, and a shiver ran down his spine. He wondered if this was what it felt like to be stalked by a predator from the shadows.

Not knowing what to expect, Aziel rested his hand on the hilt of his blade as he approached the curved rock, where he saw the group of several dozen bipedal insects spread around the crystal columns. They looked familiar. The mark on his wrist began to heat up as a dull pain began to hammer within his head. Both increased the closer to them he came.

Aziel raised a hand to his forehead, in an attempt to relieve himself from the ache. He blinked a few times before continuing unsteadily toward his curved rock. But as he got within a few feet of it, another one of the insects turned to face him.

She was different from the rest, but again looked familiar... too familiar. She stared at him, her eyes widening and her mouth opening and closing, as if struggling to speak. Her hands slowly rose toward him, tears beginning to pool in her eyes. A single tear slid down her cheeks as she said in a whisper, "It's the Aziel..."

Aziel stared at her, not knowing what to say—but then a sharp, unbearable pain exploded in his head, as if someone was stabbing him repeatedly from the inside. His right wrist began to burn from the escalating heat spreading from the World Seed's mark.

He yelled out in agony, then gasped as he collapsed to his knees. His hands clutched at his skull. He could hear movement—screaming—around him, but could not focus on what was being said.

Seemingly random images flashed through his mind before it all went suddenly black.

* * *

"Aziel, you must keep your blade in front of you. Do not give your opponents an easy opening."

The man smiled at the young boy before taking a few steps back.

"Again," he called, and they charged one another with their blades. The sound of clashing metal rang across the small square.

Aziel stared at the scene playing out before him. Was this a memory? It had a hazy feel to it, almost like a dream, and the people around him did not seem to notice his presence. But if it was a memory, then how was he watching it play out like this?

The man did not look like any race Aziel knew or had read of. His skin was a uniform shade of red, and although he looked roughly humanoid, he had enormous arms and three black eyes which Aziel saw blinked vertically.

"Good!" the man said. "Keep improving at that rate and perhaps you'll be able to help your mother sooner than expected." He knelt before the boy and gripped his shoulder. "Let's keep working on your footwork now."

My mother? was all Aziel had time to think before he was pulled suddenly from the scene and found himself in another. Here, the same man was arguing with a familiar woman in a white dress. Her large feathered wings were unmistakable, but it was the creature behind the pair that consumed his attention.

There stood an equally familiar-looking insectoid woman. Her scythe-like arms were held low and her head was bowed respectfully. It wasn't the same person he saw in his place of power, but close.

"Ascended, you don't have to do this!" the red man yelled, his massive arms flexing at his sides. Aziel could see the concern... even pain, in his eyes.

The woman in white brought her hand up, to gently stroke the man's cheek. "N'goth, you and I both know that only I have a chance against the overseer. If I can—"

"If?" N'goth interjected, grabbing her arm. "We cannot lose you, the faction won't survive it! Let the Grauda and I fulfill our sworn duty to you! Let us and the other divini—"

"No," the winged woman commanded, her tone suddenly harsh. "You and the rest must lead our forces and defend our peoples and lands. Once I'm done with the overseer, this war will be as good as over." She turned, showing the man her back. "You are dismissed, N'goth."

"Helena..."

"Don't," she interrupted him sharply.

The man's shoulders and head sank at her words. "As you command," he whispered, before turning and nodding toward the female Grauda. In silence, they made their way out.

The woman in white stayed where she was for a few moments, then sighed and ran her hands across her long blonde hair. Her white feathered wings extended and stretched outwards before folding back in again. "Aziel," she said, and for a moment, Aziel thought she was speaking to him, but she then continued. "You shouldn't eavesdrop on us like that. Come out."

Her voice held no hint of anger. The same young boy Aziel had seen engaged in sword training now sheepishly emerged from his hiding spot behind the curtains. He had grown a little since the last scene.

"I'm sorry, Mother..." he began, which caused the woman to smile and kneel before him.

"It's alright. Before I leave for battle, we need to go somewhere..." she said, stroking his arm lovingly. Although her expression stayed stoic, Aziel could see that her beautiful features were strained as she looked at him, her eyes filling with tears.

Aziel moved closer to the pair and tried to touch the person he now knew to be his mother... but his hand went through her, as if she wasn't there. He looked down at his younger self. This was around the age he had been when he first found himself in that world he had been trapped in... was that the "somewhere" she was talking about?

Before he could investigate further, he was again pulled away from the scene, and he found himself in darkness.

* * *

Aziel snapped open his eyes. He was breathing heavily and found he was still on his knees. He looked around and noticed bones, lots of bones. He was surrounded by them, a wall of them. Aziel recognized Vhal's spell, but why would he weave a Bone Shield around him?

He could hear screaming from somewhere close by. It sounded like Celia, Vhal, and his guests were yelling and hissing at one another, but he couldn't make out any of the words through the bones.

Aziel placed his hand on one knee and pushed himself to his feet. He drew out his sword, and with a single diagonal swipe, cut through the bone wall in front of him. It gave way to his blade as if made of paper. The chamber immediately fell silent, as all eyes turned to him.

Both Celia and Vhal were facing his guests, mana leaking from their hands, ready to destroy anything that came close. The insects had their weapons raised protectively around the female he had seen just before his episode.

"That is enough," he declared. He walked past them all to his curved rock, where he sat as if nothing had happened.

Celia quickly moved to his side, her hand caressing his cheek as her eyes looked him over. "Master, are you alright? You suddenly collapsed, I thought…" Her voice quivered slightly, genuine concern painted on her features.

"I am fine, Celia, do not worry… I was just surprised, that's all." He squeezed her hand reassuringly, smiling. She smiled back, but Aziel could tell she was still worried. She then moved back to take up position to his right, one hand still resting on his shoulder.

Vhal took his place to Aziel's left, his eyes flashing, but he said nothing.

The Grauda woman he noticed before knelt in front of him, and the rest of her escort followed her lead. She looked up at him with such reverence it was almost uncomfortable.

"It is nice to see the Grauda again, after all this time, and with such a young queen at their head," Aziel said.

"You *know* them?" Celia asked.

"Again…?" Vhal asked almost at the same time, his eyebrows inching upward.

The Grauda queen sniffed and wiped the tears from her eyes and cheeks. "You came back, just like in the stories," she said, her voice trembling.

Aziel smiled, though he did not know what stories she was referring to. "I remember your people," he said. "I was introduced to them when I was much younger, I believe… N'goth was your king at the time, was he not?"

The Grauda queen nodded slowly. "After Divinities' Fall, we were lost… but stories of you were shared between the different peoples… 'the Aziel' they called you… the savior."

Celia and Vhal stared at them both as if they were speaking a different language. Vhal in particular seemed piqued.

"My lord," he said, "perhaps we can ask for an explanation?"

Celia nodded in affirmation.

For once, Aziel realized he knew something that they did not. It was an odd but empowering feeling. He stood and took two steps toward the Grauda queen, who lowered her head as if not worthy of his gaze.

Aziel frowned at that. He again took a few steps toward her, then placed one finger gently under her chin to raise it.

The other Grauda stared at him with wide-open eyes, while the queen looked absolutely terrified. Her eyes shifted from side to side, as she tried to look at everything other than him.

"Take a deep breath," he said, "you are safe here; no one shall harm you."

The queen followed his advice, then finally made eye contact. He smiled as he looked into her light brown eyes and examined her for a few seconds, admiring her beauty. He noticed her face flush slightly at his attention.

Not wanting to make her uncomfortable, he withdrew his hand, then stood and turned to face his champion and faction officer.

"These are the Grauda, one of the races that made up the Kirk'nolok Collective," he said.

Vhal frowned. "I have never heard of such a faction…"

"And if he doesn't know about it, then I definitely don't," Celia added.

Aziel turned back to the queen. "You may rise," he said. The queen, who was still watching him intently, immediately did as he commanded.

"Perhaps it would be best if you explained…" Only then did Aziel realize that he still didn't know her name. "What should I call you?"

The queen smiled. "My Grauda name would be impossible to pronounce without mandibles," she said, more confidently, "but I also go by Astrel."

"I welcome you to Soul's Rest, Queen Astrel. I am Aziel." He smiled at the look of wonder Astrel was giving him. "Would you tell us about the stories you mentioned—the ones about me?"

She nodded slowly. Aziel sat back on his curved rock, gesturing for her to begin.

"After the events of Divinities' Fall, the different peoples were left without direction or purpose. With the loss of our crystals, things deteriorated quickly." Astrel's shoulders slumped as she said this.

Vhal raised his arm to stop her. "If I may interrupt Lady Astrel, what is this… Fall… you speak of?"

Astrel glanced at the lich then back at Aziel, who nodded.

"Divinities' Fall is the name of the battle which ended with the death of the divinities of the time," she said bluntly. Then she smiled as she made eye contact with Aziel. "Except for one."

Celia and Vhal looked at each other, then back at the Grauda queen.

"And this one who survived… is our Lord Aziel?" Vhal asked skeptically. "When did this happen? I know of no period in history where all the Ascended perished."

Astrel exposed her teeth and hissed before raising both her scythe arms into the air. "The young races only care about their own histories. We have inhabited these lands far longer than they have! They did not even exist at the time."

"And who are these young races?" Celia asked cautiously, keeping an eye on the queen's sharp arms.

"The so-called civilized races, of course. We Grauda are one of the ancient races that ruled over Kadora." Astrel's rage and frustration seemed ready to boil over. "But after the Fall, new races appeared and spread across the continent like a plague. We were chased away, stomped on, and hunted like common beasts by those who inherited what we had lost. And now they have the nerve to call *us* monsters."

Slowly, her features softened as her gaze returned to Aziel.

"Stories of the Aziel, the last of our Ascended, circulated shortly after the Fall. We were told he would unite us and lead us." She looked at him, her eyes wide in wonder. "So much time has passed since then, and many of the other races dismissed you as simply a myth, as something their ancestors used to keep hope alive during those difficult times. But now you are *here*..."

Celia bit her lip. "How do you know he is the Aziel that was spoken about? I mean, the name could be a coincidence, couldn't it?"

Aziel could hear the uncertainty in her voice, as if she didn't believe her own objections.

"When you called your master Aziel back at my colony, it piqued my interest enough to place my trust in a demon. But the moment I saw him, I knew he was the one." Astrel smiled in a gentle, almost motherly way, as she turned back to Aziel. "It's his eyes that mark him as our savior. Gray eyes that shine like twin moons—that was the only description the stories told of him. But the stories also told of the Aziel using a strange and powerful type of mana." Her eyes drifted to the gray Capital Crystal beside her for a moment before returning to Aziel. "I am certain he is the one."

Vhal leaned down to whisper in Aziel's ear. "My lord, I must admit, I don't know what to make of this. Even if she speaks the truth, who knows to what extent time has distorted the facts? I personally know nothing of what she speaks of, nor do I feel particularly trustful of her words. This is the first I have ever heard of so-called ancient races."

"I trust her," Aziel replied. "Although the memories I reclaimed are hazy and far from complete, I know the Grauda were allies. They have waited for so long… I believe I am duty-bound to hear them out."

Vhal stood up straight and nodded. "If you trust them, I will follow your lead. But may I ask who introduced you to the Grauda? In your memories, I mean."

"A man named N'goth. He was the one who taught me how to use this—" Aziel patted the hilt of his sword. "I know nothing of the events around Divinities' Fall, but given what Astrel has told us, along with some of the memories I have reclaimed, it seems that I was kept away—perhaps to protect me from what happened."

"There was a long war," the queen said firmly. "Divinities' Fall was simply the battle that ended a war which all sides lost. I do not know much about the war itself, or what happened to you. Nothing of that time was passed down through the Grauda queens. But if you were kept hidden, it was likely to keep you safe in case the worst happened." She placed her index finger on her lip as she looked away, thinking. "The other ancient races might know more."

Aziel thought about this. "I have large gaps in my memories, but simply seeing the Grauda brought some of them back. Perhaps it is worth seeking out other ancient races, to see if the same will happen."

"It is worth a try," Vhal agreed.

Aziel took a deep breath. There was a lot they could learn from Astrel, but he felt it was time to deal with the reason they were gathered here. "Let us get to your terms, Astrel."

The queen shifted uncomfortably. "The Grauda would not dare declare terms to the Azi— I mean to you, Lord Aziel. We will follow you freely and without condition." She stopped herself and looked thoughtful for a moment. "If you would allow for a single request, we—I—would be forever grateful," she continued softly, as if afraid to even ask.

Aziel was glad there was something she wanted. He would not

have felt comfortable taking their mana without doing anything in return. He nodded for her to continue.

Astrel shifted on her feet again, but then steeled herself and straightened her back. "Ever since the final days of the Collective, the Grauda have named no king. As the current queen of the Grauda, I ask that you, Lord Aziel, become the Grauda King." Her eyes stared at him unflinchingly.

Aziel took a second to think it over. "Was N'goth the last Grauda King?"

Astrel nodded solemnly. "Yes, he was. The Grauda have never had a king since."

Aziel pursed his lips for a moment. It seemed a reasonable, even beneficial, request. Just as he was about to accept, Vhal placed a hand on his shoulder.

"May I, my lord?"

"You have something to add, Vhal?" Aziel replied.

"Just some concerns I wish to clear up."

Aziel gestured him forward, and Vhal took a few steps closer to the queen.

"Queen Astrel, while I am sure my lord is honored by your request, would you explain what his duties as King of the Grauda would be?"

The queen looked at Aziel, as if for permission to answer. He nodded.

"The title of Grauda King can only be bestowed by the reigning queen. It gives the bearer the authority to order all Grauda, male or female." Astrel looked around at her kneeling subjects, before turning back to Aziel. "While there is no official role for the king, I would ask that you protect my people." She looked down and her shoulders shook slightly. "We have suffered for a long time, and I am ashamed to say that I was not able to alleviate... any of it."

The other female Grauda looked at their queen. Aziel could

tell that they wanted to reassure her, but didn't dare to speak in this setting.

This somber atmosphere was shattered by a snort from Celia. Everyone turned to stare at the succubus, who crossed her arms, a single finger tapping her forearm.

"Oh, stop it with the sob story already. Knowing what you went through, I think you did quite well." She turned to Aziel. "Which reminds me, there is something you should know before you decide whether to take them under your wing."

Aziel tilted his head and waited patiently for her to continue.

"The thing is," Celia said, "the Grauda are sort of at war with Whiteridge… and by extension, with the Kingdom of Maiv."

Both Vhal and Aziel stared at her. Astrel looked livid at this news.

"So that's where they were all coming from!" she hissed.

"The Kingdom of Maiv is the one to the south of here, correct?" Vhal asked. "How did the Grauda end up at war with them?"

Celia sighed, then briefly explained what she had discovered in the nobles' carriage and in Whiteridge.

Vhal looked down, stroking his beard. "Quite a dilemma… I don't think we are ready for a confrontation with a kingdom and an established divinity."

Celia shook her head. "I don't think they will have the ability to respond properly to a threat in the Wilds… as I said, the Maivian are going to great lengths to hide their activities. Whiteridge is basically a military outpost built to look like a town. I don't know about the Odanians, but the Jannatin Empire would never allow such a thing to exist and would use it as an excuse to take out the whole kingdom if they knew."

Vhal looked thoughtful. "That might be the case, but it doesn't change the fact that there are thousands of humans already there, and if what you said is true, most if not all of them are soldiers. There is also the shrine to Adara, which at the very least means their divinity knows and approves of their action."

"You think she would move to protect the town?" Aziel asked.

"If a shrine is being used by followers to donate their mana to her as their divinity, then it is linked directly to her or her temple," Astrel said before Vhal could respond. "If destroyed, the backlash that would cause is considerable, but I do not know of this Adara or how she might react."

Aziel sighed. "How many Grauda are there, Astrel?"

"Just four thousand." The queen looked ashamed, her eyes downcast. "We have recently lost one of our females... there are only fifteen of us left, including the ones still in the colony. Of the males, eight hundred are warriors and the rest are workers. We lack the resources to breed more..."

Four thousand sounded like a lot, Aziel reflected, until he factored in that they were speaking about an entire race. "What sort of resources would you need to replenish your ranks and build a new colony near Soul's Rest?"

Astrel looked to the ground for few moments, thinking. "Food is the most urgent concern," she said as her gaze returned to Aziel. "My sisters can breed and swell our ranks, but it will take over a month for our brood to grow... If we had a place with a high concentration of earth mana or a supply of earth crystals, then it would speed up the process considerably," she added hopefully.

"We will figure everything out in time," Aziel announced. "I accept your terms, Astrel, Queen of the Grauda, and would be honored to be your king."

Astrel smiled brightly, her eyes glittering with tears, but she wiped them away before they could fall.

"As for my terms, I only wish that you be loyal to the faction and for your people to become my followers," he said.

Astrel knelt again, her head bent low. "The Grauda accept your terms, Ascended King Aziel."

As soon as her declaration was done, his faction mark heated up and a notification appeared before him.

The Grauda, led by Queen Astrel, have asked to join your faction. As faction leader, you have final say over whether or not to officially admit this racial guild.

Do you accept? Yes or no.

Aziel had no idea what was meant by a racial guild, but he smiled and quickly chose yes.

The Grauda have joined the Fallen.

Warning: the full scope of the Grauda contribution to the faction cannot be accounted for until major officer positions are filled.

Aziel let out a sigh of relief as he felt the first trickles of mana enter his vessel. It seemed that since he was both the Ascended and Faction Leader, then the Grauda joining his faction was automatically equivalent to them becoming his followers. Here in his place of power, where the drain was practically non-existent, he could feel himself begin to regenerate. Though the amount of mana was still slow, Aziel couldn't help but grin... the sensation felt wonderful.

Celia nudged Aziel. "Ascended king," she purred. "I like the sound of that."

Aziel smiled back, then gazed down at the still kneeling queen. "Astrel," he commanded. "Tell your people to start moving to Soul's Rest."

He turned to Vhal, who had been silently observing from one side.

"Please show the Grauda to one of the food stores in the Imperial Wing. I also task you with aiding her in finding a suitable spot for their new colony, as well as ensuring their protection once they arrive."

The lich did not look happy about being given this task, but nodded nonetheless. "As you command, my lord," he said with a bow.

Aziel turned back to Celia, who was now pressing against him. "Celia," he said, causing the succubus to grin in response.

"Yes, Master?" she replied, resting her chin on his shoulder and staring into his eyes. Aziel tried to concentrate.

"I assume you achieved your quest objective."

Celia chuckled. "Of course. I would not have returned otherwise." She pointed at two figures wrapped in cloth that lay behind the kneeling Grauda. "One fire and one earth weaver, Master," she said, happily.

Aziel took a second to examine their vessels and smiled. He was too far away for a clear view, but he could confirm their proficiencies. "Thank you Celia, well do—"

Aziel stopped and tilted his head as he noticed a third vessel.

It was a small one, wrapped and stashed with the other items the Grauda brought with them. Whatever it was, it was not a mana weaver and it was barely hanging on to life.

Aziel stood and looked down at the queen, causing her to flinch slightly.

"There is someone hiding amongst your belongings," he said. Vhal took a step forward, raising his staff in preparation for an attack.

Celia on the other hand, seemed just as confused as the queen by his words.

"Hiding?" Astrel asked cautiously, before turning to see what everyone was staring at.

One of the female Grauda looked up and squeaked: "Food... keep fresh, for queen."

Astrel nodded and gestured with her head toward the pile of supplies, but her expression made it clear that she wasn't sure what to expect.

The female Grauda rushed toward the pile and pulled out another object before unwrapping it.

Celia hurried over to see what—or who—was hidden under it. She opened her eyes wide in surprise.

"Melody? What is *she* doing here?" Celia asked the queen.

"You know her?" Vhal asked, relaxing his guard.

"She's one of the adventurers I hired," Celia answered, and

Aziel could almost feel the relief in her voice. Celia then pointed at the other two wrapped figures. "They were all in the same party, I thought she was as good as dead when they took her."

Celia knelt and cupped Melody's cheek before checking for a pulse. The beastkin didn't react to her touch.

"She's completely out of it. Whatever they gave her is strong stuff." Aziel couldn't figure out if the creature's presence or the fact she was alive had surprised Celia more.

Aziel sat back down on his curved rock. As he did, he noticed that Astrel was staring at the ground, her shoulders trembling.

"Are you cold?" he asked, with a hint of concern.

"No my lord," she replied.

"Then why are you shaking?"

"It is nothing," she replied, finally looking up. "You are not displeased?" she asked warily, as if expecting to be struck.

Aziel tilted his head, confused. "Should I be?"

"I have brought an unknown into your place of power… even if I didn't realize she was kept alive all this time." Here she glared at her sister, who seemed to wilt beneath the weight of it. "Others would have taken offense."

"I see," Aziel replied. "Do you wish to be punished?"

"N-no, that's not what I meant!" she exclaimed, before realizing she had raised her voice to him. "S-sorry, I didn't mean to…"

They stared silently at each other for a few seconds. As if just recognizing what she was doing, the queen's eyes suddenly opened wide, and she looked away, her face turning red. Celia, who had been grinning at their interaction, suddenly burst out laughing, which only deepened Astrel's embarrassment.

The male Grauda kneeling around their queen wore confused expressions, as if unsure whether their queen was in some sort of danger, but a few snaps from the females made them relax again.

Astrel glowered at Celia before refocusing her attentions back on Aziel. "I will kill the beastkin," she said stiffly, before leveling her gaze at the female Grauda again, who now looked on the verge of tears. "Then I will have a word with my sister about this... oversight."

"No!" Celia said before glancing at Aziel. "Maybe we can keep her alive? Treat her injuries and question her about Whiteridge and their intentions?" she suggested quickly.

It was clear she cared for this girl, though Aziel couldn't guess why. "Leave her be for now," he said.

The queen nodded, and again Celia seemed relieved.

Vhal chuckled, but then his expression immediately turned serious, the sudden shift catching everyone off guard. "Lady Astrel, I believe you are supposed to bestow my lord with a title," he said.

To Aziel's surprise, the queen's whole body flushed red.

"Astrel?" he asked, concerned.

When the queen did not reply, Vhal frowned, his eyes flashing brighter.

"You can bestow the title, can you not?" he hissed. "It's a bit early in the agreement to start breaking terms."

Celia silently moved back to Aziel's side where she wrapped her tail possessively around his waist. Her eyes narrowed now, concerned about where this was going.

Aziel tried to ignore Celia's scent and his arousal at how her lean and perfectly proportioned body was rubbing against him. "What is the matter, Astrel?" he asked slowly. "Is there something you haven't told us about becoming the Grauda King?"

Astrel took a deep breath, as if preparing herself to plunge underwater. Then she stood tall and met his eyes. Aziel was taken aback by her sudden intensity.

"You must mate with me," she declared, her cheeks still flushed, but her gaze steady.

At his side, Celia froze. Aziel simply stared blankly at the queen before him. Vhal, meanwhile, began chuckling.

Celia grabbed Aziel's head and turned it to face her. "I don't care how many women you bed, but I get to be first," she hissed. Aziel felt her body temperature rise against him.

He nodded absently, still trying to process Astrel's words, but Celia smiled and released him.

Aziel took a deep breath and tried to calm his nerves. He now had a succubus who demanded his attention and a Grauda queen who he was... what, exactly? Duty-bound to sleep with? Astrel was indeed an attractive woman, but was that really enough? And how would this lead to him gaining anything?

"Astrel," he said, "while I can't complain about being with you in... such a capacity. If I may ask, is this truly a requirement to become king?"

The queen kept her back straight, though Aziel could only assume that she was as nervous and inexperienced in this area as he.

"To be king..." she said, then swallowed. "You must bed me to be king. It is the only way to mark you with my scent, the queen's scent. It is how the others will identify you as their leader."

Vhal, who was still chuckling to himself, asked, "Scent, you say?" He grinned. "And am I correct in assuming this scent needs to be... dare I say, *reapplied,* from time to time?"

That caused both Aziel and Astrel to blush.

"Ye-yes, it does," the queen replied.

Vhal turned to Aziel, with the widest grin he had seen on the lich, his enjoyment coming through even with the ravaged state of his face. "Well, well, Lord Aziel—" he began, but Aziel raised a hand to stop him.

"Spare me your comments, Vhal. This has already been a long day." He turned back to the queen. "See to your people, Astrel. We can discuss that matter once they arrive here safely."

She bowed, then retreated out of the chamber. The other Grauda got up and ran, trying to keep up with her hurried pace.

Aziel sighed, his shoulders slumping forward slightly. But before he could do anything more, Celia was upon him, wrapping her arms around his neck and pressing her soft lips against his to kiss him, deeply.

At first, he was too surprised to react. But he soon lost himself to the unexpected assault, gripping her waist and responding ardently to her kiss, only pulling free to take a much-needed breath.

Celia was so close he could feel her hot breath brush his skin. Her golden eyes regarded him with a predatory look, as her tail began to expertly make its way into and down his pants. Aziel tried his best not to gasp and moan, but the sensations he was experiencing were overwhelming.

Several throaty coughs drew their attention away. Vhal was staring at them flatly, plainly unimpressed.

"As enjoyable as it is to watch you two, perhaps you should use one of the bedrooms," he said with disdain.

Celia slid sinuously off him, then took his hand in hers.

"No time to lose," she purred, pulling Aziel toward the chamber's exit.

CHAPTER 18

KING LUCIUS MAIVANN, second son of the late king, leaned back on his throne as he listened to two nobles shout at each other.

"The people of those lands had always paid their taxes to me!" the first one insisted.

"Which only makes your theft that much bigger!" the other noble shouted back.

"Just be truthful, for once in your miserable life! You just found out we discovered a silver deposit down there, didn't you?"

"Ha, doesn't matter if I did! That farmland is lawfully mine to administer, not yours!"

The king sighed and rubbed his clean-shaven face before raising his right hand.

"Silence!" yelled a guard who stood beside him. He wore decorated plate armor engraved with three red roses in a vertical line, the Maiv royal crest. He was a member of the Royal Guard, one of twelve that guarded the king and his family at all times.

"Your King speaks!" the guard announced.

"My lords, the interior minister will review your noble charters and ensure that the disputed land is given to its rightful owner." King Lucius sighed. "The other will pay a fine of two hundred gold coins to the treasury for wasting the kingdom's time and resources over something so trivial."

The taller noble opened his mouth to argue, but was interrupted by the large wooden double doors at the end of the throne room being swung open. A heavily armored man wearing a long red cape strode into the room, his footsteps echoing against the hard stone floor and walls.

He had short blond hair and blue eyes, just like the king, and when he drew level with the quarreling nobles he sneered at them before kneeling respectfully to his liege.

"Your Majesty. I bring urgent news," he said, keeping a calm tone, but the look in the high commander's eyes told him this was a matter that needed his immediate attention.

"High Commander," the king replied. "Approach."

The large man stood and strode toward the king's throne. He nodded at the Royal Guards, who saluted him in return, before he leaned down to whisper in the king's ear. "We have received an urgent message from Whiteridge by Wind Speak device, Your Majesty. I recommend that we gather the council."

The king frowned at his highest-ranked military commander. "He used an air crystal? Is it that dire?" he asked

The high commanded nodded.

The king turned back to the two nobles, who were still glaring at each other, apparently oblivious to the exchange.

"Leave us, now," he commanded. The nobles must have noticed his expression, as they quickly bowed and left without further complaint.

The king sighed, watching the Royal Guards shut the double doors behind them. "These nobles will be the death of me," he complained.

The high commander smiled. "It's just part of being king."

King Lucius returned the smile wearily. "You can still take the throne if you want, Baelen. I will give it to you willingly."

Baelen shook his head. "I am too hot-headed for the crown. But you know that already, little brother."

The king nodded, then sighed again. "So, tell me, what is this all about?"

"Nothing good I'm afraid, but it would be best to let everyone know at the same time."

King Lucius glanced at one of his royal guards, who saluted and marched out. "Then let us go to the council room," the king said, standing and rearranging his fur overcoat.

Baelen and two of the royal guards followed him silently out of the throne room and entered a side room less than one-third of the size. It had no windows, and the walls, like all in this castle, were built of large stone blocks. At the center stood a long, thick wooden table, with several chairs placed on both sides and one slightly more ornate chair at its head.

The king walked to the head of the table and took his seat there, while the two Royal Guards took up positions by the doors.

High Commander Baelen let out a deep breath as he took his own seat. "This armor is getting too heavy for a man of my age," he complained, rubbing the back of his neck.

The king smiled and leaned back on his own seat.

A few moments later, two men and a woman entered. The first man wore a red shirt and black pants, with a heavy fur coat over them. His black hair and thin mustache shone from the numerous oils which coated them. He was the newest member of the council, having only gained his post a few years back.

"Your Majesty," he said bowing before the king.

"Interior Minister Aden, take your seat at my table," Lucius said formally, gesturing to the vacant chairs. The young man bowed then did as commanded.

Next came the young woman. He smiled at the sight of her. With every passing year she grew more beautiful. She had long blonde hair and blue eyes just like his own. An assortment of gold earnings, rings, and necklaces complemented the long, flowing red dress she wore, which was cinched tightly at the waist. It swept the floor behind her as she came toward Lucius and bent to kiss him on his head.

Lucius watched his only daughter. She resembled her mother. Memories emerged from the depths of his mind of his time with his late wife—their first meeting in the castle's gardens, the first kiss they shared, the time they spent in a servant's room's small closet to hide from their minders. She truly was the love of his life. As king he could of have had as many wives as he wanted—his advisors at the time had certainly encouraged it, and so had his wife. But no, Phea was enough for him, and after her untimely death, he couldn't bear marrying another.

"Father?" his daughter asked, concern painting her features.

"Uh," Lucius said as he shook himself out of his thoughts. "My apologies, Crown Princess Lucienne, my beloved daughter," the king continued softly. "Please take your seat at my table."

Lucienne looked at him for a long moment, then smiled, and as she took her seat beside him, the last man approached King Lucius. He was by far the oldest member of the council—he had advised Lucius's father before him and held the honor of being the longest-serving person in the castle. He was balding, with only a few strands of white hair remaining. His dark brown eyes had lost their shine, and his wrinkled face didn't hide any of the signs of the long life he had lived.

He wore a fur coat similar to Aden's, and a large amulet hung from his neck. His back was slumped forward as he walked, and he bowed as low as his old age allowed.

"Your Majesty," he said in a strong voice that did not match the frail-looking body he inhabited.

"Foreign Minister Hagen, I'm glad to see you're back on your feet. I had no doubt you would fight through that bout of sickness. Please, take your seat at my table."

The old man smiled, then nodded and made his way toward an empty chair.

As soon as he sat, the king took a deep breath. "I, King Lucius, faction leader and Adara's blessed, welcome you to my table and ask for your counsel."

Everyone bowed their heads respectfully. Seeing this, the king then reached out and pressed a metal square built into the large table.

The metal flared to light, and loud clanks sounded from behind the stone walls as the air around the table began to shimmer. These effects grew in intensity until they suddenly stopped, leaving only a light hum.

"The Dome of Silence has been activated," the king said. It was one of the few Magitech devices with a military application his kingdom was able to make use of. No one outside the dome could eavesdrop—not even the guards who stood by the doors would hear what was being said.

Unlike the more common Magitech devices which were salvaged from long gone nations such as the Caelian Empire, the Dome of Silence was one of the much rarer First Age Magitech devices. Lucius wondered how impressive and remarkable these mysterious people must have been to create such marvels.

The high commander stood, breaking Lucius out of his thoughts.

"We have received an urgent message from Whiteridge," he said.

Lucienne rolled her eyes and the elderly foreign minister let out a tired breath.

"What is it this time?" the princess asked.

"Both Lord and Lady Tiaus have been killed on their way to Whiteridge. Their daughter survived, but went missing a few days later when she left for the Wilds with a group of adventurers. She is also assumed dead," Baelen added, his expressionless face set like stone.

The elderly foreign minister visibly sagged in his seat, and Aden clenched his jaw at the news. Lucienne remained silent.

The king closed his eyes for a few moments before opening them again and asking, "How were they killed?"

Baelen's fists closed, but his expression remained unchanged. "Grauda," he spat.

Everyone reacted with shock to that news.

"Grauda? Are they certain? What happened exactly?" Aden asked.

"It would appear the Tiaus family got a bit lost and traveled farther north of the route we had given them, where they were ambushed and butchered. And yes, it is certain, there were witnesses," Baelen replied.

"The death of the Tiauses, while tragic, can be managed," foreign minister Hagen said, coldly. "They were of minor nobility without any lands to their name, it was one of the reasons why we chose them for this task in the first place—no one would ask any questions about their disappearance."

"While that may be true, it still leaves Whiteridge without a governor," Aden replied, a little timidly. "We cannot put all the responsibility on Alistair's shoulders, especially if the Grauda are back."

"I still think we should abandon this ill-advised idea of claiming the Wilds," Lucienne added dismissively. "Even with a stronghold built, the Jannatins will not accept us claiming it for ourselves. The Odanians may be supporting our efforts in the shadows, but who here actually believes they would come to our aid if things go wrong? That settlement has been nothing but trouble from the very start."

The young interior minister cleared his throat. "Whiteridge is risky, yes, but it is a risk we are forced to take, Your Highness," he replied. "If we do not expand our borders and claim the resources of the Wilds for ourselves, then it is just a matter of time until the Jannatins take us over. The Odanians, while untrustworthy as you say, now have a vested interest in a stable and strong Maiv—enough for them to put aside their historic grudges and offer their aid... in secret at least. The Jannatins, on the other hand, have been building up a military presence at our border for some time now."

"If only the empire would be so reasonable," Lucienne retorted.

"Unlike Odana, Princess, the Jannatins have far more personal and national security reasons to see us put down," Foreign Minister Hagen replied. "Your ancestor and our founder Duke Manfre took advantage of a particularly chaotic period in the empire's history to declare his dukedom independent. The Jannatin Imperial Family consider our very existence as a blotch on their honor."

The king looked to his elderly advisor. "Is there truly no way to end this madness? Over a century has passed."

Hagen shook his head. "Perhaps if things had proceeded differently, Your Majesty. The fact that we were successful in securing our independence galvanized other groups within their territories to work toward their own. The only other time anyone had been able to secure their freedom from the Jannatins was shortly after they became a true faction. And as we all know, the case of the Tijari, or the Free State of Tijar as they call themselves, was far from typical. Even now, the Jannatins are dealing with two separate independence movements. They blame us for this trend."

The king leaned back in his seat, irritably. "Yet their focus seems solely on us. Perhaps they should blockade and attack the Free State of Tijar for a change."

Aden chuckled. "Unlike us, the Tijari achieved their independence through diplomacy, and with the support of practically every other faction in the peninsula, as well as factions we have never even heard of. They control the Bank of Tijar after all. It is their currency that we, along with everyone else uses in our dealings. Not to mention their sticky gold fingers swirling around in every nation's trade and economic success. We can only be grateful for their declared neutrality. As a single city faction, they wield massive influence and power. For the Jannatins to move against them would be the same as declaring war on the whole Eastern Peninsula."

The king nodded. None of this was new to him, but that didn't change how frustrating it was. "And what of the Ejani? Hagen, have you spoken to their ambassador?"

"I have been in talks with him for the past three days, Your Majesty," the foreign minister replied. "Their position has not changed. They condemned the Jannatin for the hostile maneuvering in the region. They offered to mediate between us to avoid any hostilities from breaking out. They are willing to keep the Jannatin back as long as no evidence of aggressive actions from our side can be brought to them. With that said, they will not risk their relationship with the Jannatins for us, which makes this a symbolic gesture at best."

The king could only shake his head. While the Ejani did help his kingdom from time to time, they did not recognize Maiv as a sovereign nation, as that would risk angering the Jannatin Empire.

"They did offer to buy our finished goods," the aged foreign minister added.

"Oh?" Aden interjected. "And what's the catch?"

"They would only buy them at half their market value, and only through intermediaries," Hagen replied. "But due to the current state of our treasury, the minister of economy is practically begging us to accept this deal, as distasteful as it might seem."

The king exhaled deeply. Since its founding, his kingdom had suffered greatly from the embargo his larger and more powerful neighbors had imposed. But even under these hostile conditions, they had survived due to the trade they conducted with other nations.

That had changed two years ago. The Jannatins had raised the stakes by declaring that if anyone conducted trade with Maiv, the Empire would tax their imports. Given the choice between trade with Maiv or the Jannatins, the decision was simple. Even he couldn't argue with that.

"High Commander," the king asked, "tell me, what are the odds of us winning a war against the empire?"

Baelen scrunched his brows together in thought, then shook his head. "I don't think we have any hope of winning. We might be able to stall them at the border, but with their firepower and highly-trained professional armies… it would cost a lot of lives to do even that. And I'm not even considering the fact that we have no effective counter for their elite Cloud Knights, or their Magitech weapons."

"One good thing is that the morale of the country is still high," Aden added, with a slight smile as he rubbed at his mustache. "The population still believe Maiv will prevail against any enemy, just like we did against Odana in the past."

Hagen scoffed at that, causing the king to raise a questioning eyebrow.

"My deepest apologies, I meant no disrespect. With the state of the economy, it would be quite the stretch to call morale high. Your ancestors also did a good job—perhaps too good a job—of retelling that battle with Odana."

"A glorious victory was needed to bring the new faction together," the king said. "Even if the details were… exaggerated, somewhat, to our benefit."

"That battle is a good example of how I believe a war with the Jannatins would proceed," Baelen interjected. "Though we outnumber them, we would pay four or even five of our countrymen and women's lives for one of theirs. Our army is brave and committed to king and country, but it is undertrained and under-equipped. I dare say it would be a massacre, and this time we wouldn't win—even if we paid the terrible cost."

"Any likelihood our divinity Adara will lend us her aid?" the king asked, already fairly certain of the answer.

Aden shook his head. "Like every other divinity, our lady Adara is bound by the rules set by the Geskian Theocracy and has sworn to the Vaya Pact, Your Majesty. If she personally moved to help us, then the Jannatin Empire's pantheon of divinities will also be free to act. The unspeakable devastation such a battle would lead to…"

Aden's words trailed off before he let out a heavy breath. "And that's assuming the Theocracy itself doesn't move against us in response. No, we cannot ask for her aid, and I don't think she would provide it even if we did," he continued with a shrug of his shoulders. "As per the pact, she is only allowed to take personal action if her place of power is threatened. The Jannatins know of this and will stay clear of the Three Flames as a result. Her Order of the Flame is a different matter altogether though; I am certain she will direct them to help us in whatever capacity they can."

The king sighed again. That was something at least. It was always the same at these council meetings: doom and gloom, with little to no good news. His kingdom's struggles would continue forever, it seemed. He really thought the sudden interest from Odana in a stable and strong Maiv would change things, but their full support was predicated on them taking full control of the Central Wilds.

"I did have an interesting encounter with a known agent of Odana recently," Hagen said cryptically. "I wanted to confirm the information before bringing it up in this council, but I think it's too important not to discuss."

"You spoke with a spy of theirs?" Lucienne asked as she gave him a sideways glance.

"More listened than spoke, I would say," the old man replied. "It would seem the Princedom is now willing to provide actual support and possibly negotiate a trade deal with us."

"Really?" King Lucius replied, surprise evident in his voice. "Why? What has changed? Have they elected a new High-lord Prince we haven't heard of?"

"No, nothing like that, and the spy didn't say," Hagen replied. "But my guess is that with many of the internal struggles coming to an end within the Jannatin Empire, the Princedom is worried they might set their eyes on their old enemies. I surmise our value as a buffer against the Empire now exceeds whatever value they equate by taking full control of our territory."

Lucius nodded and tapped his golden ring against the table. "Follow up on that, Hagen. This might just be the opportunity we needed all along. Now, before we discuss how to deal with the situation in Whiteridge, any update regarding the mana anomaly deep within the Wilds?"

Baelen shook his head. "I have heard nothing from the soldier we sent to investigate for some time now, and the Archmage of the Maiv Order has also expressed his concern over the silence of his Detector... it is safe to assume they are either dead or deserters at this point." He paused. "Besides, Captain Alistair also reported that they could no longer detect the anomaly itself. Whatever it was, it seems to have passed."

"Did the others send any teams to investigate?" Lucienne asked, crossing her arms.

On the far side of the table, Hagen shook his head. "As far as we can tell, the mana burst did not reach any major cities in the United Princedoms of Odana or the Jannatin Empire. And we saw no movements in response to it. The only reason we detected it was due to Whiteridge being so deep in the Wilds."

They all sat in silence for a long moment before the king placed his hands on the table. "Does Whiteridge have the capacity to deal with the Grauda on their own?" he asked.

"The garrison is far larger than it was when the first war with the monsters started," the high commander replied. "I cannot imagine the Grauda regaining their full strength in such a short time. With the help of the adventurers there, I predict they should be able to handle it easily."

"And if they can't?" Aden asked, his eyes narrowing slightly.

"Then we rid ourselves of that failed project and act as if it never existed," Lucienne interjected.

"Lucienne..." the king warned. "We are not gathered here to discuss how to get rid of Whiteridge, but how to save and make it prosper."

"I was against this idiotic plan from the moment it was proposed, Father. Hagen said it himself: Odana are using us as a shield against the Empire, and we accept their order as if the Adara herself ordered it! Perhaps we should just stop wasting time and declare ourselves their vassal and be done with it," she added angrily. "The chances of Whiteridge's success is so low, we might be better off invading the Jannatin Empire and taking their capital."

"It is a risk we are forced to take," the king replied. "And this is the last time we discuss this, or I will exclude you from this council," he warned.

"*Exclude* me?" the princess cried, astounded. "I am your heir and viceroy! All we do is sit here and discuss how to avoid angering those damned Jannatins, while they undermine us and attack us any chance they have! They even killed my mother—the queen—right here, in this very castle! Our home! You're willing—"

The king slammed his hand down on the table and stood. He felt his face heat up as he glared at his daughter. "We don't know who poisoned Phea!" he bellowed back. "And I am still your king! You will not raise your voice to me, or I will have you arrested for your impudence. If you have nothing to add to the discussion which would benefit the kingdom, then stay *silent*!"

Everyone glanced between him and his daughter, who herself was staring at him in some mix of shock and rage. Her mouth opened then closed a few times, before she let out an agitated breath and stared down at the table in front of her.

With the room now in silence, the king retook his seat, rubbing his forehead.

"Now," he asked tiredly, "what is this council's decision regarding Captain Alistair's message and the situation in Whiteridge?"

The other councilors glanced at each other. Lucienne only shook her head mutely.

"Sending reinforcements is difficult at the moment," Baelen answered, as if nothing had happened. "Given how high the border tensions are, it would also be risky, as I am certain our troop movements are being monitored."

"Choosing another noble to take over the governorship of Whiteridge will take time," the elderly Hagen added. "We need someone competent, but who has few to no ties and little influence. A difficult set of criteria."

"What about the Royal Guards?" Aden asked. "We can send them back again—they were instrumental the last time the Grauda were a problem."

The king shook his head. "No, not when the Jannatins are on a war footing. A hole in our protection could be just what they're waiting for."

Aden rubbed his chin. "Then the decision is simple. Taking into account the high commander's assessment, we should ask Captain Alistair to keep the council up to date with regular reports on the Grauda hunt, along with any other complications, while we continue to build up our presence in the area."

The king looked at each member and they nodded in agreement. "High Commander, send our response to Whiteridge," he ordered. "There will be no reinforcements for the time being. We will, however, send some extra supplies. They will surely need them for an extended hunt. I will also release a few of the precious wind crystals we hold in reserve so that Alistair may use them to fuel the Magitech device and keep us updated by Wind Speak more freely. Tell him to ensure that they do not make too much noise or attract too much attention to themselves."

Baelen stood and saluted. "As you command, Your Majesty." Then he frowned as if just remembering something, and took his seat again. "My apologies, but due to the urgency and importance of the other points in Alistair's message, I forgot to mention the last…"

"Which was?" King Lucius asked, wearily.

"There had been a murder. One of the original soldiers sent to settle Whiteridge was found Siphoned in an alley."

Lucienne scoffed loudly again, which caused the king to glare at her, a clear warning in his eyes.

"There is a demon in Whiteridge?" Aden asked with a disbelieving frown. "How could a demon walk around a place full of military personnel and adventurers and not be apprehended?"

"The message didn't say," the high commander replied. "But it is safe to assume they don't have a suspect, or else they would have mentioned it."

The king shook his head in dismay. "Any indication of a targeted attack? Work of a warlock perhaps?"

Baelen shook his head, "There was no mention of a warlock."

"Only one victim?"

"Alistair reported only one, Your Majesty."

"Then let us hope it remains that way. We do not have the resources to deal with a wild demon at the moment. Order the captain to focus on the Grauda. He can hunt the demon down once the main threat is neutralized."

King Lucius stood, and the rest of the council members followed suit.

"I thank you all for your counsel," he said, formally. "May Adara's flames bless us and light the way of our fine kingdom."

He then shut off the Dome of Silence and made his way out of the meeting room with a heavy heart. Dark clouds were gathering above his kingdom, and if something wasn't done soon, the flood waters would come to wash all he had left, all that he loved, away…

CHAPTER 19

AZIEL SLOWLY OPENED his eyes and tried to stretch his limbs but found it impossible to do so. He looked down to see a sleeping, naked Celia curled up beside him, her head resting on his chest. Last night had been... interesting, to say the least.

His champion had taken control as soon as they entered the bedroom. The whole experience had been overwhelming. Celia had done things to him he didn't know were possible. He wasn't complaining, of course—it all felt amazing, especially the things she did with her tail.

He had simply followed her lead until about halfway through, when he had accidentally discovered her weakness. In his excitement, he had allowed his body to be infused with more mana than normal, and she had shuddered from the experience. After that, he simply kept spiking her with his mana from time to time, enjoying her yelps, jumps and giggles.

Though it was a waste of mana he could have used for other things—more *practical* things—she enjoyed it and he enjoyed her reaction, so it had been worth it.

Aziel smiled and brushed a few strands of her platinum hair from her sleeping face. She moaned in protest and pulled him in closer to snuggle into his chest, her tail tightening around his leg. Aziel sighed and relaxed. He wasn't going anywhere soon, it seemed.

He spent this time mentally reviewing what he needed to do that day. The first thing that came to mind were the two weavers Celia had secured.

Astrel had entered during one of their breaks to inform him that the captives had been placed in one of the empty rooms on the second floor under Grauda guard. Aziel grinned at the idea of learning how to use fire and earth mana, especially with how limited Soul Weaving appeared to be.

Then there were the Grauda. Right after Celia dragged him into the bedroom, Vhal had left to fulfill Aziel's orders to look for a suitable place for their colony. Astrel had already directed some of her sisters to send word and begin the process of evacuating their former home in order to settle closer to Soul's Rest. The queen herself had decided to remain in Soul's Rest, and was sleeping in the room adjacent to theirs.

He had detected her unique vessel several times during his enjoyments with Celia. Curiously, she had kept visiting their door throughout the night before returning to her own room.

Aziel's thoughts were interrupted by a sweet moan. He looked down to see the succubus stir, then smile languidly when she noticed him looking at her.

"Good morning, Master," she purred, before pressing her lips against his bare chest.

Aziel smiled then let out a slow breath as Celia's hand slowly made its way down his chest and to his member. She pushed herself against him, stretching upward to bring her lips to his as her hands moved steadily up and down.

After yet another passionate kiss, she bent and spoke softly into his ear.

"You are the first man to wake up beside me after spending the night," she whispered.

Aziel grinned. "You will have to work much harder if you ever plan to Siphon me to death, Celia," he quipped. Celia pulled back, her eyes predatory as she stared into his.

"I went easy on you, Master, this being your first time… but don't provoke the succubus. You might not be able to handle what comes next," she said, as she slowly straddled him.

Aziel shook his head, before placing his hands on her shoulders, stopping her just shy of enveloping him.

"Not now Celia, we have much to do," he warned, and she pouted.

"Oh, fine. I'll just have to teach you some new tricks tonight then," she said with a shrug, as she slowly dismounted him and stretched seductively. "We had a little peeker last night, did you notice?" she asked, innocently.

"Peeker?" he asked.

Celia laughed. "Our dear Queen Astrel couldn't wait to see what she was dealing with."

Aziel shrugged. He wasn't particularly embarrassed by others seeing him naked. He had been naked for a long time in that mind prison, after all.

He rolled out of bed and, followed by Celia, made good use of the small bathhouse adjoining each of the bedrooms. She again tried to take advantage of their nude state, but Aziel was able to resist her advances.

After last night's experience, the effect Celia had on him was more manageable. His desire for her hadn't changed, however, if anything—he looked forward to bedding her even more.

He also liked her domineering and playful attitude, and just the thought of her gave him a feeling he had never felt before… Whatever it was, it brought a smile to his face.

As they dressed, Aziel glanced at his champion. "I will be visiting our captives to see if I can learn anything from their mana. Will you be joining me?"

"Hmm," Celia pondered, as she put on her armored greaves and shoes. "Why not? I guess with all that's happening right now in Whiteridge, it would be hard for me to look for more weavers."

Together, they made their way to the levitation platforms. On the upper level, they walked side by side toward the room where their captives were being held, their hands brushing against one another as they did. The female Grauda who stood guard outside the room tensed at their approach, but otherwise did not react.

Aziel noticed that the males who stood around her wielded far higher-quality spears and were now wearing some of the leather armor they had found in the storage room. He also noticed that the leather cuirasses had been cut open at the back to allow freedom of movement for their scythe arms. Aziel didn't remember giving them permission to take what they wanted from that particular storage room, and could only assume Vhal had done so.

He unlocked the door and entered, with Celia still close behind. The room was empty except for a plate of food, a pair of buckets, and the three captives.

Aziel's attention was drawn first to a young-looking boy, who sat in the far corner. The other two captives were female. One had long black hair and wore half broken spectacles, while the other was the beastkin Celia had pleaded for.

The young boy gazed up at him, and Aziel could see the fear in his eyes.

"You are Alexander, correct?" Aziel asked, without taking a step closer to the terrified boy.

"Don't answer him!" the black-haired girl shouted, hatred dripping from her every word.

The young boy gulped. His blue eyes watched Aziel before he nodded slowly.

"I do apologize for the less than ideal living conditions," Aziel continued, trying to smile reassuringly. "I am Aziel, the lord of this place. I wish for your help in something of great importance."

"You have a strange way of treating people you wish to ask for help," the raven-haired girl replied.

Aziel turned to look at her. "I assume you are Kim. Celia told me about you."

Kim glared at him, then at Celia. From her expression, she didn't seem to recognize the succubus.

Alexander stood on shaky feet and looked down at the floor between them. "Wh-what happened to Griff?" he asked, meekly.

Aziel turned to Celia. "Is that the big one you talked about last night?" he asked.

Celia nodded.

"Ah, I see. Then Griff is dead," Aziel said flatly.

Alexander's shoulders sagged, but it didn't appear that he was surprised by the news.

"You fucking bastards!" Kim yelled. "You won't get away with this, whoever you are!"

"Let's calm—" Melody tried to say, but Kim turned quickly and scowled at the beastkin. Melody curled more tightly into her corner, her ears drooping.

Aziel watched their interaction with some interest. Given the hostility, he was glad they weren't able to weave at the moment. Astrel had mentioned they had been fed a potion to knock them out during their travel to Soul's Rest, but that was just a side effect when given in large doses. In small doses, it prevented the usage of mana for several hours. It was one of many alchemic recipes the Grauda had developed during their war with the humans, and Aziel thought about how useful and potentially dangerous such a thing could be.

"I need to take a look at your vessel," Aziel said quickly, failing to contain his excitement. Then he frowned. "It might... it will cause you some pain. But I promise to release you once I'm done."

Kim looked genuinely surprised by the offer while Alex looked far more nervous than before. "I can't use my mana at the moment; I'm not sure why."

"You were hurt, so we gave you some medication to help you recover. Unfortunately, it also may limit your use of mana for a short time," Aziel replied. "This is one of the reasons why I need to check on your vessel," he added, as an afterthought.

"Then why was I given it too?" Kim asked.

"Just to be on the safe side,' Aziel replied.

A small smile appeared on Alexander's face.

"Thank you for taking care of my wounds. You are a weaver too, right? I can sense your mana... even without Detect Magic. You must be very strong." He looked down, as if he had said something he shouldn't have.

"I am indeed a weaver," Aziel replied. "But there will be time to talk about that later." Could all weavers sense each other, he wondered? His ability to sense soul mana allowed him to do so, but what about others? Was that why Silus had called him a monster when he first laid eyes on him?

Aziel took a deep breath and cleared his head of the thousand questions that flashed through it. "Shall we begin?" he asked. Celia, meanwhile, was leaning in the doorway with a somewhat bored expression.

Alex flinched and looked up into Aziel's eyes. "W-what do I need to do, for you to... check my mana, was it?" he asked.

"Just try to relax. Like I said, this will hurt a bit." Aziel took a few steps closer and placed his hand on Alex's chest. The boy tensed at first contact.

"You will keep your promise to release us, right?" he asked quickly. When Aziel nodded, he could feel the boy instantly relax.

Kim and Melody both watched, Kim still suspicious while Melody wore a more subdued look. The beastkin's hands rested on her injured leg, which was wrapped in cloth and secured to a long stick to keep it straight.

Aziel closed his eyes and began to repeat the process he had gone through when he looked into Celia's vessel. This time, however, he tried to avoid the pain Celia suffered. He didn't know why or at what point he had actually hurt her, so he just applied more caution to the whole process.

The familiar gray, misty vessel came into view. He could tell what types of mana the boy was proficient in from a distance, but getting the kind of detail he needed required closer examination. He prodded and poked it, then slowly peeled away a small section of his vessel to take a closer look inside.

Just like Celia, the boy had a pool of soul mana within his vessel, and it circulated around his body through his veins. Unlike Celia, however, there was a distinct lack of demonic mana—only a small mote of earth mana hovering above the pool, just as he expected.

Aziel focused on the mote and began examining the details that made it different from his own. Earth mana felt exactly as Aziel expected it to: hard, heavy, and unbendable. Its underlying structure and connections looked quite beautiful, like a piece of art.

But Aziel was surprised by how little difference there was between it and his own soul mana. Although it did feel different, the changes he would have to make to produce it were the equivalent of adding an extra pinch of salt to a lake—almost imperceptible.

He began committing the small differences to memory, so he could experiment with it later. He heard a few gasps and screams from what sounded like Kim, but ignored them. As he neared completion of the task, he was practically giddy with anticipation, and hoped Vhal was right about this.

Once he had what he needed, he opened his eyes and was met by a familiar, yet unexpected sight.

Alex was on the ground, gasping for air, both hands on his chest. Aziel looked at the boy curiously, again dumbfounded as to why this was happening. He had been extra careful this time, but it hadn't seemed to matter.

"What did you do?" Kim screamed, her voice full of anger and worry.

"Be silent," Aziel commanded, his eyes narrowing. He was trying to think and there was no time for her comments and interruptions.

Kim gulped audibly, and though her eyes opened wide, she didn't say anything more.

Aziel knelt beside the boy, closing his eyes and again focusing on his vessel. It was then that he saw the issue. It was so obvious he felt like he needed to slap himself for the oversight.

The hole he had created to peer into the vessel was still there and was slowly expanding. The boy's whole vessel was quivering unnaturally.

He tried to manipulate the edges and pull them close to seal it, but that only made it worse. The vessel ripped at multiple locations, and Alex screamed. Soul mana leaked out of the many rips, and a few seconds later, the entire thing imploded.

Aziel saw a portion of the mana shoot toward him, followed by the sensation of absorbing it. With a heavy sigh, he opened his eyes and confirmed what he already knew. Alex was dead. But the state of his corpse was a surprise.

The boy was still in a fetal position, but his eyes were hollow, and his mouth was wide open, as if in a silent scream. His skin had turned a deathly gray, and his body had shrunk considerably.

Aziel heard a surprised gasp from behind him and turned to see Celia staring in shock at Alex's withered body. She strode forward and knelt beside him to take a closer look.

"What did you do?" she whispered. "He looks like someone I Siphoned."

Aziel creased his brows. Siphon? Was that what he had done? He closed his eyes and focused before opening them again.

"No," he said. "There is no demonic mana around him or coming off him. It's still soul mana."

Celia bit her lower lip as she examined Alexander's corpse. Aziel watched her, and a disturbing thought rose to the surface of his mind. Hadn't he done the same thing to her? Had he almost killed her without realizing it?

More importantly, however, he had killed this boy after promising him he would let him go. Aziel felt something heavy weigh on his heart and shoulders. He had killed before, but always in response to a threat. Alexander had been an innocent, hadn't he?

"What's the matter?" Celia asked, and he realized she was looking at him now, concerned. "You're looking a bit pale." She reached out to brush one hand down his arm fondly and smiled.

Aziel shook his head slowly then smiled back at her, deciding to keep his thoughts to himself. "It's nothing. I'm fine, my mind just wandered a bit."

Celia pursed her lips, but didn't press him further.

Aziel relived what had happened when he examined Celia's vessel. While she had reacted the same way initially, she didn't die. Was it because she was a demon? He couldn't think of a reason why that would make a difference. But then it hit him: he had healed her.

When he saw her in pain, his immediate reaction had been to use their link to channel his mana into her. She had started feeling better afterward. This was his Soul Rejuvenation in action. He had suspected this when he first read over the skill's effects, but knowing it to be true somehow felt different.

Instead of trying to stretch the vessel to close the breach like his failed attempt with the boy, he must have filled in the gaps with his mana. Celia had to take a short nap after that, probably for her vessel to recuperate from the shock, but she was otherwise completely fine.

Aziel frowned at the implications. This meant that anyone he examined in this way was going to die unless he forged a permanent Soul Link with them.

Then there was the other matter. Aziel had just stumbled upon an ability that used none of his mana and was lethal to anyone who had a vessel, which as far as he knew, was everyone.

More importantly, there was no clear way to defend against it.

Celia had gone back to examining the body, so Aziel stood and turned toward Kim, who scrambled back against the wall, her eyes wide and her lips trembling. He stepped toward her, when Celia called out to him.

"Wait!" she asked. "Are you going to do the same to her?"

Aziel thought about it, then nodded. "No matter how distasteful I find this to be, it is something that must be done. At least the faction can extract some benefit from her sacrifice."

Kim started to panic even more, but she had nowhere to go. Celia's gaze lingered on Alex for a few moments, she then dragged her hands over his face and closed his eyes before standing. "Alright, I guess," she said, her eyes meeting his.

Aziel turned and moved toward Kim, causing her to scream out in panic.

"Please! Anything but that! I'll serve you—I'll do anything!"

Aziel shook his head. "I am sorry. I promise, I will end it quickly."

Unsurprisingly, Kim didn't take comfort in his words. She kicked at him with her feet, trying to keep him at a distance.

"Do not make this any harder than it must be," Aziel said.

She threw her broken spectacles at him then kicked his hand away when he reached for her.

At this, Aziel sighed. He raised his hands, and four thick tendrils of gray mist materialized around him before shooting toward Kim and wrapping around all four of her limbs.

The black-haired girl kept screaming, her muscles flexing and her body twisting as she struggled against her restraints. Aziel bent down and placed his hands on her heaving chest.

"I am truly sorry, but I see no other way," he said, before he closed his eyes.

He could feel Celia close by, but she remained silent, watching.

Aziel again tried to focus on the girl's vessel, but something was not right. There was another vessel here, or something that mimicked one, and Aziel couldn't help but register something sinister about it.

He explored the feeling, then noticed that not only was it made up of soul mana, the vessel also had an unusual link, but one so thin he couldn't track it. He reopened his eyes to see that he was staring at Kim's right hand, which was held outstretched by one of his tendrils.

"What is that?" he asked as he gripped her hand and focused on the source of the feeling. It was a plain-looking black metal ring.

Kim tried to pull her hand back but didn't have the strength to overcome Aziel's Soul Tendril.

"It's nothing!" she cried as she tried to twist her hand out of his grip. Failing to do so, she snarled then spat on the floor. "Let go of me!"

Celia, who had come closer, gasped at the sight of the ring before her expression twisted in rage. Aziel half expected her to strike the raven-haired girl, but instead she did something even more unexpected—she turned and stormed toward Melody, who flinched in the face of Celia's intensity.

Celia grabbed the top of Melody's high-collared shirt and pulled it down, revealing a similar black metal band—only this one was wrapped around the beastkin's neck.

"You're a slave?" Celia cried out in surprise.

Melody remained silent, but hung her head in shame.

Aziel didn't understand what was happening exactly, but he pulled the ring off Kim's finger and offered it to Celia. She quickly grabbed it.

"I'm taking Melody to another room," she stated, not waiting for Aziel's permission before offering the beastkin a helping shoulder to lean on and guiding her out of the room.

When the door had closed behind them, Aziel stared at Kim, who looked even more terrified than before. She gave the distinct impression of having been caught in the act of doing something terrible. And if what Celia said was true, she had been. Aziel didn't know much about the mechanisms of slavery, but he had read enough to know he did not support the practice.

He again placed his hand on the girl's chest and closed his eyes, going through the motions of examining her vessel. But this time, he proceeded faster than he had done with Alex. He presumed that creating a bigger hole in her vessel would lead the girl to die in less time. Although she wasn't an innocent, that didn't mean she had to suffer.

The fact that this was the second time he had examined fire mana hastened the process of learning what he needed, and it was soon done.

Aziel let out a long, tired breath as his eyes locked onto Kim's remains. The longer he stayed there, the heavier the weight which burdened his heart became. *This was necessary*, he told himself. He knew this would not be the last distasteful—perhaps even heinous—act he would find himself committing in the name of his faction. He could only hope that it would be worth it in the end.

Aziel left the room and instructed the Grauda female and her two male escorts to take care of the two corpses, a duty she accepted enthusiastically. Aziel did not want to know what they were going to do to the grayed-out flesh he left behind. He would force himself to focus on other things, like the two mana types he had yet to try out.

* * *

Aziel was surprised when Celia joined him in the training hall. She said nothing for some time as he prepared to experiment, but then she let out a frustrated sigh.

"Where did you take her?" Aziel asked, still not knowing why she seemed to care for the beastkin.

Celia looked up at him, as if just now remembering he was there. "In one of the bedrooms on the second floor. Don't worry, I told the Grauda to guard the room."

"I see."

A few moments of silence passed as they stood there watching each other.

"Did I do the right thing?" Aziel asked. His eyes drifted toward the ceiling as he tried to make sense of the mixture of feelings which weighed on him.

Celia took a step toward him and pushed herself up on her

tiptoes to peck him on the cheek. "I can't say. I guess it depends on what you do from now on?"

Aziel lowered his gaze and watched her as she stared at the floor, lost in her own thoughts.

"Celia? Are you alright?" he asked.

Celia forced a smile as she met his gaze. "I'm not sure, it's happened a few times now, but when I saw what you did to Alex, I... I felt nothing. I mean I was surprised by how he died, but that was it." Celia shook her head, "before my evolution, I think I would have felt something— anything—from witnessing someone I had traveled with getting killed, even if it was for a short time. And yet..."

"Do you regret it? Me, forcing your evolution?"

Celia let out some air from her nose, then shook her head again, "I don't, I might have lost something in the process, but I also gained a lot. It's just a bit odd for things to have changed so quickly, that's all."

Another few moments of silence went by and the feelings churning within Aziel began to bubble to the surface.

"I just took the lives of two people who couldn't fight back or protect themselves, just so that I may make use of their mana," Aziel said, wrapping his hands around Celia and pulling her in for a hug, a memory of an angry human mage in the forefront of his mind. "Maybe I am a monster," he said.

Celia pulled back, her golden eyes staring into his. "Master, you are not a monster. You help me with my hunger every day, you gave your protection to the Grauda, and I don't know what Vhal is getting out of this, but I'm sure that insufferable lich is grateful too." The intensity of her gaze mounting, Celia placed a hand on his chest. "Kim was a slaver and Alex was at the very least complacent in it. *They* were not innocents, and even if it wasn't the main reason, by killing her, you freed Melody."

Aziel raised his hand and cupped her cheek. "When—" Aziel shook his head, "if I ever cross the line, I want you to—" Celia turned her head and kissed his palm. "Yes, Master. Now let's cut this depressing conversation short. How about we do something a bit more fun? What about the mana? Did you try using it yet?"

Aziel shook his head as he let out a low chuckle. "Not yet, but we will find out soon enough." He took a deep breath before letting some of his mana drift from his hand. He focused on the stream of mana and tried to modify its structure into something like fire mana, whilst making sure he could still control it—an imitation of fire mana, in a way.

It was far more difficult than he expected. While manipulating the structure of the mana was actually simple, changing it all at once was not. As soon as he changed a single aspect of it, the whole thing would start to run wild and cause a chain reaction. The result, strangely enough, was demonic mana.

Celia was looking at him with a mix of surprise and awe. "You're creating demonic mana…" she whispered, before she walked forward into the slowly growing light-green cloud. She closed her eyes, relaxed her body, and then let out a soft moan as she began absorbing it.

While Aziel was glad Celia was enjoying herself, demonic mana was not his intended result. It was a good sign, though. If he could create demonic mana, then there was no reason why he couldn't create the rest.

He was also glad Celia was absorbing it. Already, the aggressive mana was trying to infiltrate him and corrupt his own vessel. He wasn't in any danger of actually turning into a demon, but it was an irritation.

Aziel tried again, and this time he came closer. It seemed to be just a matter of getting used to each tiny change individually, then applying them all at the same time.

Over what felt like most of the day, he tried and tried again, each attempt getting him closer to the desired result, and his progress motivated him to keep going. Celia simply stood there, soaking up all his failures.

At last, Aziel wiped his sweaty brow and grinned at the stream of red mana emerging from his right hand. He had done it; Vhal had been right.

The mana cost was far higher than weaving with his soul mana, at least double, but that didn't matter in the slightest right now. He slowly weaved an activation symbol with the fire mana. The symbol glowed brightly, bursting into flames, before dying out a second later. The whooshing sound the flames created caused Celia—who still had her eyes closed, enjoying the constant supply of demonic mana—to turn around.

"You did it?" she asked, her eyes wide open now.

Aziel laughed as he created more and more fire mana. His output kept increasing until he reached the levels Celia released when she weaved her more powerful spells. He grinned and noticed Celia's eyes narrow as she licked her lips.

"This calls for a celebration, don't you think, Master?" she whispered, as she got down on her hands and knees and began to crawl toward him, deliberately swaying her hips as she did. Aziel was too ecstatic to argue with that, letting her lean into him and slowly wrap her arms around his neck.

When he kissed her, she responded by pressing her whole body against him, hard, the sudden and unexpected force pushing him backward onto the floor. Celia was quick in taking advantage of his position and straddled him, before she began pulling off his jacket. Aziel could feel her body heat as her tail drifted along his thighs then pushed itself into his pants. He let out a gasp. A loud knock on the door startled them, breaking them out of the moment.

Celia took a deep breath through her nose, before sliding off him and stomping toward the door, her tail swishing from one side to another.

"That better not be Vhal," she mumbled. Aziel sat up, knowing that was exactly who it was.

She opened the door and sneered at the grinning lich. "You are doing this on purpose," she spat. "Go away," she added, then moved to shut the door.

Vhal grabbed the door, stopping her. "Now, now, Celia. I left you to your devices last night, didn't I?" he said, the grin never leaving his rotten face. The succubus stared at him, her eyes narrowing.

"What do you want?" she asked suspiciously.

"I found something," he said, before chuckling. "I was going to show it to our lord last night, but you brought guests, and I have been busy securing a new location for their new home."

He began digging into his robes and pulled out a rather large scroll.

"I think you two will find this just as interesting as I did," he said, as his eyes locked on Aziel's.

Aziel reluctantly suppressed his arousal—Celia had really got him going in those few seconds. He pushed himself onto his feet and rearranged his clothes. As he approached the pair, he noticed that Celia still had a frown on her face. She gave him the impression of a small animal who had just lost its treat. He couldn't help but chuckle at that, as he leaned down to give her a light kiss on the cheek.

"Don't worry, we can celebrate later," he whispered into her ear, causing her to look up at him for a moment then nod, her eyes daring him to not follow through on his promise.

Aziel turned his attention to the lich. "So, what did you find?"

Vhal passed him the scroll. "Plans, my lord. Plans detailing what the imperial family meant for this place to be." The lich's grin grew even wider.

That piqued his interest. Aziel glanced around, but there were no tables in the training room. Instead, he sat on the floor and rolled the scroll open to inspect its contents.

"What..." was all he could say at what he saw. The imperial family didn't lack ambition, that was certain. The large scroll mapped out their plans to claim the Central Wilds and build it up as the new governmental center of their empire, its new capital.

It included massive infrastructure plans, such as a dam for the great Ranvine River which ran through the Central Wilds, and tunnels which cut through entire mountains. It even mapped how the region would be divided into several districts, including one dedicated entirely to the military and another for diplomatic functions. What was noticeably missing was any mention of a residential district. It didn't seem like this governmental center had any plans for actual citizens to live here.

What it focused on primarily, however, was the expansion and transformation of the Facility into the center of power and the new home for the imperial family. The fortress would be built from the inside out, starting with the interior and then building the fortifications on the outside. These would finally be combined into a massive finished structure.

There were dimensions and notes scribbled all over the plans, and from the drawing, Aziel could tell that the first stage, the interior—with the exception of some modifications to the ground floor—was more or less completed. It seemed work was going to start on the inner fortifications next, before moving to the outer fortifications—something which would have required re-forming a large section of the mountain face.

Silently, Celia sat beside him and rested her chin on his shoulder as she examined the drawings herself.

"Is this even possible?" Aziel asked, looking up at Vhal.

"They wouldn't have begun building if it wasn't," the lich replied. "The Central Wilds is called that not because it's at the center of the continent, but because it was at the center of the Caelian Empire. We are very much at the eastern coast of the continent, east of the unmapped Great Wilds behind the Great Spine mountain ranges, but the name seems to have stuck even after the empire ceased to be."

Aziel remembered the large landmass he'd seen when he was in that white room looking down at a planet below. The portion which included the Central Wilds and all the other nations he knew was but a relatively small peninsula on the eastern side of the continent.

"It is sound thinking to have a central location to govern from," Vhal said, "so I can't fault their logic. It also confirms my suspicions of what those purpose-built administration zones on the second floor were meant to house. Ministries." He pointed at a small hallway at the south eastern edge of the plans, which stretched all the way off the page. "That underground tunnel was how they moved all the materials and manpower in and out."

"Another entrance?" Celia asked. "That's probably not a good thing to have, is it?"

"A secret tunnel would be a more accurate description; its entrance is hidden behind the throne below... I found it completely by accident. If I were to guess, then the tunnel is likely to connect to the Underdark, but we won't need to worry about anyone or thing coming in to surprise us from down there. The passage is completely caved in... just there," Vhal said as he pointed at the center of the hallway on the scroll. "I found these plans down there."

Celia stared at the lich, her mouth ajar. "This place is connected to the Underdark? Isn't that really dangerous? I've heard people go mad after going in there; are you sure the cave in is enough? Wait, did the Caelians build the Underdark tunnels?"

Vhal shook his head, but did not try to hide his amusement from Celia's response. "Not at all, the Underdark is an ancient place and predated the empire by quite some time. It's true that many dangerous and deadly things stalk its halls, but I'm certain we are safe for now." Vhal raised a hand and gave his beard a long stroke. "I wonder if the Underdark existed during the time when the ancient races ruled. An interesting question to ask Astrel."

Aziel glanced at Vhal, then Celia, who had an eyebrow raised before she let out a long sigh. "Why would the empire even do this?" she asked. "Build a new capital? And use something as dangerous as the Underdark?"

Vhal shrugged. "None of the researchers or I noticed anything when we were working here. Who knows what the imperial family was doing right under our very noses, or why they would undergo building such a place in secret? Our duty was to study and ensure the mana Lord Aziel provided kept flowing." Vhal stroked his beard again. "Perhaps that was one reason? They wanted to consolidate their power, but also keep Aziel a secret? Unfortunately, even as lead researcher of the Facility, I was not privy to the happenings of the empire during my long time serving here."

Celia and Vhal kept on debating while Aziel sank deep into his own thoughts. He didn't really care about whatever this Underdark was, or the Caelian Empire, but these plans were another story. As the birthplace of the Fallen, Soul's Rest was more than likely going to be the center of his faction. With a few modifications, perhaps inheriting the empire's plan and using it for himself was not a bad idea. The only problem was how to move forward with it.

He again began reading over the notes. One positive aspect was that the design of the fortification required very little in the form of construction materials, at least when considering the scale of it. Everything was to be carved from the mountain rock, like a massive sculpture.

At the same time, how would he even do that? Perhaps earth weaving could help, but he knew he alone wouldn't be enough—it would take too long, and it would drain him of his entire mana supply multiple times over.

No, he would need both earth weavers and labor, a lot of labor. Aziel went through his memories, and one thought kept coming up: the Grauda.

Although the ancient race had learned some new things since his now reclaimed memories of them, such as their impressive depth of knowledge in Alchemy, the Grauda had a very distinct role in the past. They had very much been the builders of his mother's faction, and with their explosive population growth rates, it would take only a short time for Astrel's people to breed the labor he needed.

That, however, led to another question. If the Grauda were the builders he believed they were, then why were they living in holes in the ground? Celia's description of their nest wasn't impressive at all... This was something he would need to discuss with Astrel as soon as the Grauda were settled.

Aziel smiled and rolled the scroll back up before meeting Vhal's ethereal blue gaze with a wide grin, causing the lich to stop whatever he was explaining to Celia and look at him questioningly.

"Vhal, there is something you need to see," he said, as he let out a burst of red mist from his hand.

CHAPTER 20

CELIA SAT ON the bed in the middle of one of the many second floor bedrooms of Soul's Rest, with Melody draped over her lap. She glanced down and ran her hand through the beastkin's brown hair and smiled. A few days had passed since she had placed Melody in this room, and Celia had visited her every day since to check on her recovery.

Melody's leg was wrapped in several layers of a slightly damp cloth the Grauda had provided. Celia recognized the horrific smell coming off it—it was the same potent smell she encountered in her short tour of the Grauda colony. Whatever that concoction was, however, it worked fast. Melody was already able to put weight on her leg even if she was in pain most of the time. But yet again the Grauda provided a pink colored potion to dull it.

Celia wondered where all these recipes were coming from, but Astrel would not tell her anything. She supposed it didn't really matter. Celia was just glad Melody hadn't lost her cheerful personality. The beastkin still tried to stick to the succubus at all times, just as she had when Celia was masquerading as Miley. Celia didn't know if this lack of respect for personal space was specific to Melody, or if it was some quirk of her race. Beastkin were not a common sight in her life.

The Grauda queen had kept her distance from Celia, only

speaking to her if she absolutely had to or if Aziel commanded her to. Even then, she would simply call her "demon" and scowled at everything and anything Celia said or did.

Celia didn't let it bother her, though. It wasn't as if she needed to be friends with the arrogant bug. She instead focused her attentions on Melody.

Ever since Melody had kept Celia's dagger a secret from her party members, Celia had felt that something was off, but she never would have guessed that Melody was a slave. A battle slave, to be exact, which were usually bought by merchant caravans and nobles to provide protection.

The only reason Celia hadn't put the pieces together earlier was because Kim had been an awful slave master—not awful in how she treated Melody, but in how little control she commanded over her as her master. Melody had been able to hide the dagger from the team because Kim had not ordered her to never lie or keep secrets from them. That wasn't due to her being kind or trustful, just stupid and naïve—at least, that was Melody's opinion.

Melody wasn't loyal to them at all. They had bought her from a slave trader just before they conducted their adventurer's exam because they were desperate for a fourth member. Having slaves in an adventurers' party wasn't that rare, either; Celia had heard of some parties that were made entirely out of slaves, except for one overall master.

Celia chided herself for not studying the adventurers party she had hired more closely. The fact that Melody was a slave would have been listed in the book they provided her in Whiteridge, but she had only been interested in weavers at the time, to the point where she didn't even hazard a glance at the non-weavers of the group.

Celia tried apologizing to her for how things had gone, but Melody didn't seem to hold anything against Celia or Aziel for their actions, nor did she seem to care that Celia gave her to the Grauda as food. She really had given herself over to the life of being a slave.

There was one thing the beastkin did seem to find galling, however. The beastkin found it hard to believe that Miley was in fact Celia. Celia in turn had a hard time convincing her otherwise.

She even tried to Shapeshift back into Miley, but found that too much time had passed since she'd first come into contact with the girl. Apparently, she could only save a template for a total of ten days, one per level of the skill, a limitation annoyingly not mentioned in the skill's description. She could refresh that period by coming into contact with that person again, but that wasn't really an option seeing as Miley was dead.

Celia was finally able to convince Melody of the truth by showing her the dagger—there couldn't be more than one of a weapon that powerful, after all. She also Shapeshifted into a copy of the beastkin to prove it was possible. Celia was sure that given enough time, Melody could be persuaded to serve her master, and recent events had given her an idea as to how.

Aziel had been laying out plan after plan for the Central Wilds and how he would claim it for their faction. Celia found the whole thing amusing for the most part. She was almost certain this enthusiasm was due to Aziel being trapped in Soul's Rest for so long.

But as his champion, she felt obliged to do what she could to help her master's plan along. And one thing he didn't seem to be thinking of at all, was how expensive it would all be. If he was going to create a country out of his faction, he would need an economy, and that needed money—a lot of it.

Melody was from the Free State of Tijar, a country ruled by traders, for traders. "So, Melody, are you a merchant?" Celia asked the beastkin, as she scratched her behind her furry ear.

Melody's purring stopped as she looked up at her, her feline eyes narrowing. "I am, I mean… was."

"Was?" Celia asked curiously.

"I still have the trader skill, but I haven't done any trading in a while…" she replied, her fluffy tail wagging slightly.

Celia hesitated as she prepared to ask her next question. It was the question she had avoided asking ever since she found the band on her neck, but she couldn't delay it any longer.

"Melody... can you tell me how you became a slave?"

Celia felt Melody's whole body stiffen, but then the beastkin sighed, deflating. "When I was still in Tijar, I used to be part of my father's trading company. We were small, but we traveled all over the peninsula, even made it as far as Anoria. I loved meeting new peoples and showing them all the things we could provide them through our trading company."

Melody remained silent for a second, and Celia noticed a ghost of a smile as the beastkin recalled her past. Then her face fell.

"When my father passed away, I suddenly discovered that due to some secret dealings that went awry, his company was in debt—a lot of debt, more than I could ever pay... so I was sold, along with all my belongings and my father's company to make up for it."

Celia shook her head sympathetically. She had made sure to update her master with regards to the beastkin every night—after they had their fun, of course. Rather annoyingly, he would remain silent and only listened to her at those times, not offering her any opinion on the matter. But he was visibly interested in the intelligence Melody provided about the tension between Maiv and the Jannatin Empire.

Melody didn't seem to have any qualms talking about that, either. Her expertise in scouting made her far more observant than Celia. She had provided approximate troop numbers and composition, as well as some of Whiteridge's patrol timetables. But more importantly, she was a wealth of knowledge when it came to the current geopolitical situation between the surrounding nations.

The kingdom's intentions seemed straightforward: build up their presence, subdue the monsters that had made the Central Wilds their home, and claim it for themselves. But Celia couldn't see that resulting in anything but a full-scale war.

Were they hoping that building a stronghold here would deter their enemies from striking? Celia didn't think so. The real question was whether the Maivians were looking for a war, or simply preparing for the inevitable. Her master was leaning toward the latter.

That made her wonder what might be going on in her birth country. Did they really not know of Whiteridge? Or maybe they thought it wouldn't matter. The Jannatins were far more powerful militarily than the kingdom in practically every sense.

Celia shook her head. It was not the time to worry about those politics. With the Grauda moving in, things were about to get pretty busy around here.

Celia got up from the bed, sliding Melody off her, which the beastkin didn't appreciate. But Celia ignored that and left the room, making sure to close the door behind her. She saw the three Grauda male guards assigned to guard the door look at her curiously as she put her hand into her enchanted pouch and pull out a small black ring. She stared at it. If she wanted, she could simply wear it and order Melody to serve them…

But the magic used in slavery was an offshoot of the Demon Binding ritual. No, she wouldn't do something she so feared to another.

Placing the ring back in her pouch, she turned then recoiled in surprise, letting out a small yelp at the sight of a wisp-like creature hovering in the air in front of her. It had pinholes for eyes and a larger one for a mouth, which made it look like its mouth was open in a surprise at all times. It was kind of adorable, in fact. She moved to pet it—but then let out another yelp, this time in pain, and pulled her hand back immediately.

Warning, you have sustained a minor injury!

Not only had it somehow burned her hand, Celia felt a sudden weakness within her mana vessel—though that didn't last long.

She growled at the wisp, thinking of which spell she should use to vaporize it, until it began to speak with her master's voice.

"Celia, come meet me in my place of power immediately. We need to discuss a few things," it said.

Celia blinked rapidly, as she stared at the peculiar creature before her. She then Inspected it.

You have successfully inspected your target.

Name: Soul Wisp
Race: Elemental, Conjuration
Rank: Varied
Mana: 95/100
Level: 10

She studied the notification carefully, then sighed. Conjuration meant that this creature was born of mana, and once it exhausted its supply, it would simply puff out of existence. Swallowing her annoyance at being burned by such a creature, she made her way down to the levitation platforms, the wisp following closely behind her.

On her way down, the platform made a stop at the first floor of the Imperial Wing, where she was joined by Vhal and Astrel, each with their own wisp hovering behind them.

"Ah, Celia," Vhal said, as he stepped onto the platform. "How goes the interrogation?"

"As expected," she replied, uninterested.

Astrel stared at both of them stoically, but said nothing.

"Were you summoned by our lord as well?" Vhal asked as they descended to the ground floor in a mostly uncomfortable silence.

Celia simply nodded and pointed to the wisp behind her with her thumb. They would find out why soon, she guessed.

As they all entered the crystal chamber, Celia could see Aziel sitting on his curved rock. He had utilized the last few days experimenting with earth and fire mana, but spent practically all his spare time here so that he might regenerate.

He looked up at them and smiled. "Ah, you're here. Perfect."

"How may we be of service, my lord?" Vhal asked with a slight bow, which Astrel mimicked.

"I just wanted to tell you of my plans. You three represent the highest-ranked officials of the Fallen, after all."

Celia raised her hand awkwardly at that.

"Yes, Celia?" Aziel asked.

"I don't really have a position in the faction, Master…" she said, somewhat meekly.

"Perhaps not an official position," he replied almost immediately, "but you are my champion, a representative of my will. Your position is only second to mine."

Vhal chuckled. "That is true."

Celia found herself letting out a breath. She hadn't realized that not having a position in her master's faction had bothered her as much as it did. But now that she knew otherwise, she felt a wave of relief wash over her.

"With that settled," Aziel continued, "I wish to discuss the system of government my faction is to employ."

Celia wasn't expecting that. "Isn't it a bit early to be creating a government?"

"Possibly, but I would rather have the foundation prepared beforehand instead of scrambling to establish one when it is needed."

Celia kept any further objections to herself. Creating a system of government now felt like preparing for the arrival of a guest they didn't know existed. Perhaps this was again due to her master having too much time to himself in this place. Maybe she should start intruding into his free time a bit more, just to give him other, more pleasant things to think about.

"It is clear to me that the Fallen, unlike the factions around us, will likely not be a single or dual race majority. Instead, it will be a collection of many races—assuming we succeed in gathering the ancient races, of course."

Aziel paused to look at each of them.

"My proposal is this: I shall establish a governing council. An inner council, if you will. It will contain a chosen representative of each member race, and allow for open and unfiltered discussion so that any concerns and worries—which I am sure each of the races will have unique forms of—will be properly heard. It will also be a place which allows for discussion regarding how the faction should move forward. The council will be given the power to create laws, propose initiatives and even declare war... as long as a majority votes in favor of it. That's as far as I've gotten," he added.

Vhal chuckled again. "Where did you get this idea from, my lord?"

"Ah, it was a form of government another empire employed... the Borins, I believe their name was. It was detailed in one the books in the study, penned by the imperial family... it was mostly a criticism of that form of government, but I rather liked it."

Celia remained quiet. She didn't know why her master wouldn't just declare himself king and be done with it, but then again, this was not remotely within her sphere of expertise. They might as well have been discussing how the levitation platform worked.

The insect queen, on the other hand, seemed deep in thought.

"Astrel?" Aziel asked. "Any concerns?"

Astrel looked up, surprised, then glanced quickly away as if scared of what he would do to her if she spoke.

Aziel stood and drew close enough to gently cup her chin, forcing her face him. "Astrel, you may speak freely to me. I wish to hear your voice and opinions." The Grauda queen looked into his eyes then smiled.

"I... I confess I am concerned," she mumbled. "You are giving away all your power as Faction Leader to this council, who might do things you do not agree with." Her voice became more confident the more she spoke. "In principle, I think this council is a good idea—the Collective also had one, so that all its members could have a say in government. But we swore ourselves to you, not some council of races. I think you should preside over the meetings. Any and all majority decisions would have to go through you or your appointed Viceroy for final approval or rejection. That way, you would still be the one in power, the one with the final decision."

She glanced at Celia.

"Perhaps your champion can also take on some of the burden," she added as an afterthought.

"Nope," Celia protested immediately. She might have wanted a place in the faction, but approving laws? That was too much. "That sounds too tedious for me," she complained.

Astrel scoffed loudly at that. "Of course it would be."

Celia rolled her eyes. "It's almost as tedious as keeping track of a certain bug that keeps sticking itself to our bedroom door every night," she said, sweetly. "You know, you could simply join us."

Celia wasn't against her master having multiple partners. Such an arrangement was quite common, especially in human society. A man having multiple wives was normal in the majority of the nations within the Eastern Peninsula.

"Our master has gotten a lot of practice, you know," she purred, moving closer to Aziel. Her finger traced his jaw, then ran down his shoulders and arm. "He's gotten quite good at it now."

Aziel sighed. "Is this really the time, Celia?"

"You worry too much, Master," she said as her tail slowly wrapped around him. "I'm only trying to help."

Her master had become far more adept at controlling himself and withstanding her teasing advances. While it had been fun to play with him when he was shy and nervous, this hard-to-please version also worked for her. Celia leaned in and their lips touched for a moment before two loud coughs interrupted them.

They both turned to see Vhal staring at them. His eyes were

dimmer than usual as he leaned tiredly on his staff. Beside him, Astrel stood straight as if trying to make herself look taller and wore an indifferent expression on her face. But Celia could feel the nervous energy, and practically smell the want coming off her.

Just as she was about to toss a barbed remark, Aziel abruptly pulled away from her and stared toward the exit of the chamber.

"Someone is here," he said, before relaxing somewhat. "A Grauda female? A new one."

Astrel's antennae stood at attention as she quickly made her way down the path, only for the female in question to burst in and glance around frantically before bowing low before her queen.

"Queen," she squeaked.

"What is going on?" Astrel demanded, looking down at her sister. "You were supposed to help with migrating the colony."

The female Grauda finally lifted her head to face her queen. She looked haggard, and her breathing was labored. She must have been running for a long while. "Colony... attacked," she squeaked before looking down again. "Humans... many."

Celia could see the queen's whole body start to shake at this news.

"I thought we would have more time," she whispered, before turning to Aziel and kneeling. "Please allow me to go back to my colony and save as many of my people as I can. With my help, I should be able to save a few."

Her shoulders were trembling, and Celia could see the desperation in her eyes. She turned to see Aziel gazing down at his newest follower with an inscrutable expression on his face.

"No," he declared, his voice low. Everyone stared at him in disbelief. Was he going to abandon them? That would only leave the few Grauda who remained to repopulate the whole race.

"Mas—" Celia began, but Aziel raised his hand to stop her.

"Astrel, you will stay here at Soul's Rest. You will oversee the construction of your new home. As the last and only Grauda queen, with no other to take your place, you are far too important to risk."

"But—" Astrel tried to protest, but he again raised a hand to silence her.

"There is also the matter of officially making me your king," he said, before taking a few steps forward and placing his hand on her head and rubbing the space between her antennae softly with his thumb. "Do not fear. I promised to take care of your people, and I will."

Astrel looked up into his eyes for a few long moments. She must have seen something there, as her fearful expression dissolved into one of confidence and she nodded. But even then, Celia could tell she was putting on a brave face.

Aziel turned to Celia and grinned. "My champion, I think it's time to officially unleash you upon our enemies."

Celia grinned back at that and bowed. "As you wish, Master. I will make them suffer for coming after us."

"Prioritize the safety of my followers, Celia. Killing the humans is not your mission. You will travel to the Grauda colony and escort them back here safely." Aziel then turned to Vhal. "You will join her and act as backup. Help her when things get troublesome for the Grauda or herself."

Vhal frowned slightly. "My Lord, my place is here by your—"

"I know that, Vhal," Aziel interrupted, in a commanding tone. "But as your lord, I require your assistance in this matter. Your power will ensure success with the least amount of casualties. I will also feel better knowing you are there, especially since we don't know what we are up against. You are my insurance."

Vhal didn't seem happy about this, but bowed nonetheless. "As you command, my lord,"

Celia didn't think she needed Vhal, and honestly she didn't like the idea of having the lich there if things went south. She still didn't trust him, either, but was starting to trust that he was loyal to Aziel at the very least.

Aziel knelt in front of Astrel, who was staring at him, her lips trembling. "I…I can't put my people's survival in the hands of an undead lich and a lazy demon," she said, her eyes pleading.

Celia couldn't help but roll her eyes.

"Then put their survival in my hands," Aziel replied. "I am sending my champion and most trusted advisor, Astrel. If they cannot save your people, then no one can." He leaned in and kissed her gently on the lips, which caused the queen's whole body to stiffen and blush red, her antennae twitching erratically.

Celia found the whole thing amusing—the arrogant queen was so inexperienced in this field that she was almost childlike. Not unlike how her master had been, now that she thought about it.

She moved closer to the pair and placed her hand on her master's shoulder. When he turned to face her, she surprised him with a kiss of her own, far more passionate than the one he had just given Astrel.

Celia grinned as she glanced toward the Grauda queen, who looked like she was going to pass out with embarrassment. Then she nodded toward Vhal, who seemed merely bored as he waited for them to finish.

"Well, let's get going. We have some Grauda awaiting our arrival," she said, just as a notification appeared in front of her. From the look on Vhal's face, he seemed to have received one too.

Your faction leader has offered you a faction quest:
Evacuate the Colony.
Your faction leader has tasked you with the protection and evacuation of his faction's people and followers.
Quest objective: Evacuate the Grauda from their colony and escort them back to Soul's Rest.
Reward: Variable

Both Vhal and Celia grinned at that. But just as they turned to leave, a hand gripped Celia's shoulder, and she turned to see her master place a letter into her pouch with a smile.

"Master?" she asked.

"Make sure this is delivered to whoever is in charge of Whiteridge after you have secured the Grauda's safety," he whispered into her ear. "I must admit this is moving faster than I anticipated, but we shall take advantage of it nonetheless."

Celia stared at him for a moment before shrugging. "As you command, Master." She leaned into him for another kiss then jogged out of the chamber to catch up to the lich.

CHAPTER 21

CELIA PACED BACK and forth beneath a large tree, frustrated. Bringing Vhal had been a mistake; the lich had asked for a rest every few hours, so the same distance that had taken a few days to traverse with Astrel was going to take at least a week now. She couldn't fathom how an undead could feel tired in the first place.

"Can we go now?" she growled, as she glanced over. Vhal was leaning against a tree on the opposite side of the small clearing they had found.

"Why are you in such a hurry, Celia?" he replied, unperturbed. "The humans have surrounded the Grauda. They are besieging them, not assaulting them. A few days won't change that."

Celia seethed. "I don't know. Maybe because your lord ordered you to save them all? A few days under siege means casualties. I have seen their colony; they didn't have enough of that fungus to feed everyone there."

Vhal sighed and raised his arms in surrender. "Alright, let us be off then," he said tiredly, his signature grin noticeably missing.

Celia couldn't help but ask, "For someone who has been trapped for so long, you don't seem happy to be on the outside."

Vhal's eyes flashed slightly before he turned away. "I might have been the only person in the Facility who actually wanted to be there..." he said stiffly, a moment later. "Every second son or daughter of every noble house was to be surrendered into the service of the imperial family."

He flashed her a small smile.

"Surrendered... that's what they called it. To me it was a freedom—freedom from the politics of the imperial court—" He stopped abruptly, his eyes narrowing.

Celia had also felt it. Something was watching them, but she couldn't tell from where. She nodded slightly to Vhal. Without another word, they slipped out of the clearing and continued on their way silently.

Whoever or whatever the thing was, it had some remarkable stealth skills to be able to keep its presence hidden to this extent from two Elders. Even after a mile, it was still following them. Celia's heart started to beat faster as she tried her best not to grin.

Since she had become an Elder, every creature she had encountered had run away from her, but now the opposite was happening. She itched to try out her new abilities.

In another small clearing, Vhal stopped suddenly and turned to face the forest behind them. Celia stopped too, looking at him curiously.

"What are you doing?" she whispered.

"I will not be stalked," he spat, then began weaving with his black necrotic mana. He tossed the spell above him and said, "Detect life," before a light pinging sound began emanating from the black symbol hovering just below the crown of the surrounding trees.

Vhal closed his eyes then grinned sadistically. He again started weaving something, as a being from Celia's nightmares showed itself from behind a tree and shrieked so loudly, she had to cover her ears.

The creature had a black hairy carapace, and its many black eyes glittered in the sunlight as it stared at her. It used its eight long legs to quickly carry its bulk toward them.

Vhal yelled, "Necrotic Blast," and a ball of what looked like black tar shot forward toward the spider, slamming into its head.

The creature drew back and shrieked in pain, as its flesh started melting from the point of impact. It wobbled then slammed into a nearby tree over and over again as if trying to shake something off it, but the melting hole the spell created kept going deeper. Within a few moments, it had fallen to the ground, its legs coiled inwards.

"I feel better already," Vhal commented before taking a few steps toward his kill.

Celia stared at the corpse in disgust. "Spiders…" she mumbled. "I hate spiders."

Vhal poked it with his staff, then grinned.

"Why are you so happy?" Celia asked. Its melted head smelled awful, and its hairy black legs were making her skin crawl.

"Of course I'm happy!" Vhal exclaimed. "I have never seen an Arachne in the flesh. I think this is a crawler, one of the smaller of their kind."

"Small?" Celia cringed. This thing was the size of a large dog and it was considered *small?*

"Well, their young are smaller, of course," Vhal replied happily, before kneeling beside the corpse to examine it more closely. "Quite a hard carapace… Hmm, as expected, no venom in this one."

Celia shook her head as she waited impatiently for Vhal to finish. The crawler's many eyes and curled legs disconcerted her, and she couldn't stand being near the thing.

Vhal took his time to note down some observations in a notebook before turning to Celia and grinning again. "The good news is that this crawler seems to have been alone. The bad news is that it won't be for long, as they usually work as scouts for an Arachne cluster."

"Scouts? You mean more of them are coming?" Celia frowned suddenly, a thought occurring to her. "They were avoiding me all the way to Whiteridge and back. Why the sudden change?"

Vhal shrugged. "Perhaps they tolerated you at first, but your repeated intrusion couldn't be ignored anymore. Who knows how they think?"

Celia looked up at the trees, then nervously scanned her surroundings. The crawling sensation on her skin was still present, and her unease only intensified. This was not what she'd had in mind when she'd wanted to try out her power.

"Are you sure we aren't being watched?" she asked, her eyes narrowed as she slowly reached for her dagger.

Vhal chuckled. "No, I am not. Detect Life has a limited range."

Celia scowled. How could he be so nonchalant about their situation? They were supposed to reach the Grauda colony as quickly as possible, and now they were being stalked and hunted by spiders. Her features hardened as she glared at Vhal, who only looked back at her questioningly.

"Let's kill the Arachne in the surrounding area," Celia declared.

"And why would we do that?" asked Vhal.

"If they are willing to attack two Elders, one of which they were avoiding before, then what do you think will happen when we come through here with a large number of helpless Grauda? We may be strong, but we can't defend that many from all sides. We're only two people, after all." And killing them would also make her feel a lot safer at night, but Vhal didn't need to know that.

The lich stroked his beard thoughtfully, before nodding and grinning. "Perhaps you are right. I would rather avoid losing too many on the way back. If we ingrain fear into the hearts of these Arachne, then we might be able to use a more direct path back."

"Great," Celia said, already heading deeper into Arachne territory.

It didn't take long for the spiders to react to their presence. The paranoia Celia had been experiencing was confirmed as a cacophony of noise erupted around them. Shapes materialized out of the trees and began advancing on them. It would seem the Arachne had had them surrounded for a while, and now that the intruders had made their intentions clear, they were going to defend their territory. Violently.

"Well… this is unfortunate," Vhal said as he cast an eye over the growing number of spiders surrounding them.

"Unfortunate? That's all you have to say about this?" Celia said indignantly. She pointed at one spider, its many eyes staring back at them. "Look at that thing—it's the size of a horse!"

"It's a soldier type. Very tough, but no venom," Vhal replied casually, before pointing at another spider standing on a low branch. "That's a web spinner. Also no venom, but can throw balls of web which expand when they land… be careful of those, it will most likely mean death in this situation."

Celia stared at the lich, her mouth slightly parted. "Are you enjoying this?" she yelled. "Look at them all! I can't dodge a dozen— what did you call them?—web spinners tossing white goop at me at the same time."

Vhal chuckled. "Calm down, Celia, and look at the big picture. They do outnumber us, but we are Elders and they know it."

Celia took a deep breath, then scanned the growing swarm surrounding them. Vhal was right. Something was wrong. Why weren't they attacking?

The lich began releasing copious amounts of necrotic mana from his hands. The black mist swirled around him as his eyes flashed, and Celia could only stare in horror. He looked like death personified, and his mad chuckling wasn't helping.

"Tell me, Arachne! How will you deal when death's chill comes calling?" he cried, and the black tide of spiders retreated a few paces in response.

Those things were afraid of them! Celia couldn't help but grin. Here she was thinking they were going to be swarmed and killed, when the spiders were in fact afraid of *her*. She laughed and mirrored Vhal by releasing her fire mana too.

The surrounding spiders shrieked, then began to part slightly, catching the pair's attention.

"Arrogant trespassers," a feminine but sharp voice hissed.

Celia focused on the one figure that looked decidedly different than the nightmarish creatures around her. It walked slowly toward them, a long mane of black hair flowing from side to side with its movements.

A woman—or at least, from the waist up. Her white skin contrasted with the black pools she had for eyes, whose glare seemed to promise an agonizingly slow death. Her lean upper torso was covered with a white dress, which had a V-neck so deep Celia had to wonder how it wasn't falling off. The material looked fine and silky, and it moved gracefully with her.

But it was the rest of this woman which gave Celia pause. The white skin of her upper body differed strongly from the black chitin of the spider thorax and legs that made up her lower half.

Vhal and Celia both stopped their posturing and turned to face the stranger. Celia immediately activated her Inspection.

You have successfully Inspected your target.

Name: Asheeke
Race: Arachne, Princess
Rank: Lesser Enlightened
Level: 26

The princess was so enraged, she didn't even seem to notice Celia Inspecting her.

Vhal grinned then bowed slightly. "My, my… and who might you be?"

"Who I am is not your concern, interlopers. You will leave our territory. *Now.*" Her tone was sharp and an *or else* was implied.

Vhal laughed, and Celia glared at him. This crazy lich was going to get them killed! The princess might have been only half her level, but numbers weren't everything.

"My name is Vhal'nuel," the lich said, and paused for a moment before continuing. "I am a follower of the Ascended Aziel, whose faction will soon rule these lands, which happen to include your territory. I suggest you join us if you wish your race a prosperous future."

Celia kept staring at Vhal, trying to understand his plan. What had happened to keeping a low profile?

"The Ascended Aziel, you say," the spider woman said, before placing a perfectly manicured finger on her chin in mock contemplation. She shrugged. "Never heard of him."

Vhal turned to Celia with a bored expression. "I believe our original plan was correct. These Arachne don't seem to understand the power being directed against them. Kill them all." He then sat down and pulled out his notebook, which to Celia's disbelief, he began reading.

Celia stared at him. "Vhal? What are you doing?"

"Hmm?" He looked up at her. "Oh, this is most likely going to turn into a battle. I'm only here to help when things go bad, so until then you're on your own," he said, then went back to reading.

Celia blinked a few times, before turning to look at the spider lady, who seemed equally confused about the situation. She didn't wait long, however, the spider princess pointed at them and the surrounding spider swarm surged forward.

Celia cursed and dashed toward the lich, while simultaneously weaving a spell. She glanced up to see several balls of sticky webs reach their apex and begin their descent, aiming straight for herself and Vhal. She cursed again and skidded to a stop in front of the lich, then quickly used the glowing hot symbol she created and scribed a fiery circle around them.

The symbol marked the ground with a bright orange glow, and as soon as she connected both ends, Celia yelled, "Eruption!"

The orange markings exploded upward, as a wall of flame at least twenty feet high roared into being around them. The webbing above burned and vaporized as it was confronted with the extreme heat.

But Celia and Vhal were not spared from it, either. Surrounded by the flames, they were slowly being cooked alive. Celia groaned as the spell glowed brightly in her hand—then yelled again and pushed it forward. The symbols in her hand slowly rotated, and the walls of fire began to tilt outward.

She took a moment to glance at Vhal, who was still—unbelievably—absorbed in his book.

Then the heat inside the circle dropped considerably, while the opposite was occurring on the outside. It took a while for the walls to tilt low enough for Celia to see the other side, but she grinned when she did.

She already knew that she had killed a lot of her opponents, due to the mana her vessel was absorbing, but seeing it in action was a whole other matter. The only word that came to her mind was *mayhem*. The spider swarm had scattered wildly as they tried to avoid getting roasted by the intense heat.

Their screeching was so loud that Celia had a hard time listening to her own thoughts, but the satisfaction of finally being able to use her Elder abilities to their fullest made it all worthwhile.

It took a few more moments for the spiders to get far enough away to not be affected by the flames, which were now almost parallel to the ground.

It was a surreal situation—it almost looked like she and Vhal were standing in the middle of a sun, the flames flaring around them. It was the first time she had used this spell, as weaving it had been impossible for her as a Lesser succubus.

She looked around for threats, but even the web spinners had retreated from their high perches, their trees now blazing. She was pleased to see the charred remains of countless spiders still alight around them, but her smile faltered when her gaze fell on the princess.

The spider creature was smiling back at her, which brought back that crawling sensation on her skin again. It was a predatory smile that made it clear she was not worried about this development. The reason for her confidence became abundantly evident only a few moments later.

A massive spider appeared from behind her, its bulk barely able to fit between the trees. Its height was close to a two-story building, and Celia gaped at it. How had she and Vhal not noticed this before? Or maybe the lich had noticed, but didn't think it worth telling her about. She quickly activated her Inspection skill again and stared in disbelief at the results.

You have successfully Inspected your target.

Name: Raikkat the Destroyer
Race: Arachne, Prince
Rank: Varied
Level: 30

She clenched her jaw. This had to be some cruel joke—that thing would probably have killed her with a glance before her evolution. Celia again focused on her spell. The symbol flashed and began to spin faster in front of her hands.

She sighed in relief at the sight. Eruption was a multi-effect spell, the first time she had used one of those. Seeing that it was working as expected, Celia stared back at the spider lady with a wicked grin.

The flames around her began to coalesce into several tall pillars which Celia directed toward the large spider.

The creature didn't even have a chance to dodge them, struggling as it was to fit between the trees. The fire lances streaked through the air and slammed into its front and flank, exploding on contact. The resulting shock waves hurled hundreds of spiders into the air and flattened the area around them.

Celia took a deep breath and the fiery spell symbol finally faded from her hand. She sank down on one knee as the drain of using a rank four spell finally began to register. She couldn't remember the last time she had felt so drained of mana, and the only thing keeping her conscious was the mana she was continuously receiving from her master.

She looked to one side and saw Vhal look up, nod a few times, then go back to reading. Celia cursed under her breath. She was going to kill him after this, she promised herself.

With a grunt, she pushed herself onto her feet again and scanned her surroundings. The once green and forested area was now a wasteland. The ground was scorched, while the remains of burned trees and spider carcasses littered the area. Black smoke filled the air, reducing the visibility drastically.

There were no open flames, however. Her spell must have drawn on all the fires to power itself up and the explosions hadn't left any behind.

Celia shook her head at the devastation. What would a level six or even eight spell do if her level four spell could so utterly destroy an area of this size? She turned and took a step toward the lich, then froze as a loud crack of shattering wood rang out behind her.

Her whole body tensed as she slowly turned to see exactly what she had hoped never to see again. The giant spider was lurching toward her—singed, but not dead.

Its heavy legs dug into the ground with every step, its multiple black eyes reflecting her image. Green viscous liquid dripped from its twin fangs as it stood on its hind legs, its size blocking the sun completely. It screeched, the sound so loud she had to cover her ears with her hands, then charged her.

Celia tried to roll to one side, but her body wouldn't move as fast as she was getting used to. She looked up toward the charging colossus… perhaps using such a powerful spell hadn't been a good idea. With so little mana left in her vessel, she was in a severely weakened state. Her muscles were sore, making it difficult to react to anything.

She was stuck, and now she was going to pay for it.

The spider ignored Vhal completely and raised one of its legs to sweep the area in front of it, slamming into her. Celia felt the mana in her dress work, concentrating at the point of impact, but it wasn't enough. She was hurled several feet in the air—straight into a burnt-out tree. She broke through it and continued forward, finally skidding to a halt on the ground. She gasped as her organs tried to keep themselves from imploding from the force, and a notification flashed angrily before her.

Warning: you are suffering from critical injuries and require healing!

As if reacting to the notification, Celia sensed the link with her master suddenly expand to allow more of his mana through. As it did, she felt his Soul Rejuvenation work hard on healing the myriad of injuries she was now suffering from. She tried to stand, but a loud snap sounded from within. Celia yelled out in pain as she grabbed her side in shock before she let out a wheeze.

Blood trickled down her head and over her right eye, forcing her to close it. Gritting her teeth, she pushed through the pain, dragging herself toward the remains of a burnt tree to lean back against it. That single blow would have more than likely killed her if it wasn't for the protection her enchanted dress offered her. She could hear the giant spider's screeching, but right now another enemy was the focus of her attention.

The spider lady stood before her, but she wasn't smirking anymore. She must have been caught in the explosions, since her silk dress was damaged and some of her long black hair looked to have been burned off. The princess glared at her, and from this close range Celia could see sharp canines appear from between her lips.

"You will pay for this, succubus!" she hissed, her eyes twitching. "I will make sure you suffer a long… slow… death." She raised one of her black legs and slammed it down on Celia's.

Celia screamed in agony, her voice only overcome by the loud and horrific cracks that resounded from her leg.

Warning, you have sustained a severe injury!

As Celia glared at the spider princess, she noticed something behind her and tried to speak—but instead began to cough violently, the sharp pain in her ribs causing her to wince between bouts.

The princess turned to see what Celia was looking at... and saw Vhal standing there, a huge grin on his face, as a thin hollow circle of glowing black mana hovered above him. To one side, the large spider sat, its belly flat on the charred ground as its many eyes stared at the lich, unmoving. It looked like a giant grotesque statue.

"Still alive back there?" Vhal asked rather cheerfully.

"Fuck you, Vhal!" she shouted back, before yelping as a loud pop signaled the repair of one of her cracked ribs. *Damn*, she thought. Soul Rejuvenation worked fast.

"Good... good," Vhal said, unaffected. "It wouldn't do for my lord to be disappointed in me after my first mission. Good work, Celia, very good. Even I didn't think you could last this long, but now it is my turn."

"What is that?" The spider lady pointed at the black circle above them. "And what did you do to the prince?"

Vhal looked at the giant spider. "Ah. So this is a prince class Arachne? Too bad it had to die... they are quite rare. I would have loved to study him closer... but, then again, so is a princess," he added with a shrug.

The spider lady's glare grew in intensity. "You think that because you killed a prince, you can challenge me? I will tear you apart bone by bone, undead!"

Vhal shook his head. "Poor, unfortunate thing. I have already destroyed what remained of your cluster. You are the only one left... but enough of this," he said, raising a single hand to point at her.

The spider lady didn't wait for him to finish. She charged forward, dodging from one side to the other. Her speed was astounding—in her weakened state, Celia found it difficult to keep track of her movements—but then the princess slammed into the ground just a few yards away from Vhal. Her speed and momentum causing her face to bury itself into the ash-filled soil.

She twisted and began screaming in pain, her body arching upward. Her voice was filled with so much anguish that Celia had to look away from her writhing form.

Vhal, on the other hand, was still grinning as he took the opportunity to close the gap between them. "Poor creature, how easy it was to bait you." He looked up, and the black circle slowly lowered down to encircle them. "All you had to do was stay still and you would have survived... well, perhaps not survived, but at least lived for a while longer."

Celia grunted as she felt her leg snap back into place, and she grabbed a nearby stick and used it to push herself upright. She took a painful step closer. The princess's screams of agony had died out now and had been replaced by whimpers and the sound of feeble weeping. But as Celia took a second step, Vhal turned toward her.

"Stop there, or you will suffer the same fate," he warned.

That was when it made sense at last. The black circle was having an effect on the area below it. She still didn't know what it was, but Vhal had needed the princess to distance herself from Celia, so he had goaded her into charging him by acting as though he was going to direct the spell toward her. Instead of disrupting Vhal's plan, the princess had fallen straight into his trap.

Even from this distance, Celia could see the blood start to flow from the princess's eyes and ears. She was silent now. It had been a slow and cruel death, one which Celia did not want to experience.

As she watched, Vhal swiped his hand in the air, and the black circle burst into a cloud of necrotic mana and began to disperse. "It's safe now," he said, leaning down to examine the dead princess.

Celia took a few tentative steps forward. "What *was* that?" she asked, noticing the spiders lying dead around them, without any visible burn wounds.

"Dullumar's Ring," Vhal said, as he stood.

"Dullumar…?" Celia asked.

Vhal shrugged, "Some people like to name spells they create after themselves. Dullumar was a particularly nasty fellow. This spell causes any living body in its vicinity to start breaking down from the inside."

Celia winced at the thought. How would it feel to have your own body betray you and attack your insides? She shuddered as she remembered the princess's screams.

Vhal looked her up and down. "You're hurt."

Celia had to stop herself from smacking him. "Thanks to you! Did you have to wait until I actually took a hit?"

"Now, now, Celia, I was just following orders. I must admit, though, I didn't think you would weave an Eruption spell. I wasn't aware you even knew of it."

Celia scowled. "How about you follow the *spirit* of the order instead of its literal wording? I don't think Master meant for me to come to any harm."

"Ahh, perhaps you are right. My apologies then, Celia. I will make sure I don't repeat the same mistake." He bowed slightly to her, but Celia knew better than to trust the lich's sincerity.

She leaned heavily on her branch. She was so sore, and not in the mood to argue. "Why did you mention Aziel to her? I thought we were trying to limit information about him, for his protection."

Vhal stroked his beard before answering. "I thought perhaps the Arachne might also be an ancient race. You saw how Astrel's disposition changed after she heard our lord's name."

Celia shook her head. "Astrel already told Master they weren't. I could have told you if you simply asked."

Vhal chuckled. "Ah, I suppose it matters not now." He gestured at the devastation around them. "Nothing survived to speak of our lord anyway."

Celia couldn't help smirking at that—before she doubled over in pain again. "This is going to take a few hours to completely heal, even with Master's Soul Link…"

"We should keep moving," Vhal suggested. "There is no guarantee that these were all the Arachne in the vicinity. We have sent a powerful message for them to find, but should not give them the chance to retaliate."

Celia nodded in agreement. The spiders terrified her, and she was under no illusion that if Vhal hadn't intervened she would be dead. Given the pure hatred and rage burning in the princess's eyes, it wouldn't have been a pretty death, either.

With one last look at the field of spider corpses, Celia wondered if there were any crystals she could have harvested if she'd had the time. They both then quickly pushed on through the heavy brush and ancient trees of the Central Wilds toward the Grauda colony and the men besieging it.

CHAPTER 22

AZIEL FROWNED AS he tried to make sense of what had happened. Celia's link had suddenly opened up and his mana began channeling through it at a much higher rate, a veritable flood in comparison to before. While the change had lasted only a short period of time, it came as a shock.

He hoped something awful hadn't occurred, but the fact that the link was still there gave him some peace of mind. That meant Celia was alive, at least.

There was no use worrying about something he couldn't control, so Aziel refocused his attention on the scroll in front of him.

He wanted to create a new and safe home for the ancient races, and perhaps any other race who had been suffering from persecution or worse. The problem was that, like the Grauda, any ancient race was probably woefully under-developed and only a shadow of their former selves.

Aziel had had more memories of the Grauda return to him over the last few days, mostly in dreams. They came in short fragments and were nowhere near as clear or intense as the first time, but they did reinforce his initial impression of his newest followers. The Grauda had indeed been highly skilled and valued within the Collective. They were among the best builders of their time—constructing massive towers, dams, canals and large cities at record speed.

But how much of those abilities remained amongst today's Grauda? Would they be able to reclaim their former skills and become the master builders they had once been?

He wasn't certain, but he was fairly sure Astrel would know. As queen, she must know of this history. While certain information would have been lost over time, this part of their heritage—their main contribution to the Collective—would surely not have been.

So why hadn't Astrel mentioned it? Was it for some nefarious reason? Or was she worried about creating an expectation in Aziel's mind she might not believe they could deliver on?

He was leaning toward the latter. Astrel had offered him kingship of her race. Betrayal or deceit would be exceedingly difficult when all her people would answer to him just as much—if not more—than to her. But then again, he was not king yet.

Aziel had spent some time cataloguing the crystals within his place of power. Other than the eight massive Capital Crystals, there were a few hundred of considerable size, ranging from the size of his outstretched hand to three to four times that. The vast majority, however, were small to tiny. Looking down, Aziel's gaze rested on a crystal he had found earlier. It was the size of his fist, one which would usually be used for long-term projects, such as fortifying a castle if it were an earth crystal. He activated his All-Seeing Eye and a notification appeared before him.

You have successfully Analyzed your target.
You have successfully Detected the magic within your target.

Soul Crystal
Type: Crystal
Mana: 3,250/3,250
Purity: 100%

He picked it up. Like the rest of the soul crystals, it was pure mana. He had noticed this difference when he examined the smaller crystals from the library. The purity of all these other crystals ranged from two thirds to one-half. For whatever reason, his crystals—even the massive Capital Crystals—were pure and whole. He again activated his All-Seeing Eye, this time targeting the closest Capital Crystal.

You have successfully Analyzed your target.
You have successfully Detected the magic within your target.

Soul Capital Crystal
Type: Crystal
Mana: 626,400/626,400
Purity: 100%

Ownership: Aziel

Skill:
Crystal Link
Mana Well

This wasn't the first time he had inspected the crystals during his mostly solitary time within his place of power, but still, Aziel couldn't help feeling excited at the sheer amount of mana they contained, and he had eight of them.

The crystal was already linked to the many soul crystals within this chamber. Focusing on it brought a sense of a web of thin mana links with the Capital Crystals at its center. The other skill, Mana Well, on the other hand, simply meant that the Capital Crystals would create 1% of its maximum mana per day, essentially recharging themselves and releasing any excess into the chamber.

Aziel exhaled as he gathered his thoughts. After Celia and Vhal's departure, Astrel had taken his advice and spent the majority of her time at the new Grauda colony site to help organize the dig with only short visits from time to time to Soul's Rest. Other than the few male Grauda guards and Melody, he was the only detectable vessel remaining in Soul's Rest.

He looked at the many crystals around him. He had spent every possible moment here to take advantage of the mana he was receiving from the Grauda. The feeling of it pouring into him was electrifying—perhaps even addictive. But the amount was still small. He would need a lot more if he hoped to gain the ability to move around freely on the outside.

He estimated that if his vessel was full, he would be able to walk around for a week and a half, perhaps two, before he would be forced to return here. That range would of course increase considerably if the Central Wilds became part of his faction. And that was a great motivator to expand.

Aziel stood and made his way toward the nearest crystal column and placed his hand on its surface. It hummed at his touch, and he could feel the mana within it. He stared at it as a thought came to him. Vhal had explained that soul crystals were quite resistant to change, unlike the non-crystallized version of his mana. But he also believed that Aziel's direct control over soul mana might be the missing key to achieving what he could not.

Aziel studied the Capital Crystal in front of him, but quickly stopped himself. Experimenting with a Capital Crystal was asking for trouble. He instead made his way to the edge of the large chamber and pulled free one of the smaller crystals that protruded from the wall.

He closed his eyes and tried to change the mana within into fire mana. But just like when he had tried to look into the crystals before, it felt as if this one was covered by a thin sheet of fabric. He could only see the general outline of the structure, which made changing it that much more challenging.

Unlike raw mana, where he could see the details and track the changes he was making, modifying the crystals would be akin to working blind. And if his previous experiments were any indication, a mistake might turn his crystal into a demonic one—and who knew what kind of mayhem such a thing would cause.

Aziel returned to his seat, where he placed the small crystal on his lap. While there was a massive supply of soul crystals here, losing any of them would be a heavy price. He knew of no way to replace them. And more importantly, they all helped maintain his place of power, even the smaller ones.

He rubbed his forehead as a slight headache started to develop. Glancing down at the small crystal again, he wondered if there was another way to create one. If so, then he would be able to experiment and learn how to modify them without risk.

His fingers traced the edges of the crystal, thinking hard. He was so focused on the crystal that he didn't notice someone approach him.

"Lord Aziel?" a familiar voice said.

Aziel tensed, before letting out a small breath. "Astrel, you're here."

The Grauda queen looked at him curiously, then knelt before him.

"I am, my lord."

Aziel tilted his head as he examined her clothes and dirtied skin. "Were you digging?" he asked.

Astrel paused before answering. "We are few here. Everyone needed to assist."

"I see," Aziel was fairly sure the queen wasn't supposed to dig. Females generally did not. He sighed. As more and more time had passed, he had noticed Astrel's overall behavior change. She didn't sleep and kept to herself even more than usual. He guessed that digging was just another way to distract herself from the fear and worry she must be experiencing. Perhaps changing the subject was the best course here.

Aziel picked up the small crystal to show her. "I am attempting to change the nature of this crystal, but it's harder than I expected." As he explained his dilemma, Astrel listened to him quietly and didn't move from her spot.

Finally, she asked curiously, "If you can change your mana into any other, then can't you do the reverse?"

Aziel looked at her. Could he? He had never even considered this. He stood and, without thinking, kissed the top of Astrel's head. The action caused her scythe arms to twitch, and Aziel had to force himself not to flinch away from them.

"Thank you." He smiled, which caused the edges of her lips to inch upwards too. "If you are right, then I might be forever in your debt."

"Don't say things you might regret, Faction Leader," she replied dryly, catching him by surprise.

He had not yet been able to work Astrel out. She kept largely to herself, but anyone could tell that she was different with him than with the others. More reasonable, one might say, less guarded. But this was the first time she had actually quipped with him.

But even as he thought this, Astrel's face turned a few shades darker, as if just realizing what she had done.

"Regret, you say? Quite confident, aren't you?" Aziel said and grinned at her shocked expression. Her overall demeanor gave the impression that she was about to flee. "Wait here for a moment," he added, "I'll be right back."

He strode out to the library in hopes that a bit of space would give Astrel some time to calm down. Aziel perused the empty shelves at the edges of the library and collected a few fire crystals he needed before making his way back.

Astrel still stood exactly where she had been, and Aziel stopped midway to his curved rock to appreciate the view the beautiful queen presented. His eyes took in the shine of Astrel's darker-colored skin, well-defined body and shapely legs.

She turned just then and smiled nervously. "Find what you were looking for?"

Aziel smiled before taking his seat. "Fire crystals," he explained. "I know how their structure looks, so I thought it would be easier to revert them to soul mana, if it is indeed possible," he added, selecting one crystal to work with.

Astrel took a few steps closer to him, to get a better view. Aziel focused on the fire crystal and tried to imagine the structure of the mana within it. Like his own crystals, it was mostly guesswork.

When he felt confident enough, he gripped the crystal in his hand and forced the mana within to morph. The crystal shook in response, before it began to heat up. Moments later, the fire crystal started to flash, and a crack formed on its surface.

Aziel stood abruptly, causing Astrel to squeak and take a step back in surprise. It was a sound he had only heard her sisters make before, and hearing it come from her made him pause, before another flash from the crystal refocused his attention. Hurriedly, he threw it as far from them as he could. It was just in time—as a moment later, it exploded in the air. Aziel was tackled just as the shock wave pushed him back against his seat.

He winced then opened his eyes to see Astrel on top of him. Her arms wrapped around him, the tips of her twin scythes sunk into the rocky ground to stabilize them. She looked at Aziel and her mouth opened slightly. They were so close Aziel could feel her warmth, her breath, and from the way Astrel's eyes were now glancing away from him, she noticed how close they were too.

She quickly pushed herself off him and knelt.

"Forgive me, my lord I—I just reacted. I wasn't think—"

"Stop," Aziel commanded, and the Grauda queen looked up at him, worry painted all over her features.

He knelt in front of her and she quickly ducked her head, but Aziel sighed and put his hand under her chin. "My apologies, Astrel. Things didn't go as planned, and I placed you in danger."

He smiled and took advantage of her position to kiss her softly on the lips.

Astrel froze, her eyes wide open. Even when their lips parted, she remained that way for a few moments before raising a finger to slowly trace it over her lower lip. Aziel watched, then let out a soft chuckle as he patted her shoulder. "Perhaps you could give me some space so that I may try again?"

It took a moment for her to collect herself, but then she nodded once before standing and returning to her former position. She watched warily as Aziel picked up another fire crystal and sat back down on his seat. His shoulder ached where he must have knocked it against the rock. "I'll be more careful," he promised.

Again, he tried to adjust the structure of the mana within. But unlike his soul mana, over which he had complete control, fire mana was… different. It was chaotic and unruly. Aziel tapped the crystal a few times, then released a wisp of soul mana around it. The fire crystal shone brighter, but it didn't absorb the mana.

Aziel frowned. The reaction was peculiar: it was as if it wanted to absorb his mana, but something was stopping it from doing so. He wondered if there was another way, perhaps a link? Aziel shook his head; there was no point in trying to run before mastering how to walk. He instead activated his All-Seeing Eye, and a notification appeared before him.

You have successfully Analyzed your target.
You have successfully Detected the magic within your target.

Going back to his original plan, Aziel tried to force the change. Like before, it grew warm in his hands. Small streaks of light played under the surface, growing brighter. He turned away and found Astrel staring at him. Her body was tense, poised, ready to jump to save him again.

Her complete willingness to risk herself for him brought about a warm feeling inside. It motivated him to push harder. Failing now would most likely lead to her injury, and he couldn't have that.

The brightness of the crystal continued to intensify as he focused on speeding up the conversion, until he was forced to close his eyes to protect them from the glare—but then, suddenly, the heat vanished.

Opening one eye slowly, he risked a glance at the crystal in his hand. Its dim gray glow captured his attention. He had done it; he had converted it into a soul crystal! Aziel grinned, then laughed as he brought it closer to his eye to get a better look. There was a noticeable size difference. It was smaller, but also felt different, unclean. He again activated his All-Seeing Eye.

You have successfully Analyzed your target.

You have successfully Detected the magic within your target.

Soul Crystal
Type: Crystal
Mana: 130/130
Purity: 37%

It had lost half of its purity during the conversion. A steep price, but what had worked, exactly? The only answer seemed to be speed. He had to complete the conversion before the crystal became too unstable and exploded. Perhaps doing it even faster would retain more of its purity? He had to experiment with this more. Focusing on the new soul crystal, he began modifying it again, this time back into fire mana.

Now that he knew it was a race against time, he worked hard on modifying the mana within it quickly. The process was easier now that he knew what he was doing, but it was still much tougher than working with normal atmospheric mana. Within a minute, the soul crystal had reverted back to fire, and he grinned triumphantly. He again used his All-Seeing Eye to see the results of his efforts, and to his surprise, there was no loss at all. The new fire crystal remained at 37% purity.

Aziel pondered this. Converting the crystal from fire to soul resulted in a sizable loss in purity, but the reverse didn't. Perhaps it wasn't speed at all, but the conversion into soul mana that was the issue.

He decided to attempt a different angle. A shortcut. He grabbed a different fire crystal and tried converting it directly into earth. The mana didn't respond to him. Frowning, Aziel increased the pressure, in hopes of forcing the change. Almost as soon as he started, he knew he had made a mistake.

Instead of converting, all the mana within the fire crystal activated at once. What began as a small glow quickly expanded into a man-sized sphere of fire, with him at its center. At first, nothing seemed to happen. There was no pain, no heat, nothing. Flames swirled and roared around him. Aziel looked down and watched in fascination as a thin translucent barrier covered his entire body. His armor was protecting him, nullifying the magical flames. It only lasted for a few moments though. The barrier flickered, the enchantment was draining the mana within the suit as it struggled to keep the unending and intensifying onslaught of the fire at bay. Aziel screamed.

Warning, you have sustained a severe injury!

He tried to move, to release his mana, but he couldn't, all he could do was grit his teeth. Pain, and the smell of burned flesh engulfed him.

Then, there was another sound. A loud hiss. Something grabbed his shoulder and pulled. He was tossed out of the inferno and onto the ground, gasping.

From the corner of his eyes, he watched the sphere of flames which had gotten large enough to engulf the curved rock and much of the space around. Astrel strode out from behind it, her chitin skin was darker, but not burned. She ran to him, pushing him onto his back, her eyes frantic as she examined his many burns.

"I—I'm sorry, I—" Aziel tried to say, his voice rough.

Astrel shook her head, "Don't speak. Just stay still."

It would seem his screaming had gotten the attention of the entire mountain fortress, as more than a dozen Grauda strode into the chamber. Astrel grabbed something a male Grauda had offered her and shoved it into Aziel's mouth. "Swallow," she commanded.

Aziel did as she asked. He was already starting to feel better as his Soul Regeneration got to work healing his many wounds, but whatever Astrel had given him had numbed his body to the pain.

With the help of two Grauda, Aziel sat up and let out a breath. "Thank you, Astrel,"

Astrel didn't respond, her eyes still looking over his burns. Aziel glanced over her shoulder to see the last remnants of the flames disappear. A thud sounded from beside him and Aziel turned just in time to watch Astrel dunk her hands into a large vat one of the males must have brought. She nodded at the two Grauda who supported him and they both reacted by laying him back on the ground and stripping off his armor.

"I'm sorry, my lord. I will accept any punishment you deem

worthy, but I must do this," she said, then wasted no time as she began to slather his burns with an unknown slimy substance.

Aziel grunted from the sting then grimaced at the awful stench. Astrel didn't let up as she pushed her fingers into his wounds, making sure the torturous slime penetrated deep into his skin. Holding back his protests, Aziel closed his eyes and instead let the queen do as she pleased. At least he learned a valuable lesson from this. Shortcuts aren't worth it.

CHAPTER 23

SEVERAL HOURS AND a long relaxing bath later, Aziel once again sat on his warmer than usual curved rock. With his skill and the smelly but effective Grauda ointment, his burns had already healed without a trace. Leaning back, his fingers played with a small soul crystal, and he noticed Astrel staring at it.

Aziel smiled then shook his head. "Don't worry, I won't do anything reckless."

He figured as long as he converted a crystal into soul mana before anything else, he should be fine. Even with the steep cost in purity, the ability to convert crystals would be extremely helpful, especially once he could learn how to use all the other mana types. He could use them to strengthen himself and his followers.

His gaze drifted across Astrel's face, and her magnificent black hair which cascaded down her shoulders and back. This woman ran into a raging fire to save him, and Aziel had no doubt that he would have perished if not for her intervention. He noticed her skin had reverted back to its natural brown color. She was strong, brave, beautiful, and she was his... Aziel's adventures with Celia had opened up a new world. Arousal and sex had never been a part of him before meeting her, but now, it seemed to be the first thing to cross his mind.

He wondered if his Mark of the Succubi trait was working on Astrel. It was a fair assumption that it was. He had made his peace with the trait's effects. What made it acceptable to his mind was the fact that it did not *create* an attraction, only enhanced what was already there.

One thing that did concern him was what Astrel's inclusion in his sex life would mean. Celia didn't seem to mind him having more than one lover, and had actually encouraged it, constantly telling Astrel to join them in his bed. But the few romance novels he had skimmed over from the great library were about one man and one woman, with the inclusion of a third, or even a fourth causing much strife and heartache. But whenever Aziel hinted at the subject, Celia would make it clear in no uncertain terms that such strictly exclusive relationships were a feature of past cultures and fantasy, with monogamy being a relatively rare choice occurrence. This was especially true with people in power.

"Astrel, are you alright?" he asked, still twirling the crystal in his fingers. The question caused her to look at him, but her face made it clear she was still deep in thought.

After a moment, she nervously clasped her hands together in front of her before straightening her posture again. Aziel had seen her do that a few times now, and it usually meant she was going to ask for something she didn't think Aziel would agree to.

"My lord," she said. "I realize this might be dangerous, but can you make an earth crystal?"

"I suppose," Aziel said looking down at the crystal, then back at Astrel. "I don't see why not."

Astrel swallowed audibly. "You know, Grauda females can increase their fertility by being close to earth crystals," she said, so softly he needed to lean forward to hear her words.

It took a moment for Aziel to process what she had said, and he distinctly remembered her mentioning something similar before. Did she want to increase her fertility? Was she asking what he thought she was asking him?

"You wish to enhance your fertility, Astrel? Do you want to have a child?" It was something he had never thought about. Wait, did that mean Celia could get pregnant? Aziel's heart felt about to burst out of his chest and he swallowed hard.

Astrel smiled, not realizing his inner turmoil. "While I would be fortunate to do that, as Queen I cannot have children, I can only choose the next queen. I was asking for my sister's benefit."

"Do you by any chance know if Celia is pregnant?" he asked. He hadn't exactly been careful about where he placed his seed during their nightly activities. While learning that sex with Astrel would not lead to children was a relief, was he too late when it came to Celia?

His state of near panic was halted when Astrel burst out laughing. Her laughter was almost musical, and this was the first time he had actually heard it, but Aziel only stared at her in utter confusion.

"I'm sorry, my lord," she said with a warm smile. "I never expected the legendary Aziel to worry about such things. Demons can't have children either."

Aziel let out a breath he had been holding and closed his eyes, trying to relax. The relief of hearing that was overwhelming—he had been considering stopping all sexual contact. It wasn't that he was against the idea, it was just too early and too dangerous to raise offspring. He wondered if having no possibility of reproduction was something that bothered Celia, or Astrel for that matter, but thought better of bringing up such a topic.

He opened his eyes again only to see Astrel's face close up. She had moved so close that their noses were nearly touching. Smiling, she traced a finger down the side of his face, then over his lips.

"The demon was right, you worry too much about needless things," she whispered before pulling back a few steps.

Aziel had a feeling Astrel had enjoyed his panicky episode a little too much. But seeing the troubled queen smile was well worth it.

Clearing his throat, he tried to get back on topic. "Just so I understand this correctly, if you have a supply of earth crystals, then that would help your people breed more quickly?"

Astrel nodded once. "Earth mana helps with our fertility and also helps our young grow faster. In the days of the Collective, the Grauda use to breed and lay their eggs around earth crystals. It sometimes reduced the incubation period by half."

Aziel realized that he had no idea how the Grauda bred, but for once, he didn't really want to know. He was certainly glad Astrel looked more like him and less like the males of her race. He wasn't sure he would be able to lay with her otherwise. He could feel his heartbeat speed up at the thought of sex, and he realized how much he was looking forward to it. Celia had succeeded in corrupting him into her way of thinking.

What he did know was that compared to others, the Grauda were fast breeders, with the only real limiting factor being food. While most of the food stores they had found in the Imperial Wing were rotten, there were still a considerable number of nonperishables there. It was enough to perhaps give the Grauda some breathing room to expand until their fungal farms became self-sustainable.

If what Astrel was saying was true, then all his concerns regarding labor could be soon solved. Not only that, he would also be able to arm his workforce, and having a standing army was crucial if claiming the wilds was to be successful.

"Astrel," he announced. "I'm opening the rest of the food stores for your use. Take all that you need in preparation for your people's arrival—and for the coming population boom."

The queen nodded then smiled, but her joy didn't reach her eyes.

Aziel was again reminded of the pain she was experiencing, and he could only imagine the horror going through her mind. Knowing her people were trapped and besieged was taking an obvious toll on her.

Aziel extended his free hand and she looked at it questioningly.

She then tentatively placed her hand in his, and Aziel slowly pulled her toward him.

"Do not worry, Astrel, your people will be safe, and I will ensure a future for you and the Grauda." He smiled at her warmly. "I will bear this burden with you."

Astrel stared at their joined hands, then looked up into his eyes. Her body quivered slightly, and her lips parted, as she visibly battled with herself about what to say.

"Please," she whispered, "I can't lose them." She collapsed to her knees before him, her shoulders shaking as she began to weep silently.

While Aziel had known how hard this time apart from her people had been on the young queen, and how she had been working in anticipation of their reunion, he had not expected the dam to break so suddenly. He reached out, placing his hand gently under her chin and pushed upward so she may face him. He looked down into her eyes with a smile, as his thumb drifted up to wipe away a tear that made its way down her cheek. She looked at him pleadingly, as light from the crystals around them reflected off the tears collecting in her light brown eyes.

"Let it out, Astrel," he said softly. "You have stood strong all these years, supporting your people in their time of hardship and suffering. When they arrive, they will need you to be strong for them again and lead them through this time of great change for your race." He gently stroked her head before continuing. "For now, let your pain out and unburden your heart."

His words opened up a floodgate of emotion as Astrel's crying grew in intensity. She pushed herself up to wrap her arms around him and buried her face into his shoulder. She let out a wail so full of pain and loss it made his spine shiver.

Aziel embraced her. Other than when she pulled him out of a firestorm and covered him with ooze, Astrel had been hesitant of touching him, treating him like the hero she thought he was. A figure from their legends. It was as if touching him or even looking at him too closely would shatter this shred of hope he somehow represented to her and her people. Hugging him like this was a good step forward, he thought.

It took some time for Astrel to calm down again. Aziel simply held her close and rubbed her back, while whispering encouraging words into her ear, trying to assure her that she was no longer alone. He and the others of his faction would help her and her people recover from their troubles.

It was one thing to hear that they had been hunted and killed for so long, but witnessing Astrel's pain had made it all too real. She had watched as her people were encircled, starved, then killed by the thousands within their own homes. She had experienced the loss of her queen, and had been appointed queen herself at a young age to lead the survivors away from the massacre. Ever since, she had gone about her duties alone. And now it was happening all over again, and she couldn't do anything about it.

A dark and fiery hatred grew in Aziel's heart as he held her close. These humans of Whiteridge, and by extension the Kingdom of Maiv, had destroyed the lives of his followers and were now trying to finish the job. But this time, things would be different. This time, they would have to deal with him first.

Aziel felt the mana within him swirl as the fury in his heart swelled. He was tired of hiding. He knew any rash decision would put more of his followers at risk, but perhaps it was time to act? The letter he gave Celia should get things going. He would need to make a statement, a statement the world could not ignore.

The Central Wilds would be his home, he resolved, and the home of all the peoples and races who wished for his protection from the greed and politics of the human world—not just the ancient races. He would gather more followers to build a powerful faction and govern them fairly. More importantly, he would bring death and fury to anyone who wished any ill to him or his own.

These dark thoughts were interrupted by a sniff and the loosening of Astrel's grip. Aziel looked down at her to see her honey-colored eyes stare back at him, a gentle smile gracing her face. The sight washed away all the rage that consumed him, as if it had never been there to begin with.

"A shameful display…" she mumbled, as she wiped the last of her tears away.

Aziel smoothed her hair. "There is no shame in being truthful to yourself," he replied. "We all have our moments of weakness, and I hope you will be there when it is my turn to show mine."

"The Grauda and I will always be by your side… my king," she whispered, before straightening up.

Aziel smiled at her, then grabbed the largest soul crystal he could reach. He quickly went through the motions of modifying the mana within it, feeling Astrel's gaze upon him as he did. While the process took longer than with the tiny crystal he had used for testing, it did not take as long as he thought it would, given its size.

Satisfied with his work, he took her hand and drew it toward him, palm up. "I hope this crystal will be of use to you," he said. "I admit I am ignorant of the more intricate details of your race's ways, but this is the least I can do for the time being." He placed the fist-sized earth crystal on her palm.

Astrel stared at it for what felt like hours. Aziel was worried she was going to start crying again, but instead another beautiful smile appeared on her face, before she leaned down and brushed her lips against his.

"Thank you," she whispered, then turned and hurried from the chamber.

Aziel sat there frozen, staring at her receding form. His whole body shivered. Her kiss had been… different, more tender in comparison to Celia's passionate and hungry ones. He shook his head to free himself from the trance-like state he was in, then leaned back in his seat with a chuckle.

It was nice to see Astrel the person rather than the queen. He hoped she would continue to let him see her this way in the future.

Shaking himself, Aziel brought up his personal log and grinned. With the Grauda contribution and all the time he had been spending in his place of power, his vessel was almost full. Just a few more days and he would be ready.

But right now, there was something he had to take care of. He wished Celia could be here for this, but he would just have to do it himself.

CHAPTER 24

AZIEL RAPPED ON the wooden door before opening it and entering.

"Hello, Melody," he said.

The brown-haired beastkin's ears pricked up at the sound of his voice. She was coiled on the bed, not unlike a cat, he thought.

She opened a single eye to look at him. "I wasn't paying much attention before, but you're actually more good-looking than I imagined. And believe me, with the way Celia speaks about you, I had high expectations."

"Oh?" he said with a smirk. "Does Celia talk about me often?"

Melody didn't move from where she sat. She kept looking at him with one eye closed. "I'm going to assume that was rhetorical."

Aziel snorted, then shook his head.

"I'm guessing you finally meeting me means you have come to a decision?" she asked.

Aziel sighed. He had been reluctant to trust Melody. Not only was she an adventurer, she had also killed Grauda. But Celia certainly did trust her. She had defended the beastkin at every opportunity. Aziel scratched the back of his neck. He supposed she was right, Melody had been a slave after all, and the worst he could accuse her of was defending herself. Celia had also begged him to offer Melody a position in his faction, one that would make use of Melody's trade skills and connections in her homeland.

Aziel had to admit that Celia made some good points. He would need a way to bolster his faction's finances to pay for what was to come. There would be a point where loyalty to him and his faction would not be enough, and he had a distinct impression that other races might not be as open as the Grauda when it came to working without some form of economic return. He also knew from the extensive reading he had been doing that wealth and trade could be just as powerful as standing armies at getting what he wanted from others.

He would need currency, and lots of it. Annoyingly, for all the riches and extravagance of the Imperial Wing, there wasn't a single piece of actual currency to be found. He could start chipping the gold off the wall's gilded ornaments and forming them into solid coins. But the coins Celia had shown him from the looted noble carriage were very much marked and while it was faint, Aziel could feel a hint of magic within them. He also had to admit that the intelligence Melody had provided him about his now enemies had been useful.

"Before we get to that, there is something I wish to discuss with you," he said.

Melody glanced up at him, finally opening her second eye before letting out a small yawn.

Assuming that meant she accepted, Aziel went straight to his questions. "How much do you know of Maiv's divinity—Adara, I believe her name was."

The beastkin furrowed her brows before she shrugged. "As much as anyone else, I guess. She's a fire Ascended, and her place of power is located in the largest of the volcanos that make up the Three Flames. She has her own guild, the Order of Flames, and visits the capital every now and then to check up on the Capital Crystal and meet the king. That's really all I know."

Aziel nodded. The Three Flames were a trio of ancient volcanos to the southeast of the Kingdom of Maiv, just by the coast. He had seen them in maps in some of the library's books.

"Do you know anything of her strength? What would she do if, let's say, I attacked her followers or shrine? Would she come to their aid?" This was the point he really wanted to know.

Melody scratched her cheek in contemplation. "Hmm... it would be abnormal if she did take action—in person, I mean. I don't know about her Order of Flames, though," she added a moment later.

Aziel looked at her curiously. "What do you mean?"

"I've never heard of an instance where a divinity took direct action to protect his or her followers, other than some stories that took place during the dark times after the fall of the Caelian Empire." Melody scratched her ear a few times, thoughtfully. "They say a divinity will only protect their followers when they face total annihilation, or if another divinity threatens them, but even that might not be true."

Aziel looked at her in horror. Never acted? So these Ascended lived off their faction's followers' mana and limited themselves to charging their Capital Crystals—a job that needed so little effort, Aziel could probably do it in his sleep?

Aziel cleared his throat as he tried to hold back his outrage. "Wouldn't the divinity be in trouble if their followers were annihilated? I would think it logical to intervene out of necessity, then."

Melody nodded in agreement. "Most of the time the divinity simply joins the winning side. Both Adara and my home country's divinity were part of the Jannatin Empire's pantheon before gaining their independence. The only recent example, if you can even call it that, was what happened to Ishna Noan." She began stroking her tail, patting down any stray strands.

"Ishna Noan...? Aziel asked. The name was familiar, but he couldn't remember where he'd heard it.

Melody smiled sadly before replying. "It's the dark elven city-state to the northwest of here. It was the last place to fall to the Blight that ravished the northern territories. As I understand it, their divinity wouldn't help fight off the undead hordes no matter how much they begged. He instead abandoned them and fled the city. The results were devastating."

Aziel clenched his jaw. He couldn't understand why an Ascended would act like this. These people chose them as their divinity and supported them with their mana. Yet, when they were needed the most, they wouldn't help? At all? His mother certainly hadn't stood by. Even when N'goth pleaded with her to, she had actively aided her followers in battle.

"What happened?" he asked, already knowing the answer.

"Not many details are known, but the city is in ruins now. The royal family of Noan, after whom the city was named, were killed during its defense along with a large portion of their population." Melody shrugged. "The survivors escaped and were given…" Melody paused looked to one side, "refuge… by the other factions. That was around a hundred or so years ago."

Aziel didn't know what she was insinuating, but he shook his head in disgust. He had expected his equals to do more. What made it worse was that although he was trapped in his place of power, he assumed they had not been—and still they did nothing. Were the divinities just a prize for who won a war at the end? His heart went out to those dark elves who had apparently suffered so grievously.

"What happened to their divinity? The one who abandoned them."

Melody shrugged again. "No idea, but most people believe that other divinities hunted him down."

"Good," he declared. If that were true, then at least the divinities did something right. "I, however, will not remain idle to the happenings of the world around me. I will protect and lead my followers myself, and their fate will also be mine."

Melody smiled. "Celia was right about you. Just don't go dying anytime soon, or I won't be able to fulfill my bargain with her." She leaned back against a pillow. "That's if you'll have me."

Aziel crossed his arms, about to reply—but then sensed a vessel dash away from Melody's door. He had been so distracted he hadn't noticed it before, an oversight that irritated him, and now it had escaped too fast for him to examine it closely. But given which room he sensed it flee into, Aziel had a good idea of who it was. All he could do was sigh again.

"Melody, how long would it take for you to reach your home country and broker the trade deal you discussed with my champion?" he asked.

The beastkin smiled brightly then pushed herself off the bed and onto her feet. "My leg has healed up quite well, those Grauda have some great healing remedies. If I move unhindered… maybe two weeks? I don't know how long it would take to broker a deal. A few more weeks, perhaps? That's assuming you have something to draw a merchant lord to the table."

Aziel rubbed his chin as he thought about that. The first things that came to mind were his crystals. He was sure they would fetch a good price—but no. They were his edge over his opponents, and he didn't want to advertise his unusual mana too much and risk attracting the wrong type of attention.

Giving up the highly enchanted prized imperial weapons was not an option either, and he couldn't ask the Grauda to sell their Alchemic recipes. The books of the great library and study were definitely not for trade, so what was left?

While Melody combed the unruly fur of her tail, his mind raced through the contents of Soul's Rest—until it was stopped short by a single item. Aziel grinned at the thought.

"Melody," he said, his tone catching the beastkin's attention. "What do you know of aranite?"

Melody looked at him as if he had lost his mind. "It's a metal that goes by another name: gods' steel. It is supposed to be better than true silver—oh, and it doesn't exist."

Aziel's grin grew wider and Melody watched him uncomfortably.

"Why?" she asked.

"How much would you say a single standard ingot of aranite would sell for?"

Melody chewed on her upper lip, as she went through what appeared to be some mental calculations in her head.

"Well, a standard ingot of true silver usually goes for about a thousand, thousand five-hundred Tijari gold pieces, on average... so something as rare and legendary as aranite would go for at least double that, I would imagine," she stated matter-of-factly.

"And is that a lot of gold?" Aziel asked curiously.

Melody snorted. "A lot? That's *more* than a lot. There's a reason why true silver is only in the hands of royalty—it takes a nation to afford something like that, and a rich one, too."

Aziel grinned. During breaks in his training, he had experimented with his sword's active enchantment. He was delighted to find it cut effortlessly through rock, steel, and even the enchanted leather armor. He finally tested it against the storage room's aranite gate, and to his surprise, the blade was able to chip a small shard out of it—but not without effort. He had had to use it more like a saw than a sword to achieve even that.

Aziel plunged his hand into his pouch and pulled out a small metallic shard from within, which he presented to Melody.

"This is a piece of drained aranite," he stated. "Take it with you as evidence, and state that the Fallen are willing to accept a trade deal for the stuff."

Melody stared at the tiny shard in her hands. From her increasingly shocked expression, Aziel figured she must have used Analyze on it, which was forcing her to accept it as the metal she hadn't thought existed until now.

"How...?" she muttered.

"That is not important. Get a good deal and I will offer you a position in my faction which will report directly to me and my appointed Viceroy. Is that acceptable to you?"

The beastkin only stared at him. "You would give me, a slave, a position with direct access to the faction leader if I complete this task?" she asked, skeptically.

"You come with the recommendation of my champion. Also, aiding my faction when it is young and powerless means you can reap greater rewards when it rises," he added, with a smile.

Melody looked down at the shard in her hands again, and Aziel noticed her tail flick from one side to the other. "I'll do it," she whispered, before repeating it again more confidently as she met his eyes.

"Good. Your gear will be brought to your room, and then you will be released. I'm sure a scout such as yourself will be fine alone, and won't get lost in the Wilds?"

She simply nodded.

Pleased, Aziel turned to leave—but then paused. Melody's mentioning her status as a slave had reminded him of something which had bothered him ever since he had detected that ring on Kim. He swung back around and the beastkin's ears twitched as he approached her, her tail stiffening.

"Do not fear me," he said, as he pulled down the high collar of her shirt to see the dark band that encircled her neck.

Melody fidgeted nervously, and he presumed she felt ashamed of it. Ignoring her discomfort, Aziel placed his hand on the band and frowned. It was made of simple iron, but he again felt that sinister energy emanating from it. He closed his eyes and took his time examining the small vessel. Just like before, he recognized the soul mana coursing through it—it just felt different to his own, like it was tinged with something else. A ritual perhaps? Vhal hadn't gotten around to explaining rituals to him, so he couldn't be certain.

He focused on the vessel within the band and saw that the soul mana reacted to his will. Instinctively, he drew it toward him and the vessel stretched in response. An idea came to him, and Aziel put it into action immediately. Just like every other vessel he had inspected closely, he began ripping holes in it. The slave band's vessel quivered once, then imploded.

Aziel opened his eyes and saw Melody staring back at him with wide-open eyes. He glanced down at his hand and saw that the iron band had cracked and shattered. Its many pieces lay on the floor between them.

Aziel pulled his hand back just before Melody pounced on him, hugging him and rubbing her head against his chest. Aziel froze, not knowing what to do.

"Thank you," she cried, her tail wagging excitedly.

"You're... welcome..." Aziel replied slowly.

"I'll do it! I'll make sure I complete this task for you!"

"Good." He separated himself from the excited beastkin and strode to the door. There he stopped, his back still facing her. "But do not think that I will not come after you if I find out you have betrayed me," he added coldly, then left the room.

*   *   *

As soon as he had witnessed Melody leave Soul's Rest, Aziel made his way to where that mysterious vessel had disappeared into.

"Astrel?" he called softly before knocking the door twice. "How are you feeling?"

She didn't answer, but just when he was about to call again, the door opened slightly to reveal the Grauda queen.

Aziel smiled. "May I come in?"

She took a step back, letting him push the door open and join her inside. It was his first time here, but he was not surprised to see it was identical to all the others. A large bed stood at the center, with a dresser and cabinet by the wall. Carpets and other decorative items were on display all around. A single light crystal shone from the ceiling, providing ample lighting.

Aziel sat on the edge of the bed and faced Astrel, who was still standing by the door.

"Were you avoiding me?" he asked with a smile.

Astrel looked up with her eyes wide. "No!" she cried. "I would never—"

Aziel raised a hand to stop her. "I didn't mean it that way. I simply noticed you leave in such a hurry when I was speaking to Melody, and I thought something might be wrong."

Astrel looked down at her feet again.

"I… I overheard what you said… I just needed time to process it," she replied, meekly.

Aziel tried to remember which part of the conversation she was referring to. He didn't think Astrel cared about the dark elves, so perhaps it was something else. "I can understand why it would be upsetting to hear of the … indifference… that Ascended seemed to show…"

Astrel shook her head, then her face lit up in a smile Aziel had never seen before. His heart started beating faster at the sight of it. Astrel looked so relaxed and at peace, she almost looked like a different person.

"Astrel?" he asked.

She walked over to him and reached out to cup his cheek, but then hesitated. She stared into his eyes for a moment, then finally seemed to muster the courage to gently stroke his cheek with her thumb.

Aziel was entranced by her beauty and tenderness. "Astrel?" he asked again, and her smile grew wider as she sat beside him on the bed.

"You are truly the Aziel… my Aziel," she said in a hushed tone. "You still hold onto the ways of the ancient Ascended… you are the last of the ancient Ascended. You don't know how relieved and happy I was to hear you speak of protecting your followers. I was so happy I felt my heart was going to burst. I ran to give myself time to calm down, that is all." She then looked away. "I'm sorry," she added.

Aziel placed his hand on hers, causing her to face him again. "I promised to protect you, Astrel, and I will keep my promise," he said, with as much conviction as he could.

Astrel withdrew her hand slowly, then pushed him gently down on the bed before sitting astride him. Her whole body seemed to have grown a shade darker, and he could feel her trembling.

"I... I am ready to give you what I promised, my king," she whispered, a tinge of fear coloring her voice.

Aziel observed her for a moment. Astrel was indeed a beautiful woman, but though she said she was ready, she still looked afraid. How could he claim to protect her while asking her to do something she feared? He pushed himself up and Astrel slid down and ended up sitting on his lap. He placed his hands on both her sides to steady her, and her trembling stopped. For a long moment, they looked into each other's eyes.

"You don't have to do this now, Astrel," he said. "I can wait."

The queen looked at him in confusion, but then her beautiful smile returned.

"You misunderstand, my king," she said, placing a hand on his chest just above his heart. "I want this... I just don't have... any experience."

Aziel didn't think it was physically possible, but her face flushed even darker after that admission. He couldn't hold back his laugh, which caused her to frown slightly.

"My apologies, Astrel. I did not mean to offend you. Do not worry about experience—before I met Celia, I knew almost nothing about sex other than it resulted in children." He laughed again, and Astrel smiled then joined him with light laughter. "We can take it slow, and learn about each other at your pace," he added.

The queen nodded and leaned down to kiss him, their lips met and this time she didn't pull back. As their breathing grew heavier and their passions flared, their hands began exploring then undressing one another.

Aziel had a much easier time of it, since Astrel's dress consisted of a few pieces of loose fabric. His hands slowly ran over her toned body and the strange sensation of her soft chitin skin.

Astrel, on the other hand, had to deal with his multilayered armor suit. She moaned at his touch, then actually hissed in frustration between kisses. The longer it took, the more frantic her clawed hands became, and Aziel worried she would simply rip his suit off if he didn't do something about it. Gently, he began to help her undress him.

Astrel nervously looked away as she tried to control herself, her antennae twitching wildly and her scythe-like arms stretching backward and outwards like a pair of wings.

As soon as he was free of the armor, Astrel pulled him tightly to her. Only the sound of the door swinging open made them stop, turning to see one of the female Grauda look very apologetic as she quickly shut the door. The both giggled at that, before continuing their eager explorations.

CHAPTER 25

ALISTAIR SAT ON a tree stump facing a makeshift table, which was covered with stacks of documents and a large, roughly-drawn map. He stared at the markings depicting land elevations, supply lines, and defensive positions around the Grauda colony.

They had found the colony much quicker than he anticipated. The Grauda had fallen back almost as soon as the adventurers went out to hunt for them, obviously hoping to elude them. But one party quite literally stumbled onto their colony, where they lost all members except for one. Luckily, the injured survivor had been able to run back to Whiteridge and report his findings.

Alistair reread the transcript of the last message he had received from his high commander. The Jannatin Empire were amassing at the eastern border of the kingdom, where they were accumulating supplies—a sure sign of their intent to march. He had been ordered to end the Grauda threat as soon as possible to ensure that Whiteridge was ready for a possible war.

He was still bitter about the minimal support his government had offered to help exterminate the beasts, but Alistair was never one to shrink away from a challenge. The few supplies and weapons that had been sent were distributed immediately before they marched. Marth, his predecessor, had been of great help. She had taken command of the garrison in Whiteridge and took care of the supply lines from there, freeing him up to get rid of these abominations.

This Grauda colony was far smaller than the one they fought when they first settled here, but that didn't mean it wasn't dangerous. The probe attacks they had sent had been blocked quite ferociously by the insects.

To avoid unnecessary casualties, Alistair had decided to settle for a siege to weaken the enemy. He was confident that he and his men would outlast them. He looked down at the transcript again and tapped his finger against it.

"If only we had the time…" he grunted. But this message changed everything.

He looked up as the flap of his tent was pushed open, then scowled.

"You're late, as usual," he said.

Rook, his deputy, unbuckled his sword belt and placed it on a side table before sitting down on another tree stump across from him.

"There has been another Arachne attack," Rook reported, as he tiredly ran his hand across his hair. "A small one, but they are getting more frequent."

Alistair rubbed his forehead. Ever since they had arrived here, those damned spiders had been attacking. He couldn't figure out why the Arachne would be this far south of the Webbed Woods in the first place, but there had been no fewer than five separate attacks since the siege began.

He had split his men and the participating adventurers into four camps and placed them to the east, west, north, and south of the colony. His men were to patrol the areas between each camp to ensure no Grauda could escape or have any chance of bringing in supplies. This time he would ensure their annihilation.

But with these constant attacks, he had had to divert more of his men to defend the outer perimeter from the Arachne.

They usually attacked at night. The first attack had been

particularly horrible. The northern camp was caught completely by surprise, resulting in twenty-four casualties—but even more horrifying was the thirteen that went missing. Alistair shivered at the thought of what those poor men and women might be going through.

"How many this time?" he asked with a sigh.

"Only two dead," Rook replied, exhausted. "It was the smallest attack to date, but a tree hopper serpent poisoned a man at the eastern camp whilst he took care of business in the bushes. I haven't been able to visit him, but it appears he will need to be sent back to Whiteridge for proper healing."

Alistair closed his eyes as he pinched the bridge of his nose in frustration. "What about the tunnel?"

Rook shook his head. "The earth weavers are confident the Grauda are digging one, but they can't seem to pin down where it is exactly."

Alistair narrowed his eyes, one hand reaching up to clasp a small metal necklace around his neck. "Let me be clear, Rook, that tunnel must be destroyed before they reach wherever they are aiming for. These monsters will not escape again."

Rook nodded and turned to the maps on the table. Alistair hoped his deputy could not see how his hand was trembling at the emotions flooding him.

The first Grauda war had been brutal. The fighting took place in the thick, unforgiving forests all across the region, and they hadn't known much about their enemies at the time. The Grauda had tunneled under their frontlines and emerged less than a mile from Whiteridge. The town was still new, and the walls had not been completed then, with most of the people still living in tents.

The attack had been swift and cruel; the Grauda swept through the area like a wave of death and gore, biting and decapitating everyone in their path. More than half of the people who had settled in the new town were killed in a single night, before they were able to organize themselves and beat the attackers back.

By the time Alistair and his company had returned, the attack was already over. The Grauda had collapsed the tunnel behind them to ensure no one could pursue.

In the devastation that met them, Alistair had lost what was most precious to him—his wife and young daughter. His daughter was only thirteen, and she and her mother had been savagely mutilated as they tried to hide beneath the covers. The vivid image of his daughter's body, her blonde hair matted with blood as he cradled her in his arms... the memory still haunted him.

Marth, who was the captain at the time, had allowed him some time to grieve. The attack was a massive blow to morale. There was even talk of abandoning the whole idea of settling the Wilds. But Alistair begged Marth not to listen. His pain and sorrow had been replaced by an uncontrollable hatred for the bugs. His daughter would be avenged, he swore.

That massacre did lead to the king forbidding families to settle in Whiteridge, however. From then on, only soldiers and military support professions were allowed to come. It was only a few weeks ago when that restriction had been rescinded, only for the Grauda to show themselves again.

Alistair came out of his reverie still clutching the necklace. It had been a gift from his late wife to his daughter, who had worn it at all times. It was the only remaining possession of hers that he still had. He ground his teeth as an all-too-familiar anger consumed him.

"Call the camp leaders," he commanded. "We need to discuss our assault."

Rook looked at him curiously. "Assault, sir?"

"We will end this tomorrow."

His deputy hesitated, but then nodded in confirmation. "I will send runners to summon them immediately," he said, standing and saluting smartly. He picked up his sword belt and refastened it around his waist, but just as he reached out to pull the tent flap, another man stormed into his tent.

"Captain!" the man cried. His breathing was labored, and his leather armor was dirtied with blood and so much mud it was as if he had rolled his way to the command tent.

Alistair stood. "What is it? What happened to you?"

The soldier looked into his eyes, and Alistair could see the fear written all over his features. "The north, east, and western camps are all under attack!"

"Those damn Arachne don't know when to quit!" Rook grunted. "We should just go after them after we get rid of the Grauda."

"No! It's not the Arachne," the soldier said, his eyes darting around the tent. "It's the undead, hundreds of them."

Alistair blinked. Rook was wearing the same dumbfounded expression he probably had. "Undead?"

"Yes sir!" the soldier confirmed.

Rook shook his head in disbelief. "We must be cursed, for the Arachne, the undead, and the beasts to all attack us while we besiege the damn bugs."

Alistair placed his hand on the hilt of his sword and strode toward the exit, before stopping in his tracks. "What's your name?" he asked.

"Milton, sir."

"Well, Milton, Rook. Follow me, I need to see this for myself."

The two men saluted and followed him out of his tent. At that moment, the alarm bell began to ring. Men and women ran into and out of their tents to gather their weapons and don their amour, while the guards rushed toward the entrance of the camp to defend it.

A short woman armed with a bow ran toward him and pulled up short. "Sir! Undead spotted—they're charging toward the entrance of the camp."

Alistair frowned. Four camps attacked by undead at practically the same time? This was a coordinated attack... but who could even do this? He had never seen the Grauda or the Arachne use necrotic mana. Could there be Jannatin necromancers using the chaos to attack them now?

Unlike the king and his council, Alistair was under no illusions that the Empire did not know about Whiteridge. No matter how careful they had been, someone would surely notice something; someone would talk. He had always wondered why the Empire made no move to attack them, but maybe this was the moment it began.

He unsheathed his sword, and Rook and Milton did the same.

"We will kill these creatures quickly before sending reinforcements to the other camps," he commanded. "Let's go."

They ran together toward the sound of fighting, their group growing as more men and women joined them. By the time the camp's entrance came into view, their numbers had swelled to over two hundred. Alistair directed them into formation.

"Footman to the front and archers behind!" he yelled, and his men reacted immediately.

He took his first look at the battle playing out before him and opened his eyes wide in surprise. While the majority of the undead were mere skeletons and zombies, the lowest and least powerful of necrotic monsters, mixed amongst them were more powerful beings. He saw several specters and even a banshee. Those monsters were immune to ordinary weapons—only magic or the elements could harm them.

A girl who couldn't have been more than seventeen of age ran up to him and offered him a piece of paper. "Sir, the Inspection report," she said, her hands shaking slightly which made the document tremble.

"Right," Alistair said distractedly, already reading it. "Good work." As soon as those beasts had arrived, his scouts had Inspected them. It did not surprise him to learn that they were conjured beings, made entirely of magic. Their nature, numbers and the presence of specters confirmed without a doubt that they had been conjured by powerful necromancers. It had to be the Jannatin Empire behind this.

The only anomaly was the banshee. She was a true undead creature, not a conjuration.

Name: Nora the Crazed
Race: Undead, Banshee
Rank: Lesser Enlightened
Level: 19

A level 19 Banshee; how was that even possible? A summon, perhaps? No, not even the famed necromancers of the Jannatin Empire could actually raise a creature this powerful. Alistair grimaced as he tried to purge his mind of such thoughts. There was no point in analyzing this now.

Alistair glanced behind him, gesturing for two earth weavers to come forward. He pointed out the banshee and specters. "Focus your spells on them," he commanded.

He turned back to his soldiers, who didn't look as confident as they had been only a minute before.

"Be brave! We will beat the monsters back into whatever hole they crawled out from. Adara's flame will protect you from evil," he said confidently, before yelling, "Archers! Take them down!"

The back row of archers raised their bows and let loose their arrows. They arced above the gap between the two forces that would soon become a killing field, before landing in a cluster of undead.

The monsters were too distracted by chewing the guards who had been too slow on the retreat to notice the arrows heading toward them. The first wave brought down some zombies and the few skeletons unlucky enough to receive an arrow to their joints.

Alistair frowned. He knew arrows were not particularly effective against these types of undead, but if even a few were killed, it could save lives.

Alistair turned his attention to the specters present, who were hovering just above the ground. They were almost transparent but glowed a faint blue, with dark-blue outlines that took the form of different types of animals. There was even one that resembled a human among them, but it had no facial features that he could see. Arrows would do nothing to them, their ghostly forms were immune to any physical weapons. They moved slowly, which was a blessing, as touching them resulted in a painful death for most.

The banshee was another matter altogether. While she shared the same basic features as specters, she was very much a female humanoid. Her legs faded out just before reaching the ground, and her hair floated on an unseen wind around her.

What made banshees particularly lethal was their ability to weave. This bumped up their threat level significantly, as one weaver could do a horrendous amount of damage.

Alistair ordered the archers to set their arrows aflame and focus on the specters. While the arrows wouldn't hurt them, the fire would. He just hoped his archers could take out all of them.

As his men dipped their arrows in oil, the undead dispatched the last of the gate guards and began their shuffle onward. He noticed the banshee grin and saw blue mist leak out of her hand, before she began to draw symbols in the air in front of her.

Alistair turned to his men and raised his sword above him. "Fear nothing, Maiv's finest! Adara is with us!" he yelled, before activating the small enchanted fire crystal embedded into his sword.

His blade erupted into flames, and his soldiers roared as they readied themselves for the coming battle. Alistair took a deep breath and—just as the archers let loose their flaming arrows—ordered the attack.

His soldiers yelled out a final war cry then charged behind him toward the unorganized line of undead, who continued shuffling forward, unperturbed by the wave of humanity accelerating in their direction.

Ahead, Alistair saw the fiery arrows shoot through the specters. The creatures made no sound, but their forms flickered with every hit. Some flickered out into nothing.

The banshee screeched as an arrow hit her side. She glared at the line of archers before tossing her completed spell toward them. "Frost Nova!" she shrieked, and a small bolt of ice shot toward the group before slamming into the earth amongst them.

A circular wave of ice erupted from the epicenter, shooting off icicles the size of a man's arm in all directions. Alistair stared at the chaos that followed, as the once organized line of archers scattered in all directions to avoid the deadly ice. Some screamed and ducked, while others were impaled and fell.

More than twelve men must have died from that one spell. Alistair ground his teeth together when he saw the banshee grin wickedly and began weaving with her water mana again. Then he and his men were crashing into the undead, the sound of shattering bones and metal slamming into flesh resounding around him. This was nothing like a fight between disciplined armies—it was a brutal brawl.

The zombies used their weight to push down their victims, while skeletons swung their improvised weapons wildly. A cacophony of noise assaulted Alistair as he swung his flaming sword horizontally, cutting cleanly through two skeletons, their bones collapsing into a heap at its touch.

Rook, who had never left his side, used a torch to keep one of the specters away while Alistair flanked it and stabbed at its center repeatedly until it flickered into nonexistence. Another loud crash sounded from somewhere nearby, followed by agonized, fearful screams.

He turned to Rook. "We need to get rid of that banshee!"

Rook nodded, and the two men charged through the chaos. They passed more and more men impaled or covered in ice. The ground beneath them had turned to mud, and their feet sank into it. Alistair cursed as he glared at the banshee before him. She merely opened her arms wide to encompass the dead and dying, as if presenting her grisly work to him.

At this distance she would destroy him, he realized. His movements had been slowed considerably due to the terrain, and it was obvious that his men were trying to avoid her.

He scowled at their stupidity. Leaving a weaver to do as she pleased was just asking to die. He looked around and cursed when he found his two earth weavers entombed in ice.

Rook gripped his shoulder. "I'll distract her," he shouted over the noise of the battle, gesturing to a javelin he must have scavenged from a body on the way.

"That won't harm her," Alistair shouted back. "You know that!"

"I have my tricks," Rook replied cheerfully, pulling a small bottle of oil from his pack.

Alistair chuckled a little, then turned back to the banshee, who was no longer smiling. He gripped the hilt of his sword tighter—he knew he needed to end this quickly, as the fire crystal would not last much longer. He raised his sword and charged forward, his feet sloshing across the muddy soil. The banshee screamed, a loud and terrifying scream that caused his bones to rattle. It took everything Alistair had to stop himself from curling into a ball—instead, he forced himself toward her.

The banshee began weaving another spell, but just as she was about to toss it, a flaming javelin streaked through the air and flashed through her chest, before burying its point into the mud behind her. A small explosion followed, and the banshee screamed again—but this time in pain as her form flickered in and out of existence.

Alistair grinned, impressed. Rook's small bottle of oil had worked wonders. He reached the banshee just as her form shimmered back into existence and thrust his sword into her chest. The banshee screeched, and Alistair felt a chill as ice began to form on his arms where it came in contact with her ghostly body.

Warning, you have sustained a minor injury!

He yelled out in pain then pulled back just in time to avoid an icicle which exploded out of the mud only inches from him. He again lunged toward the banshee, but another icicle blocked his path and Alistair growled. This bitch had to be running low on mana by now, surely. He sidestepped yet another icicle then saw what she was doing—the banshee was using her free hand to weave the smaller spells that were holding him back, but her focus was not on him.

Alistair turned and saw Rook running toward him. He screamed a warning, but he could already see the bolt of ice streaking toward his friend. The spell hit the ground just in front of his deputy, and Alistair hoped it was just a simple ice bolt—but a moment later it exploded, and ice erupted from the point of impact.

Time slowed as two icicles stabbed right through Rook, lifting him several feet into the air. Alistair heard the banshee's laugh, and he bellowed out in rage.

He turned and her laughter stopped. As she began weaving again, Alistair ran toward her with everything he had. The banshee tried to stop him with icicles yet again, but her mana reserves were running low, she was slower now, so he easily dodged them.

Alistair raised his sword above his head, activated his fire crystal again, and slashed down at the same time that he yelled, "Cleave!"

The flames which surrounded his sword flared up and roared angrily as they engulfed the banshee. She screamed and flickered, but Alistair had had enough. He slashed and stabbed at the ghostly woman until all that was left was a small orb of glass that glowed a faint blue.

A spectral core, he realized. It was a material used in several alchemic concoctions and sold well in the capital.

Alistair leaned down and picked it up slowly. The sounds of battle had begun to die down around him, as the last of the undead were picked off by his soldiers. But Alistair felt empty inside. Even without looking, he knew that he had lost many men and women… too many. Not to mention that his deputy was amongst the dead.

His camp was by far the most protected and well-manned. If the others had been attacked in the same way, then it was likely they had not survived.

Alistair dropped the core onto the muddy ground and stepped on it, plunging it deep into the mud. He then turned to face his people. He could see that more than half of them were missing, and a third of those still standing were injured in one way or another. Alistair swallowed as he thought about the ramifications.

It would be impossible to maintain the siege now, not without major reinforcements. There were simply too few of the task force left to maintain the patrols required. There was also the matter of the Empire's necromancers. That they had not shown themselves during the battle was both a blessing and a curse.

On the one hand, their absence had most likely reduced the overall casualty figures, which were already atrocious. But on the other, there were still enemies out there capable of conjuring specters and summoning a true undead banshee.

Alistair knelt beside his deputy's still form and slowly shut his eyes. "You have fought well, my friend; I will tell your family of your bravery this day." He sighed at the thought of that conversation. When this was all over, he would have to inform many parents that their sons and daughters were dead.

Alistair stood and ordered his remaining men to collect the dead, before glancing down at his sword. He frowned at the empty slot that had housed his fire crystal. He would have to get another one, and the king's court would not be happy. Just as he began to sheathe his sword, the camp's alarms sounded again.

"What now?" Alistair cursed. His men were tired and demoralized. Just one glance made it clear that they didn't have another fight in them. He spotted a familiar soldier sprinting toward him.

"Captain!" Milton yelled as he drew close enough to be heard. "The Grauda are attacking! Thousands of them! It must be the whole colony!"

Alistair shook his head. This was just too much. The attacks were too coordinated to be a coincidence, and if Milton was right that the whole nest was emerging, then they had been waiting for the moment to strike. But the Empire helping the Grauda? He must be going mad.

"Form up!" he yelled, then hurried toward the other side of the camp, from where he could already see black smoke rising.

These Grauda worked fast, but he would be damned if he didn't kill a few of the savages before they got him. His soldiers were hesitant, but in the end they did what soldiers did best: follow orders. Without a protest, they formed up behind their captain and marched straight toward what they must have known was likely to be their last battle.

As they came closer, it became clear that Milton had not been exaggerating. There were thousands of Grauda running around, looting and killing anyone they found. They had gone for the food supplies first. Many of the figures he saw were only half the size of the usual Grauda fighters. Were they their young? Alistair didn't understand why they would risk their young when their soldiers alone could overwhelm them at this point.

"Hold and get into position!" he yelled, and his men and women quickly formed ranks with swordsmen in front and archers behind. Unlike the undead, arrows were effective against the Grauda and he grinned at the idea of finally killing some of the vicious monsters who had torn apart his family. He would finally have his revenge.

The Grauda didn't bother to organize into any formation. They simply charged forward in a swarm, with the intent to swallow them whole.

Alistair raised his sword in the air. "Loo—" he began, but was cut short by an icy feeling in his chest. He looked down to see five thin, black, blade-like objects sticking out of him.

Warning: you are suffering from critical injuries and require healing!

Alistair didn't need the notification—he coughed out so much blood it splashed on the ground. All the soldiers were staring at him with shock in their eyes. He turned to see his assailant and frowned.

"You… you traitor," he gasped, every word causing waves of pain to spread through his chest, as his lungs began to fill with his own blood. The blade-like objects were pulled from him, allowing Alistair to collapse to his knees. His soldiers were still stunned into inaction, and even the archers had their arrows only halfway drawn as they stared at the scene unfolding before them.

"I am truly sorry for this, Alistair," Milton said. "But I have a mission to complete." He then raised his arms above his head and slowly lowered them, and the most beautiful woman Alistair had ever seen manifested in front him. He forgot about his pain as he stared into her golden eyes, which shone brighter and brighter. His mind felt clouded, but he could see from the reactions of his fellow men, this beauty wasn't a hallucination due to his injuries. She was real.

The woman smiled the most beautiful smile, and Alistair smiled back, then tried to wipe the blood from his mouth. What was he doing? What were they all doing staring at this woman, in the middle of a battle? Were those *horns* on her head?

Each time some hint of lucidity returned to him, it was as if a weight the size of a mountain pushed it back down… and he was again entranced by her.

"That's it, just look at me," she said, as she stroked her finger down his cheek. Her touch was electrifying, almost enough for him to ignore the grotesque sound of snapping and ripping that was coming from all around him.

"Don't worry, it will all be over soon," she whispered into his ear. Dumbly, he nodded his acceptance.

His vision started to fade as his body began to lose any ability to function. He struggled to stay awake… and then whatever spell the demon had placed on him lost its power as his brain began to die.

The last thing he saw was the Grauda rip into his people, as they all stared at the demon in wonder. They didn't fight back when the insects cut their throats and bit into their flesh. They didn't even scream. They did nothing but stare.

* * *

Celia sighed as Alistair finally slumped to the ground. Her plan had worked flawlessly, and as far as she could tell, they had not lost a single Grauda. Vhal's Army of the Dead skill was just the diversion she had needed to speak to the Grauda in their nest and gather them together.

The undead he conjured were far more effective then she had initially accounted for, which made using her Charm on the few remaining humans much easier. It still took a lot out of her to keep so many under control, however. Some of them did resist, and it was not unlike juggling, as she had to keep reapplying her Charm to them.

Killing Alistair had been difficult, but it had to be done. At least a stab to the heart was far better than letting the Grauda have their way with him. It really was the only mercy she could offer him.

She glanced around now at the gory and dismembered remains of the soldiers that had come here to fight. The Grauda had been starving when she found them down in their tunnels, and they were now eating everything they found. It was a feeding frenzy, with the humans as the main course.

Trying not to watch for too long, Celia walked back through the bodies to the other edge of the camp. Vhal was there, along with all the female Grauda who had stayed behind in the colony when their queen left to meet Aziel.

"Quite vicious," Vhal said, grinning widely as she approached. "Almost makes using my Summon Undead worth it. Using it comes with a price, you know."

"It was the only way to ensure the Grauda survived *and* keep our identities a secret," she replied.

Vhal shrugged. "Perhaps." He pointed at the scene behind her. "They must be acting on pure instinct."

"They were starved. The humans brought this upon themselves," Celia said flatly. She stared at the watching females. "Well? How long are you going to stand there? Get your males under control. We need to get moving."

The females nodded and spread out to do as they were told.

Vhal leaned on his staff and stroked his beard, thoughtfully. "I honestly thought they wouldn't listen to us."

"They saw me talking to their queen, so they know who I am. And they were the ones who asked for help, remember?" she replied, stretching her arms over her head. "This is the last time I use a male disguise," she continued, caused Vhal to look at her curiously.

"It's… too real," she complained, which elicited a chuckle from Vhal.

"Are the differences causing you some discomfort, Celia? I would have thought you of all people knew how to handle the equipment," he quipped, his grin was so wide it looked unnatural even for him.

Celia stared at him blankly. She wasn't in the mood for their usual back and forth. She just wanted to return to Soul's Rest to be with her master and, well, rest.

A female Grauda approached her and nodded. Celia looked around, confirming that the females had already calmed their males down. She had to admit she was impressed by how fast it had been. It couldn't have been easy to calm a frenzied swarm.

She pulled a small letter from her pack and showed it to the Grauda. "Send a group of your fastest warriors and capture a human that escaped from one of the other camps. Give him this letter. Follow him and make sure he delivers it to Whiteridge."

The Grauda female looked at her curiously. Celia had no doubt about what was going on in her mind. She was deciding if following this sort of order from a non-Grauda was acceptable.

"The letter is from your future king," she added, and the female

Grauda's antennae twitched, before she reached and grabbed the letter. Vhal, on the other hand, frowned.

"A letter? What is it about?"

Celia grinned. "Feeling left out, Vhal?" she said, before striding past him to lead the Grauda on their march home. She could feel his stare boring into her, but she was tired, her muscles ached, and her head hurt. That Mass Charm had taken a lot out of her. Besides, the letter was sealed. She didn't know what was in it any more than he did.

CHAPTER 26

AZIEL SCRATCHED HIS head as he sat in the study, poring over books and documents relating to governing as well as urban planning. It was all far more complicated than he ever thought it was going to be. And more importantly, it was frustrating.

These books all contained information regarding human settlements, and a few described elvish architecture. Nothing even remotely considered the needs of beings such as the Grauda, the undead, or demons. He supposed that it made sense in a way, but that didn't make it any less annoying.

He shut the book and let out a deep sigh before rubbing his eyes. Celia and Vhal should be back any time now, if things had gone to plan. He really hoped they did. He didn't want to upset an already concerned Astrel. The thought of the Grauda queen brought a smile to his face, as he recalled the last few days.

Astrel had insisted on coupling multiple times. It was to ensure her scent stuck, she said, but he was suspicious of her reasoning. By the end of their first encounter, the reaction of other Grauda to him had changed drastically, shifting from a strange mix of fear and restraint to outright adoration and respect. They practically hung on his every word now, to the extent that it made him feel a bit uncomfortable about the kind of responsibility that entailed. Not to mention the trait he had received as a result.

King of the Grauda
Class: Title
You have been chosen by the reigning Grauda
Queen to lead their race.

Effects:
Ability to command all Grauda with the author-
ity of the queen.

Aziel smiled as the runes began to fade. It wasn't as if he was going to refuse her offers. Not only was she beautiful, but having sex with someone even less experienced than himself was something of a relief.

Astrel and Celia were completely different in that sense. When he was with the feisty succubus, it was a battle for domination—a battle he would lose every time if he didn't start using his mana as a weapon. Their sessions were also instructional as much as they were about passion, as Celia used their time together to teach him some tricks of the trade, so to speak.

Astrel, on the other hand, was completely submissive in bed. She let him lead and did what he asked at all times. It had been a bit frightening at first—he was used to Celia taking on that role—but he quickly grew to enjoy it. It was far more relaxed than the full-on experience Celia represented... not that he didn't also enjoy that. In the end, they balanced each other out quite well in his mind.

Just as he put down the book in his hands and leaned back in his chair, intending to take a short break, a knock sounded from the door. It opened, and the queen entered. Her soft chitin skin shone, and her hair was wet, giving off a floral scent. He examined her up and down, then smiled as his eyes met hers. She smiled back and made her way to his side.

"Enjoyed the bathhouse?" he asked. She nodded, taking a seat at the desk and glancing at the books in front of him.

"Planning to build a city for the humans?" she asked mockingly as her fingers delicately opened the book's cover, then let it go to slam shut again.

Aziel chuckled softly. "With all the information available, it would be easy to do so, I think. But unfortunately, no. We can still learn from them, I suppose."

Astrel placed her hands in her lap. "You really are going to try and build a country for us? The civilized nations won't make it easy."

"As if I need their permission," Aziel scoffed. "The Central Wilds will soon belong to us. And if they decide to oppose me and those I consider my own, then I will simply remove them from the board." He sat up straight. "Which reminds me, I wished to ask you about the other ancient races. Do you know who and where they are?"

Astrel hesitated, looking down at her feet. "Many of the ancient races I was told about either died out after the Fall or were hunted into extinction." She looked up, and Aziel could see the pain in her eyes. "As far as I know, the other two races that made up the Collective are no longer with us."

Aziel placed his hand on top of hers, and gently stroked them. Astrel looked up and smiled slightly.

"But that doesn't mean no others exist. My mother told me of the Ogre'i. They are still somewhere in the Wilds, I believe…" She paused for a moment before continuing in a less confident manner, "There were also rumors a few years back of a Valkyrie being sighted, but I haven't seen any evidence of them."

Aziel narrowed his eyes as a familiar tingling sensation started in his head. He frowned as the tingling morphed into a brutal hammering—and then his brain exploded in pain.

Astrel looked at him in concern, gripping his hand in hers as he closed his eyes and clenched his jaw in an attempt to fight through it. This agony was exactly the same as the episode he had gone through when he first saw Astrel... but to his dismay, no new memories followed, just the harrowing pain.

Thankfully, the experience only lasted for a few heartbeats. Aziel let out a sigh of relief and looked up at the concerned Grauda queen to reassure her with a small smile.

"My king?" she asked, her hand still gripping his tightly.

"I am fine, Astrel, don't worry. Just tell me who and what the Valkyrie are. Everything you know." If just the mention of their name had given him that reaction, then they had to be important.

Astrel gazed upward, as if in an attempt to gather her thoughts. But then she shook her head slowly and frowned.

"The Valkyrie are... or were... powerful beings of light. They had large feathered wings, and the stories say they were the most beautiful people that ever lived. Their whole species served a single Ascended of light, and they acted as her honor guard, but they were also known for how private and secretive they were." She paused. "The stories I was told say that they were the first to describe you as the Aziel after Divinities' Fall, but not much is really known about them."

Aziel thought about this. Her description came awfully close how his mother looked in the memories he recovered. The real question was, why would the Valkyrie spread rumors of his possible return?

Were they looking for him? And if so, were they his allies or enemies? Of course, that was assuming they still existed. He was also frustrated by his missing memories—he had assumed that learning more would have triggered something, but nothing had happened.

And there was another problem. From his memories, it was

clear the Collective, and therefore the Grauda, served his mother's faction. But Astrel didn't even seem to know who this Ascended of light had been. While a story being told over and over again from one generation to another meant details would be lost, could that be true of something as important as who led their faction?

He swallowed his questions for now, then stood. "Come, Astrel. There is something we must do."

* * *

Once inside his crystal chamber, Aziel looked at Astrel with a serious expression, which caused the Grauda queen to freeze.

"Kneel," he commanded, and she did as he asked without hesitation. "I would like you to swear fealty," he said, and at his words, Astrel's whole demeanor changed.

She gazed up at him and nodded. "I, Astrel," she began, "last queen of the Grauda, swear fealty to my lord and king, Aziel. I offer my body and soul to your service, to be commanded in any way you see fit."

Aziel placed his hand on Astrel's head, before declaring, "Astrel, Queen of the Grauda, I accept your fealty; you will be the first of my inner council to advise me and represent the interests of your people. Serve me and your people well, and I will ensure you are properly rewarded."

Astrel stood, a proud smile on her face. "I will serve you well, my king."

Aziel smiled back. "I have no doubt that you will. We should now speak about our future plans. As you are the only member of the inner council so far, your opinion in these matters is vital."

He walked with her to the curved rock at the end of the chamber, where he took his seat.

"Once your people arrive, which should be soon, you will begin repopulating your race," he said. "I am uncomfortable with the Grauda being in a perpetual state of near extinction."

Astrel bowed, but he could see her blush slightly—perhaps

wording it so bluntly wasn't the best idea. As their queen, she mostly likely blamed herself for their current state, but it was something that bothered him, and he needed it rectified as soon as possible.

"As you wish, my king," she said.

"Good. Now let us get to the role the Grauda will take on as members of the Fallen."

Astrel looked at him curiously. "Role? My people are to fulfill all the roles, are they not?"

"For now, yes. But the Grauda have a specialty I want to discuss. I have a distinct memory of the Grauda being builders." He paused as Astrel's shoulders stiffened. "Is there a reason why that is no longer the case?"

Astrel smiled sadly, her posture relaxing, "You are correct. We Grauda do indeed have racial inclinations and specialized skills when it comes to construction. I did not mean to hide this from you, my king, I—" her voice was growing more frantic, and Aziel raised his hand to stop her.

"I am not upset, Astrel. I only wish to understand," he said.

Astrel nodded slowly. "The Grauda can build like any other race, but our skills allow us to build faster and more precisely. We can see the structural weaknesses and strengths of rock and other construction materials. We just couldn't access these abilities... until now." A small smile appeared on her face as she met his eyes.

Aziel was at a loss. "So you *can* build the structures I remembered?" he asked.

"Yes, my king. This skill set has been locked to us ever since the events of Divinities' Fall. It requires us to be part of a faction and also have a king... when my people gain the skill points needed, they will have the ability to build whatever you desire."

Aziel blinked, was it really that simple? He couldn't help but grin—it was as if a weight had been suddenly taken off his shoulders. With this, most of his plans could finally go into action. As for levels... the next step should solve that.

"I am pleased—" he tried to say, but Astrel's antennae suddenly shot up, and she turned to face the entrance before sprinting toward it without a word.

Aziel stared at her, dumbfounded, then jumped up himself and followed. As he got closer to the door, he sensed the thousands of vessels gathering outside and making their way down the long hallway. There were so many he couldn't distinguish them from one another—they all blended together.

He caught up to Astrel halfway down the passage, just as she threw herself at the leading group of female Grauda and hugged them tightly. The surrounding males and females clicked their mandibles in what Aziel could only hope was happiness. He smiled as a sense of relief washed over him.

Before he could do anything else, he felt himself being tackled to the ground and quickly flipped onto his back. A succubus sat astride him, a huge grin on her face.

"Master..." she purred, before she dove forward to kiss him.

"Celia," he tried to say, between kisses, but she placed a finger on his lips to quiet him.

"Hmm... floral..." she hummed, then opened her eyes wide and grinned down at him. "You took the stubborn queen didn't you?" she asked excitedly. "About time. I thought you would never get down to it, at the rate things were going."

Aziel looked at her curiously. "You're not upset?" Although Celia had said she wouldn't be, before and after the fact were completely different scenarios.

Celia tilted her head slightly. "Should I be?"

"No...?"

"Then I'm not. But, Master, I completed my quest and was awarded an extra point of Reflex from the World Seed!" She licked her lips as her eyes roamed his body. "Now I want my real reward," she said, leaning forward to trail kisses down his neck while her tail played with the growing bulge in his pants. She giggled. "Looks like you're more than ready."

Aziel struggled to keep his thoughts in order. His whole body was screaming at him to just let her do as she pleased, but there was a whole race of people he had to greet. Not to mention they were in the middle of a crowded hallway.

"Celia," he whispered.

"Mmm…" she moaned, then went back to nibbling on his ear.

"Let's continue this in the bedroom, after I'm done with the Grauda," he said, but even he could hear the hesitation in his voice.

Celia lifted her face up to his and smiled knowingly. "Master," she purred, then leaned in, only to yelp as she jumped back in surprise.

Aziel quickly took the opportunity to get back to his feet, preparing himself to counter her inevitable tackle. Instead, he looked down and saw Celia looking back at him with hazy eyes, a dreamy expression on her face he had never seen before.

"Master," she mumbled. Her body twitched as another moan escaped her lips. "That's not fair."

Aziel looked at her, then back at his hands. He had spiked her with his mana, and although he did use more usual, this was a far stronger reaction than he expected.

"Ah, my lord, you're here," a voice called out.

Aziel looked up to see Vhal pushing his way through the Grauda, only to stop suddenly as he stared down at Celia who was slowly recovering from her ordeal.

"Hmm," he said.

"She will be fine… I think," Aziel said, as Celia curled herself into a ball and shuddered.

Vhal's interest seemed to fade almost as quickly as it had appeared. He nodded and bowed to Aziel. "We have completed the mission, my lord. We lost four Grauda males on the way here due to an Arachne attack, but otherwise all went well, considering."

Aziel frowned. Astrel had briefly told him of the Arachne and the danger they posed. But they were now actively attacking him? He was just about to ask Vhal for more details when he noticed the growing crowd of Grauda gathering around them. They were looking at him with that familiar mix of awe and devotion, which was uncomfortable.

Being their king was going to take some getting used to. He glanced around until he found Astrel and called to her to lead them to their new home, before picking Celia up from the ground.

The succubus moaned but wrapped her hands around him as he lifted her, her head tucked between his neck and shoulder. She was completely out of it, and Aziel could only smile as he made his way back to his place of power, with Vhal close behind.

There, he lay Celia down on his seat before asking Vhal what had happened. The lich took his time explaining all that had occurred, including the Arachne attack, the battle, and that his letter had been delivered.

"What was in that letter, my lord?" he asked curiously.

Aziel grinned. "A threat, of course."

Vhal's eyes flashed and he grinned too. "Oh? And what did you threaten them with?"

Aziel put his hand on Celia's shoulder to steady her; she had gone to sleep and was now slowly sliding down the curved rock.

"It's simple, really. I told them that the Grauda King had returned and would destroy them for all their crimes against my people. I told them I wished to meet their Faction Leader or his Viceroy in Whiteridge a month from now to discuss terms, or I would send word to every nation in Kadora about the Maivian military presence in the Central Wilds."

Vhal seemed to enjoy this. "Then you have decided it's finally time to reveal yourself to the world?"

"I have," Aziel replied. "Vhal, I need you to help Astrel organize the Grauda. Help them settle as soon as possible, give them access to the armor and weapons that they may need. We have three weeks to get them into shape for a possible war with the humans."

He opened his palm and let out a cloud of soul mana, which quickly solidified into several Soul Wisps.

"My Soul Wisps can last for just under a week. I will need you to show me where Whiteridge is, so that I can monitor activities there." Aziel leaned down to pick Celia up again. "I will take her upstairs and will meet with you shortly."

Vhal bowed again. "As you wish, my lord."

Aziel arranged Celia in his arms, and he smiled as he looked down at her peacefully sleeping face. He then slowly made his way to their bedroom.

Gently placing her onto the bed, he leaned down and kissed the top of her head. "I'm sorry, I'll be sure to make this up to you later," he whispered, but just as he was about to draw back, he felt something slither around him before tightening around his leg. He glanced down to see Celia's tail wrapped around him, and then he was gripped and tipped back onto the bed.

"That was mean, Master," Celia purred as she climbed on top of him. "But I will forgive you, since being carried around by you was pleasant," she admitted with a mischievous grin.

"You were awake?" Aziel asked, surprised.

"Mmm-hmm," she said as she pressed her body against his. "I think I'll have you make this up to me right now," she purred, between kisses.

Aziel inhaled as he felt her hands slowly make their way down his chest, her tail moving expertly to remove his pants. She had become quite adept at dealing with his armor. Knowing there was no point in fighting her, he smiled and pulled her close to whisper in her ear.

"You win, Celia, but you have to promise we will only do this once… I really do need to take care of the Grauda."

Celia smiled shrewdly, as she turned her head and licked the side of his neck. "I promise," she whispered.

Aziel chuckled to himself. She was never going to keep that promise.

CHAPTER 27

THE WEEKS THAT followed were a flurry of activity as the Grauda made themselves at home. Vhal, as ordered, opened up all the resources of Soul's Rest to them—with the exception of the dimensional bags and the Imperial Family's personal weapons, which were too valuable. The Grauda did not seem to mind, happily accepting whatever they were given.

As expected, Astrel's mood had significantly improved since her people's arrival. She even asked if Aziel could provide her with some additional earth crystals; apparently, after so long without breeding, her sisters had become overexcited and may have overdone things. With Aziel's help, she rather giddily reported that the Grauda population would more than double in the next month or so.

This was a fact Aziel didn't need confirming. Even in their pre-hatched state, the new Grauda provided him with a small amount of mana. He was amazed by how the tiny eggs Astrel showed him could become full-grown Grauda in a matter of weeks, given enough earth mana.

What excited the queen even more was when Aziel identified certain eggs as providing him with slightly more mana than the rest. When the first one of those hatched, it became clear why that was.

They were females. It appeared the increased earth mana had

also increased the abysmally low female birth rate. Astrel explained that the growing number of females meant she could now afford to appoint regents.

It was a point Aziel had not even considered—how impossible it would be for Astrel to control so many Grauda on her own. With a set of regents, Astrel could delegate tasks and even expand into other colonies, with her new proxies reporting back as needed.

Despite Astrel's earlier concerns, all the humans they had killed during the massacre meant that many of the Grauda were able to assign some new skill points to their building abilities. Immediately after, they started fixing what Astrel described as the weak, unsupported, and dangerous walls that made up Soul's Rest.

Aziel was thankful to the Grauda's newly unlocked racial skill, Wondrous Builder, as it helped avert a problem he hadn't even known about. A cave-in within his place of power would have been, to put it mildly, problematic.

Another unexpected and pleasant development was that Astrel's and Celia's relationship seemed to have improved greatly. The Grauda queen was grateful to the succubus, especially when she heard that it was her plan that allowed for the almost complete survival of her race. Calling them friends might be overstating matters, but there was an improvement there.

Vhal, on the other hand, spent this time looking through and decrypting the grimoires within his office. This provided a veritable mountain of useful spells Aziel could weave with his earth and fire mana.

Unfortunately, this activity revealed a personality quirk of the lich, to the dismay of everyone who called Soul's Rest home. Vhal seemed to have no control over his rather loud and spine-chilling laughter, which he unleashed on the echo-prone fortress whenever he made a breakthrough.

One of those discoveries, however, did solve a problem which had concerned Aziel ever since his proposal to Melody and her departure from Soul's Rest for her home country.

Aranite—or gods' steel, as she had called it—was something he had an ample supply of, given the three large gates made of it. But therein lay the problem; Aziel could not sell massive gate-sized slabs of the material. He needed ingots. He tried heating them up in the hopes of melting them, but as suspected, nothing happened. The aranite didn't even begin to glow, no matter how much heat he exposed it to.

While his blade was able to chip pieces away if he activated its enchantment, that method would not result in ingots, and Aziel wasn't sure his blade would survive that much contact with the rare metal.

It was after this last failed attempt that Vhal had offered a solution. In his reading of the earth grimoire, he had stumbled upon a spell named Shape Metal. A functionally rank-four spell, it did as expected—it had the ability to re-form metals.

Aziel tried it on the aranite and the metal resisted at first. Aziel felt the lingering mana within the metal work to deny the spell's effects, but after he empowered the spell, he finally started to get some results.

Luckily, the aranite was already almost completely drained. Otherwise, he was certain that even the empowered spell would not have worked on it. It took over a week for Aziel to weave the spell a sufficient number of times to re-shape the gates into the over three thousand mana-drained aranite standard ingots. These were stacked and stored within the now empty storage rooms, which had previously housed the emergency rations the Grauda had so enthusiastically taken for themselves.

When all these preparations were finally complete, Aziel made his way through Soul's Rest, checking on the hundreds of Grauda workers digging into mountain rock, helping to bring his plans into existence.

While they were progressing faster than expected, Aziel was under no illusion about how long it would take to complete. The

Grauda had no weavers, and without the ability to weaken or even sculpt the hard mountain rock using earth mana, this project would continue for years.

As he entered the hallway leading to the outside, he unexpectedly bumped into Astrel.

"My king." She greeted him with a warm smile.

"Astrel. Are you returning from the colony?"

She nodded. "There had been another Arachne sighting nearby. I wished to make sure they were not a threat."

"These Arachne are becoming a problem," Aziel said, annoyed.

Astrel shook her head, "Your champion and head researcher did annihilate one of their clusters, but even then their behavior is abnormal. The Arachne have always been aggressive but only within their territory and sometimes along their border. These types of random attacks are unlike them."

This was an issue neither could work out. Aziel was comfortable with ignoring the Arachne for the time being, but with two separate Arachne attacks on the Grauda colony in the last week, he was forced to take this threat more seriously.

The attacks had been small in scale, considering. Aziel responded by sending his Soul Wisps deep into their territory.

What he witnessed there had raised more questions than answers. There were large clusters of roaming Arachne. But instead of defending their homes, they were actually attacking each other… and rather brutally so. Aziel could find no pattern or reason for this behavior.

"Do be careful," he said. Astrel smiled and leaned forward to give him a quick peck on the lips before hurrying past without a word.

Aziel shook his head and chuckled before continuing on his way. With the Arachne mostly busy tearing themselves apart, it was a matter he could deal with at a later date. His focus now was entirely on Whiteridge, and by extension, the Kingdom of Maiv.

There was good news on that front, thankfully. It would seem the humans had taken his threat quite seriously, as not long after the delivery of his letter, large-scale preparations went into effect in and around the town. Fortifications were being hardened, patrols had been doubled, and even the ditch dug around the town was being expanded. He was amazed by how many humans there still were in the town. He assumed after such a crushing defeat, their numbers would have diminished. But it seems the host sent to deal with the Grauda had not been their entire force.

A few days ago, his wisps had spotted something even more important.

An elegant carriage had entered Whiteridge with an armed escort, which relieved him. As the days passed, he had grown anxious that the Faction Leader or Viceroy might not agree to meet him. Their presence was an integral part of his plans, after all.

He had moved his wisp close enough to the carriage to see a blonde-haired beauty step from it and make her way into the unfinished fort. When he described the woman to Celia, she was quick to identify her as the Crown Princess Lucienne of the Kingdom of Maiv, Viceroy of the faction of Maiv.

Celia explained that in her time within the kingdom, paintings of the princess were placed in inns and other public places within every village or town she visited, even more so than the king, but she didn't know why that was the case.

As Aziel continued down the passage that led to the entrance of Soul's Rest, he thought about what the princess's presence in Whiteridge meant. It was time to move on to the last stage of his plan and claim the Central Wilds for the Fallen.

At the threshold of the mountain, he stopped and took a deep breath. White moonlight painted the ground and leaves of the forest before him, but his body and mind couldn't appreciate the scene's beauty. All they did was increase his fear of what the outside represented: danger. Danger of being drained of his mana until he was nothing but a husk.

Closing his eyes, Aziel tried to calm himself as he took his first step outside the mountain since his encounter with the dryad.

Carefully, he took another step, followed by another... until he felt the drain begin to take effect. With the mana he was receiving from his followers counteracting it, the drain was not nearly as strong as last time, but that didn't make the feeling any more comfortable.

Aziel opened his eyes and saw that he was alone in the now debris-free clearing, just a few yards from the tree line. Astrel must have ordered her people to remove all the rocks and broken stumps.

He glanced back at the open doorway of his home, then up at the starry night sky. An unfamiliar sky... a new sky. Unlike the one he had stared up to inside his prison world, this night sky was bursting with color, and the full moon that dominated it bathed the world below in its light.

But even in the presence of such celestial beauty, Aziel could only frown. It worried him how different his perspective had become since he was last here. Instead of appreciating the new world he had now become a part of, all he could see were the perils awaiting him and his people.

He stared at the stars and wondered how many of them stared back at him. How many of them were massive metallic fortresses masquerading as stars? It was an uncomfortable question he had struggled with ever since learning of the World Seed's quests. They had made clear just how much influence the World Seed had over their lives.

By bestowing some missions with more rewards than others, the World Seed was effectively directing their decisions in a very real way—who knew to what end.

Then there was the question he didn't know if he could even ask. Who or what were the Overseers or Archivist? He didn't dare speak of them. He didn't know which part of his experience in that white room he was threatened not to reveal. Aziel didn't even know if the people around him could answer if he did ask. No, he would not satisfy his curiosity if it meant a possible death by a beam of red light from above.

The sound of rustling and crunching leaves brought him out of his thoughts, and he turned to see Celia approaching him. Her golden eyes shone even more brightly at night.

"Master? Should you be out here?" she asked with a hint of concern.

Aziel smiled. "It's alright. A few minutes won't make a difference." He sat on the ground, his back against a tree. "Care to join me?"

Celia sat beside him, resting her head on his shoulder. Aziel responded by wrapping his arm around her and pulling her close. What followed was a few moments of silence as they stared at the heavens above.

"I never thought I would ever experience something like this," Celia whispered softly.

Aziel dropped his head to look at her, but she was still gazing up at the moon above, its light revealing every detail of her beautiful face.

"Girls in my village always dreamt of meeting a man, having some fairy tale adventure and raising a family... It was something my mother always talked about, but then..." she paused for a moment, and her eyes looked down to the ground. "Well, that dream became impossible for me," she said, her voice more solemn.

"Celia," Aziel began.

"Wait, let me finish." She sighed, as her eyes met his own. "I never told you of how I became a demon, have I?"

Aziel slowly shook his head. Celia took a deep breath, as though steeling herself.

"It was a long time ago," she began. "It started with my father arriving home drunk one night. He was often drunk, you see. But this time, something was different; he looked crazed, his eyes... they were so red. He started yelling at my mom and smashed her dressing table to pieces. I was so scared. My parents often fought, but they never got violent. But this time... I just stood there, frozen." Celia shivered. "I watched as he grabbed and threw her to the ground. I watched as she screamed, and he pummeled her to death."

Aziel placed a hand on her shoulder.

"When I finally gathered the courage to try to pull him away, I knew it was already too late. I clung to him, sobbing. I just wanted him to stop... he tried to push me away, but during our struggle, I felt it. I was... pulling something from him."

Celia shut her eyes before continuing.

"I heard awful gurgling sounds as his breathing got slower and hoarser. Finally, he stopped struggling, and there was all this power... all this pain. I fell unconscious after that, and when I woke, I found myself curled up on the floorboards. I thought for a moment it had been just a cruel nightmare. But then I saw myself, transformed. I saw them."

Celia opened her eyes then, forcing herself look directly at him as she spoke.

"My mother was a mess. Her skull had been caved in, her arms and hands were bloodied from when she tried to protect herself. But my father... my father's skin had turned gray. He was all shriveled up—as if someone sucked all the fluids from his body. In my desperation, I had done something impossible, I Siphoned him, without even knowing how or what that was. I don't remember much of my actual transformation, just the pain,"

Aziel didn't know how a non-demon could have weaved a Siphon, but Celia certainly believed she did, and she turned into a demon as a result. From the tremble in her voice, he could tell she was deeply ashamed of her actions, and that she had feared what his reaction might be.

"I ran," she whispered. "After my transformation into a succubus, I was in a never-ending cycle of survival. It was all I thought about, nothing else mattered. But that all changed when it led me to you."

The edges of her mouth edged upward.

"With your link, survival was no longer an issue. I didn't need to strive for it, you just *gave* it to me. Things, feelings I never thought possible for someone like me. All of a sudden I had things like relationships, happiness…" Her voice trailed off as she again looked away from him. "All I'm saying is that I'm happy here… happy here with you."

Aziel took her face in his hands and kissed her, stopping her from saying another word. It was unlike any kiss he had shared with Celia—it was tender and soft, so different from the hungry kisses they usually shared.

As their lips parted, their eyes met, and they stared at one another for a moment in silence before Aziel whispered, "I want to say I am sorry for all the hardship you had to go through in the past. But everything that happened has led to you being here, with me. And it might be selfish, but I won't apologize for that. I am… truly lucky and blessed to have someone like you by my side, Celia."

It was a feeling he had been struggling to understand, but even though he was certain the link between them had influenced their relationship in many ways, at the moment he said those words, he felt a weight lift from his heart and he knew it to be true.

Even in the moonlight, he could see Celia's face turn pink as she averted her gaze. Aziel saw her take a deep breath and her shoulders relaxed. A moment later, she leaned into and kissed him again, but this time more in line with her usually passionate ways.

She pulled away with the most radiant smile he had ever seen on her, and he couldn't stop himself from smiling back.

"Let's go back," she said with a mischievous wink. "Astrel is probably waiting for you in your bed."

Aziel looked at her curiously, and Celia picked up on it immediately. "Ah, I know it's my turn. But I felt bad, with her staying back and all." She gave him a knowing smile. "I expect you to use all that I taught you—she won't see you for a while, you know."

Aziel remained quiet for a moment. By morning, Celia, Vhal, and himself, along with six hundred heavily armed Grauda would march toward Whiteridge to meet Lucienne. Ignoring her vehement objections, Aziel had ordered Astrel to stay behind to keep charge of the repairs of Soul's Rests and see to its protection.

The idea of taking turns in his bed had been entirely Celia's, and he thought better of intruding into whatever deal she arranged with Astrel.

Aziel chuckled. "I'll be sure to make my teacher proud," he said, which elicited an exaggerated nod from the succubus.

"You better," she said, offering him a hand to help pull him up, which he accepted gratefully.

As they walked back through the clearing toward the open doorway of their home holding one another's hands, Aziel couldn't help but take one last look at the stars above and wonder how things would turn out.

CHAPTER 28

AZIEL AWOKE TO a now-familiar but very much-loved scene: Astrel entwined at his side, her head resting on his bare chest. His first thought as he kissed the top of her head was that she really did smell like flowers. She stirred at his kiss, groaning before looking up at him sleepily.

"My king," she murmured with a yawn, before slowly sitting up on her knees. She rubbed her eyes then looked at him with sudden focus, something was on her mind.

Aziel smiled. "I know you want to come with me, Astrel, but I need you here."

The Grauda queen practically deflated at his words. "But my king... my place is by your side, leading my warriors into battle," she complained, as she began unwrapping the cloth from around her scythe-like arm. It was something she had put into practice to protect the bed and him from any accidents.

"I know, and trust me when I say that I would much prefer you be at my side at all times." He emphasized his words by drawing her hand to his lips and giving it a kiss. "But you and I both know that Soul's Rest cannot be left unattended for so long."

Astrel sighed then nodded. "I know... I just," she sighed again before straightening her back and looking at him sternly. "You must promise to come back to me unharmed, my king." Aziel had to wonder what she would do if he broke that promise, but was not foolish enough to ask. Instead, he leaned in and kissed her gently on the lips.

"I promise," he whispered. "I do have a lot to come back for, after all." He stood and began to pick up the pieces of his armor and suit. Astrel simply smiled at him.

* * *

Adjusting his collar, Aziel strode into his place of power with Astrel following closely behind, to find Celia, Vhal, and six hundred Grauda male warriors awaiting him.

All the Grauda present wore the full leather armor provided to them over their hard chitin exoskeletons, and each wielded a steel-tipped spear. Each also had a bow strapped to their back and a quiver of arrows attached to the side of a belt, for quick access when needed. The Grauda didn't seem to have any natural inclination to archery, and from what little Astrel had told him of their training, they were not great marksmen over long range. Even so, this would allow them to have some kind of projectile weapon to use during ambushes whilst also keeping their spears instead of using them as javelins as they had been doing so until now.

The troops were divided into groups of one hundred, each led by a single female equipped with the same armor and weapons, but with a golden scarf around their necks not unlike the one Aziel wore. They had found hundreds of them packed in the boxes within the main storeroom, which they now called the armory. Vhal explained that they had been worn by military officers to help distinguish them from the rest of the soldiers, and Aziel saw no reason not to continue using them as such.

The male Grauda stared at him with their black, beady eyes, while the females wore the same look of awe Astrel had when they had first met. He wasn't sure how long they would treat him that way, but if Astrel was to be believed, it was going to be a long time. It was just how their race saw their king, she explained.

"My lord," Vhal said with a slight bow, offering him a red book. "I brought it, as requested." It was not the actual grimoire, but a copy which contained all the spells Vhal had decoded from its original so far.

"Good," Aziel said as he tucked it under his arm. "I'll be needing it."

"May I ask what for?"

"You'll see. I'm fairly sure you will enjoy it," he said, smirking.

Vhal chuckled as he positioned himself to Aziel's right and didn't press for more. Celia, however, had latched onto his left side and purred.

"I really shouldn't have given up my turn," she whispered haughtily. "I really missed you last night, Master…"

"Do not worry, Celia," he said. "We will have plenty of time on the way there and back."

The succubus grinned and pressed herself even closer. "Oh, I know…" she purred, before pulling back.

Aziel smiled at her antics, turning just in time to see Astrel step forward to kneel before him, causing the rest of the waiting Grauda to kneel as well.

"They are ready, my king. The Grauda will make you proud," she announced confidently.

Aziel gently placed his hand on her head. "Of that, I have no doubt. But if I have my way, they won't have to," he added.

The inquisitive looks from his followers at this only made him chuckle, as he pulled up his log to confirm his mana levels were indeed full. He had spent a lot of time calculating and measuring in order to fulfill his goals. If everything went according to plan, he should have just under a third of his mana left by the time he returned to Soul's Rest, and at that point, the Central Wilds would already belong to the Fallen.

"We will only take a break at night for sleep," he commanded, as he rested his hand on the hilt of his sword. "We must get there as quickly as possible. Time is not our friend."

He turned to Vhal, and the lich nodded his head in acceptance. "As agreed, I will hold the rear and ensure no enemies impede us from behind."

"And I'll scout ahead and take out any threats in our way," Celia added. "I estimate we should get there in three days' time, given one single rest per day."

Aziel grinned. "Well then, let us be off. I have a princess looking forward to meeting me, and I'd hate to keep her waiting." And with that, he led his troops out of the crystal chamber and into the Wilds in the direction of Whiteridge.

*　*　*

Celia's estimations turned out to be correct, as by the third night they had reached the outskirts of the town. Their forces had been spotted some time ago, since Aziel detected a few vessels close by, which must have been their scouts, who were maintaining just enough of a distance that it would be difficult to catch them.

That didn't matter to Aziel, however; he wasn't planning on a surprise attack, after all. What did matter to him was his mistaken assumption about how the drain on his mana would work.

He had made his calculations based on his experience when he first left the mountain, and simply estimated the rate of increase as he moved farther away from his home.

But even his worst-case scenario hadn't gone far enough. Instead of a steady increase, the drain increased exponentially over the distance, with large jumps at what Aziel could only call random distance thresholds. The first was at about thirty or so miles, when the drain increased by a factor of two. This had kept repeating every now and then. By the second night, he had to actively meditate to keep himself in check. Of his followers, only Celia seemed to have noticed that something was wrong, but he kept reassuring her that everything was fine.

This mission had to be completed no matter what. His faction could not stay in the shadows forever, and first impressions were everything.

With the increased drain in mind, his revised estimate would leave him with just under a fourth of his total mana by the time he made it back to Soul's Rest... and that was taking into account the massive reduction of the drain he would enjoy if he successfully claimed the Central Wilds.

But Aziel had confidence in his plan. Things would work out, he was sure of it. Now, as night gave way to day, he stood with Celia by the tree line facing the town of Whiteridge, his Grauda force hidden in the thick brush and trees behind them.

He placed a hand on Celia's shoulder. "Are you ready?"

She frowned. Aziel had explained the main thrust of his plan to her, and she had expressed concern regarding several points.

"I am, Master, but are you sure there is no other way?"

"Not if we are to claim the region in a timely manner. And not if we ourselves are to avoid casualties and a protracted war with the humans," he replied, curtly.

Celia looked at him for a moment then nodded. Without another word, she raised a white flag to signal to the town their intention to talk.

The humans must have been expecting them, as only a few minutes passed before the gate opened and a carriage pulled by two white stallions approached them at a steady pace. It was joined by four figures on horseback.

Celia planted the flag in the ground before her, and Aziel pulled her closer to him as they waited for the guest to arrive. "Remember your part," he whispered. Again, she simply nodded.

The human party drove right up to them. Aziel shook his head; these humans didn't think of him as a significant enough threat to meet closer to town, instead coming all the way to his forces. They would live to regret that, he thought, as the carriage door opened.

One woman and one man jumped out, each taking up position to one side of the carriage door. Then the female guard offered her hand to the last occupant, who gracefully accepted it. As the human he knew to be the princess emerged from within, Aziel noticed Celia's expression change for a moment, before her smile returned as if nothing had occurred.

The princess wore an elegant red dress and had her blonde hair swept back in a bun, with a single jeweled rod speared through it. A quick glance at her vessel told him she was a fire weaver, and the only weaver in the party before him. She took a few graceful steps down the small staircase and onto the grassy field before looking Aziel up and down then doing the same to Celia a moment later.

Aziel noticed her gaze linger on him a bit longer than appropriate and had to force himself not to smile. The crown princess, heir to the Kingdom of Maiv, was attracted to him. It seemed his succubus trait had started to work on her immediately. Unfortunately, he knew that budding attraction was not going to survive what he had planned.

"Princess Lucienne," he said, bowing his head slightly. "It is a pleasure to meet you. And might I add that the stories of your beauty were quite understated."

The princess pulled a stray hair back from her face and tucked it behind her right ear, smiling. "That's charming of you to say. But I have not had the pleasure of hearing your name?" she added sweetly.

"Ah, my apologies, I have forgotten myself." Aziel looked directly into her light blue eyes. "Lord Aziel, King of the Grauda, as promised."

The princess raised an eyebrow. "You claim to be a lord, but have not told me your house's name."

"That is because I am not a noble, my lady. I simply take the title of lord because my followers call me so."

The princess seemed surprised. "If being a noble had such a low barrier to entry, then we would have nothing but nobles, don't you think?"

Aziel shrugged, trying to hide his impatience. "Perhaps. But we are not here to speak of such things, are we?"

"Ah, yes, the King of the Grauda and his threats. Rather brutish, don't you agree? I honestly thought I would be meeting a dirty ruffian or one of these creatures I have heard so much about, not a well-dressed gentleman and his... concubine," she said, eyeing Celia, who simply smirked and glued herself even tighter to Aziel's side.

"Apologies, I must have lost all my manners today," Aziel said. He nudged Celia forward slightly, so she might bow. "May I introduce Celia, my succubus."

Celia did bow, though perhaps a little too low, as all the men in the princess's escort either stared at her now-exposed cleavage or respectfully diverted their gaze.

"A warlock, then," Lucienne said, unamused. "Didn't know your kind lurked so deep in the Wilds."

"I have my reasons," Aziel said, as Celia returned to his side.

"And is one of those reasons the Grauda? I must say, I'm am quite confused by this entire matter. How could someone such as yourself become king of such a monstrous race?"

Aziel kept his face blank. "Monstrous, you say?"

"Why of course," Lucienne said, matter-of-factly. "Just the description of them makes my skin crawl," she added, and literally shivered at her own words.

"Then perhaps we should get down to terms, Princess? I'm sure being in close proximity to my... monsters... is unpleasant for someone of your stature."

Lucienne actually seemed abashed, which surprised him. "Ah, my apologies, Aziel. I of course did not mean any disrespect."

For all her consolatory words, Aziel did not fail to notice that she neglected to call him lord. "None taken. Shall we?" he asked, and at a nod from the princess, two of her guards produced a pair of chairs from the carriage, which they placed facing each other.

"Please, have a seat," Lucienne said. When he had done so, she placed her hands on her lap and began. "We had to take considerable efforts to ensure my presence here was not noticed by the same people you threatened to inform of our activities… With that said, it is obvious that we do not wish for word of Whiteridge to be known, and I'm sure you simply want an end to hostilities between ourselves and your Grauda. I am willing to give you that, if they move out of the general vicinity of Whiteridge."

She smiled at Aziel in a way that made it clear she thought she was doing him a favor by offering such terms.

Aziel shook his head. "There has been a misunderstanding, princess. I am not here to discuss a truce, but your surrender."

The princess stared at him for a moment, then slowly breathed out through her nose.

"I knew this whole thing was a waste of time," she said, "but Father insisted I take it seriously. Surrender, you say? And why would we do that?"

"The reasons were made clear in my note, princess," Aziel replied flatly. "You will surrender your faction's claim to the Central Wilds, or face the consequences."

It was Lucienne's turn to shake her head. "I grow tired of this already. How would your beloved Grauda fare in the open where they could not hide—and against manned walls, no less? You can throw your Grauda against us and watch them die if you wish, or you could take this negotiation seriously," she said.

Aziel remained stoic. "My terms remain as they are, princess."

Lucienne sighed in dismissal, but just as she was about to stand Aziel drew his blade and pointed it at her neck. His movements were so fast and seamless that none of her guards had been able to react in time.

At this signal, Celia's eyes grew brighter, and all but one of the guards froze in place as her Charm took effect.

"Princess!" the remaining one cried, pulling out his sword.

"Don't move!" Aziel commanded, but the guard charged. Aziel activated his sword's enchantment, and the ornate blade glowed white, humming in his hand.

Lucienne reflexively pulled her head back as he swung his blade wide, a pale line of translucent air mana trailing behind it as it sliced clean through the guard's chest and armor as if he was not there. In one fluid movement, Aziel returned the tip of the still-pristine blade to its position at the princess's throat.

The guard he had struck paused, sword still held high, before he fell to the ground, his body severed in two cleanly-cut pieces.

Aziel glared at the princess, whose face had drained of blood.

"I did tell him not to move," he said, and she swallowed.

"This is disgraceful," she stuttered, feebly. "We came here for talks, and you would draw your blade?"

"Any notion of civility and honor went out the window when your people started placing rewards on the heads of mine," Aziel stated, his voice cold and unforgiving. "So, let me say this again, princess. Surrender your faction's claim to the region to me, or face the consequences."

Someone within the town must have noticed the exchange, as at that moment a bell began to sound from that direction, but Aziel didn't flinch. He kept his gaze fixed on the princess, who was again swallowing hard.

"I can't do that... not without my father's approval..." she mumbled.

"You are the viceroy and have the authority to do so," he said, his voice flat. "Surrender it."

The princess's eyes twitched, and she looked at him in disgust. "Who are you?" she cried. "Some Jannatin dog using monsters to his advantage? I will never surrender anything to you!"

Aziel tilted his head at that, momentarily confused, then

laughed. "Ah, my mistake. I see I failed to properly introduce myself. We are not Jannatin. I am Aziel, Faction Leader of the Fallen."

The princess blinked, as she tried to process this. "The Fallen?" she asked. "The new faction?"

"Indeed. Now, this is the last time I will ask. Surrender your claim to me… immediately."

The princess didn't reply. She glared at him, and though the fear was still visible on her features, she still shook her head slightly.

"So be it," Aziel said, and lifted one arm in the air.

Several Grauda ran out of the trees and quickly disarmed the Charmed guards, before grabbing the princess and forcing her and her escort down on the grass.

Celia, who had been petting the horses during this time, now took a few steps toward Aziel with a worried look on her face.

"Are you sure there is no other way?" she asked softly.

Aziel shook his head. "I gave them a chance to back down, and now they will suffer for their crimes."

Celia glanced at the disarmed humans, then back at him before she nodded reluctantly. With a sigh, she moved out of his sightline, bringing Whiteridge back into view. The bell had fallen silent now, and he could see activity in the towers as men and women prepared for whatever was to come.

Aziel pulled the red book from an inner pocket of his jacket and turned to a page he had marked. He took a few moments to reread Vhal's comments and the decrypted symbols required for the spell he needed. He had to get the symbols and order right, or things might unravel badly for both him and his followers. A failed attempt at this spell would leave only one option open—a real battle.

Aziel glanced at the princess and remembered her words. She was right; his Grauda would not fare well in this open field and against walls guarded by trained soldiers, and such a battle would not send the message he needed the other factions to receive. He tried to refocus on the book, but a wave of fatigue made the words blur in front of him. Time was quickly running out.

He shut the book and returned it to his inner pocket. He could hear the guards behind him, now released from Celia's Charm, gabbling in confusion as they tried to understand what was going on. But Aziel took a deep breath and raised both hands toward Whiteridge, shutting out everything but the task before him.

First, he began to release copious amounts of fire mana, creating a red cloud that grew larger and larger until it began to curl and roil. He grunted as the mana began to form the activation symbol, taking shape in the air in front of him.

"What are you doing?" Lucienne screamed, but he ignored her. As a fire weaver herself, she must have known that the amount of mana Aziel was releasing was too much for a simple fireball.

Aziel instead began to focus on the second symbol, then the third. One after the other, red symbols began to form before him, their glow vivid and shimmering. By the fifth, his vessel began to quiver under the strain of both the increasing cost of the spell and the ongoing drain.

A bead of sweat formed on Aziel's brow as he formed yet another empower symbol and added it to the last, before starting work on the next. He felt the muscles of his arm burn and his legs begin to tremble under the crushing sense of weakness that was slowly engulfing him. Again his estimations had been off—the spell used far more mana then he thought it would. But it was too late to stop now.

By the time he was done, a glyph made of a total of eight symbols glowed ominously before him, its very presence causing the air to swirl around it. It waited for him to release it upon his foes.

Aziel glanced back at the princess, who seemed to be in some sort of daze as she stared at the rank seven fire spell he had just woven. He also noticed her female guard look in the direction of Whiteridge, terror on her face.

"Your Highness, please!" the female guard screamed. "I beg you, my husband is in there!"

The princess didn't respond.

Aziel didn't let that perturb him. He began to raise his hands, and the finished symbol responded by glowing brighter and larger. With every inch it grew, it pulled more mana from him, and just as Aziel felt that he could not take the strain any longer, he let out a visceral grunt and pushed it forward.

A loud sizzling noise followed as the symbol burst into flames and scorched everything in its wake. It kept glowing brighter until it suddenly collapsed into itself and formed what looked like a small sun, which shot into the air above Whiteridge at a blistering speed.

All eyes followed the ball of flames as it disappeared into the clouds. A moment of silence followed as everyone held their breath, waiting for something to happen.

And then it did.

A deafening bang echoed across the land, followed by an explosion from above. The clouds suddenly and violently parted to make way for the massive symbol that was hiding behind them.

It was the exact symbol Aziel had woven, but it had expanded to a size that easily covered the entire town below, its red glow painting everything in the surrounding area in its light.

"I can't do it," he heard the princess say, behind him.

Aziel turned and saw her look at him, an expression of total defeat on her face. None of her former confidence remained.

"I can't do it, there must be something else," she pleaded. "Just… stop this madness,"

"There is nothing else, princess. You and everyone else must learn the consequences of going against me and my faction. Those people will serve as an example and will pay the price for your crimes and unwillingness to submit."

Without breaking eye contact with her, he clenched his fist and opened it again. Aziel again grunted as another portion of his mana was suddenly sucked from him and an ear-splitting noise rang out from the symbol in the sky above.

The symbol began to crack across its lines. Those cracks gave way to more cracks, until the whole creation shattered into what looked like tens of thousands of tiny little shards. Only their glow and sheer number made them visible from this distance.

At that same moment, the gates of the town swung open and a group of seventy or so people ran out. Aziel swung around when he sensed their vessels approaching—they were indeed soldiers, he saw, but they didn't seem to be armed. They were simply trying to run. Behind him, the same female guard began screaming.

"Kaeden! Run!" she yelled, and a Grauda male prepared to slam his spear into her—but Celia grabbed him to stay the blow.

Aziel looked at her curiously, but she did not explain, so he focused again on the spell. Sending out the last of the mana required to release it, he struggled with the effort, then let his hands drop to his sides as he tried to control his now labored breathing.

What came next happened slowly. Instead of the spell simply activating all at once, the fiery shards began to fall in a more staggered manner, almost like a light drizzle, soft and harmless.

Then the first tiny shard smashed into the side of the half-built fort at the top of the ridge. It exploded, a chunk of the stone wall flying outward from the force of the blast—and this was followed by another explosion, then another.

A cacophony of noise followed, as what had started as a drizzle turned into a heavy downpour, with each tiny red shard exploding on contact, consuming houses, inns, and people.

Even the initial screams that could be heard from the town were drowned out by the explosions, and Aziel, his people, the princess, and the bound guards all stared in silence at the complete destruction of Whiteridge. Large plumes of black smoke rose, replacing the once serene blue skies, and thunder and purple lightning erupted above. By the time the last shard completed its descent to the ground, the landscape as far as they could see was lit by the raging fires that engulfed the town and surrounding area.

Aziel stared at the aftermath, his heart pounding. He had known what his spell would do—he was under no illusion about its destructive capacity—but even with the constant stream of mana he was getting from people he killed, the amount paled in comparison to spell's mana cost. His vessel continued to tremble painfully. He had to finish this, and now.

He turned to Lucienne and stared down at her. "Princess," he said.

She met his gaze slowly as ash began to fall from the sky.

"I swear to you that I will march to your capital and do the same to every town, every city, every hamlet I find on my way. I will grind your faction to dust... or you can swallow your pride and give up your claim... *now*," he said, doing everything he could to hide the desperation in his voice.

"You're a monster," the princess whispered.

"Only to my enemies," he replied, coldly.

Their attention was diverted by a hiss from one of the Grauda males. It was the same female guard as before. She was trying to push her way through the Grauda, and as Aziel followed her frantic gaze, the reason became clear.

The group of humans who had run out of the town had survived. They must have lain low until the spell's effects had passed, and they were now fleeing from the flames behind them.

Aziel sighed and took a few steps forward before raising his hand to the sky. This was followed by a few loud clicks from the Grauda, and one full division ran out of the forest with their bows in their hands. They quickly readied themselves to let their arrows fly toward the helpless humans.

The princess stared in utter shock at these preparations, and the female guard wore such a pained and hopeless expression that Aziel hesitated for a moment before he steeled himself again.

Just as he was about to give the order, he felt a hand grip his arm. Celia was at his side, her lips pressed tightly together.

"Don't," she whispered, her voice full of pain. "Your message has been delivered, anything more... anything more would just be cruel."

Aziel stared into her golden eyes, his expression blank. "If those people were us, they wouldn't have stopped."

"I know..." she said, and she let go of his hand in order to clasp her arms around him.

Aziel sighed, and the fury he had not noticed growing within him began to fade as he slowly lowered his hand and wrapped it around Celia. The female Grauda who led the archers clicked her mandibles twice at the sight of this, before she and her division slowly melted back into the forest.

Gently, Aziel separated himself from Celia and glared at the princess who flinched at his gaze.

"Surrender your claim," he said, his voice low and full of promise. "Do not force me to repeat what has happened here."

The princess blinked, her face tinged with the red glow of the flames from Whiteridge. "I'll do it," she said, her voice trembling, as she tried to fight the tears welling in her eyes. "If you promise not to harm my people, I'll do it."

Aziel knelt in front of her and, tenderly, wiped away the single tear that lay on her cheek. She stiffened at his touch.

"I know you might find my next words hollow," he said softly. "But I did not enjoy taking their lives. I firmly believe that this was a necessary evil and a repayment of debts... I promise to not harm your people as long as they do not harm me or mine."

The princess didn't reply. Taking her silence for consent, Aziel opened his faction log and approved his faction claim to the Central Wilds.

A notification appeared:

The Fallen have met the required prerequisite and have claimed the region known as the Central Wilds.

All other claimants have been notified. Total number of current claimants: four.

The princess's eyes became distant for a moment, before the circular mark on Aziel's wrist began to heat up again and several notifications flashed before him, the gray runes appearing one after another.

The Kingdom of Maiv has renounced it's claim to the region known as the Central Wilds and instead offer it's support to the Fallen's claim.

The Fallen now has a majority claim.

Congratulations, your faction has claimed the Central Wilds.

Further options have been unlocked in your faction log.

Warning, newly claimed region has not yet been pacified.

Aziel let out a sigh of relief as his trait came into effect, and he felt the massive drain on his dwindling mana taper off into a barely noticeable trickle. He couldn't believe how different the feeling was. After days of constant and ever-increasing draining, his body had become almost accustomed to the sensation. This change felt wonderful.

Bringing up his log, he winced at what he saw. Barely fifteen percent of his total mana was left. Making it back in time would be a challenge, even with his new claim.

Clearing his throat, he placed a hand on Lucienne's shoulder.

"Collect your people and return home, princess," he said softly. "My Grauda will escort you to the edge of the forest. I hope this is the last and only reminder I need to give you."

The humans didn't waste any time doing as he commanded. The princess and her guard quickly collected the survivors and made their way south. Aziel assumed they were heading for Golan, the capital.

He again glanced at what had once been Whiteridge and the still-raging fires... then up at the black clouds that now completely blocked the morning sun from reaching them. Aziel knew the likely ramifications of his actions, but he still believed they had been necessary.

The surrounding nations needed to fear and respect his faction. He needed every human to know that the Fallen were here to stay and would bring complete destruction to any who opposed him. They couldn't guess that this display of power had almost drained him of his mana.

A familiar chuckle sounded from behind him, and Aziel turned to see Vhal approaching.

"Simply marvelous, my lord," Vhal said effusively. "A masterful use of the empowered Crystalline Fire spell."

"Can we go home now?" Celia interrupted. "The ash makes me sneeze."

"Yes we shou—" Aziel eyes opened wide as a piercing pain shot through his core.

He fell to one knee and clutched his chest, as he felt the drain on his mana explode back to its previous levels. The shock and suddenness of it caused his vessel to shake and churn as it attempted to regulate itself quickly to control the leak.

Warning: you are suffering from critical injuries and require healing!

Aziel felt his muscles contract, and his fingers and toes curled inwards as he screamed out in pain. He could hear Vhal and Celia shouting something, but no meaning came to him. In his short moments of lucidity, he was able to feel the heat radiating out of his wrist and read the runes that flashed before him. He tried to swallow a lump that had developed in his throat as he felt overwhelmed at the unfairness of it all.

He was going to die, and it was all due to the World Seed moving against him.

Kadora Announcement: Region claiming requirements have been added.

Warning: the Jannatin Empire has contested your claim to the Central Wilds. Due to there being a number of other claimants equal to your majority claim, a total of three days will be given to decide whether to support or reject the contested claim.

Warning, your faction has lost control of the Central Wilds.

Aziel looked up to the darkened sky. His last act in this world would be the destruction of an entire town. He had failed, and as his vision began to darken, the last thing he saw was Celia's tearful face, her mouth opened wide in a scream.

CHAPTER 29

AZIEL FLUTTERED HIS eyes open—then instinctively covered them with his hand to protect them from the bright light that shone from above. He groaned from the pain which shot through his right arm as he moved it. He was tired, and terribly confused, but there was one overwhelming sensation that eclipsed all others: a deep ache. Everything ached.

He glanced to one side and realized that he was back in one of the bedrooms within Soul's Rest. But how did he get here? He closed his eyes again in an attempt to organize his thoughts, but all he could remember was the agony and his submission to his inevitable death. His wrist began to heat up as a notification appeared before him.

Warning: you have gained a new condition, Wounded Vessel. Mana cost of all spells and skills increased by 100%. Condition will remain until Vessel has been given sufficient time to rest.

Aziel sighed. That was to be expected, he supposed. He shifted his body and grunted as another twang of pain shot through him, but it was the soft groan that sounded from his side which caught his attention. He turned to his right and saw a familiar figure seated beside his bed, her head resting on her folded arms.

He smiled at the sight of the succubus, then frowned when he noticed the state of her hair and face. Celia must have been through a storm for her hair to be in such a mess, and the puffiness under her eyes made it clear she had been crying.

He slowly raised his arm, wincing at how difficult even such a small movement was, and gently touched her arm.

"Celia," he said, and was surprised by how hoarse his voice was. He sounded like he hadn't had a drink of water in weeks.

Celia moaned in response, then buried her head more deeply between her arms.

Aziel felt too weak to move his arm again so he coughed as loud as he could, making Celia jerk upright. She stared at him, her mouth opening and closing, as tears began to well up in her eyes.

"Celia—" he tried to say, but instead was slapped across the face so hard, he felt his brain wallop the side of his skull. Her movement had been so fast he didn't even have a chance to react.

Aziel shook his head and turned back, only to be slapped again.

The third time he was prepared for, and he used all his strength to raise his hand in time to grip Celia's arm before the strike. But instead of stopping there, she lunged forward at him and began slapping him with her other hand.

Aziel grunted as he tried and failed to catch her other arm, while she kept pummeling him.

Then, just as suddenly as it all started, the assault stopped.

He felt Celia sag and her head drop until her forehead touched his own. Her eyes were now closed, but Aziel stared at her, seeing her tears and feeling her body shake.

"I… I thought I'd lost you…" she said between sobs, her voice cracking.

Aziel was stunned into silence.

"You suddenly fell and started screaming," she managed to say, "you passed out… We didn't know what to do, but then your skin started to shrivel up…"

"Celia… I—" he said, but was again cut off as she abruptly pulled her head back from his.

"I had to Shapeshift into a horse to get you back here in time! Do you know how it feels to be a horse?" she yelled, glaring at him. The sudden change in tone made him swallow whatever he had been going to say. "How dare you... you let me depend on you... then go and do something so reckless!" she hissed.

Celia's hands, which had been gripping his clothes, now balled into fists as her shaking grew in intensity. "You were turning gray by the time we got here, just like someone I'd Siphoned. Three days... Three days you were out cold!"

Aziel glanced at his hand as if to confirm her words. His skin looked normal, if a bit dull and dry, but he had no doubt that Celia was telling the truth. His vessel had grown so thin it had begun to use his lifeforce to heal itself, creating a certain death spiral.

By bringing him back here, close to his place of power, Celia had saved his life. And at that moment, an awful thought came to the forefront of his mind. By getting him here, Celia had saved her own life... Aziel wasn't sure she had even realized this, but he remembered Vhal's warning about the possible lethality of severing mana links all too clearly.

Not only had he gambled with his own life, but Celia's too. A swell of self-hate flooded him, and his whole body sagged. Perhaps he wasn't cut out for being a faction leader. He had taken a massive risk and for what? Absolutely nothing, the World Seed made sure of that. Aziel closed his eyes as rage flowed through him. Why was this happening? What did he ever do to deserve this? But then, Aziel let all his frustrations out with a shuddering breath. The World Seed can wait, there was something more important to him he had to deal with right now.

"Celia... I'm sorry," he said, his voice soft. "I promise I'll be more careful in the future."

He saw Celia's hands unclench, and she reached out to cradle his face in her palms.

Aziel stared at the complex expression on her face. It seemed to be a mixture of fear, anger, and worry—but just as Aziel thought she was going to scream at him again, she smiled.

"You better be," she whispered, "or I swear to any and all the powers who are listening that I'm going to chain you to this bed and never let you out of my sight." She then leaned in and kissed him, hard.

Her body pressed hungrily against his, and all that kept things from descending rapidly into full-blown sex were Aziel's grunts of pain.

When their lips finally parted, Aziel let out a breath of relief and exquisite frustration. He was glad Celia wasn't angry at him, but one glance at her grin made him think that his relief had been premature.

"Vhal and the Grauda army should be back later today, but that won't matter because you have a queen to deal with," she said, giving his cheek a light pat. "Only reason I won't stay mad is because of what I'm sure Astrel is going to do to you."

Aziel looked around quickly, which caused her to laugh.

"She's not here, not for a little longer, anyway. She gathered up a group of Grauda and took off into Arachne territory. She was going on about wanting to kill something or other."

Aziel swallowed as he remembered his promise to the Grauda queen to come back safely.

"Was she... that upset?" he asked nervously.

Celia shuffled about, tucking herself under the sheets, and then hugged his side, not caring that her movements made the pain in his aching muscles flare. She traced her middle finger down his chest and began to draw random figures there before she spoke again.

"Well, she was worried sick at first—you should have seen how the Grauda react when their queen is in such a state, they practically went mad trying to find things to cheer her up." She shook her head, then placed her hand flat on his chest. "Once you started to get your color back, however, she... well, let's just say you should avoid laying with her for a while. We can't have you losing something important now, can we?" She emphasized her words with a gentle squeeze of his manhood.

Aziel swallowed again. So many thoughts raced through his head that he stopped feeling the pain of Celia's nuzzling. He couldn't think of a way to make it up to the Grauda queen.

He let his head fall back on the pillow, as he gave up looking for a way out. He probably deserved Astrel's wrath. It was his failure to gather all the information regarding how claims worked. Although the World Seed had tried to kill him before, he had gravely underestimated its willingness to intervene. His failure to take the Seeds possible actions into account had brought him to this point.

This thought gave him pause. As if waiting for him to realize this, he began to feel the slight heat coming from his wrist. He quickly focused on it and several notifications appeared before him—and he simply stared at the runes, amazed.

The United Princedoms of Odana have renounced their claim to the region known as the Central Wilds.

The Jannatin Empire's counter claim has failed to secure enough support. The Fallen retain their majority claim.

Congratulations, your faction has claimed the Central Wilds.

Further options have been unlocked in your faction log.

Warning, newly claimed region has not yet been pacified.

Aziel stared at the gray runes. It would appear the Seeds' attempt at thwarting him had failed. Even so, he couldn't fathom why the Princedoms of Odana would do such a thing. What did they gain by giving Aziel what he wanted? Then again, he didn't know much about the country, other than that it sported a massive slave economy.

There had to be something he was missing? Or maybe they simply didn't care about the region as much as they had let others believe. Aziel mulled it over in his head for a few more moments. They might have not wanted to support the Jannatins, perhaps that was the key. Aziel shook his head; it didn't matter right now.

His gamble, as reckless as it had been, had succeeded.

Aziel wondered why Celia hadn't said anything, but then remembered that she had no official position within his faction. As the only appointed officer, Vhal was the only other person who would have received a notification about it, and he was currently still somewhere in the Wilds.

When he shared the news with Celia, she didn't seem nearly as excited as him.

"This doesn't mean that what you did was right," she practically growled at him, and Aziel had to concede to that, but then quietly brought up his faction log as Celia tucked herself into bed again.

He hadn't had a chance to take a look at these further options, and he wanted to see what it was before another rule he didn't know about came into effect to take it away.

He quickly focused on a new rune which read *Regions*, and a moment later a map of the Central Wilds suddenly manifested before him. He scanned it quickly, wondering what the strange overlays over certain areas of the map were.

He received his answer a moment later, when his eyes came to rest on the list of flashing runes right below the map.

Warning: several unaffiliated racial guilds of significant influence are operating within your region. Regional appointments are disabled until the region is completely pacified.

It then went on to list the names of four guilds, followed by which overlay represented their area of activity.

The first one was no surprise to him; the Arachne, who operated the western section of the inner valley.

The second was the Sister Groves, which Aziel assumed—based on their location to the southeast and what little he knew of them—were the dryads.

The next so-called unaffiliated guild was completely foreign to him.

Gorshak's Horde, which had territories dotted all over the southern half of the map, with a larger area visible to the southeast.

But it was the last guild that really caught his attention.

The Ogre'i. Their territory spanned a large section of the mountains to the east.

Aziel distinctly remembered Astrel mentioning their name as members of the ancient races. He knew already that he wanted them to join his faction—and perhaps meeting them would help him reclaim another portion of his memories.

The only problem was that he wouldn't be going anywhere soon. The throbbing pain still radiating from his body made sure of that. He didn't know how long it would take him to recover, but now that he had mana and his Soul Rejuvenation hard at work healing him, he was sure it wouldn't take too long.

Taking another quick glance at the map, Aziel grinned at the advantage he now had. By successfully claiming the Central Wilds and gaining access to this map, he had basically been given the location of all major threats in the area.

His grin only lasted a moment, however, as the door to the bedroom suddenly swung open and Astrel strode in. She glanced around the room until her eyes met his own.

She still wore her traditional clothing, but they—along with her scythe arms—were caked in blood and gore. Her entire body looked as if someone had thrown a bucket of viscera at her—even her face had bloody marks on it.

Her eyes narrowed at the sight of him, then she turned and set down the round shield held in her left arm, and followed that by placing an impressive looking spear that Aziel was certain was one of the imperial family's weapons beside it.

Astrel's eyes locked on him again, and he felt a cold chill at her expressionless face. It was the same face she used to give Celia before they had bonded, and being on the receiving end of it made his already weakened core shiver.

"My king," she said, her voice flat and emotionless. "You are awake."

Aziel glanced down to see Celia extricate herself from his side, then wink at him as she made her way toward the door.

"This is my cue to go," she said, and as she passed Astrel, Aziel heard her whisper, "Just don't kill him." Then she was gone, the door shutting firmly behind her.

A few moments of silence followed as Aziel and Astrel stared at one another.

He was the first to look away, and he put his hand to the back of his head nervously. "Astrel, I'm so—"

The Grauda queen quickly closed the distance between them, her sudden movement interrupting his thoughts. She looked at him for a long moment, her eyes cold, before leaning forward and kissing him deeply, her lips pressing against his.

Caught completely by surprise, Aziel didn't react fast enough to kiss her back. He only stared at her as she broke the kiss and stepped back.

"I am glad you are awake, my king," she said with a slight smile, before her expression turned hard again. "But we shall have words regarding your recklessness." He noticed her antennae stand up straight and her bloodied scythe arms twitch.

With a swallow, Aziel nodded. He didn't know what she was going to do with him—or more accurately, *to* him—but he knew he probably deserved it. All he was going to do was apologize to her repeatedly until she accepted it, and hopefully he would come out of the other side still whole.

With that in mind, he surrendered himself to his fate. As the queen advanced on him, he comforted himself with thoughts of the next steps his faction would take on its road to power.

EPILOGUE

FIVE-THOUSAND FOUR-HUNDRED AND thirty-one, she counted to herself. Her blood-red eyes reflected against the next droplet of water as it gathered more moisture from the surrounding rocks. Slowly, it stretched under its own weight.

She had no idea how long she had been in here. The sound of water dripping and the rattle of the chains suspending her in the air by her wrists were the only things keeping her company in the dark.

Except that wasn't strictly true. There were always the torturers, who took pleasure in tearing her apart from time to time only for her cursed body to heal so they could do it all over again.

The pain didn't bother her any longer; she had lost count of how many nails, toes, fingers, tongues, and limbs they had torn off her. Now that she thought about it, however, she hadn't had a good lashing for a good while. She wondered if they had grown bored with it.

Her thoughts went blank as the water droplet freed itself from the stone surface above. Just as it began its descent to the rocky floor, she heard a familiar voice behind her.

"Traitor," it said, but she couldn't see the speaker. Instead, she felt his hand brush across her naked back, before his nails dug in hard and gouged at her flesh.

But she didn't scream—she didn't even flinch. She would not give them that satisfaction… not any longer.

The man laughed, and she heard the metal clank of his sabatons striking the stone floor as he made his way around her and into her field of view.

He had black hair, which was combed slickly back, and complemented by a thick mustache and goatee. Like her, he had white, pale skin, and blood-red eyes, and his grin exposed the sharp canines which were a hallmark of his… *their* race.

Vampires. She had been turned into one by the very person who stood before her—and for what? Petty revenge over events she had played no real part in.

"I have good news, Traitor," he said, as his hands worked the mechanisms which controlled the chains that kept her feet off the ground. "The Empress has completed her evolution and awakened."

That news caused her to blink. Nevani was awake? The vampire must have noticed her reaction, as he laughed cruelly.

"Oh, I know you've been looking forward to seeing her. And guess what, Traitor? You have been summoned!" He laughed again as he slammed the mechanism with his hand, and she fell to the ground hard. The heavy chain that had held her followed, slamming into her head and body with a bone-crushing thud.

The man didn't wait for her to recover. Instead, he grabbed her by her dirty, sweaty blonde hair and dragged her across the rocky ground and up a flight of stairs. She didn't make a sound or even whimper as her skin scraped across the rough ground—instead, she closed her eyes and kept her mind deliberately blank.

A backhanded smack to her face forced her back to the present, and she looked up to see the same man scowling down at her. He then turned away and knelt on the ground.

"My Empress, I have brought the traitor," he said, his voice low and respectful.

"Excellent," a familiar voice sang, her tone smooth and dripping with malice. "You may return to your post, Sukan."

"As you command, Empress," he said, then stood and bowed his head, before taking up a position on one the side of the room.

"Valery Novaul." She felt a delicate finger slide under her chin and push up. She didn't fight it as she rose up from the floor and onto her feet. "It has truly been too long. My, have you grown since we last saw each other."

The Empress's hands dropped to caress Valery's collarbone before cupping her breast.

"You filled out in all the right places," she added, as her red eyes inspected Valery's body. Then she gripped Valery's jaws tightly and sneered. "I've always hated how you Novaul girls got so... pretty."

Valery kept her passive expression with difficulty as she examined the women before her. Empress Nevani had hair as black as night reaching down to her waist, and her white skin glowed healthily, in a way rare for a half-undead demonic creature.

She wore a tight black dress, and as Valery's eyes traced its gold linings, she noticed a small human boy drenched in blood on the floor behind the Empress.

The Empress noticed her looking and grinned. "Oh, I got hungry when I awoke. Things got a bit messy, I'm afraid... you wouldn't like a taste, would you?" she asked, innocently.

Valery swallowed. She had been given drops of blood from time to time, barely enough to keep her alive and fuel her healing. Her body shivered and her mind clouded over at the sight of it—at the *smell* of it.

The Empress *tsked*. "Now, it's quite rude to not give your full attention to your liege, don't you think? But then again... it runs in the family, doesn't it?" Her eyes narrowed as they met Valery's.

"I had nothing to do with that," Valery said, but just as the last word passed her lips, the Empress's hand moved—too quickly for her to keep track of—and pinched Valery's tongue between two of her fingers before squeezing.

Valery felt the Empress's nail pierce her tongue and the taste of her own blood flooded her mouth.

"Empress," Nevani hissed.

Valery blinked, then quickly corrected herself. "I had nothing to do with that... Empress." Her voice came out slightly distorted, due to her tongue being held captive.

"Good," the Empress said, then released her, allowing Valery to swallow the blood that had pooled in her mouth.

"You know, Valery, when Sukan first brought you to me, I actually felt bad about this whole thing. I mean, you were but a teenager, taken from your home... but now I can see the resemblance." The Empress's brow and nose crumpled in disgust as she looked at Valery coldly. "You look just like her."

"I am not my sis—" Valery began, but was abruptly knocked to the floor by the force of a slap.

"I don't recall giving you permission to speak," the Empress hissed. She narrowed her eyes, as if reading something in Valery's face. "Do you know what it was like? To come back home to the capital to find it in turmoil... to walk up to the throne room and find your father—the emperor, *your emperor*—kneeling on the floor with his own blade buried deep into his chest?"

She bent down to grab Valery by her neck, pulling her up and off her feet. Valery's weight didn't seem to bother her at all.

"And who do I find pushing that blade deeper into him?" she growled, as her nails dug into Valery's flesh. "My best friend, high commander of our empire... one I used to call sister. But she didn't stop there, did she? No, she sent her treasonous lackeys after me. Too bad my captain of the guard was more than a match for them."

The Empress gestured briefly to Sukan, who stood still and silent by the wall.

"My only regret was not getting my hands on her before the

people she supposedly rebelled to save, murdered her. At least I have you to pay for your family's sins."

"Kill me then," Valery spat, her annoyance boiling over, but the Empress just laughed.

"Don't worry, I will. But not before you witness me reclaim my throne and undo all your family died for," she said, before letting go of her throat. Valery fell to the ground, gasping, as the Empress turned to Sukan. "Is it done?"

The black-armored vampire nodded. "We gathered more than we needed, and our agents are in position, my Empress. We only await your orders." He dug something out of his pouch and offered it to Nevani, which she accepted with a smile.

"Always the overachiever, isn't he?" she murmured, before turning to Valery and dangling the item in front of her.

"Know what this is?" she asked, and Valery saw she held a vial of red liquid. It looked like a potion of some kind, but the liquid inside it was too thick…

"Blood?" she asked cautiously, not knowing where this was going.

The Empress laughed. "Yes, blood. Your blood, Valery."

"My blood? Why?" Valery asked, as a deep sense of anxiety seeped into her heart.

The Empress shook her head. "To use, of course."

"I don't understand."

A deep sigh escaped the Empress, as she took a seat on an ornate-looking chair. "Tell me Valery," she asked, her tone as demeaning as if she was talking to a child, "what happens when a non-vampire consumes a little vampire blood?"

"They go mad… violent," Valery replied, as her worries flared.

"See, you aren't as stupid as you think, once you put your mind to it. So, what happens when a non-vampire consumes a *lot* of vampire blood?" the Empress asked.

Valery gulped, as Nevani's plan became clearer in her mind. "They turn into thralls, then vampires," she whispered.

"They do, don't they? You have some personal experience of that, after all." Nevani chuckled. "It's ironic, isn't it? Your treasonous house led to the fall of mine, and now the last survivor's blood will lead to its resurgence… it's almost poetic."

A million thoughts ran through Valery's head as she tried to think how that was possible, until just one remained. "The blood from my torture… you collected it," she said, dazed.

The Empress laughed again. "Yes. My loyal Sukan did just that. But now that my evolution into an Elder is complete, things will soon get busy." Her eyes scanned the carved stone walls around her. "I grow tired of the Underdark and its incessant whispers. These ancient tunnels and ruins bore me, and I do miss the sun. It's about time we moved back to the surface."

Whispers? What whispers? What was she talking about? But before Valery could ask, the empress turned to Sukan again and flicked her hand.

"Let it begin. Start small and with the Ejani—they are the greatest threat, and I wish to have my revenge on them first."

"As you command, Empress," Sukan replied. He pulled out a small device from his pouch then inserted a tiny white air crystal into it. He then raised it to his mouth and began to whisper orders.

"See? the death you wanted may come earlier than you expected," Nevani said mockingly.

"You will never get what you wish, Nevani," Valery hissed in defiance. "I may not have been part of what brought you and your corrupt family down, but those people up there are better for it."

The Empress swiftly disappeared from her sight, and Valery suddenly felt very cold. She looked down to see the Empress's arm protruding from her abdomen, her hands clasped around Valery's intestines.

Valery coughed, blood spilling out of her mouth, as she felt the Empress's breath on her ears and cheek.

"Look at what you made me do… all that wasted blood," Nevani whispered, then dragged her fangs across her neck before slowly pulling her arm out of Valery's body.

Valery collapsed to her knees, her hands moving to cover the gaping wound in her middle as her breathing grew heavier. The Empress paid her no mind, crossing slowly back to her seat before leisurely crossing her legs. She looked thoughtful for a moment then smiled.

"You know, my father used to love telling me stories of our empire…" she mused. "There is one phrase in particular he always repeated."

Valery swallowed, and to her dismay felt her cursed body begin to heal again. "What?" she managed to cough out.

The Empress's smile became a sadistic grin, as she said, "Always remember, the Caelian phoenix never dies."

Aziel
Hidden
Ascended
Level 91

Mana: 10,300/10,300
STR: 28
REF 25
MND: 35
VES: 206

Skills
Soul Rejuvenation (Lvl 10)
All Seeing Eye (Lvl 10)
Long Blades (Lvl 10)
Soul Link

Traits
Soul Weaving
Ancient Being
Soul Infused
Ascended's Domain
Mark of the Succubi
King of the Grauda

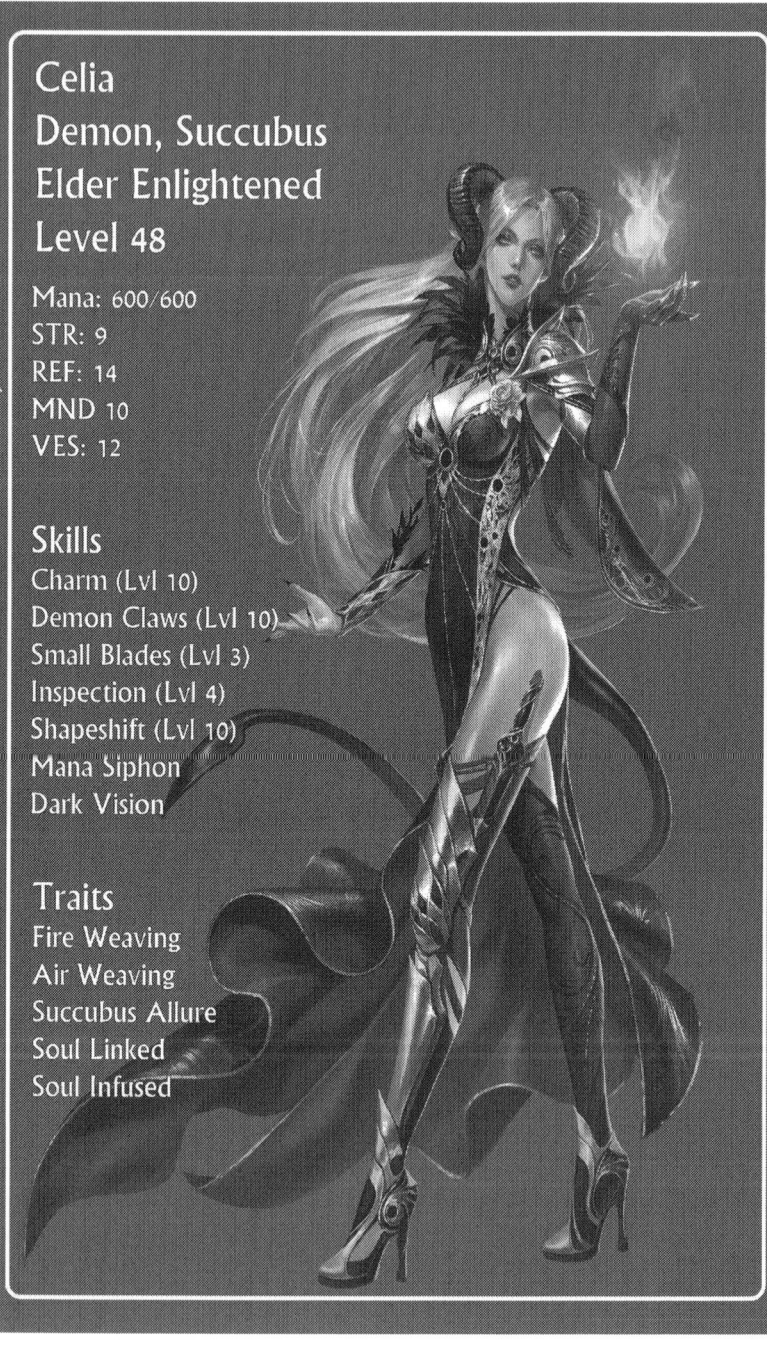

Celia
Demon, Succubus
Elder Enlightened
Level 48

Mana: 600/600
STR: 9
REF: 14
MND 10
VES: 12

Skills
Charm (Lvl 10)
Demon Claws (Lvl 10)
Small Blades (Lvl 3)
Inspection (Lvl 4)
Shapeshift (Lvl 10)
Mana Siphon
Dark Vision

Traits
Fire Weaving
Air Weaving
Succubus Allure
Soul Linked
Soul Infused

Astrel
Grauda, Queen
Greater Enlightened
Level 28

Mana: 250/250
STR: 10
REF: 11
MND 6
VES: 5

Skills
Keen Sense (Lvl 2)
Power Strike (Lvl 2)
Poles (Lvl 4)
Shields (Lvl 4)
Inspection (Lvl 2)
Alchemy (Lvl 3)
Wondrous Architect (Lvl 1)
Grauda Scythes
Dark Vision

Traits
Queen of the Grauda

Printed in Poland
by Amazon Fulfillment
Poland Sp. z o.o., Wrocław